RED
RAIN

R.L. STINE

A TOUCHSTONE BOOK
PUBLISHED BY SIMON & SCHUSTER
NEW YORK   LONDON   TORONTO   SYDNEY   NEW DELHI

Touchstone
A Division of Simon & Schuster, Inc.
1230 Avenue of the Americas
New York, NY 10020

First Touchstone hardcover edition October 2012

TOUCHSTONE and colophon are registered trademarks of Simon & Schuster, Inc.

For information about special discounts for bulk purchases, please contact Simon & Schuster Special Sales at 1-866-506-1949 or business@simonandschuster.com.

The Simon & Schuster Speakers Bureau can bring authors to your live event. For more information or to book an event contact the Simon & Schuster Speakers Bureau at 1-866-248-3049 or visit our website at www.simonspeakers.com.

Designed by Akasha Archer

Manufactured in the United States of America

10 9 8 7 6 5 4 3 2 1

Stine, R.L.
  Red rain / R.L. Stine.
      p. cm
"A Touchstone Book."
I. Title.
PS3569.T4837R43 2012
831'.54—dc23
                              2011044273

ISBN 978-1-4516-3612-3
ISBN 978-1-4516-3614-7 (ebook)

For Jane

But Zeus sent from heaven a show'r of blood-stain'd rain. In sign of many a warrior's coming doom.

—The Iliad

Prologue

By morning, the hurricane had passed. But not before destroying every home, every building, every life on the island.

Lea lowered her hand from her eyes and waited for them to adjust to the yellow-gray glare. The light reminded her of a sickroom, a hospital room, that chilling light that carries no warmth at all.

No clouds in the sky, but the sun was hidden, lost behind the swirling dust and mist and chunks of dirt that clogged the air.

The light feels dirty.

Now, two dogs began to wail. Not in pain. Howling a mournful song. Sharing the horror of what they saw.

Lea took one step, then another, concentrating on keeping her balance.

Stay on solid ground. Don't stumble and fall off the edge of the earth, into the ragged piles of death. Keep moving and you won't be buried here.

Lea's thoughts were a jumble. No way to straighten them out, not with the dogs howling and the children crying, and the corpses all witnesses, all of them, lying so still and watching the living in silent accusation.

Her sandals sank into a deep puddle of cold water. She kept walking. Ahead of her, she could hear the rush and roar of the waves. She was walking to the beach without realizing it.

The winds and thundering rains had burrowed deep trenches in the sand. Lea stumbled and slogged through them, not seeing them, paying no attention to the mud and wet sand that invaded the bottoms of her jeans and clung like wet plaster to her legs.

The sweaty mist carried by the wind off the raging waves didn't revive her. It seemed to blind her even more, as if she were stepping into a whirling, warm cloud, swallowed by it, vanishing. The roar drowned out the howls of the dogs. Drowned out everything, even its own sound. A kind of noisy hollow silence Lea never knew existed.

The beach was soaked and soft, *soft as quicksand,* she thought. And as her sandals sank deep into the muck, she pictured herself sinking down . . . down . . . until she disappeared forever into a dark, quiet world.

In the water, a canoe bobbed crazily, upside-down. Something pale and flimsy tossed on the waves. Was it a sail? A bedsheet?

Something crunched beneath Lea's sandal. She stopped with a gasp. She pictured a human hand. "Oh no."

She lowered her eyes to the sand. Tentacles. A pile of wriggling creatures. She jumped back. Struggled to keep her balance. No. They weren't moving.

Salt air off the ocean made her eyes water. When she could finally focus, she recognized them. Starfish. Dozens of them. Stiff and already dry. A pile of a hundred dead starfish, trailed by hundreds more, a long line all down the shore. They must have been washed from the sea by the storm.

Lea bent to examine them. She had never seen so many starfish. Never imagined so many would travel together. Travel together to their deaths.

She picked one up. Prickly. Nearly as hard as a seashell. She turned it over in her hand. The arms so stiff. As if it had never been alive. She dropped it onto the pile.

This has to be a symbol of bad luck.

But how can the luck get any worse?

She was still leaning down, her eyes trailing the long line of starfish corpses, when she felt the first warm drop on the back of her neck. She brushed it away with the palm of her hand and stood up.

A high wave crashed onto the beach, more violent than the others, sending up a spray of white foam before retreating. Lea felt another warm drop, this time on her forehead.

She took a step back from the ocean, shoes squishing on the mucky sand. A soft patter made her gaze around.

It had started to rain. She felt a few warm taps on the top of her head, another on her forehead. She raised a palm and felt warm raindrops on her skin.

Gazing up, she saw only white glare. No rain clouds. But the raindrops made a *pit-pit-pit* sound on the sand all around her. And the shoulders of her sweater were already wet. And her hair—

She uttered a soft cry and squinted into the falling rain. Something strange. Something not right. Like the dead starfish all gathered in a line on the shore.

Something wrong with this rain. The brightness of the sky and the darkness of the raindrops . . .

Very wrong.

Lea began to shiver. So unnatural. The darkness of the raindrops . . .

As the storm grew stronger, it became easier to see that the raindrops were red. A shimmering deep scarlet.

"Holy shit," she murmured. "It's raining *blood*!"

She raised both palms and watched the red raindrops bounce onto her skin. Fascinated and horrified, she didn't move. Stared at her hands as the red drops trickled down her palm. She lifted her eyes to the raindrops falling all around her.

Red . . . As if the blood of all who had died here last night was raining down on her. The blood of all the victims pouring doom over the island, a final terrifying drenching good-bye.

It soaked her hair and poured down her face. Bloodred raindrops pattering down from a cloudless sky. *A blood rain.*

Where had she heard that phrase before?

Yes. She had read about a blood rain in southern India several years ago. For real. The sky had opened up and red rain poured down on a village. And the people were terrified. Lea remembered.

They were frightened that the red rain was the onset of the world's end.

Now sheets of rain fell, driven by the gusting winds off the ocean. *Like red curtains, blowing and parting and closing again.*

Yes. Red curtains of rain all around her.

So wrong. So unnatural and wrong.

And as the billowing blood curtains appeared to part, two boys came stepping out. Two blond-haired boys with bright blue eyes, walking solemnly side by side.

Identical blond boys, wavy hair brushed straight back off their broad, gleaming foreheads, bare-chested and barefoot, wearing only ragged, torn white shorts stained by the red raindrops.

Their faces glowed pink. Not a healthy pink but a reflection of the red rain falling around them. They gazed straight ahead at Lea, unblinking, faces drawn, their expressions stern, wooden, unreadable.

Angels, she thought, unable to move, forced to stare back at them. *Like blond angels.*

Two angels floating out from a curtain of blood and horror.

How strange to see these two rays of light appear from all this darkness. Strange even for this island of mystery.

Pale chests and arms, white as angel feathers. Hands tucked into the pockets of their stained shorts.

Glowing figures, they moved in unison, walking together lightly over the soaked sand. Blue eyes locked on Lea. Closer.

Until Lea was forced to cut the spell. She blinked a few times. Then, squinting harder at them, she called out, shouting over the roar of the dark rain, "Can I help you?"

PART ONE

Two Days Earlier

1

BLOG POST
BY LEA HARMON SUTTER
Travel_Adventures.com

(*April 10*) Well, here I am on this island everyone calls mysterious and frightening, and I hope you are as curious as I am to find out if any of the stories are true. I tend to be skeptical. I have a bunch of older brothers who loved making up stories to terrify me, and I quickly learned not to believe any scary story anyone ever told me.

I suppose it's odd to begin a travel blog by saying that no one comes here. But before I can begin to describe the unique charms and dark mystique of Cape Le Chat Noir, I really have to start with that fact.

No one comes here.

Of course, no one really believes the island is cursed. But there are too many frightening stories from its past to ignore. The dozens of Spanish ships that mysteriously sank off the island shores in the 1600s? The rumors of dark-magic rituals? The stories—that many believe to this day—of the living dead walking the island in broad daylight?

If you are an adventure traveler like me, those all seem like *good* things!

But the fact is, no one has paid much attention to this island of whitewashed shacks, tall pine forests, fishing villages, and eccentric islanders—despite the fact that you can almost reach out and touch the place from the Outer Banks beaches of South Carolina.

Located a hop, skip, and a splash from the Cape Hatteras National Seashore, vacationers have avoided Cape Le Chat Noir like—shall I say it?—a black cat crossing their path.

For you history nerds, here's the 411: The island was annexed by the English sometime around 1650. They had little interest in it. Too small and too far from the mainland. Most English settlers chose the Roanoke Colony to the north (and we all know how that worked out).

Small groups of nomadic American Indians found their way to the island. Spanish pirates arrived later, sometimes unhappily, because they watched their ships go down just offshore.

Yes, this part of the ocean is known as the Graveyard of the Atlantic. You can Google it. Don't bother to look for a *reason* why all the ships sank. No one can tell you. But this was the beginning of the island's bad reputation.

When French traders arrived and heard the stories, they gave the island its unlucky name. I haven't been able to find out what they were trading. Most likely rum or some concoction like it. The islanders I've met seem to drink from morning till night. And if that's your idea of travel adventure, go ahead—pack your bags.

I've saved the best (or worst) for last. Here's the most interesting historical detail—and it's definitely creepy. Especially with frightening forecasts of a big hurricane heading this way.

I don't want to talk about the hurricane now. I'm pretending it's not going to happen.

You see, Le Chat Noir was devastated by one of the most powerful storms in hurricane history. It was the Labor Day Hurricane of 1935. And I have every finger crossed that history is not going to repeat itself now.

I heard the story of that dreadful hurricane shortly after arriving at Cape Le Chat Noir and stepping off the bouncing, wooden dock. Believe me, folks—it did not exactly make me feel as if a welcome mat had been put out for me.

The jeep-taxi to take me to my hotel was late. Squinting in the bright sunshine, I glanced around. The dock area seemed to be deserted, except for two ragged-looking fishermen setting off in a tiny flat-bottomed skiff. Definitely no official tourist greeter waiting with a rum punch or even a friendly smile.

I spotted a tiny brown shack across the dirt road with the sign *Tea Shop*. So, with suitcase, laptop case, and camera in hand, I made my way there to wait for my ride.

Inside, the room was dimly lit, with red neon lights over the mirror at a bar and small gas lamps on each table. The tables were round cylinders, like conga drums. Wall posters from tea companies provided the only cheeriness. I liked a poster that showed a grinning Chinese child holding a big steaming cup, and the words *How Long Since You OOLONG?*

The place was totally empty. I took a seat at a table near the bar. I coughed, hoping it might summon someone from in back. A wooden overhead fan squeaked as it slowly made its rounds.

An old woman emerged—white bristly hair under a black bandanna, pale skin tight over her cheekbones, silvery gray eyes, a little hunched over. She wore a long black dress, not exactly island wear. Without asking, she set a cup of dark tea down on my table with quavering hands.

"Thank you." My voice sounded muffled in the heavy air of the tiny room. The squeaking fan seemed to grow louder.

"Why have you come?" Her voice was velvety smooth, much younger than her looks. Not exactly a friendly hello, huh, folks?

I stammered an answer about writing a travel story about Le Chat Noir.

"There's a big storm on the way," she said. "Hurricane Ernesto. Didn't you hear about it?" She had no accent at all. Her eyes were so glassy, I thought she might be blind. But then I remembered she had set the teacup down on the little table with ease.

"Yes. My husband warned me not to come here in hurricane season," I said, inhaling the bitter steam from the cup.

Mark is so sweet. He always wants me to stay home. But exploring my backyard would make for a dull travel blog, don't you agree?

Well, to cut to the chase, the woman told me her name was Marguerite. She procured her own cup of tea, sat down across from me, stared unblinkingly into my eyes, and began to talk in her smooth whisper of a voice.

"The hurricane of 1935 didn't have a name. They didn't name them then. But it didn't need a name to be remembered."

I blew on the cup, then sipped the tea. "You mean it was a bad one?"

She nodded. Her throat made a rattling sound. I pretended not to notice.

"The storm showed no mercy. It swept over the Outer Banks, up to Chincoteague Island and the Virginia coast, flattening everything in its path. Nothing was left standing on this island. Not a house, not a shack, not a bait shop, not a teahouse. All shattered. All ruined. Even the lighthouse on the south shore was toppled over, into the ocean."

I tsk-tsked. "That's horrible."

"My friends . . . people I knew, members of my family . . . Many were crushed, buried, drowned. I was a child. I saw the corpses. They were floating in lakes and rivulets caused by the storm. Even at my age, I knew the horror. I knew the pain, the suffering. No one could decide where to pile the bodies. They lay sprawled in the sand and sea grass and on piles of wreckage. The corpses . . . They were feasted on for days by seagulls and starving dogs."

She took a long sip of tea. Her throat rattled as she swallowed. She gripped the cup with both hands, I guess, because her hands were so shaky.

I felt a shiver go down my back. The story was terrifying and sad, but her whispered voice made it even more frightening. I had to remind myself that this took place in 1935.

"I was a child but the pictures never faded from my eyes. The island was devastated. Turned to rubble. But it took only *weeks* to rebuild Le Chat Noir. Why? Because of a miracle. You might not call it a miracle, dear. You might call it a *nightmare*."

She waited for me to react. Her silvery eyes still hadn't blinked.

I set down the cup. "What do you mean? What kind of nightmare?"

She swallowed. She leaned closer, close enough for me to see the thick layer of powder on her tight cheeks. "Le Chat Noir returned to normal in weeks. Because the *old* dead—the dead from centuries past—came back to life. All the dead of the island returned to help rebuild it. No eyes, flesh rotting, bones yellowed and broken, they floated up from their flooded graves and went to work. They joined the survivors to bury the recent dead and restore and rebuild Le Chat Noir.

"When the job was done, did they return to their graves? No. The dead were proud of their handiwork. And they enjoyed the sunlight. It healed them and made them look almost normal, so normal most of them could blend in with the living. They decided to stay."

I squinted at her. "The dead? The dead people stayed?"

She nodded, her expression solemn. She reached across the table and squeezed my hand. Her hand was dry and hard, like solid bone. "That's what makes Le Chat Noir special, dear. It's the only place on earth where the living share their space with the living dead."

I glanced down at my empty teacup. The tea leaves on the bottom appeared to form an X. Of course I didn't believe Marguerite's story. But it left me feeling strange, kind of cold and tingly.

She smiled for the first time. Her smile cracked the powder on her cheeks. Placing both hands on the table, she pushed herself to her feet. "I see you are thinking about my story."

I nodded. "Yes. It's . . . frightening."

Her smile faded. "Not that frightening, dear. I died ten years ago, but I'm doing pretty well. Can I bring you another cup of tea?"

My mouth dropped open.

A dry laugh, more like a cough, escaped her throat. "I'm only teasing you. I see your ride is outside. Enjoy your stay on our beautiful island."

2

Lea sat on the edge of the bed, smoothing her hands over the tropical-colored, flowery quilt, letting the warm sea breezes tickle her face. The lace curtains fluttered at the open window of the rooming house. White and yellow daisies floated in a glass bowl of water on the bed table beside her.

The small, second-floor room was bright with afternoon sunlight spreading across the blond-wood floor, and spotlessly crisp and clean with a vague aroma of coconut in the air. Red and blue starfish dotted the wallpapered walls, appropriate since the place was called Starfish House.

The two-story, shingled house with a sloping red-tile roof stood on a low, grassy dune overlooking the Eastern shore beach and a row of white fishing huts along the water.

Is this the calm before the storm? Lea wondered. *Or has Hurricane Ernesto changed its course?*

She didn't want to check. She didn't want to spoil her first day.

She could hear the hushed voices of her hosts drift upstairs from the front desk. An hour before, when the jeep-taxi dropped her off at the front door, they had both come bursting out, clapping their hands and speaking rapidly and excitedly in French, almost dancing around Lea and her two bags.

Maybe they are just warm, excitable people, she thought. *But they're really acting as if I'm their first guest.*

Macaw Henders and her husband, Pierre. They owned the six-room inn. She was a big woman, Spanish-looking, with cocoa skin, round, black eyes and straight black bangs across a broad forehead.

She wore an expansive red-and-fuchsia housedress with feathery sleeves and collar and a red bandanna over her hair. Lea had to suppress a laugh since it really did look like bird plumage.

In contrast, Pierre was as thin as a pencil, balding, with brown eyes deep-set in a serious face. One of those people who always looks worried, Lea figured. No way to determine how old he was. He could be thirty or fifty.

A soft knock at the doorway startled Lea from her thoughts. She stood up as Macaw appeared, holding a tray with a white china cup. She handed the cup to Lea. Lea gazed down at a foamy, dark brown drink. She expected the cup to be hot, but it was cold.

Macaw smiled, revealing a gold cap on one front tooth. "Go ahead, Madame Sutter. A welcome drink. Take a small sip to start." She spoke in a lilting singsong.

Lea took a small sip, then another. Coffee with vodka? No. But definitely potent and sour. She could feel the warmth slide down her throat, into her chest.

"Macaw, what is this drink called?"

The woman hesitated. She ruffled her feathery housedress, much like a preening macaw. "Kill-Devil," she said finally, lowering her eyes.

Lea laughed and gazed into the cup. "Kill-Devil? Do you know why?"

"Because it's powerful enough to kill the Devil?"

Lea took another sip. She was starting to like the bitter taste. "This is a lovely room," she said, gesturing with her free hand. And then blurted out without really thinking about it, "Am I the only one staying here?"

The woman nodded.

"But, why?"

Macaw's smile faded. She pretended to be interested in something on the tray. "I guess they have their reasons, Madame Sutter."

3

BLOG POST
BY LEA HARMON SUTTER
Travel_Adventures.com

(April 11) The bad news is that Ernesto still has its sights on Le Chat Noir. The hurricane is slow-moving, about fourteen miles per hour, which is even more bad news, because the longer it stays in one place, the more damage it does.

The only good news is that it gives me a little time to find some kind of adventure to write about before I have to duck and hide.

I'm writing this post on my iPad. I can feel the emergency vibes. People are boarding up their windows and pulling their boats onshore. The sky has turned an ugly lead color, and the wind feels heavy and damp.

My hosts, Macaw and Pierre, were reluctant to let me leave the house. I'm not sure they understood that my job is to go out and do risky things so I can write about them.

I'd been in touch (by email) with a woman who lives on Le Chat Noir, named Martha Swann. Martha told me about an island ceremony called *Revenir*, which is French for "to come back." She explained that the *Revenir* ritual is part of a practice called *Mains*

Magiques—Magic Hands. She believed the French traders picked it up somewhere and brought it here with them. Martha wrote that it is a must-see.

I told my hosts I wanted to attend a *Revenir* ceremony, and they reacted not with horror but with definite disapproval. They both started shaking their heads, as if it would persuade me to drop the idea.

"It's all a fake," Macaw insisted. "They put on a show. The priest—he performs it every week."

"It's bad for the island," Pierre agreed. His eyes took on a sadness. "These magic rituals, they make us look foolish. Primitive."

"Why scare the people away?" Macaw said. "Why not talk about the beauty here? The natural beauty. Not the *unnatural*."

"I know it isn't real," I said. "I'm not going to write that it's real. But I think my readers will find it interesting. You know. It's all about life and death, right? It's been practiced for hundreds of years. It's so . . . colorful."

"We don't want to be colorful," Macaw said in her red-and-fuchsia dress.

After a lot of begging and pleading and explaining, they finally agreed to find a guide to take me to the ceremony.

He turned out to be a sandy-haired, boyish, tanned young man in khaki cargo shorts and safari jacket, who seemed so shy and spoke so softly I never did figure out what language he was using. I believe his name was Jean-Carl. He always looked away when he spoke to me, as if he was ashamed of his job or where he was taking me.

He drove me in an open jeep over the one single-lane paved road that leads to the center of the island. The road was lined on both sides by amazing cabbage palmettos. Their clusters of long leaves gleamed, even in the darkening light of the sky. Talk about magic! The trees were flowering, the yellow-white blossoms flashing by like tiny lights.

I didn't see any other car traffic. Jean-Carl parked the jeep in the shade of a clump of palms at the edge of a sandy path, and we began to walk, the soft sand tickling my feet as it flowed over my open sandals.

I tried to ask Jean-Carl questions about what I could expect to see. But again, he seemed embarrassed or else just painfully unsuited to his job. He kept repeating the word *scary* and shaking his head.

Of course, that only heightened my anticipation. And when we reached a small crowd of people—men and women of indeterminate age in colorful beach caftans and robes—I was ready for my *Mains Magiques* adventure.

4

Lea estimated twenty people in the crowd, mostly men. They stood at the edge of the thick rain forest, inside a circle of the strangest palm trees she'd ever seen. "What are those trees called?" she asked Jean-Carl.

He gazed at them, blinking a few times. He didn't answer.

What a great guide. I don't think he speaks English.

A well-dressed, middle-aged woman with pink cheeks, short blond hair, and pale blue eyes turned to Lea. "They are called jelly palms, dear."

Lea studied the very fat trunks topped by long, delicate leaves that looked like feathers. "Y'all can make jelly from the dates," the woman said. She had a definite Southern accent. "The dates are big and juicy and very sweet." Then her eyes went wide. "Are you Lea? From Long Island? I'm Martha Swann."

Lea gasped. "Martha? Really? Hi. How did you recognize me?"

"From your Facebook photo. I feel like we're old friends."

"Wow! I mean, wow. How nice to meet you. See? I took your advice. I'm here. I always think these rituals are a hoot, don't you? They're almost always like from a bad horror movie. Hope I don't burst out laughing."

Martha pursed her lips. "I don't think y'all will laugh at this one." She glanced around. "My husband, James, and I come often. It's . . . really miraculous. We've even gotten to know the priest." She raised a finger to her lips. "Look. I think it's starting."

Lea turned and stepped forward, into the circle of people. They had gathered around a fallen log, smooth-barked, about ten feet long. A sun-bleached skull was placed in the center. *A human skull. No. It's an animal head. A goat, maybe.*

She turned to Jean-Carl to ask, but he had moved away to the other end of the log. She mopped her forehead with the back of one hand. The center of the island felt much steamier than the outer beach areas. She suddenly found it hard to breathe.

These weird ceremonies make me giddy.

She listened to the buzz of quiet conversations. Two older men in white robes and sandals appeared to be having an argument. A woman in a blue chiffon caftan stepped between them.

The crowd grew larger. Now there were maybe forty people standing in the circle around the log. Lea hadn't seen them approaching. They seemed to have emerged from the trees.

She turned and saw five people striding quickly on the path. Four of them were obviously American tourists. The two men were paunchy and pale and wore blue-and-red Chicago Cubs baseball caps. One wore a Budweiser T-shirt with a beer can emblazoned across the front.

The two women with them were slender and dressed in shorts and flowery tank tops. They had cameras hanging around their necks and were being led by a tall, serious-looking guide, dressed in khaki cargo shorts and safari jacket, like Jean-Carl.

Lea was startled. Actual tourists on Cape Le Chat Noir! She had the urge to say hello. To interview them and ask how they came to be on the island and if they knew what this ritual was about. But their guide led them to the other side of the circle.

People talked quietly, but the conversations ended when the priest—a tall, bald man wearing a long red robe tied with a yellow sash—stepped out from behind a fat-trunked jelly palm. He had a red face and shocking white-blond eyebrows that moved up and down on his broad forehead like furry caterpillars. His eyes were silvery gray, metallic. He had a tattoo of a blue five-cornered star on the crown of his bald head, almost big enough to be a skullcap.

Weird-looking dude.

He stepped into the circle, carrying a long wooden tray. On the tray were coconut halves, flat side up. Without uttering a word, he stepped up to people and raised the tray to them, offering a coconut half. Lea quickly realized that he was approaching only the men in the circle.

He handed coconut halves to six men. She could see that the insides had been carved to form a cup, and each cup contained a dark liquid. It looked a lot like the Kill-Devil drink Macaw had given her when she arrived the day before.

Lea felt a chill as the priest eyed her for a long moment. She couldn't read his expression. He flashed her an almost imperceptible smile. Then he moved to the center of the circle and gazed at the men holding the coconut cups.

"It's the Black Drink," Martha murmured in her ear. She leaned close and whispered surreptitiously, as if she was breaking a rule. "The Black Drink. Be grateful, dear. In the ceremony, the priest gives it only to the men."

"Why?" Lea whispered back.

Again, Martha raised a finger to her lips. Her eyes flashed in the gray afternoon light. She returned her gaze to the priest.

Lea glanced down the line to the tourists. All four of them were busily snapping photos with their cameras and phones.

The red-robed priest gave a signal, and the six men raised their coconut cups high above their heads, as if offering them to the sun. They all chanted something . . . in French?

Lea struggled to understand. She had studied French for two years at Northwestern. But this didn't sound like any French she'd ever heard.

When the six men finished, the priest chanted for a long time, mumbling to himself and moving his hands slowly in a strange sign language. The sleeves of his robe swayed beneath his bone-slender arms.

Lea kept her eyes on his hands. They appeared to take on a life of their own, like small, pale animals floating in the air.

Birds uttered harsh cries in the rainforest behind them. A gust of hot wind made the feathery palm leaves slap and scrape.

We need pounding drums here. Ominous background music.

She scolded herself for being so cynical.

The skin on her arms tingled. She wiped sweat off the back of her neck.

The air is so heavy and wet. Perhaps we are feeling the first winds of the hurricane.

She crossed her arms tightly on her chest to steady her heartbeat. *I certainly don't want to be out here in the middle of the island if the damned hurricane hits.*

The priest finally finished his low chant. He nodded. The six men lowered the cups to their mouths and drank the dark liquid down.

Lea heard soft cries in the crowd. Muttered words.

The men stood silently, swallowing even after lowering the cups to their sides. Palm leaves slapped loudly above their heads, as if clapping.

The sky darkened from pale gray to charcoal. The wind picked up, fluttering robes and skirts, lifting Lea's hair behind her head, making a howling moan as it swirled through the shivering trees.

Special effects, Lea thought. *The priest chants and the wind starts to howl. Very dramatic.*

But she wasn't prepared for what happened next.

As she squinted into the fading light, the six men all began to groan. They coughed and rolled their eyes. Their faces reddened. They bent their knees and knelt.

Bending low, faces purple, they uttered hideous choking sounds. Then rasping moans from deep in their throats. Their stomachs bubbled and heaved.

And they all began to vomit at once.

5

Groaning, moaning, bleating like sick sheep, all six men heaved together. At first they spewed a dark liquid and then the chunky orange and yellow of their undigested lunches.

Hands on their knees, heads bowed as if praying, they puked their guts out in a chorus of animal groans and splashing liquid.

Lea grabbed her throat. She felt her breakfast rise. Her stomach churned. She held her breath, swallowing hard, swallowing, struggling not to heave along with them.

This was no act. They weren't faking it. No one could fake those ugly sounds, those horrified expressions. She covered her ears from their choked gasps and bleats and retching moans.

The sour smell rose into the humid air and swept over her. She stared at the thick piles of yellow-green vomit, spreading puddles on the sand. Still holding her breath, Lea started to turn away.

But Martha held her by the shoulders. "It isn't over. It just started."

Just started?

A shudder ran down Lea's body. Her legs suddenly felt rubbery, weak. She forced herself to watch. The six men bleated and choked. They grabbed their throats. Their eyes bulged in panic. Their faces darkened from red to purple to a sick blue.

She cried out as the men collapsed to the ground. One by one, they folded up, coiling into themselves. Uttering strangled sighs, they dropped facedown into their own vomit. They sprawled awkwardly on the ground, eyes bulging, gazing blankly. Their arms and legs twitched, as if they were getting electrical shocks; twitched like grotesque puppets that had lost their strings. Then stopped.

No one moved.

Swaying in the gusting wind, the feathery palm trees slapped and applauded. The birds had stopped their shrill symphony.

The red-robed priest knelt beside one of the fallen men. The star tattoo on his scalp appeared to wriggle, alive, like a blue octopus. He placed two fingers on the man's throat. Minutes went by.

"*Il est mort.*" Announced in a whisper.

"Oh my God," Lea murmured. She suddenly realized she had been hugging herself tightly for some time. Down by the tight circle of onlookers, she heard the startled cries of the four tourists. No one else made a sound.

The priest moved to the next victim sprawled facedown on the sand, a young man with short red hair and a boyish, freckled face. He rolled the man onto his back. After a brief examination, the priest repeated the words. "*Il est mort.*" Flat. No emotion at all.

Lea turned and saw the two men tourists snapping photos with their phones. The women had their hands over their faces, blocking out the death scene.

"Is this for real?" the man in the Budweiser shirt boomed. "Hey—are they really dead?"

No one replied. All eyes were on the tall, bald priest until he knelt over the last of the six victims.

"*Tous sont morts.*"

Lea forced herself to breathe. She suddenly felt dizzy, the blood pulsing at her temples. She had hoped to write about travel adventures people would find exciting. But *no way* she wanted to watch six men drink poison and vomit themselves to death.

Squinting into the graying light, she could see clearly that the six men weren't breathing. Their chests showed no movement. No rise and fall. No movement at all. Their eyes bulged, gazing blankly like glass doll eyes. Their mouths hung open, frozen in their final gasps for breath.

Still, no one on the island moved or made a sound. She glimpsed Jean-Carl across from her in the circle. He had his head down, hands jammed into the pockets of his cargo shorts.

The tourists had stopped their picture-taking. One of the women was crying. Budweiser Man wrapped her in an awkward hug.

The priest, still expressionless, turned to face the crowd. His blond caterpillar eyebrows had gone stiff and still.

He clasped both hands in front of him. Lea noticed for the first time that his fingernails were painted black. He began to chant: "*Revenir . . . Revenir . . . Revenir . . .*" Softly at first, then louder, urging the audience to join in.

"*Revenir . . . Revenir . . . Revenir . . .*"

The chanting voices echoed off the trees of the rain forest. The chant continued for two minutes . . . three . . .

Lea screamed when she saw a hand move. On the ground. Fingers twitched.

"*Revenir . . . Revenir . . . Revenir . . .*"

The chant continued, no longer a word, just a low, breathy sound.

Another dead man blinked his eyes. Another raised his head an inch off the ground. A short groan escaped his throat. More hands twitched. Like crabs testing the sand.

"*Revenir . . . Revenir . . . Revenir . . .*"

As Lea stared in disbelief, the six dead men sat up. They blinked rapidly and shook their heads, tested their jaws, squinted at the chanting crowd.

The chant ended suddenly. People rushed forward to help the men to their feet. In seconds, they were all standing, taking small steps, still looking dazed, wiping chunks of vomit off their shirts and shorts and robes.

The priest raised his hands high above his tattooed head. "*Les hommes sont revenus,*" he announced. "The men have returned."

The six men were walking steadily now, making their way to the path. The circle of onlookers broke up, people heading in all directions. Lea listened to the excited conversations. Some people were laughing. The ceremony was over.

Lea shut her eyes. Again she pictured those men bent over, their streams of vomit splashing onto the grass. Their gasping, terrified faces. Their bodies coiled lifelessly on the ground in front of her.

And as rain began to patter down, she thought of the 1935 hurricane and the story of the dead returning to life to repair the devastating damage. The living sharing their space with the unliving.

Huge raindrops rattled on the palm leaves, like assault rifles. Loud as thunder. The wind swirled around Lea, pushed her right, then left. She planted her feet, determined not to be blown over. A suffocating wind rushed over her face, made her gasp for breath.

It came on so suddenly. I thought we had time.

Hugging herself again, she ducked her head and searched for Jean-Carl. Nowhere in sight. Perhaps he had run to the jeep.

A strong blast of wind bent the palm trees till they were nearly horizontal. Lea's shoes sank into the mud as she stepped onto the path.

She felt a hand on her shoulder. Gasping in surprise, she spun around. "Martha?"

Martha had a canvas tennis hat pulled down tight over her hair. Her sweater was already soaked through, matted to her body. "Better come home with me." She had to scream over the roar of the wind.

Lea blinked through the sheets of rain that swept over her. "No. My stuff—"

"Better come with me, Lea. This is going to be bad. It's going to be real bad."

6

As Hurricane Ernesto slowly made its way north, Mark Sutter was ending his book tour close to home at HamptonBooks in Easthampton, Long Island.

The store occupied a gray shingle building near one end of the long row of shops on Main Street, a few doors down from the Ralph Lauren store, a country antiques store, an old-fashioned toy store, and the Hamptons' branch of Tiffany's, all closed and deserted on this rain-tossed April night, before the summer people had arrived.

Mark arrived early, shaking out his umbrella and squirming out of the Burberry trench coat that no longer seemed to be waterproof. He liked to watch his audience come in, liked to size up the crowd before he spoke to them.

Crowd. Would there be a crowd on a night like this? He saw a few rain-bedraggled people in one of the long, narrow store aisles. A good sign.

A smiling, middle-aged woman hurried out from behind the front counter to greet him. "Hi, Mr. Sutter. I'm Jo-Ann, the manager. Welcome. You're early."

She was a mouse of a woman, small and gray, with lips the same color as her skin. She was probably forty, but she looked ten years older. She wore a loose-fitting gray turtleneck over black corduroy slacks.

"I like to come early and hang out a bit," Mark said. "You know. Chat with people. Kind of size up the crowd."

"Well, make yourself at home. We've already sold several books, and we got a lot of phone calls. I think there'll be a crowd." She squinted at him. "How does it feel to be controversial?"

Mark laughed. "I'm enjoying it, actually."

She nodded solemnly. "Of course you are."

Mark wondered exactly what she meant.

"Sometimes it's good to stir people up," she said. And then quickly changed gears: "Can I get you a bottle of water?"

"No. I'm fine."

"Sure? I have plenty of water."

"No. Really. I saw enough water driving here."

His joke fell flat. He knew it wasn't much of a joke. He shouldn't try to be funny. No one expected it of him. But what was this obsession with water? In every city at every bookstore, they tried to shove bottle after bottle of water at him.

"The rain is from the hurricane," she said, "but we're lucky. I have the radio on. They said it's veering out into the ocean. We'll just get the rain."

"Hurricane?"

She squinted at him. "You didn't hear? It's a big one. Down South."

Mark felt his throat tighten. "My wife is down South. On an island. I didn't know. I had my iPod in the car. I—"

"Maybe you should try to call her." She turned and saw the line of customers at the front counter. "I'd better get back." She gave his wrist a quick squeeze. Like saying *Good luck*. Then she turned and made her way back to the other two clerks at the counter.

She stepped behind one of the cash registers and pulled on a pair of tight white rubber gloves. *To protect herself from money germs?*

Mark slid his BlackBerry from the pocket of his jeans, raised it to push Lea's number. Then stopped. No bars.

I'm sure she's okay. I'll phone her after the book signing.

He stepped toward the back and leaned against a bookshelf where he could watch customers enter. He could see a gauzy reflection of himself in the front window, floating over the pyramid of display copies of his book. A gust of wind rattled the window and sent rivulets of rainwater streaking down the glass.

"Where do I put this?" A man in a brown rain slicker and canvas tennis hat shook his umbrella in a red-haired store clerk's face, sending a spray of rainwater over the front counter. The young man pointed to the tall can by the door, already jammed with wet umbrellas.

The store was small, narrow and deep with two aisles leading back through tall wooden bookshelves. Rows of low-hanging fluorescent lights sent down a pale glare, making everyone look a little green. At the back, a steep stairway led upstairs to the author event area.

Mark felt his skin prickle. He rubbed his stubbled cheeks. The air in the store felt hot and damp despite the cold blasts every time the door opened. He could smell the ocean.

In a few hours I'll be home.

He could hear a low mumble of voices from upstairs. A respectable crowd on a stormy Wednesday night in Easthampton. *Please— let there be fifty people.* That's all an author cares about. A crowd big enough not to be embarrassing. Please—not four people who all choose to sit in the back row.

To his relief, he saw several couples lined up at the cash register. They all had his book in their hands. Did they look happy? No.

They've all come for a fight.

He turned back toward the front door and felt his stomach rumble. Not from stage fright. He looked forward to another confrontation. If only he could keep them from shouting this time.

He suddenly pictured the young woman in Boston who turned purple and started to tremble. That was *awkward.* And the angry couple who followed him to the parking lot and refused to let him get into the car until they had their say.

His stomach churned again from the bacon cheeseburger he had eaten too fast at Rowdy Hall, the noisy, crowded hamburger joint across the street. He always ate too fast when he was alone.

I'll be home tonight.

His house in Sag Harbor was twenty minutes away, maybe a little longer if the storm continued. He had driven to the bookstore directly from MacArthur Airport in Ronkonkoma. He hadn't had even two seconds to stop at home and say hi.

Ira and Elena. When did he see them last? Two weeks ago? He talked to them on the phone every night, and he Skyped them when he could. But the conversations were always forced and hurried.

Elena was okay. Even at the gawky age of fourteen, she bobbed merrily through life like a kite in a strong wind. Ira was the sensitive one, always overthinking everything, so shy and serious. Poor guy. Sixth grade. His first year in middle school.

Mark should have been there to help him get through it. Or Lea. But she was away, too. He hated it when they were both away at the same time.

"When you write a travel blog, you kind of have to travel," Lea had said.

"I'm not accusing you of anything," he had countered. "I'm just saying . . ."

"That one of us should stay home."

"No. I'm just saying it's a *shame* that one of us isn't staying home."

That made her laugh. "I love your subtle distinctions. I wasn't a psych major like you, darling, but I know when I'm being guilted."

Guilted?

No way he could convince her to stay home till he got back. *Travel & Leisure* had let her go. Budget cutbacks. The usual thing. Now Lea was determined to produce the best adventure-travel blog in the universe, build a huge audience, collect millions in advertising, and show her old bosses what a mistake they had made.

She was ambitious. And she was a fighter. The youngest of seven, with four brothers and two sisters, Lea was used to fighting for what she wanted.

And so . . . they went their separate ways, and Mark's sister, Roz, stayed with the kids.

Mark had to admit, the ten-city book tour was not as glamorous as he had imagined. And he was taken by surprise by all the anger waiting for him at every bookstore. After all, he'd only written a book. He hadn't *murdered* anyone.

He wasn't naïve. He knew his book would spark controversy. But he never dreamed that parents would react with such alarm, as if he were threatening parenthood itself.

Which maybe he was.

Because of all the controversy, *Kids Will Be Kids* was at the top of the nonfiction bestseller list. Exactly what he had strived for. He wanted to reach as many parents as possible.

He wasn't trying to become famous by stirring things up. He believed his studies of his young patients validated his parenting theories.

He glanced at the clock, then watched more rain-soaked stragglers push into the bookstore. Someone tapped his shoulder. The red-haired store clerk—*Adam,* it said on his ID badge. "Mr. Sutter, can I get you some water?"

"No thanks. I'm good."

"You sure?"

He turned to the steep wooden staircase. He could hear the crowd up there shifting, folding chairs squeaking, the mumble of voices. Someone laughed loudly.

Showtime.

7

Not quite ready. He made his way toward the bathroom behind the office in back. A large man in a gray hoodie and faded jeans blocked the aisle. He was scanning a shelf of fiction, but turned as Mark approached.

"Hi. Are you here for my book talk?"

The man shook his head. "No. I'm not much of a reader. I'm here for my wife."

"Your wife?"

"Yeah. She heard there's a new James Patterson." He swung back to the bookshelf. "You're not him, are you?"

"No. No, I'm not. Sorry."

Sorry? Why did I say sorry?

Mark edged past him into the phone-booth-size bathroom and checked the mirror. Brought his face close and grinned. He rubbed his front teeth with one finger. No hamburger or lettuce there. Nothing hanging from his nose.

He smoothed a hand over the stubble on his cheeks and brushed back his short hair, his hazel eyes dark in the dim light from the ceiling. He wasn't admiring himself. He was *preparing* himself.

Lea called him Gyllenhaal. She said he was a dead ringer for the actor. Flattering? Yes. A two-day stubble, short, dark hair and big eyes, and he was Jake Gyllenhaal to her.

I love you, Lea.

Only thirty-nine but even in this bad light, he could see patches of gray spreading over the sides of his hair. No problem. A psychologist doesn't want to be *too* good-looking. He needs some maturity. Some authority.

He wore a trim black suit jacket over dark, straight-legged denim jeans. His white shirt was open at the collar. Not too formal. He wanted to appear open and friendly. They would see he wasn't a stuffed shirt. He was a young father. A child psychologist with a serious point of view. But casual. Even likable?

He grinned. He should wear a suit of armor. The lions were waiting upstairs to rip him to shreds and devour the remains.

His stomach churned again. Maybe it wasn't the cheeseburger. Maybe it was the two Heinekens.

Up the stairs, Mark. Go get 'em.

He used the wooden banister to pull himself. The steps creaked beneath him. He practiced a smile. It didn't feel right. Tried a smaller one. Above the mumbling of the crowd, he could hear rain pattering against the sloped skylight window in the ceiling.

The stage area came into view as he reached the top. A good crowd. The folding chairs were all filled. And a row of people stood behind them. Some leaned against the bookshelf walls. Two young women had made cushions of their coats and sat cross-legged on the floor to the side of the podium.

At least a hundred people. No. More like one fifty.

So far, a success. Jo-Ann flashed him a smile from beside the podium. Good. The store manager was pleased.

He surveyed the crowd. Mostly couples. Parents. Some gripped his book in their laps. To have it signed or to throw at him? They watched him warily as he moved toward the podium.

"He's young," someone whispered, just loudly enough to be heard.

"Does he have kids?"

"If he does, can you imagine what they're like?"

A cell phone erupted and was quickly cut off. He saw three very old people, frail, hunkered in the front row, still in their raincoats, shopping bags on the floor in front of them. Regulars, probably. Lonely people who come to every bookstore event.

Jo-Ann started to introduce him. There were hurried footsteps on the stairs. More arrivals. She wrapped her hand around the microphone as she talked, and it made an annoying scraping sound.

"—already seem to be familiar with our guest author and his book, so I expect a lively discussion tonight."

Mark heard a few people snicker at that.

"Some things you may not know about Mark Sutter," Jo-Ann continued. "He's a Sag Harbor resident, not a summer person. He and his wife live here year-round with their two children."

She read from a handwritten index card. One hand held the card. The other squeezed the microphone as if trying to get juice from it.

"Mr. Sutter was born on Long Island in 1973. He grew up in Great Neck. He has a BS in Child Psychology from the University of Wisconsin. Mr. Sutter has a national reputation. He has contributed to many major psychology and science journals. *Kids Will Be Kids* is his first book, based on studies he made over the past five years observing his own juvenile patients and their parents."

She finally let go of the microphone and motioned to Mark with a tight smile. "Let's all welcome tonight's author, Mark Sutter."

Tepid applause. Mark forced the practiced smile to his face and took two steps toward the podium.

Jo-Ann turned and wrapped her hand around the microphone again. The applause died quickly. She waved Mark back. "Oh, I almost forgot," she said, "while I have you all here. Such a nice crowd. It's so wonderful to see people come out on a rainy night to discuss books."

Mark shoved his hands into his jeans pockets and waited. He studied the crowd. A twentysomething couple in the second row had their heads down, tapping away on their phones. Behind them, a large man in a Yankees cap and blue-and-white Yankees jacket had the *Daily News* open in front of him.

Rain pattered the skylight window. Mark glimpsed a flicker of lightning high in the green-black sky. He blinked—and saw someone he recognized in the third row. A young woman in a short blue skirt over black tights and a white tube top.

His eyes took in the gleaming white-blond hair. Blue eyes. High cheekbones. Red-lipped smile.

She didn't register at first. Mainly because she didn't tell him she'd be there. The improbably named Autumn Holliday, his assistant. She realized he had finally spotted her. She smiled and her eyes went wide. She gave him an excited wave.

Why did she get all dolled up for this?

Autumn always showed up at his office in jeans and oversize rock-band T-shirts, her hair tied carelessly back in a ponytail. Now he couldn't help but stare. She looked like one of those stunning Nordic ice-queen fashion models.

"Autumn? What are you doing here?" He mouthed the words silently.

"—Thriller Night here at HamptonBooks," Jo-Ann was saying. "I think you'll all want to be here. Our guest author will be Harlan Coben, and if you were here last year, I'm sure you will remember how funny and charming Mr. Coben can be. So . . . don't forget next Saturday night."

Mark forced himself to turn away from Autumn. Jo-Ann was waving him back. This time there was no applause. He could feel the tension in the room.

Lightning flickered in the skylight above. People shifted their weight, sat up straighter, squeezed the books in their laps. The couple in the second row tucked their phones away.

Somewhere in the back, a baby cried. Mark suddenly realized there were several babies on laps, swaddled like tiny mummies.

Mark placed his hands on the sides of the podium. The microphone was a little too low. He leaned into it. "Good evening, everyone. Thanks for coming out on such a lovely night. Instead of a reading tonight, I know you all probably have a lot of questions. And I thought we could begin by discussing—"

Several hands shot up. They were too eager.

Here we go again.

"Are you Dr. Sutter or Mr. Sutter?" From a chubby, coppery-haired man standing behind the seats, wearing an ugly chartreuse turtleneck and gray sweatpants.

"I'm Mr. Sutter. I have a BS degree in child psychology. You can call me Mark."

"So you're not a doctor?" Accusing.

Before Mark could answer, a woman in the front row, her arm cradling a swaddled baby. "Why do you think children don't need parents? Why do you think they should grow up wild and undisciplined and untrained?"

Mark forced his smile to grow wider. He had learned a lot at the other bookstore appearances. The trick was not to get flustered. Remain calm. Be quieter and saner than the audience.

He glimpsed Autumn, her brightly lipsticked lips pursed, eyes narrowed with concern.

"Have you read my book?" he asked the woman in the front row.

She nodded. "Some of it."

A few people snickered.

"Well, I think you are misrepresenting what I wrote. I believe children need parents," he said. "My problem is with *too much* parenting."

"There can't be too much!" a man yelled from somewhere in back. The outburst drew some short applause.

Mark ignored it. "Basically, what I have found is that children thrive and grow happier and more creative with *less* parental supervision. I'm not saying we should ignore our responsibility to teach them the basics of what's right and wrong. We all must instill a good moral sense. But we all know about helicopter parents these days, who hover over their kids wherever they go. These control-freak parents hinder the natural creative growth—"

"Kids *need* to be controlled," the same man shouted.

"Kids *want* to be controlled," the woman with the baby contributed. "They don't *want* the kind of freedom you are talking about."

The audience seemed to erupt. Mark kept his smile, waited for them to settle down, tapping his hands on the sides of the podium.

"I appreciate your point of view," he said finally. "But for my book, I studied my patients and their parents for five years. My observations led me to believe what I wrote here. I believe parents should act like guides—but not like cops. Children need their parents to be warm and loving. But they also need to be independent from them."

The woman with the baby spoke up again. "You mean parents should act like friends—not like parents?"

"Friends love and support you," Mark replied. "What's wrong with that?"

Another eruption of angry voices.

Autumn was shaking her head, her hair shimmering like a silver helmet in the light. She stared at him wide-eyed, concentrating, as if sending him a psychic message of support. His one fan.

She has nice tits. How come I've never noticed? Because she's twenty-three?

"Let me give you an example from the book, the boy named Sammy. Sammy is ten. His parents treat him as an equal. They let him decide what to eat. They let Sammy decide when to go to bed and when to wake up. They let him decide how much time to spend playing video games or watching TV.

"As a result, Sammy is not only happy but well behaved. Mature. He has a confidence that I don't see in most ten-year-olds. You see, the extra freedom given Sammy by his parents has allowed him to—"

A vibration against his leg stunned him, and he stopped in mid-sentence. It took him until the second buzzing tingle to realize it was the phone in his jeans pocket.

Probably his sister, Roz, wanting to know when he'd be home.

He ignored it. It buzzed three more times before it shut off.

"A lot of doctors don't agree with you," a woman against the wall spoke up in a raspy smoker's voice. "I read a review by a psychologist in the *Times* who said your ideas are dangerous."

The phone buzzed again. The vibration sent a tingle up and down his leg. Roz wouldn't call back. Someone was being insistent.

"Excuse me," he said, grabbing the phone from his pocket. He squinted at the screen. *Lea?*

"I'm really sorry. I have to take this." He backed away from the podium. "My wife—she's on an island. . . ."

He turned away from the audience. Behind him, mumbled voices and grumbling. He raised the phone to his ear. "Lea? Are you okay?"

A deafening howl made him jerk the phone away. Then he heard her voice, high, shrill. "Mark—the hurricane . . ."

He could barely hear her over the static and whistling. "What? What did you say?"

"Ernesto . . . It . . . It's *horrible,* Mark."

She was screaming over the roar. She sounded frantic.

"The hurricane? Are you okay?"

The howling stopped.

A jarring silence.

He pressed the phone to his ear, so hard it hurt. "Lea? Are you there? Lea?"

8

Mark's hand trembled as he set the phone down on the podium. His whole body tensed. He tried to swallow, but his throat had closed up.

She sounded terrified.

He kept his eyes on the phone.

Call back. Call back. Call back, Lea.

The baby in the front row started to cry. The woman shifted it in her lap and stuck a plastic pacifier in its mouth. The crowd had grown quiet. Maybe they could sense that he was shaken. He found a bottle of water on the shelf inside the podium, twisted it open, and took a long drink.

"Sorry about the interruption." He stared at the phone. "My wife is on a tiny island off the Carolinas. I think she's in the hurricane. We were cut off."

He raised his eyes to the skylight. Waves of rain rolled over the glass. Jo-Ann leaned against the bookshelf on the wall, arms crossed tightly in front of her sweater. Her eyes were closed.

"Where were we?" Mark tried to start again.

They slumped in their seats now. The tension had gone out of the room. It was as if he had absorbed it all. His mouth felt dry.

He tasted half-digested cheeseburger in his throat. He took another swig of water to wash it back down, spilled some on his shirt.

Call back. Call back.

"I know what people call me. They say I'm the opposite of the Tiger Mom. They call me the Teddy Bear Dad."

That got a few snickers. The crowd seemed to relax just a little.

"But I'm not talking about *no* parenting. My idea is *less parenting*. The examples in my book show that children can be nurtured without being bossed, guided without realizing they are being guided. My theory is that parents who are *friends* to their children will be friends for life and will not encounter—"

An explosion of thunder, close enough to rattle the skylight window, ended that thought. The lights flickered. A few people gasped and cried out.

This was a problem of living on Long Island's East End. The power lines were all strung through the trees. He wondered if Route 114 was flooded. The drive home could be longer than he had hoped.

He was talking without really hearing himself, wishing he could wrap it up, sign their books, go home and try to reach Lea. But they had come with questions and he couldn't cheat them of a chance to spout their disapproval.

Do you raise your own children this way? Are you always their friend and not their father?

Can you tell us some firsthand examples of parents who tried your way? Didn't some of the kids become spoiled brats? Total monsters?

You really think kids should be raised like wild animals? Were you raised by wolves?

That question was greeted by laughter. It made Jo-Ann open her eyes and seemed to break the tension. Mark let out a long breath. A good place to end.

He thanked everyone for their opinions and for coming out on such a dreadful night. He could sense disappointment. They had come for the kill, but he was too distracted to do battle. They hadn't even wounded him.

About half the crowd left, funneling down the creaking stairway without having a book signed. Those who lined up for his autograph were quiet and polite, except for a small, frail-looking woman in a ragged gray trench coat, who glared at him through square spectacles and said, "You could do a lot of harm with this book." She then asked him to sign the book "To Megan."

By his count, he sold thirty or forty books. When the last customer, the man in the Yankees gear, made his way to the exit, Jo-Ann patted his shoulder. "Good job, Mark. That wasn't easy."

He sighed. "This is my last stop on the tour. Now I'm going to stay home for a while."

The phone, secured in his jeans pocket, remained a silent hunk of metal and plastic. Scenes of Cape Le Chat Noir rushed through his mind, fragments of photographs Lea had emailed him. He saw the wide yellow beach. Fishing boats bobbing in the calm water offshore. Small, square white cabins with red clay roofs . . .

"Your raincoat is in the office. I'll get it for you." Jo-Ann made her way to the stairs.

Mark stood up, then froze for a second, surprised to see Autumn lingering near the back row of seats. She had a shiny violet-colored slicker folded over one arm. She smiled and hurried toward the podium.

"I . . . didn't expect to see you here," Mark said.

She giggled. "I wanted to surprise you." The blue eyes flashed. The smile suddenly became teasing. "Did I surprise you?"

"Well . . . yes."

She swept her hair back with a quick toss of her head. "You were very brave." She squeezed his hand.

Just a light squeeze, but it seemed strange to him. Like a rehearsed gesture.

"Brave?"

"Well, yeah. I mean, when I proofread your book, I didn't really know it was, uh, so controversial. I couldn't *believe* tonight. It totally made people angry. But you handled every question. I was— wow—so *impressed*."

"Thanks, Autumn. Nice of you to come tonight." She lived in

Hampton Bays with her sister, he knew, nearly an hour's drive from the bookstore in Easthampton.

He started to the stairwell. "Are you coming to work tomorrow? There's mail to answer. And a few things . . ."

She shifted the raincoat. The white tube top had slid down, revealing the tops of creamy-white breasts. "Mark? Would you maybe . . . um . . . like to get a coffee? Or a drink?"

She's flirting with me.

He felt a flash of heat in his cheeks. "N-no. I mean, I really can't, Autumn. I haven't been home in so long. And I have to call Lea. We were cut off and . . ."

She nodded. He couldn't read her expression. Her face went blank, revealing nothing, except that the light faded from those deep blue eyes.

She nodded. "Just wanted you to know I'm here for you. You know. If you need anything?" Her pale cheeks turned pink. "See you tomorrow morning." She spun away, swinging the violet slicker onto her shoulders, and hurried to the stairs.

Mark watched her go. The coltish legs in the black tights. The silver-blond hair disappearing under the shiny rain hood.

She was definitely coming on to me. If I had gone for that drink with her . . .

Don't even think about it.

He tried phoning Lea from the car. Rain pelted the windshield. He let the engine run, waiting for the cold air from the heater to turn warm. The long row of stores were mostly dark. The street was empty.

The call went right to her voice mail. He left a short message. "Call me back. Where are you? Love you."

Why didn't she answer? Why did she sound so frantic when she called?

Maybe Roz would know. Maybe Roz had heard from her too.

The wipers set a tense rhythm. He pulled away from the curb and guided the car down Main Street through the torrents of rain. In the mirror, he glimpsed three or four people, huddled under black umbrellas, stepping out of the movie theater across the street.

In front of him, the Ralph Lauren store windows were brightly lit. Cruise wear on display.

He made the right onto 114. His tires sent up waves of rainwater on both sides of the car.

Maybe Roz will know what's up with Lea.

His poor sister. Five years older than Mark, she had shown up on his doorstep nearly a year ago with the one-year-old kid in tow and nowhere to go.

Talk about bad luck with men. Only it wasn't bad luck. It was poor choices. You didn't need a psychologist to see Roz had a problem in that area.

Mark could see the black eye she had tried to cover up with makeup. And the nervous tic with her eyes . . . that was something new.

"I'm giving up men," she had said as he and Lea helped carry her bags into the house. "Maybe I'll try women."

"What does that mean?" Ira had asked.

"She's making a joke," Mark told him.

Her son, Axl, with the bush of curly brown hair and the pudgy cheeks and freckles, started to cry.

"Naming your son Axl is looking for trouble." Yes, Mark had really said that to her over the phone the day after Axl was born.

Of course, Roz had laughed. She always laughed at Mark when he was too earnest. "If Axl has problems, I'll send him to you, Doc," she said.

They had a strange relationship, he thought. She was the older sister but in many ways he played the older brother. Not the older, *wiser* brother. Her razor-sharp sense of humor would never allow him to be that. She always cut him down to size even when he was helping her.

It worked. They had always been close. Their parents had been so absent, they had to cling together from the time they were little, and that habit stuck. Now here she was with the black eye and the trembling chin, holding back her tears with all her strength.

Her boyfriend, Axl's father, had left and taken her car and her savings.

Lea said, "The guesthouse in back is empty. Why don't you live there for a while, Roz, while you're getting yourself together? Ira and Elena will love having Axl around."

"Only if I can do something to earn my rent." From Roz. "You know. If I can help out somehow?"

Which is how she got to be the nanny. And damned good timing, too, since Lea and Mark were traveling so much lately. The kids didn't take long at all to adjust to little cousin Axl. Now age two, he was so cute and so preposterously curious. How could anyone resist him?

"What that mean?"

"Why?"

"What you doing? Why you doing that?"

It was so interesting to see the little guy's brain churning away. Ira and Elena didn't question much. They seemed to accept everything as it was. They had always seemed too into themselves to be explorers.

Roz seemed happy in the little guesthouse with its single bedroom and bath. In fact, Mark had never seen her so consistently cheerful. She had her straight black hair cut short and bought some young-looking clothes.

She found a part-time job doing office work for some real estate lawyers in Sag Harbor. And she proved to be an efficient and loving nanny. The kids quickly learned to laugh at her sarcasm and sharp insults. They ate all their meals together at the long wooden table in the kitchen. One big happy family.

Of course, Mark was wary. He always began to feel wary whenever things began to go right for his sister. He knew that a new boyfriend on the scene could change it all.

He wanted Roz to have a real life of her own. Actually, he felt the house was a little crowded with the two of them always there, and it was harder to spend quiet time with Lea or with Ira and Elena. He didn't want to keep her there forever as a kind of indentured servant. But he knew Roz needed time to heal before heading off to the next chapter of her life.

All these thoughts while sailing his small BMW through the

dark waves of Route 114, squinting through the rain-washed windshield. The rapid *smack-smack-smack* of the wipers the only sound except for the splash of rain waves off the sides of the car.

No phone. No phone ringing.

Lea, where are you?

And then a sharp turn through the opening in the low brick wall. The crunch of the gravel driveway beneath the tires. Mark eased the car to the side door. Cut the lights. Turned off the engine. Watched the wipers settle down into place.

Then he pulled the raincoat over his head and burst out of the car. To the door on the run. Shoes skidding on the wet gravel.

He reached for the knob but the door swung open. A sliding rectangle of light revealed Roz in jeans and a long, baggy brown sweater. Her eyes were red-rimmed. He smelled alcohol on her breath.

"Oh, Mark."

"Roz, hi. Have you heard from Lea? Has she called here?"

Roz gazed at him for a long moment. "I don't think she can," she said finally, her voice a whisper.

9

With the winds rattling the windows, Lea stood with her phone pressed to her ear. "The connection is lost." She turned to the Swanns, Martha and James. "I heard Mark, but I don't think he could hear me."

An explosion of thunder made all three of them jump.

The lights flickered and went out. "I have plenty of candles," Martha said. "And a kerosene lantern."

She had more in common with Martha Stewart than just her first name, Lea thought. She seemed to be a perfect host and home-maker, calm and competent, despite the howling winds that made Lea want to scream.

James was soft-spoken and low-key, too. "No phones, no inter-net," he said calmly, like checking off items on a grocery list. "We probably won't have power for long. We won't be able to communi-cate with anyone for days."

"How can you be so calm about it?" Lea's voice came out shrill, tight.

James's slender, lined face flickered into view as Martha got one of the candles glowing. His eyeglasses reflected the orange light. "Martha and I have seen a lot of storms since we moved here."

"Maybe none like this," Martha murmured. Another candle flared.

The Swanns had lived in Charlotte, North Carolina, all their lives. James owned three pharmacies there, two of them inherited from his father. But he never really enjoyed running a business. When Walgreens made him an offer he couldn't refuse, he sold them his stores and retired.

Martha, a photo researcher, freelanced for Reuters and other news agencies. The internet meant that she could work anywhere, so it was no problem for her to move. Ten years ago, the two of them had picked up and moved to Cape Le Chat Noir, just because it seemed the wildest, most unpredictable thing they could do.

A crash outside—shattering metal and glass—made the candlelight flicker.

"Whoa. That sounded like a car. Think this wind is strong enough to pick up cars?" James shook his head.

The oil lamp sent an orange glow over the Swanns' front room. Long blue-black shadows crept over the floor and walls.

The room had an arching, dark wood cathedral ceiling. Two rows of track lights beamed down on the living room area, all wicker and blue and green aquatic colors, in the front facing the road. A long dining room table, covered in a flowery tablecloth, divided the living room from the kitchen.

Sliding glass doors and an enormous kitchen window revealed a panorama of the beach and ocean inlet out back. James had boarded up the window against the approaching storm. But the glass doors showed the tossing, battling waves, an eerie, unnatural green against the charcoal sky.

The shifting shadows on the walls made Lea think of Halloween. She realized she was still gripping the cell phone and tucked it into a pocket, surprised at how hard her hand was trembling.

She stared through the glass doors at the dark ocean waves raging high, foaming angrily.

"People are going to die," she said.

The Swanns nodded but didn't reply. James fiddled with the neck of his black turtleneck sweater. Martha carried a flickering oil lamp to the window ledge in the kitchen.

"Why are you taking that back there?" James called.

"It might light someone's path," Martha said.

"I'm worried about Macaw and Pierre at the rooming house," Lea murmured. "It seems so rickety and frail."

Martha nodded. "You're much safer with us, on the west beach. The inlet is protected, Lea. And our house is solid. Not wood. It's thick Virginia fieldstone. We had it shipped from Charlotte when we built the house. We knew it could withstand hurricanes."

Lea shivered. "You're both so nice to take me in tonight. I mean, a total stranger—"

Martha laughed. "I feel like we're old friends. So many emails."

"Well, you're both very sweet," Lea said. "I don't know what I would have done. . . ." Her voice trailed off. She suddenly pictured Ira and Elena, so far away.

Earlier, Martha had prepared a magnificent dinner. Conch salad and salt oysters fresh from the ocean that morning, followed by a spicy-hot gumbo of rock shrimp, scallops, and lobster. A true feast. Along with a very dry Chardonnay from a winery on Hilton Head Island.

It should have been a delightful, relaxing time. But Lea kept glancing out the back doors at the flocks of birds flying frantically back and forth in the darkening sky, chattering and squawking in a panic, as if they didn't know where to light.

James was talking about Carolina wineries and how they had to import their grapes from all over. Lea tried to concentrate. He spoke so softly, she had to struggle to hear.

After coffee, they watched the progress of the storm on the Weather Channel until the power went out with a startling *pop*. Then, in the candlelit darkness, they talked loudly over the roaring winds, straining to pretend all was normal.

"I'm worried about my kids," Lea said. "And my husband, of course. They won't know if I'm okay."

"They'll get things up and running soon after the storm," James said. "You'll be surprised. The army will be here. The national guard. Hurricanes on the Carolina coast . . . people have experience with them."

"Do you have kids?" Lea realized she hardly knew a thing about her two hosts. Her emails with Martha had been all about life on Le Chat Noir.

"We have a son. In Phoenix," Martha said. "He's thirty. Not quite a kid."

Lea squinted at her in the candlelight. "You don't look old enough to have a thirty-year-old."

Martha's dark eyes flashed. "Flattery like that will get you a friend for life."

"He's still 'finding himself,'" James added, making quote marks with his fingers. "A lot of thirty-year-olds are still teenagers these days. He—"

"*We're* the teenagers," Martha interrupted. "Running away from home to a tiny island?"

"I wanted more kids," Lea said. "I come from a big family. Four brothers and two sisters. I really wanted a houseful of kids. But after Ira was born, the doctor said we couldn't have any more. I was so disappointed. Heartbroken, really."

Her words were greeted by silence. Martha and James stared at her, their faces appearing and disappearing in the flickering light.

Too much information.

Rain pounded the house, as loud as thunder. The wind howled like a wild animal. But the house was solid as promised. The ferocious winds tried but couldn't collapse it. James praised the strength of Virginia fieldstone. Martha spoke calmly about going down to the beach after the last hurricane and watching the incredible waves.

Lea could hear things breaking outside. Cracks and heavy thuds. She fought to hold down a rising feeling of panic. She held her breath, as if she could will it away. Held her breath until her chest ached.

It will be over soon. I think the winds are already slowing.

She screamed at the cracking sound above her head. Plaster snowed down on the three of them from the high cathedral ceiling.

"It's trying to take the roof," James said. His eyes were wide behind his glasses. Even in the shadowy light, Lea could see his calm was broken.

Lea pressed herself against the living room wall, praying for the roof to hold, for the winds to stop raging. She shut her eyes tight and thought about Mark. And Ira. And Elena.

Were they thinking of her? Were they horribly scared?

She shuddered again. It could be *days* before I can reach them and tell them I'm okay. *Will I be okay?*

Another cracking sound above their heads. Another stream of powdery plaster came floating down. James staggered forward, eyes wide. His mouth dropped open. His knees folded. He started to fall.

Martha grabbed him by the shoulders, struggling to keep him on his feet.

"The roof . . ." he breathed. "It's . . . coming down."

A terrifying *craaack*. A rumble like approaching thunder. A shower of powdery plaster.

Everything shaking. Everything.

Lea screamed as the world came crashing down on her.

10

Lea struggled to pull herself up from the ringing darkness. Her head throbbed as if about to explode. Waves of pain rolled down her back, her arms and legs. Blinking in the gray light, still unable to focus, she gazed up.

"Oh my God!"

The sky appeared so close, glaring through the jagged hole in the ceiling. She raised her head, feeling dizzy. Underwater, her clothing soaked and the couch beneath her like a furry wet animal. She brushed shingles off the couch. Still struggling to focus, she saw jagged pieces of the ceiling strewn over the room.

Martha and James bent over her. Their faces were tight with concern, ghostly pale in the heavy gray light washing down from above.

"Lea? You're coming to? Are you okay?" Martha looked twenty years older. Her hair hung in damp tangles over her forehead. Her eyes were red-rimmed and wet.

Lea pulled herself to a sitting position. The room spun around her. She tried to swallow, but her mouth was too dry.

She squinted at the shards of wood and broken shingles scattered crazily around the couch. Piles of wet plaster on the carpet. Like cake flour. A snowstorm blanketing the furniture.

"The roof—"

Martha gripped her hand. "Take it slow, Lea. Just breathe. Don't try to get up yet."

"What happened?" Martha and James slid in and out of focus. Lea smoothed a hand over her hair, trying to rub away the pain.

"Part of the roof fell in," James said, gazing up at the sky. "You got hit by some slate shingles. It knocked you out."

"We were so worried." Martha squeezed Lea's hand. "It just came crashing down on you. We put you on the couch and—"

Lea shuddered. "I . . . think I'm okay. Just a headache. The dizziness is going away."

"Oh, thank God," Martha said.

"We all got soaked," James said, his voice hoarse, croaky. "But we were lucky." He glanced away, as if trying to force down some heavy emotion. Despite his attempt, a sob escaped his throat.

Martha held on to Lea's hand. "So glad y'all are okay. We were scared. You were totally out. Look. You might have a bump on your head, but it didn't even break the skin."

Lea brushed back her dark hair with both hands. "Wow. Guess I'm lucky. I feel okay. Really."

"It's morning. The rain stopped a few hours ago," Martha said. "The winds—"

James motioned toward the broken ceiling. "The rain. It soaked everything. The house will never dry out."

"But it's still standing." Martha turned to her husband. "I think we may be the fortunate ones. I . . . I'm afraid to look outside."

James shivered. "I need dry clothes." He started toward the bedroom. His shoes squished on the carpet.

Martha followed him. She turned back to Lea, her face almost apologetic. "We've been up all night. Maybe James and I should catch a few hours sleep. Before . . . before we face what's out there."

"Yes. Don't worry about me." Lea shook off another wave of dizziness. "You two are so kind. I'll never forget this. I'll be okay. Get some rest."

"Help yourself to anything in the fridge. We have to finish it before it spoils. There won't be any power for a long time." Martha uttered a long sigh.

They disappeared down the hall to their room.

Lea watched streams of water run down the wall. Stretching her arms above her head, she stood up. Suddenly alert.

Beyond the glass doors in back, tall waves continued to battle, crashing against each other, tossing off islands of foam. The water's roar seemed to be inside her head.

I have to go outside.

She had to see what the storm had left behind. She stepped unsteadily to the door, shoes sliding on the wet surface.

I'm a journalist. I have to document this for my blog. Maybe I can sell the photos to a news network.

But she wasn't prepared for the horrors a few steps from the house. The fallen trees and flattened houses. Everything crumbled and broken and down.

The people covered in plaster dust and mud, scrambling over the wreckage, searching house to house for survivors to rescue, finding only bodies.

She wasn't prepared for the howls and cries. The half-naked man who ran over the debris on the street, screaming as blood flowed down his back like a scarlet cape. The pale white baby feet poking out from under the collapsed wall of a house.

I'm a journalist.

She raised her phone to her eye. Steadied it. Focused on a man carrying two corpses over his shoulder. And . . .

Oh no. She studied the phone. Out of power. Dead. She stared at it. Shook it. No way to charge it. No way.

So now she wasn't a journalist covering the tragedy. Now she was just another victim.

Men were already piling bodies where the little white post office had stood.

Lea saw arms and legs dangling from beneath crushed, collapsed walls.

She shivered. Each breath she took burned her nostrils and made her throat ache. The air was choked with dust and dirt that hadn't settled.

I'm alive.

The island had been flattened. She squinted into the billowing gray light. The houses and shops were piles of trash. Splintered boards strewn everywhere. Fallen walls fanned out on the rain-soaked ground like playing cards.

Fifty-two Pickup.

She thought of the cruel card game her brothers used to tease her with when she was little.

"Want to play a card game, Lea?"

"Sure."

"Let's play *Fifty-two Pickup*." Then they'd raise the deck high and let all the cards tumble to the floor. "Okay. Go ahead, Lea. Pick them up."

That's what it looked like here. Playing cards tossed and scattered over the earth.

Is that how she would write it? Could that be the lead to her story?

I can't write it.

She slumped onto the trunk of a fallen palm tree and wrapped her arms around herself. *I can't write it because I don't believe it yet. And I don't want to write about such nightmare and heartbreak. Where would I begin? How would I ever describe an entire island crushed and flattened as if stomped on by a fairy-tale giant?*

Fairy tales and childhood card games were flashing through her mind. Obviously, because she wanted to escape. She wanted to go back to somewhere safe and clean and nice. It didn't take a genius to figure that out.

She suddenly pictured her father sitting in his Barcalounger in the tiny living room back in Rockford, holding the newspaper in front of him, folded down the middle the way he always read it, and shaking his head. Reading and shaking his head, his face twisted in disapproval.

You'd be shaking your head today, Dad.

How could she write about the corpses they were pulling out from under the debris? Dead faces, locked in startled expressions. She watched the mud-covered workers stack the bodies like trash bags in the town dump.

The smell . . . Already. The sour smell of death.

And the sounds. Moans and shrieks and anguished cries rang out in the dust-choked morning air like a horror-movie soundtrack. The pleas of the injured waiting to be rescued. The survivors discovering their dead. The sweating, cursing men digging, pawing, shoveling into the rubbled houses. The groans of the men hoisting more corpses onto the pile.

It seemed to Lea that everyone left alive was howling in protest. Everyone who could move and make a sound was screaming or crying or wailing their disbelief and anger.

I should be helping.

She jumped to her feet and started to walk toward mountains of debris where the road had been. "Oh!" She stumbled over something soft.

A corpse!

No. Clothing. A tangled pile of soaked shirts and shorts strewn over the grass.

What about my *clothing?*

Were her belongings scattered with the wind? Was Starfish House still standing? Had Macaw and Pierre survived?

Lea shuddered. The rooming house was on the other side of Le Chat Noir, the eastern side, the exposed side where the ocean could show its storm fury. Starfish House felt fragile even in calm weather, she thought. The Swanns' stone house had barely survived intact.

She felt a stab of dread in the pit of her stomach. Suddenly, it was a struggle to breathe. No way Starfish House could still be standing. But Macaw and Pierre?

She couldn't phone, of course. She remembered she had been talking to Mark—or *trying* to—last night when the service crashed.

Mark. What was he thinking right now? What was he doing? What had he told the kids? He had to be in his own nightmare . . . not knowing . . .

And no way to tell him.

My poor Ira and Elena.

Ahead of her, she saw an upended SUV, windows all blown out, sitting on the flattened roof where a little food store had stood. The SUV looked like an animal on its hind legs, standing straight up on its back bumper. Lea shook her head. Hard to imagine a wind strong enough to lift an SUV off the road, onto its back end, and drop it onto a building.

She spun away from it. But there was nowhere to turn to escape the horror.

The man lumbering toward her caught her by surprise. He was tall and broad and drenched in sweat, thinning brown hair matted to his red forehead. His T-shirt was torn and stained with brown streaks. His shorts were rags.

His eyes were wild and his mouth was moving rapidly although Lea couldn't hear his words. His arms were outstretched, his mud-smeared hands open to grab her.

He's crazy. He's out of his head.

Move!

But there wasn't time.

With a menacing groan, he grabbed her by the shoulders. He pulled with surprising force, nearly dragging her off her feet. She inhaled the rank odor of his body and his mud-caked clothes.

He groaned again. She wasn't strong enough to resist. He was pulling her away from the others, dragging her out of view, grunting and groaning like an animal.

"Let go! Let *go* of me! Please! What are you going to do? Please—let *go*!"

11

The radio squealed. Andy Pavano nearly lost his grip on the wheel.

"Vince, turn it down or something. Sounds like you stepped on a cat."

"Hey, I'm always kind to animals. Can you hear me now?"

"The rain is messing with the radio." Andy slowed the patrol car around a curve but still sent a tidal wave of rainwater washing over the narrow shoulder.

"It's these old Motorolas, man. They're not even digital." Vince said something else but the signal broke up.

"Vince, what did you say?"

"I said maybe you could talk to your uncle about springing for a new radio system."

"The chief isn't my uncle," Andy snapped. "He went to school with my cousin, that's all."

"Okay, okay. You're both Pavano. So it's an honest mistake, right?"

Headlights from an oncoming car blazed over the windshield. Andy tried to squint through it, but he couldn't see a thing. *Turn off your brights, bastard.*

He opened his mouth in a loud burp. The meatball hero from

that Italian place on Main Street . . . What was it called? Conca d'Oro? . . . it hadn't gone down yet.

He swerved to avoid a lake of rainwater that glimmered darkly over the right half of the road. He could feel the wind push the car sideways. "Vince, this rain is killing me."

"There's a hurricane, Pavano. Down South. A big one. It pushed out into the ocean, but we're getting the sloppy seconds."

Andy snickered. "Vince, you're a poet. Sloppy seconds? That doesn't even make sense."

"Hey, what makes sense?"

Andy joined the Sag Harbor Police Force three weeks before, but it was long enough to know that *what makes sense?* was the height of Vince's philosophy.

"The wind is trying to blow this fucking Ford off the road."

The radio squealed again. Then Vince's distorted voice: "Language, dude. Remember? People listen in. Civilians. Shut-ins. Keep it clean."

"Okay, Mom."

"You city guys don't know how to drive. How long were you a New York City cop?"

"I was a Housing Authority cop."

"Ooh, I'm wetting myself. I'm so impressed. How long?"

"None of your business, Vince. What's up with the chitchat? You just lonely?"

"I've got a wife, an ex-wife, and four kids, man. How do you get to be lonely? Tell me."

Andy didn't have an answer for that. He had an ex-wife, too. The lovely Susannah. One of the reasons he moved to Sag Harbor.

All My Exes Live in Texas.

Someone should write one like it about New York.

All of Andy's philosophy could be found in country songs.

He thought about Sari. Her dark hair falling over her forehead. Those beautiful eyes, oval and green like cat eyes. He should turn around and maybe drop by her house.

That first visit was awkward. No. Worse than awkward. *She was ice. She tried to freeze me.* All that talk about how she was in love, how she was going to get married. To a guy who owns the tennis shop in Southampton?

No. That's crap. No way that was going to happen.

Now she'd had time to think about him, get warmed up to the idea of Andy being around again.

Sure, he blew it the first time with Sari. Maybe this time . . .

"Pavano, what's your ten-twenty?"

"I'm east on Noyac. Am I going in the right direction?"

"Maybe you need a GPS. Like the summer people. You're still a tourist, Pavano. Why don't you talk to your uncle about getting a—"

"You're going to keep calling him my uncle, aren't you."

"Yeah, probably. My sense of humor, you know. Riding this desk you need a sense of humor."

"Riding this desk? You been watching *Cops* again?"

The car rumbled past the turn at Long Beach. The rain formed a heavy curtain. He couldn't see the bay. No cars in either direction. Who would be out driving in this?

"So tell me again where this house is, Vince."

"It's a left on Brick Kiln, then a left on Jesse Halsey. Go to the end. Take a right on Bluff Point Road."

Andy sighed and shifted his weight in the seat. "Got it. You know, I didn't sign on for shit like this. I came out here for peace and quiet. Maybe a domestic or two. A deer down on the road, someone steals a stop sign or takes a leak in a supermarket parking lot."

"That sounds a lot like whining, Pavano."

"Left on Brick Kiln, right? Okay. I'm here. I'm not whining, Vince. But, look—you're riding a desk, as you so colorfully put it. And I'm—"

"Got another call. I'm out. You're not the only cop out tonight, Sergeant."

"Just about."

The Sag Harbor Police wasn't exactly a big force. Vince on the desk nights, the chief, and how many patrol guys? Four? Andy ran through their names in his head. Three Italian, one Irish. He made the left, then the right.

"Vince? You still there? I can't do this. It's making me sick. Really. I'm going to lose my supper."

"Not in the car, please. If you're going to blow chunks, stick your head out the window."

"I have a weak stomach. Really. It's in my physical report. You can check it."

"Please don't make me cry. My mascara will run."

"I can't see a thing, Vince. It's total darkness here, and the rain—"

"You can do it. Just follow the regulations. Go to the house. Show them your ID. Say what you have to say. Then go throw up."

"Why did I get this, Vince? I don't even know where I'm going."

"No one else would do it, Andy. That's a ten-four."

The radio made a loud click. Silence.

Bluff Point Road curved around the south side of a part of the bay known as Upper Sag Harbor Cove. The houses were far back from the road, hidden behind trees and tall hedges. Ahead of the clicking wipers and the splashing currents of rain, they rose up in the windshield like dark walls, blacker than the sky.

How'd they expect him to find the house? Oh. There. On the right, near the end of the street.

He made a sharp right, and the tires spun over the wet gravel drive. *Slow down. You're not in a hurry for this.*

Behind a low brick wall, the house stretched across a wide lawn. A big modern house, gray shingles, with a terrace between the house and the garage. Small windows on this side. The side facing the bay was probably mostly glass. A single light cast a faint glow over the front door. Two well-trimmed evergreen bushes rose on both sides of the entrance.

Andy stopped the car near the front walk and cut the wipers and the headlights. He sat motionless for a while, staring at the rainwater rolling in waves down the windshield. Thunder crackled somewhere far in the distance.

He realized he had his hands balled into tight fists. The meatball hero weighed heavily in his stomach. *You're forty, Pavano. Maybe you need a better diet.*

It wasn't age. It was tension. Sure, he was tense. Who wouldn't be?

Who on earth would want to do this job?

He glanced into the mirror. Saw his eyes gazing accusingly back at him.

Get it over with.

He picked his cap up from the passenger seat and pulled it down over his thinning hair. He had an umbrella, but it was in the trunk. He pushed open the door, slid his legs around, and climbed out of the car. He was drenched before he got the trunk lid open.

Perfect.

The umbrella caught and refused to open.

Even more perfect.

He spun away from the car, slipped on the flagstone walk, caught his balance, and jogged to the safety of the overhang above the front door. Lights were on, but no sign of any movement in the front window.

Water rolled down the brim of his cap. He shook his head hard, then pressed the bell. He could hear it chime inside.

Footsteps. Then a man pulled open the door and stared out at him in a pool of bright light. "Yes?"

Andy gazed at the man's startled face. He was dark and had a stubble of beard on his cheeks. He reminded Andy of . . . reminded him of that actor . . . He had just watched *Brokeback Mountain* a few weeks before. Not his kind of thing, although the scenery was pretty.

And, yes. This guy looked just like that actor with the funny name. He wore designer jeans and a white dress shirt. He held a can of beer in one hand.

"Can I help you, Officer?"

Andy nodded solemnly. "Perhaps I should come in?"

A woman appeared behind the man. She had short black hair and a drawn face, kind of weary-looking. She had a baggy brown sweater pulled down over black leggings. "Who is it, Mark?"

"A police officer. I don't understand—"

Andy felt his throat tighten. Gusts of wind blew the rain under the overhang.

Just get it over with. No way you can make it any better.

What was he supposed to say first? What was he supposed to ask them? He couldn't think straight.

"Sir," he started, raising his voice over the wind, "I'm sorry. I'm afraid I have bad news."

The man and woman both gasped. Her mouth dropped open. The beer can slid out of the man's hand and hit the floor.

"I'm really sorry, sir," Andy said, suddenly breathless. "But they sent me to tell you that your wife has been killed."

12

The woman let out a cry and grabbed the banister beside her, struggling to hold herself up.

The man made a choking sound. He blinked several times. He turned and grabbed the woman's hand.

"I'm sorry, sir," Andy said, lowering his eyes. Rain pelted the back of his uniform shirt.

"How—" the man started. He made the choking sound again. The woman started to sob, burying her face behind the man's shoulder.

"It was a traffic accident." Andy kept his eyes down, partly not to see their grief. He had to force his voice to stay steady. "On Stephen Hands. Near 114. The Easthampton police—they didn't want to tell you on the phone. They asked me—"

The man's expression changed. His eyes went wide. He raised a hand to say halt. The woman lifted her head and squinted at Andy. Tears glistened on her pale cheeks.

"That can't be," the woman choked out. "You're wrong."

"My wife . . . she is away," the man said, staring hard into Andy's eyes. "She's on an island off South Carolina. She isn't in Easthampton."

Andy's throat tightened again. He swallowed hard. "Mr. Hamlin, I was told—"

"He's not Mr. Hamlin, you idiot!" the woman screamed. Her hands balled into tight fists. "He's not Mr. Hamlin. Oh, I don't believe it. I don't fucking believe it." She pounded the banister.

"I'm Mark Sutter," the man said. He slid an arm around the woman's trembling shoulders. "Roz, please—"

But she pulled away and flung herself toward Andy, furiously shaking her head. "How could you *do* that? How could you *be* so stupid? Why didn't you ask our names first?"

"I . . . was nervous," Andy said. "I should have done that. Really. I didn't mean—"

Could I just dive headfirst into the bay and drown myself now?

"I think you want Bluff Point," Sutter said softly. "This is John Street."

"Oh my God." The words tumbled out of Andy's mouth. "I am so totally sorry. I hope . . . I mean . . . The rain. It's so dark. . . ."

What could he say? "I'm sick about this, sir. Ma'am." He really did feel sick.

They glared at him, both breathing hard. Sutter reached for the doorknob.

"I can only apologize," Andy repeated. "I'm new out here, and, well . . . I'm so sorry. If you'd like to report me to my chief, I can give you my ID."

Roz spun away. She disappeared into the house. Sutter shook his head. "You should get out of the rain, Officer."

Andy nodded.

The door closed. He heard the lock click.

He stood there for a moment, letting the rain batter him.

Perhaps I'll laugh about this in a few weeks. Tell it like a funny joke.

He suddenly found himself thinking of the *Police Academy* movies. The cops were all total idiots.

I should join them.

He sighed and strode slowly to the car. No reason to run. He couldn't get any wetter. He slid behind the wheel. A cold shudder ran down his back.

The radio squealed. "Pavano, you there?" Vince's distorted voice.

"Yeah, I'm here."

"How'd it go?"

13

"Let go of me! Please! Don't *hurt* me!" Lea cried.

Mumbling crazily to himself, the man dragged her to a pile of boards and stones. His eyes were wild, bulging wide, his gaze darting from side to side. He didn't seem to hear her cries.

He's gone crazy from the storm.

What does he plan to do to me?

Then she saw the bare-chested boy, a stream of long hair hanging down over his face. His mud-drenched shorts clung to his hips as he bent over a pile of rubble. He appeared to be struggling with something in the pile.

As the man pulled her nearer, Lea heard the shrill screams. And saw the openmouthed, terrified face of a woman peering up from below a ragged crisscross of boards.

The boy had her by the hands and was tugging with all his strength, crying and tugging, trying to free her from beneath the caved-in house. The woman tossed her black hair wildly, her head tilted back in pain, and she shrieked in agony.

"Help," the man grunted, letting go of Lea. He motioned toward the screaming woman. "Help me."

He lifted the boy out of the way. He gave Lea a gentle push and motioned for her to take one of the woman's flailing hands.

I must have been the first person he saw. He's obviously in a total panic.

She gripped the woman's hand tightly. It felt cold and damp, like a small drowned animal. She gave the hand a gentle squeeze—and the woman screamed.

Startled, Lea dropped the hand and jumped back. Her heart was pounding in her throat. She had to open her mouth to breathe.

Don't panic. You can do this.

The man motioned Lea to grab one corner of a slab of drywall. Lea grabbed it. They tugged in unison and managed to slide it a few inches off the woman's chest.

The woman shrieked and wailed, batting her head from side to side.

Lea pulled up on a broken two-by-four. The man grabbed it from her and heaved it aside.

Then he turned back to the woman and wrapped his big hand around hers. The woman screamed again. Lea knew she'd hear these screams in her nightmares. Screams that seemed to have no end.

The man gave Lea a signal with his eyes. Working in unison, they forced the woman nearly to a sitting position. Then the man reached behind her back. Lea took her hands and gave a hard pull. With a moan of pain, the woman rose up, rose up in Lea's hands. Rose up . . .

Lea heard a wrenching sound. Like fabric tearing.

She gasped as the woman came stumbling out, falling toward her. Her face showed no relief. In fact, it twisted into a knot of agony. She pulled her hands free from Lea and shrieked in an inhuman animal wail: "My leg! My leg! My leg! My leg!"

Lea gasped. The woman was balanced on one leg. Blood poured from an open tear in her other side.

"Oh my God!" Lowering her gaze, Lea saw the ragged flesh of the woman's other leg trapped beneath the pile of debris. A white bone poked up from the torn skin.

No. Oh no.

The other leg. We left it behind.

It's torn off. I pulled it off. I pulled her leg off!

Blood showered the ground from the open tear in the woman's body.

"My leg! My leg! My leg! My leg! My leg!"

The man stood hulking in openmouthed shock. Fat tears rolled down the boy's red, swollen cheeks.

Heart pounding so hard her chest ached, Lea searched frantically for help. No one. No one around.

What could even a doctor do?

She and the boy and the weeping man took the woman by her writhing shoulders and lowered her gently into her own pool of blood. They stretched her out on the dirt, and the man dropped down beside her, soothing her, holding her hand, cradling her head till she grew too weak to scream.

Lea staggered away. She knew she couldn't help. She stumbled away, holding her stomach with both hands, gasping shallow breaths of the heavy, salted air. She wandered aimlessly into the wails and screams, the moans, the howls of disbelief, the symphony of pain she knew she would hear in her nightmares.

I'm not here. I'm asleep in our bed at home. I have to get Ira and Elena to school. Mark, give me a shove and wake me up. Mark?

"My babies! My babies!"

The woman's shrill howls shook Lea from her thoughts. She turned and saw a grim-faced worker holding two tiny lifeless figures, cradling one in each arm, as if they were alive. But their heads slumped back, eyes stared glassily without seeing, arms and legs dangled limply, lifelessly.

The shrieking woman, tripping over the jutting wreckage of her fallen house, followed after them, waving her arms above her head. "My babies! My babies!"

Lea lowered her eyes as they passed by. *I'm in Hell.*

Suddenly, she pictured Starfish House. Was the little rooming house still standing? And what of Macaw and Pierre? Were they okay? Had they survived? Her laptop was there. Her clothes. All of her belongings.

How to get across the island? James's truck was useless. The road would be impassable. She could walk, but it would be a walk of endless horrors.

A steady drone, growing louder, wormed its way into her consciousness. A hum quickly becoming a roar.

"Help is already on the way."

Lea turned to see James behind her. He had changed into baggy gray sweats. His eyeglasses had a layer of white powder over the lenses. Behind them, his eyes were bloodshot and weary.

She followed his gaze to the sky and saw the helicopters, five or six of them, pale green army helicopters, hovering low, moving along the shoreline.

"They probably can't believe what they're seeing down here, either," she murmured. She shivered.

James lowered his hands to her shoulders. "Are you okay, Lea?"

She nodded. "I guess."

His eyes locked on her, studying her. "No, I mean, really. Are you okay?"

"I . . . I'm upset. No. I'm horrified. But I'm okay, James. I was just thinking about Macaw and Pierre. . . ."

"Martha and I will walk you to your rooming house. It won't take long. Maybe half an hour."

"But—"

"If there's a problem there, you can come back and stay with us." He kept staring at her, as if searching for something she wasn't telling him.

Lea pictured the little white building with its bright yellow shutters and the sign over the entryway: *Starfish House*. She saw Macaw in her bright red-and-fuchsia plumage; Pierre, bored, hunched over the front desk, thumbing through a magazine, humming to himself.

"Yes. I hope there's no problem," she said.

But there was a problem. A sad and sickening problem.

14

Staring at the wreckage, Lea hoped she had made a mistake. *Maybe I'm in the wrong place.* But the sign still stood, crooked on its pole: *Starfish House.* The two-story house had toppled forward. The walls had collapsed on themselves, folded like an accordion on its side. And now the whole house lay in a broken, ragged heap, a low mountain of soaked and cracked boards and crumbled shards of drywall.

"No. Oh no." Lea covered her face with her hands. She turned to James and Martha, expecting them to be close, but she saw them across the road, helping to pull someone out from under an overturned car.

"No. No. No."

She stepped onto the fallen front door. It sank into the wet ground. She caught her balance and started to shout. "Macaw? Pierre? Are you here? Can you hear me?"

Boards cracked and settled. A window casing toppled onto its side. Lea screamed and jumped back, thinking the house might fall on her.

"Macaw? Pierre?"

No answer. They must have gotten out safely before the house fell in.

But what was that splash of red from under a fallen slab of wall? A scarf?

Stepping carefully, Lea made her way onto the pile of debris and climbed closer. She stopped with a gasp when she saw the hand lying so flat . . . the hand, smeared with dark blood, reaching out from under a wall board . . . the hand open as if waving . . . waving good-bye?

Lea's stomach churned. She fought the sour taste rising to her mouth. "Macaw?"

She stumbled forward, grabbed the side of a wall, and hoisted herself higher on the pile. "Oh no. No." The splash of red was the sleeve of a dress.

Forgetting safety, Lea dove toward it. She slipped on a broken board. Banged her knee on something sharp. Ignoring the pain, she climbed to the red sleeve. She could see more of the dress beneath the edge of the wall board.

"Macaw?" Her voice trembling and tiny. "No. Oh no. Macaw?"

She stared at the pale hand, on its back, like a dead bird.

Macaw was trapped beneath a slab of wall board. Lea's stomach lurched again. She could feel the cold fear prickling her skin. She didn't think. She grabbed the top corner of the slab—and pulled. Hoisted it up.

It slid more easily than she had imagined. She almost toppled over backward.

She raised the wall board. Gazed down. Down at Macaw's lifeless face. At the puncture . . . the puncture . . . the blood-smeared puncture in her eye.

Lea gasped. She opened her mouth to scream, but couldn't make a sound.

The nail at the corner of the board—the rusted eight-inch nail, fatter than a pencil . . . Lea stared at the nail, then down to the blood-caked puncture in the dead woman's eye socket.

And she knew. She knew that when the wall fell in, the nail had been driven into Macaw's eye . . . eight inches . . . driven through her eye and into her brain.

15

Lea felt a sharp stab of pain in her right eye. She uttered a cry and pressed a hand over both eyes. Sympathy pain. It happened every time Ira or Elena hurt themselves.

The wall board fell from her hand and smacked the tumble of boards at her feet. The pile rumbled and slid beneath her. Eyes still covered, she struggled to keep her balance. Waited for the pain to fade.

A dog howled. She heard shrill, alarmed voices behind her.

"Mes enfants? Avez-vous vu mes enfants?"

"Do you live in the village?"

"The village is no more."

Dazed, Lea wandered away from the voices. No way to escape. She could go only as far as the beach. And even there, the moans and howls of stricken people mingled with the crash of the waves. The beach was littered with death, a long line of dead starfish.

As if the stars of heaven had fallen to the sand.

And then the red raindrops came down, soft at first, then in curtains like a waterfall of blood. The blood of the hurricane victims raining down, although there were no clouds in the sky.

And the twin angels emerged from the red rain. Two identical blond boys, so frail and thin, with glowing blue eyes, sad eyes.

They walked over the rain-spattered sand toward Lea, seemingly oblivious of the red drops falling around them.

"Can I help you?" she called. *They're so beautiful. So beautiful and sad.*

They didn't answer. They stopped and lowered their heads. They stood there perfectly still, blond hair gleaming so brightly as if the rain hadn't touched it. Their thin bodies appeared to tremble.

She took a step toward them, sandals sinking in the sand. "Are you cold? The rain. Where are your shirts?"

"It's all gone, mum," one of them said. He raised his blue eyes to her.

"Gone?"

The rain pattered more gently. The red curtains dissolved into raindrops. The world brightened to a yellow-gray glare. She wiped rain off her forehead.

"Our house is gone, mum," the boy said. He had a high-pitched voice, more like a five-year-old. *They have to be ten or twelve,* Lea thought.

"Where do you live?"

He shrugged his slender shoulders. "Nowhere now."

His twin let out a sigh. He kicked a wet clump of sand with a bare foot.

"You mean—?"

"It's all gone, mum. All of it."

Lea was staring at them so intently, she hadn't realized the rain had stopped. She swept her hands back, squeezing red water from her hair. Behind her, she could hear excited voices. Alarmed voices. People shouting about the blood rain.

"What's your name?"

"Daniel, mum. This is my bruvver Samuel."

Samuel nodded but didn't speak.

Lea wanted to hug them. Wrap them both in her arms. Tell them everything would be okay. *My heart is breaking for them. I don't think I've ever felt this strange emotion.*

"Can I help you? I mean, are you lost? Can I take you to your house?"

Daniel shook his head. "We don't have a house anymore," he said in an even tinier voice.

His brother sighed again. His blue eyes were watery, but his face revealed no emotion at all.

Is he in shock? she wondered.

"Where are your parents?"

"Gone, mum."

"Gone? Do you mean—?"

"Dead, mum. In the storm, don't you know. We lost them."

"Oh my God."

We lost them. What a grown-up way to say it. Not childlike at all.

What could she say? Trembling in their baggy little shorts, they looked so small and frail and frightened. Again, she felt the powerful urge to wrap her arms around them and hug them. Protect them from this whole nightmare.

But of course that was impossible. She couldn't protect *herself* from the nightmare. Once again she saw Macaw's dead face with the nail puncture through her splattered eyeball.

"Is there someone else in your family? Aunts and uncles? Your grandparents?"

They shook their heads.

"No one," Daniel said. His twin still hadn't spoken. "It's just us now, mum."

Lea spun around. Where were James and Martha? She couldn't see them from the beach.

Waves crashed against the shore. An upside-down canoe was carried onto the sand and tumbled to a stop against a steep sand hill. Seagulls soared low, chattering loudly.

"I'll take you to your house. You can get some clothes," Lea said.

"It was washed away," Daniel said, lowering his eyes. "All of it. Everything. Washed away. Samuel and I, we watched it go."

Samuel nodded.

"And you have no one? You're all alone?" Lea realized she was repeating herself. She didn't want to believe it.

"Just our friend." Samuel spoke up for the first time. He had a high, little boy's voice like Daniel.

"Friend?"

Daniel stepped in front of his twin. "He means me, mum. I'm his only friend." He gave Samuel a scowl. "His brain right now is kind of like shepherd's pie. You know. Everything all mixed together like."

Lea waited for Samuel to reply. But he lowered his eyes again and remained silent.

These two beautiful boys—what will happen to them now?

Ira and Elena flashed into her mind. She pictured them getting ready for school. The gulped-down breakfast. The yawns and groans and protests. The lost homework. The wrestling with Axl, Roz's funny child. Axl liked to jump on their backs and ride them around the room, especially when they were in a hurry and had no time for him.

Was Roz worried about Lea? Thinking about her right now?

Mark should be home from his book tour by now. Would he drive the kids to school or leave it to Roz? Or did he keep them home to watch the hurricane news on TV? Were they suffering? Not knowing if she'd survived . . .

Were they trying to reach her online? Her laptop was buried somewhere in the wreckage of the rooming house. Wreckage.

"Can you help us, mum?"

Daniel's tiny voice broke into her thoughts. He stepped forward and took her hand. His hand felt soft and cold in hers. He gazed up at her with pleading, wide eyes.

They're so adorable. Angels. Really.

"Can you help my brother and me?"

Lea squeezed his tiny cat's paw of a hand. And she felt something.

She didn't know what it was at first. She was trying hard not to think about what had happened here and what she saw all around her. But holding the boy's soft hand, she felt a strong connection.

It was so sad. So sad and overwhelming. She didn't want to

think at all. She wanted to push it all away. Yesterday. Today. This dreadful morning. Push it away forever.

But she felt a powerful attraction to this boy and his nearly silent brother. Something warm and soft and real. Two creatures who really needed her. And this crazy feeling that *she* needed *them*.

"Yes. Yes, I think I can help you."

16

Later, Martha warned her that she was being too hasty. "You don't know anything about these boys. You are acting on pure emotion. You need to wait till you can think about it clearly. Do some research. Try to find out something about them."

"They're so sad and alone, Martha. They break my heart. Really."

"All the more reason to take it slow," Martha insisted. "I know you said you feel a connection, but—"

"Not just a connection. I can't describe it. It's something like love, I guess. I mean, love at first sight. No. That's crazy. But I just feel. I don't know what I feel. I just feel I could be a good mother to them and—"

"Look how mixed up you are, Lea. At least let me do some research. That's what I do, you know. Let me see what I can find out before you take them home with you."

But Lea, not persuaded, couldn't wait to talk to Mark.

"Mark, it's what we wanted."

"You're breaking up, Lea. Are you on your cell?"

"No. The national guard set up some special lines. I had to wait in line an hour. No one has phones or internet or anything."

"I read online they're working on it. They've got the coast guard and the national guard and—"

"I only have a few minutes, darling. We don't have time to discuss the news. These two boys—"

"You can't just snatch them away from their home. I don't understand—"

"I'm not snatching them. They don't have a home. They lost everything here. Their family. Everything. They're adorable, Mark. They will fit in fine in Sag Harbor. They—"

"I know you want a big family. You always said it. And we talked about adopting. But this is different, Lea. This is too weird. I mean, to come home with two strange boys. I don't like it. I really don't."

"They're not strange. They're frightened and confused. But they're so sweet, Mark. They—"

"There are laws, Lea. The authorities there in Le Chat Noir—"

"What authorities? There aren't any. The island governor was killed in the hurricane. They found his body a few hours ago. There's no government here. There's no police. No offices. Nothing left."

"Lea, I'm sorry, but I really think this is insane. I think—"

"Mark, I'm taking them to safety. You can't imagine what it's like here. It's Hell. It's really Hell. I've got to make sure these boys are safe. We can search for relatives after I bring them home. But I feel something for them, Mark. It was this instant thing. I can't leave them here to die."

"I suppose we could talk to people here. Immigration people? What country are they from?"

"Country? They're from here. This island. They're American. We don't need immigration people."

"I don't want to do this, Lea. You're upset. You've had a terrible scare. You're not thinking clearly. You sound to me like you might be in a little bit of shock."

"Stop it, Mark. I'm not in shock. These two boys need us. They—"

"But we don't know anything about them."

"Mark, what do you want to know? They're adorable little twelve-year-old twins. Blond and blue-eyed. I'm not bringing home two-headed aliens from another planet. What are you afraid of? Think they have some kind of flesh-eating island disease? They lost their family. They're orphans. Someone has to adopt them. So—"

"It's going to be a hell of a shock for Ira and Elena. And Roz. And—"

"They all know we want a big family."

"But it's so sudden, Lea."

"So you're agreeing? I can bring them home?"

"No. I'm really opposed here. Bringing two island boys to Sag Harbor and expecting them to fit in with our family? No, Lea. Really. Think about it. Wait till your mind is clearer. You know. Calmer. Sleep on it."

"Sleep on it? You're joking. Don't you want me to come home? I have to get off the island. Today is the last day for the rescue boats. Tomorrow will be too late."

"But Lea—"

"Listen, honey, it could be your next book. Really. Two or-phaned boys from a tiny island are taken to live with a middle-class family in Sag Harbor. Think of the possibilities, Mark. A study by you of how the boys adapt. What challenges them and what changes them and how they fit in with a family of strangers—and how they change the family. It could be a terrific follow-up book. And don't tell me you already have an idea, because I know you don't."

Silence.

"Well? You know it's a good idea, don't you, Mark? Think of the wonderful anecdotes—"

"Anecdotes? It's our *life*, Lea. It's not anecdotes. What if these boys—"

"They're sweet and sad, Mark. It's so tragic. They saw their parents carried away by the floodwaters. They lost everything. But they're adorable. I'm not exaggerating. When you see them, you'll fall in love with them, too. They're going to change our lives. You'll see."

"Daniel, you have to tell the woman about Ikey." Samuel stood at the open doorway of the fisherman's shack, white boards planked together to form a one-room shelter with a flat roof low overhead.

"She's not a woman. She's our new mum." Daniel lay on his back on the flat cot against the wall, hands behind his head.

"Ikey is fishing on the dock," Samuel said, pointing toward the water. "I can see him from here. You have to tell Mum—"

Daniel shook his head. He had a strange, smug smile on his face. As if the conversation was funny. "Ikey can't come. Mum won't take three of us. She only wants two."

"You don't know that. Did you ask her?" Samuel's voice rose with emotion. He wanted to wipe the smile off his brother's face. He stepped into the shack, ducking his head under the thick web of fishing nets hanging from the already low ceiling. "Did you ask her?"

Daniel pulled a segment of rope net down to him and twirled it around his hand. "Ikey isn't pretty like us. Mum doesn't want him."

"But she has to know—"

"No, she doesn't!" Daniel sat up quickly, blue eyes flaring angrily. A snort escaped his throat. Like an animal show of anger.

Samuel took a step back. He knew his brother's temper well. It taught him caution at an early age. Arguing with Daniel was such a waste of time. But he had to try. Someone had to look out for their little friend. Samuel had protected Ikey before. From others.

How could he protect him against Daniel?

"We will have a swimming pool," Daniel said, lying back down, twirling the fishing rope again. "Our own swimming pool, Sammy. And lobster to eat every night. And we'll wear new jeans and rule the school. That's what we always wanted, right, boyo? To rule the school?"

Daniel giggled, as if he'd said something hilarious. His head swung from side to side on the cot as he giggled some more.

Samuel felt his throat clench. Daniel was being Daniel again.

He took a deep breath. "I want to bring Ikey. Ikey is like our brother. He's our only friend. He's like family, Daniel."

"Family? Are you joking with me, lad?"

"No, it's not a joke."

Samuel scratched his chest. The new mum had found them jeans and T-shirts. But the clothes were stiff and scratchy. Samuel had sensitive skin. He needed soft fabrics or he'd break into a rash all over.

"We are starting a new family," Daniel insisted. "You. Me. The new mum. The new dad. A new bruvver and sister. A new family, Sammy. We'll swim all day in our own pool. We'll go fishing in the bay. That's what Mum says. And we'll rule the school. Like heaven. You want to go to heaven, don't you, Sammy? We're moving to Heaven."

Samuel made two fists. "I hate it when you talk stupid like that. You think it's cool, but it isn't. It's sick."

Daniel tossed the rope at the wall. He snorted again.

"I'm going to tell the new mum about Ikey," Samuel said, showing unusual courage. He knew he'd soon back down.

"Then she won't take us." Daniel swung around and leaped to his feet in a quick, graceful motion. He flashed Samuel a grin as he pushed past him and strode out of the little shack, onto the grassy approach to the beach.

"Where are you going?" Samuel turned to follow him.

"I'm going to explain to Ikey," Daniel replied without turning back.

"Explain to him? But—wait!"

Daniel trotted to the sand. Samuel could see Ikey sitting hunched at the end of the short dock in a beam of sunlight. Feet hanging over the side, fishing pole dangling beside him. Ikey smiled and waved as Daniel approached.

"Wait, Daniel."

Samuel sighed. He walked inside the shack and slumped to the damp floor. He scratched the sleeve of the starchy T-shirt. Mum seemed nice. She was pretty with that straight black hair and the shiny dark eyes. Almost like a movie star. But if all the T-shirts were this scratchy, it wouldn't be heaven.

At least their new home was near water. The ocean and the bay,

Mum had said. The place was called Long Island. That was good. Samuel had always lived on an island. Maybe it would feel like home right away.

What did that mean—feel like home? He'd never had a home. He'd never had parents. At least, not parents he could remember. Daniel was kind of his parent. Even though they were the same age.

Thinking this gave Samuel a bad feeling in his stomach. What kind of parent was Daniel? Very bad.

Samuel heard a short cry and a splash outside.

Oh no. Please, no.

A few seconds passed. Samuel sat up as Daniel strode back into the shack. He ducked his head under the fishing nets and dropped onto the cot. His face was a total blank. Eyes dull and lips pressed tightly together.

"What about Ikey?" Samuel's voice came out shrill and tight. "Did you explain? What did you tell him?"

"Don't worry about it," Daniel said without any emotion.

"But what did you say? What did you tell him?"

Daniel shrugged. That strange smile played over his face again. "No more Ikey," he said. His mouth did a strange quiver. Like a tic.

"Huh? No more Ikey? What do you mean?"

Daniel's smile grew wider. "No worries."

"But, Daniel—" Samuel couldn't find the words.

"No more Ikey," Daniel repeated in a singsong.

Samuel peered out the doorway to the dock. The dock was empty now. No boy sitting at the end. No fishing pole.

"No more Ikey," Daniel said. "So, no worries. Come on, bruvver." He jumped up and, putting a hand on Samuel's shoulder, guided him outside. "Big smiles now. Come on. Sweet smiles. Sweet. Be excited, lad. Let's go tell our new mum how excited we are."

PART TWO

17

Here he was at the Bay Street Theatre, just across from the bay in Sag Harbor, Andy Pavano and Vince's cousin Cora, in town from Bath, a little town in Maine, where she waitressed at a barbecue restaurant and took classes at Bowdoin, studying for a degree in social work.

Andy got all that info in the first five minutes when he picked her up at Vince's house and drove into town on a foggy, drizzly Saturday night. She talked quickly, with a slight Maine accent he hadn't heard much before, and kept tapping his shoulder as she talked, as if trying to keep his attention.

Cora wasn't bad-looking. She had sort of a bird-beak nose, but her eyes were round and pretty. She had the kind of smile that showed her gums, a toothy smile Andy liked. She was small and girlish—*except for her truck-driver laugh,* he thought. But maybe she just laughed like that because she was nervous. She said she'd never been out with a cop before.

"It's not really a date," he said. "Vince just thought we'd have fun together." Then he felt like a total dork for saying that. He could feel his face grow hot, but she didn't seem to notice.

She had to be five or ten years younger than him. Thirty maybe. She dressed young, like a college girl, in black tights and a purple square-necked top that gathered at her waist and came down low like a skirt. She didn't have much on top, he noticed. Her dark hair was short and layered.

Andy parked on the pier and they walked past a little lobster shack, closed for the night, and B. Smith's, a large, bustling restaurant overlooking the bay. A crowd stood at the entrance, waiting for the outdoor tables. Enormous white yachts lined the pier along the side of the restaurant.

The aroma of barbecued chicken floated out from B. Smith's kitchen, and Cora made a face. "Don't take me near a barbecue place. Sometimes after I've been at work in the restaurant, I have to shampoo three times to get the smoke out of my hair. Dogs follow me home because I smell like pulled pork."

Andy laughed. She had a good sense of humor about herself.

"You and Cora should hit it off," Vince had said the night before. "You're both in-tell-ect-u-als." That's how he said it, pronouncing every syllable. Was he being sarcastic? Probably.

Andy had told him he liked to read mystery novels and police procedurals, and Vince had teased him ever since, calling him Sherlock and telling him he should smoke a pipe.

Vince wasn't a Neanderthal, but he pretended to be. He thought it was part of his role as a small-town desk cop.

Cora seemed to think she had to tell everything there was to know about her before they got to the theater. Maybe she just had a thing about silences. Andy knew he wasn't keeping up his end, but it was hard to get a word in, and he was getting to like her soft schoolgirl voice.

She'd had a long affair with a guy in Bath she met at the barbecue restaurant. He said he was in the music business and seemed to know a lot about music clubs and new acts. But it turned out he sold jukeboxes and pinball machines, and he was married.

After she broke it off with him, he stalked her for a while, sitting outside the restaurant in his car and phoning her again and again, leaving threatening messages and muttering obscenities. When she changed her phone number, he finally went away.

"Did you call the police on him?"

She shook her head. "I didn't think they'd do anything. Usually, the police don't do anything in stalker cases till the woman is raped or stabbed in the chest."

"Usually," Andy agreed. "But sometimes a couple of cops can go to the guy's house and—you know—reason with him a little." Andy waved a fist.

Cora stopped outside the theater. "Have you ever done that?"

Andy stared at her. "Well, no. But I saw it on *Law & Order*." They both laughed.

The play was called *Whodunnit?* Cora accused him of only having one interest in life. "Do you only go to plays about cops and crime?"

"I don't go to many plays."

The play wasn't great. It was supposed to be a comedy, but people weren't laughing. The mystery was impossible to solve. The murderer could have been any one of the six people onstage.

Andy hated stories like that where you didn't stand a chance of figuring it out. The culprit could even be the nearsighted police inspector hamming it up on the old-fashioned living room set.

Cora seemed to be enjoying it more than he was. She kept squeezing his arm every time something surprising took place. She laughed when the police inspector stepped on his eyeglasses and stumbled blindly over the tea cozy.

At intermission, Andy led Cora through the chattering crowd, out the doors to the walled terrace in front of the theater. Horns honked as traffic rolled by. The air smelled tangy, salty as the sea. He was about to ask if she wanted to skip the second act and go get a bite to eat when he saw Sari walk out of the theater.

Something pinged in his chest. A real physical feeling. Like a hard heart thump. Or an alarm going off.

Cora was saying something, tapping his shoulder, but he didn't hear her. He heard a rushing sound in his ears like water washing over a steep waterfall. How could Sari still have this effect on him?

She wore a short, white tank dress that clung to her body, showing off her long legs and her trim waist. Her black hair fell loosely behind her shoulders.

And who was the guy she was arm-in-arm with? Was he *the guy?*

That shrimp. He was at least a head shorter than Sari. Wearing a geeky black-and-white wide-striped shirt like a referee wears and white chinos torn at one knee, and a rope belt. Some kind of gold necklace hanging in front of his chest. And a tennis hat. The fucking guy wore a tennis hat with the name of his store on the front to the theater!

Andy lurched toward them. He saw Cora reach for him with both hands, startled by his sudden escape. But he wasn't moving on brainpower. This was some kind of weird primitive force propelling him, the rushing waterfall in his ears sweeping him away.

"Andy?" Sari let go of the shrimpy guy, her dark eyes flashing surprise.

Andy nearly knocked over the tall sign announcing *Whodunnit?* with photos of the cast. He caught his balance and took her by the elbow.

The shrimp peered out from under his tennis cap, eyes wide with surprise. He had freckles and a wide, innocent face. Reminded Andy of someone from an Archie comic book.

"I need to speak to Sari," Andy explained to him.

He expected more of a reaction. But the guy just shrugged and flicked his eyes toward Sari.

She didn't resist as Andy pulled her away, to the side of the theater. A few people turned to watch. He glimpsed Cora behind him, arms crossed now, following him with her eyes till he disappeared around the corner.

Sari giggled. "Are you crazy? We have to go back."

He backed her against the wall. Her skin felt soft and warm. Her eyes glowed even in the darkness here. He felt a rush of feeling, so powerful he had to take a deep breath.

She had hurt him so much the first time. Caused him so many feelings he didn't know he had.

And now here they were again. Here he was, feeling this insane rush of emotion, leading him . . . where?

"Andy, you look funny. What is your problem? You don't have anything to say to me—do you? We have to—"

"I'm back," he said.

And then he was kissing her. Kissing her. And she was kissing him back. And he felt the electric tingle of her fingers on the back of his neck. Just that light touch could make his head explode, he realized.

He kissed her harder. She wasn't resisting.

When the kiss ended, they stared dumbly at each other. Her hands slid off his neck. With a shiver of her shoulders, she slithered out from between him and the wall.

A long silence. Yes, his heart was pounding, and yes, the blood was throbbing, pulsing in his temples. But he didn't hear it now.

Silence. Silence.

And then she shook her head, sending her hair flying loose. She slowly rubbed a finger over her lips, as if wiping off the kiss. "That didn't mean anything," she murmured. "Hear me?"

Then she grabbed his head, pulled his face close, and kissed him again.

18

Andy didn't hear much of the second act. He was aware of Cora squeezing his arm a few times. Was she trying to snap him back to reality? He didn't want to go back. He could still smell Sari's perfume, like oranges, sweet oranges. He could still feel the silvery touch of her fingers on the back of his neck. The whisper of her hair falling over his cheeks.

Cora turned slightly away from him, eyes straight ahead, her lips pursed. She clasped her hands tightly in her lap. She was giving up. The characters moved across the stage, making broad hand gestures, shouting accusations at each other.

After the second kiss, Sari had repeated her warning. "That didn't mean anything, Andy. Please believe me." Then she turned away with a funny, short sigh and went running back to the shrimp.

When he saw her grab the guy's hands and lean down to kiss him on the cheek, Andy had some evil thoughts. Maybe arrest him for being unsightly. Then beat the guy to death with one of those new titanium tennis rackets.

It wasn't the first time he had thought of using his profession to settle a score or right a personal wrong. But of course he had never done anything like that. He was a good person and a good cop. A few free counter lunches were the only perks he had ever allowed himself.

He couldn't help it if his brain got overheated every once in a while. You can control your actions but not your thoughts. And yes, he had violent thoughts.

But the most violent moment of his life? It was back in the living room of the little two-family house in Forest Hills when his father, after too many Budweisers (for a change), settled an argument by punching his mother in the jaw. And Andy, maybe seventeen at the time, had grabbed the old man by the shoulders and shoved him hard, sent him staggering headfirst into the stone mantel. He could still hear the *smack* of his dad's bald head, the gasp of surprise, see the darkening line of blood on his forehead.

He'd expected the old man to spin around and come snarling back at him. But instead, he coiled his body, curled into a cowering position against the flowered wallpaper. To his shock, Andy realized his father was afraid of him.

It should have changed everything. But it didn't. Anthony Pavano was a bully. His son Andy wasn't.

Then Andy did twelve years as a New York City cop. Nothing as violent as that impulsive moment.

And why was he thinking of it now in this theater with people laughing all around him? Onstage, the nearsighted inspector was interviewing a coatrack. Andy glanced around, searching for Sari. But he couldn't locate her in the dark.

He really needed a smoke. He could feel the pack of Camels in his jacket pocket. Cora probably wouldn't approve. Who was Cora? He had to remind himself.

The play ended finally. Yes, the nearsighted inspector had committed the murder. But he was too nearsighted to realize it. At the end, he arrested himself.

Andy climbed to his feet and started to follow Cora across the aisle toward the exit.

"Very clever," a woman said behind him.

"Too clever," the man with her said.

"Did you guess the ending?"

"Yes. About an hour ago. But I still enjoyed it."

"It's one of his lesser works."

"All of his plays are lesser works."

Into the cool night air. A chatter of voices as people hurried to their cars. Cora walked along the sidewalk toward the pier till they were away from the crowd, then turned back to him. "It wasn't very good, was it." Said with a shrug and a sad smile.

"I don't think I laughed," he said. His eyes were over her shoulder, searching for Sari. How had she disappeared? He just wanted a glimpse of her.

"It was supposed to be sophisticated," she said. "But the actors camped it up too much, don't you think? If they'd played it sincere . . ."

He didn't want to discuss the play. He wanted to catch one more look at Sari and have a slow, soothing smoke. He wanted to burn his throat and let the smoke make his eyes water.

No. He didn't know what he wanted.

But when he heard the shrill shouts, he suddenly snapped alert. He turned toward the cries. From the pier? He spun away from Cora and took off running.

19

He heard shouts for help. Shrill cries. And, in the circle of light from a tall streetlamp, saw a small group of people wrestling against the side of the darkened lobster shack. He didn't realize they were children until he was a few feet from them.

"Stop! Police!" he boomed.

He stepped in something soft. Glancing down, he saw a smashed ice cream cone on the pavement beneath his shoe. Another cone lay near it, ice cream still round at the top.

"You dumb shit! You dumb shit! You pay me back!" a blond-haired boy in a blue Southampton sweatshirt was screeching.

A big dark-haired kid, nearly twice his size, had him by the front of the sweatshirt and swung a meaty fist above the boy's face. "Shut up! Shut the fuck up, liar!"

Two or three other kids stood back a few feet and watched. They were all shouting angrily at the big guy.

Not even teenagers, Andy realized. Their voices hadn't changed.

"You fuck! You pay me for that cone!"

"You want a cone? I'll shove it up your ass! You think I can't? You want to dare me?"

Kids!

The big kid started to lower his fist to the smaller boy's midsection. Andy stepped between them and absorbed most of the blow on his side. The kid had a pretty good punch.

"Break it up. Police."

He grabbed the big kid by the shoulders of his gray hoodie and pushed him backward.

"Get off me, asshole. You don't look like no police."

"Sag Harbor Police," Andy said, as if that would convince the kid. "What's the fight about?"

The blond-haired boy pointed to the asphalt. "My ice cream cone. He tried to take it."

"Liar!" the big kid screamed. He lunged at the smaller guy again. Andy caught him and stood him up.

"Ethan is telling the truth!" a girl cried. The others joined in agreement.

"You're Ethan?" Andy asked.

The blond kid nodded. He had tears in his eyes. He brushed back his straight blond hair with one hand. His whole body was trembling. Andy saw he was struggling with all his might not to burst out sobbing.

"And what's your name?" Andy asked the other kid.

No reply. Instead, a sullen stare.

"Derek Saltzman," the girl said. "He knocked down my cone, too."

"I'll knock *you* down, too," Derek told her.

"You're not going to knock anyone down," Andy growled. "What's your problem?"

"Derek is mean," the girl said. "He's always picking fights."

"He's always stealing our stuff," Ethan said in a trembling voice.

"Fucking liars," Derek muttered.

"Nice language," Andy said. "How old are you?"

"Old enough," the kid muttered, still offering up the surly glare.

He has a face like a bulldog, Andy thought. *And a personality to match.*

"He's twelve," the girl offered.

"And how old are you?" Andy asked Ethan.

Ethan took a step back. He didn't take his eyes off Derek. "I'm twelve, too."

Cora stepped up beside Andy. "What's going on?"

"Kids fighting," he told her. "Over ice cream."

"I didn't take their ice cream," Derek snarled. His fat cheeks puffed in and out like a blowfish. "They're total liars."

Andy noticed he cleaned up his language with a woman present.

"Then how did the cones end up on the pavement?" Andy asked.

Derek shrugged. "They dropped them."

"Liar!"

Cora squinted at them. "Why are you kids all alone out here? It's ten o'clock at night."

Before anyone could answer, hurried footsteps clicked over the asphalt. Andy turned to see a red-haired woman running awkwardly toward them on high, spiked heels. She was tall and lean and had a white jacket tied around her shoulders, which flared behind her like a cape as she ran. Gold bracelets jangled up and down one arm.

"Derek?" she called breathlessly. "What's going on?"

She stopped a few feet from Andy and Cora and eyed him suspiciously. "Who are you? Is there a problem?"

"I'm a police officer," Andy started. "I—"

"Police? What did he do? Who are these kids?" Her voice was throaty, hoarse, a smoker's voice. It rose with each question. Her chest heaved up and down beneath her violet sweater. The bracelets matched a gold chain with a jeweled heart that hung from her neck.

"I didn't do anything," Derek said, jutting his fleshy jaw out defiantly.

"Is he your son?" Andy asked.

She nodded. Then she brushed a strand of coppery hair off her forehead. "Yes. Derek Saltzman. He's my son. I'm Elaine Saltzman. I left him for ten minutes by the ice cream store." She pointed toward the end of the pier.

"These kids say your son tried to take away their ice cream. I think there was some kind of scuffle."

"Liars!" Derek shouted.

"We're not lying!"

Mrs. Saltzman squinted at Ethan, seeing him for the first time. "I know you. You're Ethan, right?" She turned back to Andy. "He's in my son's class. What happened, Ethan?"

Derek lurched forward. He raised both hands as if to give his mother a shove. "Why do you ask *him*? Why don't you ask *me*?" In a whining voice that made Andy want to cover his ears.

He glanced at Cora. Her eyes were on one of the tall, white yachts at pierside. Three people had come onto the deck to watch the confrontation.

Bet Cora is impressed seeing a cop in action, Andy thought wryly. *Spilled ice cream is a felony in this town. Ha. Wait till I slip the cuffs on the kid. She'll be all over me.*

"Derek tried to take our cones," Ethan reported. "When we said no, he knocked them to the ground."

"Stupid liar! They knocked *my* ice cream to the ground!"

Mrs. Saltzman stared down at her red-faced son. "Are you telling the truth?"

She didn't wait for him to answer. She wrapped her hand around Andy's arm and led him across the pier. She waited for an SUV to pass, then pulled him to the side of a parked car, out of her son's hearing.

"Derek has problems," she murmured, fingers still tight around Andy's sleeve. She leaned against him and brought her face close to his. He could smell her flowery perfume and a whiff of alcohol on her breath. "Ever since his father left, he's been angry, very troubled."

This was definitely more than Andy wanted to hear.

"Mrs. Saltzman, I really have to be going. Why don't you just solve this thing by buying cones for all three kids?"

She blinked. Did she expect him to get tough or something? She was still holding onto him. A strong breeze off the bay fluttered her hair.

"Good. Okay," she said. "I just wanted to explain. I mean, these days sometimes Derek acts out. But he's basically a good boy. He has a good head on his shoulders. A good head. Really."

Of course, neither Andy nor Elaine Saltzman, nor anyone on the pier that night, had any idea of what would happen to Derek's head a few weeks later.

20

"My parents say we'll have a house in Malibu. That's where they are right now. In L.A., buying it. It's right on the ocean. See, you go out the back door and you're on the beach."

"That's awesome, Ruth-Ann. Can I come live with you? I mean really."

"It's like being on vacation all the time. Only you live there. And there are celebrities all over the beach. You know. Movie stars. And TV. And you just hang out with them."

"You think Johnny Depp could be your neighbor?"

"No way. He's too old. They don't let old people in Malibu."

The girls both laughed. They sat almost side by side on Ruth-Ann's bed, talking and texting each other at the same time.

"Dylan Sprouse?"

"You like him? I like the other one."

"They could be your neighbors. You could hang with them and they'd ask you to be on TV. And you'd be a star."

"No way, Elena. I'm only fourteen. I don't want to be a star till I'm sixteen."

That made them both laugh again.

Elena Sutter and Ruth-Ann Glazer had been friends since third grade, and best-best friends for two years since sixth grade, mainly since they shared the same sense of humor, although Ruth-Ann was the real wit, sharp and sarcastic. And because they lived two houses down from each other and were in the same eighth-grade class at Sag Harbor Middle School, and because they looked so much alike, they could be sisters.

They agreed that Ruth-Ann looked like the older sister, because she was at least four inches taller than Elena, and already had the beginnings of a woman's body, meaning she had breasts, and wore her hair in a more sophisticated, layered look, which she acquired during one of her many trips with her parents to L.A.

They were both pretty and smart and popular. They both had an easy way of getting along with other kids, and of not getting in their own way when it came to success at school. They were both spoiled but not in an obnoxious way. They knew how to get whatever they wanted from their parents and still allow their parents to think *they* were the ones in charge.

Elena was a miniature fourteen-year-old version of Lea, her mother. Creamy-white skin framed by straight, black hair, serious dark eyes, a delicate face and a wiry body, perfect for the gymnastics classes that she was becoming more serious about.

They tapped on their phones for a few minutes without speaking. Elena's phone bleeped. She squinted at the screen. "Ethan."

Ruth-Ann lowered her phone. "Ira's friend Ethan? What's he want?"

Elena shrugged. "Nothing. Just said 'sup." She thumbed the keys rapidly.

Another bleep. "He wants to come over. His PlayStation broke."

"Tell him no way. Tell him your brother Ira isn't here. He's at your house. Ethan pretends he wants to hang with Ira. Then he just stares at you. Like a sad puppy dog."

Elena laughed. "He *does* look like a puppy dog." The light from her phone gave her face a pale tint. "Hey, I'm not kidding about Malibu. Your parents would let me come with you, right? Just for the summer, I mean."

Ruth-Ann studied her friend. "You're joking. You're getting two new brothers, and you want to come live with me?"

Elena scrunched up her face. "Why do I want two new brothers?"

"Because they're hot? Show me that photo again." She grabbed Elena's phone and began shuffling through photo screens. She stopped at the twins' photo and brought it close to her face.

Elena grabbed it away from her. "You think they're cute? I think they're blond freaks."

"You're messed up, Elena. They are totally hot. I mean, for twelve-year-olds. Check out those smiles. Those dimples on this one's cheeks. What's his name? Danny? Adorable. They could be on TV. Really."

Elena stuck her finger down her throat and made a gagging sound.

She squinted at the photo. Daniel and Samuel. Wavy blond hair, almost white. And those big blue eyes. Wearing red T-shirts way too big for them. And those sick, sweet smiles.

"Like they're posing as angels," Elena said. *Where did that thought come from? Weird!*

"Where are they going to stay?" Ruth-Ann studied the photo. "Are you changing rooms? They're not moving into the playroom downstairs, are they?"

"No way. Dad fixed up the attic. He made it really awesome. He bought them a laptop and a TV, and he got them a Wii. He said they've had a tough life. He wants to make things nice for them."

"Tough life? No kidding. They lost both their parents, didn't they? And their house? And all their stuff?"

Elena nodded. "I think Dad wants to write a book about them."

Ruth-Ann handed the phone back to Elena. "For real? You know, my parents were talking about your dad's book. Did you read it?"

"Not really. Just kinda looked at it."

"Mom said the book says parents should let kids do whatever

they want. Just let them be free. My parents made jokes about it. They said it would make a great sitcom."

"Is that all your parents think about? Sitcoms?"

"Well, yeah. Their show was picked up for another year. All they talk about are jokes and scripts and stuff."

"Ruth-Ann, do you watch it?"

"Of course not. No way."

They both laughed.

Elena twisted the phone in her hand. "My dad's book isn't true. He is stricter than your parents. I mean, he doesn't let Ira and me do what we want. I always have to trick Mom into letting me go places. Or Roz. Roz is the easiest because she's busy worrying about Axl."

"I forgot about Axl. It's gonna be crowded in your house, Elena. I mean, a mob."

"That's why I want to come to Malibu with you guys."

"How is Ira taking the new brothers thing? Is he freaking?"

"Of *course* he's freaking. Ira freaks when his shoelace comes untied."

"Now you sound like my parents. They'd like that joke. They'd type it into their BlackBerries right away."

"It's no joke. The poor kid is totally stressed already. I mean, he thinks sixth grade is really hard."

Ruth-Ann snickered. "Wait till he gets to eighth."

"He hates his teacher. Miss Montgomery. Did you have Montgomery?"

"No. I had Price, remember?"

"Montgomery acts real nice. She's real pretty and she's very sweet, but she gives hours and hours of homework every night. And then she doesn't even collect it or go over it or anything. Ira says she just makes you do it."

Ruth-Ann snickered. "Tell Ira to suck it up."

Elena sighed. "I think he really misses Mom and Dad when they're both away. Roz is great. But . . . you know."

Elena's phone rang, startling her. She stared at the screen, but she didn't have to. She recognized her dad's ringtone.

"Hi, Dad. Oh. Okay. Okay. I'm coming. Bye."

She clicked the phone shut. "It's my new brothers. They're here. I gotta go." She jumped to her feet and strode out of the room. She was making her way down the stairs when she heard Ruth-Ann's shout.

"Hey, Elena—good luck."

21

At LaGuardia Airport, Mark hugged Lea and held her close, wrapped her up like a prize that had almost been lost. He wanted to plant a hundred kisses on her face. The strong emotion welled in him, taking him by surprise. He was usually so level, no tidal waves of feeling rocking his calm.

But he let her go when he saw the two blond creatures gazing at him. *My new sons?*

Yes, they were beautiful boys. Their deep blue eyes were almost unreal. And Lea's description—angels—came pretty close to describing the sweetness, the innocence on their pale faces.

So why didn't he feel some kind of immediate connection with them? The wave of emotion seemed to pull back, leaving him with an empty feeling as he stared at the boys over Lea's shoulder.

He didn't want them here. He had argued with Lea almost until their plane had taken off. But he hoped that when he saw them . . . when he actually saw the two angels, he would fall for them the way Lea had, and his doubts and objections would fade away.

What a disappointment that their hopeful blue-eyed stares only aroused a feeling of dread.

And now, after the long drive to Sag Harbor, here they were in his house. About to meet his kids. About to join his family.

Just like that. Two strangers to take care of and worry about. And love.

The boys seem really happy to be here, Mark thought. *They haven't stopped smiling.*

Guiding them to the living room, Lea stood behind them, as if backing them up, or maybe blocking any retreat. Her expression was tense. Mark noticed her eyes were bloodshot. She had one hand lightly on Samuel's slender shoulder.

Ira stood halfway up the stairs, his chin on the wooden banister. He stared down warily at the two boys, gripping the banister tightly with both hands as if holding on for dear life.

He's staring at them like they were circus freaks. I told Ira to give them a friendly welcome. Did he forget?

"Ira, come down and say hi to your new brothers." Mark motioned him down.

"Hi," he said, without budging from his perch.

"Ira, come down." Lea's voice sounded tight, shriller than usual. "Can't you shake hands?"

"Kids don't shake hands." Ira's reply.

The twins gazed up at him with those sweet smiles on their faces. Their blue eyes appeared to glow. *Like jewels,* Mark thought. *They are extraordinary-looking.* He thought of beautifully crafted dolls.

Except they were so skinny, so gaunt. The red T-shirts and long white shorts hung on them like scarecrow clothes. Their flat white sneakers were as long as clown shoes.

We've got to buy them clothes. Then see about putting some meat on their bones.

The twins stepped forward, almost in unison, and gazed around the living room. "How nice is this?" Samuel said. "We never had a couch." He put a hand on the back of the green leather couch and squeezed it. Mark saw that when he removed his hand, he left a sweat stain on the leather.

Daniel turned back to Ira on the stairs. "Do you like to swim?"

Ira scrunched up his face, as if he had to think about it. "Not if the water's cold."

Is he going to say anything friendly or positive?
Guess it'll take time.

"Where do you like to swim?" Daniel asked Ira. He was definitely trying to break the ice. "In the bay or in the ocean?"

"My friend Ethan has a pool," Ira said, chin on the banister. He didn't move from behind the bars of the banister, safe in his cage up there.

Roz came bursting into the room from the kitchen, holding Axl by one hand as the chubby, dark-haired boy toddled beside her. She wore a long blue denim sleeveless dress and was barefoot, as usual. Axl had a little sunburn on his arms. She had taken him to the bay beach this morning.

"Welcome! Welcome!" Roz threw her arms around Daniel and hugged him, then pulled his brother into a hug, as if they had known each other for years. Roz wasn't usually this demonstrative, but she had told Mark she planned to do all she could to welcome the boys into a warm home.

Axl stuck out his stubby arms toward the twins, as if he wanted a hug, too. To everyone's surprise, including Axl's, Samuel picked the two-year-old up in his arms and hugged him. Axl grabbed a fistful of the boy's blond hair and tugged it hard. Samuel laughed and spun Axl around.

His twin watched the whole thing with a dimpled smile. When Samuel returned Axl to the floor, Daniel pointed at the toddler. "He's funny-looking."

Roz's happy expression changed. "What did you say?"

"He's funny-looking. His face makes me laugh."

Roz moved toward Axl as if she had to protect him. "He has a perfectly nice face. And his hair is coming in nice and curly."

"He's funny-looking," Daniel repeated. "No lie."

Lea stepped toward him and spoke up. "Sometimes it's better to say something nice," she said.

"Sometimes." Daniel's smile returned. He exchanged a quick glance with his brother. "But the laddy looks like a chimpanzee, don't you know?"

"Panzee," Axl repeated. He giggled. He seemed to like the word. "Panzee."

Roz started to say something but restrained herself. "Well, I hope you boys like it here. Welcome to our family."

"We like it already," Samuel said. "We never had a couch."

"Mark, show them their room," Lea said.

But before Mark could move, the front door swung open, letting in a burst of warm sunshine, followed by Elena. She stopped at the door and called to the new arrivals. "Hey, guys! You're here!"

They turned and studied her.

She swept into the room and shook hands with both of them at once. "Oh, wow. How do I tell you apart?"

"I'm the smart one," Daniel said.

"He's the weird one," Samuel told her.

"You can tell them by the dimples," Lea offered. "See? Daniel has those dimples on his cheeks and Samuel doesn't."

"Weird," Elena said. She squinted at them. "Do you always dress alike?"

"Your mum bought us this," Daniel said, tugging at the baggy red T-shirt. "We lost our clothes. We lost everything." His voice cracked on the last word. He lowered his eyes.

"Don't worry." Lea stepped up behind them and put a hand on each one's shoulder. "That's the first thing on my list. We'll go shopping and buy you all the clothes you need."

They turned their heads and smiled up at her.

Lea sighed. "Oh, I'm just so happy you are both here. Look at me. I have tears in my eyes." She walked over to Mark and pressed her face against the front of his shirt. "*Thank you,*" she whispered.

"Panzee," Axl offered.

Daniel reached down and picked Axl up again. Axl poked his nose against Daniel's nose. "Chimpanzee," Daniel said.

"Panzee." Axl repeated the word.

Daniel lifted his eyes to Roz. "Do you feed him lots and lots of bananas?"

Roz squinted at him. "Excuse me?"

"You know. Chimpanzee food?"

Again, Mark saw Roz restrain herself. "I guess I'll have to get used to your sense of humor, Daniel."

Samuel snickered. "Daniel doesn't have a sense of humor. He's just strange, don't you know."

"Chimpanzee," Daniel and Axl said in unison. Then they both giggled.

Daniel turned back to Roz. "He's my new pet."

Roz's mouth dropped open.

Daniel twirled Axl above his head. Axl laughed. "Yes, boyo. You're my new pet. Gonna slip you lots and lots of peanuts."

"Panzee," Axl repeated and tossed back his head and giggled.

"Look how sweet they are," Lea whispered, leaning her head against Mark's shoulder and squeezing his arm. "They're being so nice to Axl. Isn't that the sweetest?"

"I'm not sure Roz would agree with you," Mark whispered back, watching Daniel twirl Axl faster and faster. "She looks upset."

"They're just being playful," Lea said, tears glistening in her eyes. "They don't know they insulted Roz. They're not trying to be mean."

The twins appeared to like their attic room. Mark had hired some local carpenters to add walls and finish the ceiling and carpet the floor and paint the room a comforting pastel blue-green.

The eaves were low, so they all had to duck their heads. He and Roz had gone to Hildreth's, the old department store in Southampton, and bought soft-looking, comfortable, homey furniture for the room. And twin beds, which Mark placed side by side at the end of the attic, with the window looking down to the backyard.

Now they were bouncing on their beds, giggling and raising their hands to the low ceiling. Watching them, Lea clapped her hands and let out a gleeful cheer. "They like the room, Mark." She kissed his cheek. Her face was wet from her tears.

Mark playfully tugged her hair. "I'm glad you're so happy."

"I *am* happy. I just know we're doing the right thing. I have such a strong feeling. . . ."

Elena stood behind them at the top of the attic stairs. She appeared to be studying the twins as if they were zoo specimens. Ira had chosen not to join them up here.

Earlier in the week, when Mark broke the news to Elena that Lea was coming home with two orphaned boys, he was prepared for some kind of strong reaction. He didn't expect the shrug he received and the muttered "Whatever."

Then she quickly added, "As long as they stay out of my room and don't annoy my friends."

That broke the tension. "They're going to be a little strange at first," he warned her. "They grew up on a tiny island. And they've been through a lot of tragedy."

Elena rolled her eyes. "Dad, they're twelve, right? *Of course* they're going to be strange."

They both laughed.

He knew Elena would take it in stride, as she did everything. There would definitely be problems with her along the way. A teenager with *three* younger brothers in the house? No way there wouldn't be conflicts and fights and tears. But Elena could always be counted on to ride out any emotional wave.

Ira was a different story. Take him to town for lunch and talk to him again? Tell him he had to pitch in and make this work? Tell him the family really needed his help?

Mark knew he'd just roll his eyes and say, "Tell me something I don't know."

Or worse: "Shut up, Dad. You're a jerk."

The twins were on their backs now, sprawled on the beds, luxuriating, sinking their heads into the pale green pillows. The room was pale blue and green, water colors, soothing and perhaps, a reminder of their island home.

Roz and Mark had put a lot of thought into all this while Lea was working to bring them off the island.

"Let's show the boys the rest of the house," Lea said. "Come on, get up, guys. We'll give you the grand tour."

Elena led the way downstairs. Her room was at the near end of the hall. She pushed the door open so the boys could take a glimpse. Above her bed, she had a framed poster of a girl gymnast, arms outstretched, flying high in the air. The closet door was covered with cutout photos of actors from the teen-trauma TV shows she watched on her computer. Skirts and jeans and colorful tops were strewn all over the floor. Elena had a lot of good qualities, but she wasn't neat.

"Nice room," Daniel said. He pushed Samuel out of the doorway to get a better look. He pointed to the gymnast poster. "Is that you?"

Elena rolled her eyes. "I wish."

Daniel started into the room, but Elena pushed a hand against his chest. "Two words to remember about my room, guys," she said.

They trained their blue eyes on her. "Two words?" Daniel asked.

"Keep out," she said.

They both burst out laughing. As if she had made a hilarious joke. They laughed and shook their heads. Daniel raised his hand for Elena to slap him a high five.

"You're funny, Elena," he said. Samuel nodded agreement.

"I'm serious," Elena insisted.

"Let's move on with the tour," Mark said. He guided the boys to the next room. His office. He pointed out the desktop PC and his shelves of psychology books, and the piece of moon rock on his desk. They took a quick glance but didn't seem at all interested.

At the end of the hall, Elena said, "This is Ira's room."

The boys shoved each other as they eagerly trotted down the hall. Their too-big sneakers made floppy sounds on the thick, white carpet. They all burst into Ira's room.

He lay sprawled on the bed, white earplugs in his ears, tapping away on a handheld game player. He didn't stop or look up as everyone invaded his room.

"Ira?" Mark called. "Earth calling Ira. You have visitors."

Ira tapped away, eyes on the game player.

The twins walked around the room. Daniel strode to the two windows, pushed back the gray curtains, and gazed down at the front yard and the street. Afternoon sunlight poured in, making his blond hair glow.

Ira's room was bare and undecorated. The walls were plain white. On the narrow strip of wall between the windows, he had a small, framed photograph of himself shaking hands with New York's governor, after Ira had won a state citizenship essay contest.

No other art or decoration in the room except for a small black stenciled octopus on the wall over his headboard. Mark didn't understand the octopus. Ira wasn't into sea life at all. In fact, he was timid and frightened around the ocean.

A low bookshelf stood beside the long white counter that served as his desk. The closet door was closed. No dirty clothing on the floor.

Ira didn't like clutter. He said keeping his room white and bare helped him concentrate on his homework. Nothing to distract him. And he said it helped him sleep at night because there were no scary shadows.

Samuel studied Ira's laptop. Photos of Ira and his friends on a class trip shuffled on the screen, Ira's screensaver. Daniel moved to the bed and sat down on the edge of the white quilt.

Lea tugged the earplugs from Ira's ears. He sat up straight, blinking in surprise. "Hey—"

"We're showing Daniel and Samuel the house," Lea said. "Do you want to tell them anything about your room?"

Ira shook his head. "Not really."

"Awesome room," Samuel said. "Sunny. Like an island morning, you know?"

Lea leaned toward Mark. "Don't you love their accent? Sometimes the way they talk . . . it's like poetry."

Daniel stepped up to Ira. His face turned serious. "Can I have your room?"

A short laugh burst from Ira's throat. "Huh? I don't think so."

Lea took a step toward Daniel. "You like Ira's room, sweetheart? It's kind of bare, don't you think?"

Daniel didn't respond. He wrapped a hand around Ira's upper arm. His eyes locked intently on Ira's startled face.

"No. Really," Daniel said, lowering his voice. "Can I have your room?"

Ira raised his eyes to Mark. A pleading glance. Mark felt too stunned to react.

"I'll have your room," Daniel repeated, patting Ira's shoulder. "Okay?"

22

"Mark, be reasonable. It's a perfect solution. I can't believe you're the one being the hard-ass about this." Lea's hands were clenched into tight fists over the kitchen table.

Mark reached across the table to take her hand, but she snapped it out of his reach. "I think I'm being the reasonable one," he said.

"I think *I* am," Roz insisted. She had put Axl down for his nap and joined them in the kitchen for what had started out as a quiet discussion and, much to Mark's dismay, quickly elevated into a shouting match.

Ira was sulking in his room. Elena had taken the twins on a walking tour of the neighborhood to show them the bay. The boys were hopping up and down with excitement and had no idea of the conflict they had caused among the three adults.

Lea took a breath and started another attempt to persuade Mark. "You saw the look on Ira's face when the boys wanted his room. He was *sick*. He was about to have a fit."

"Of course he was," Mark started. "He had every right—"

"So then they saw the guesthouse and totally fell in love with it," Roz interrupted. Mark gazed at the dark stains on the front of her sweater. Axl was constantly using her sweater as a napkin.

"They don't know *what* they want," Mark said, turning to Lea. "How could they? It's like they stepped onto another planet."

"They know they want to live in the guesthouse," Lea said, jaw clenched, eyes about to tear up again. "And Roz has agreed to move up to the attic."

"It's better for me anyway," Roz said. "I can keep a closer watch on everyone if I'm staying inside the house. And the attic is even roomier—"

"And that way, Ira will keep his room," Lea said. "That's so important. I wouldn't do anything to hurt Ira's equilibrium."

"No! No way!" Mark jumped to his feet, nearly knocking over his chair. "I built the attic room for the boys. They should be in the house. We don't know anything about them. We have to take special care of them. We can't have them living by themselves in their own house, even if it's in the backyard. That's *crazy*."

Lea motioned with both hands for him to calm down. "We want to make them happy, Mark."

Mark felt his throat tighten. "So you'll do *anything* they want? Is that your idea?"

"Mark, stop shouting. Can't we sit here and have a calm discussion? Roz and I agree—"

"Leave Roz out of this. We're the ones adopting these . . . these . . ."

"Leave me out of it? I thought I was part of this family. God knows, I'm the one spending most of the time with the kids."

Mark patted her hand. "Sorry, Roz." He turned to Lea. "I'm not trying to be difficult. I see how happy you are. I see you already have strong feelings for these boys. You know I didn't want them here, but I'm going to try, Lea. I'm going to do everything I can. But you can't just give in to them. You can't give them everything they want. They don't know—"

"You saw them pleading and pleading to live in the guesthouse. You saw how excited they were."

"I just think it's too soon to have them living on their own. We don't know how they're going to adapt. We don't know if we can trust them. We don't know—"

"They won't be living on their own. No way. They'll be with us all the time. We'll—" Lea gasped. Her eyes were over Mark's shoulders. "Oh no."

Mark spun around and saw the twins huddled in the kitchen doorway. He felt his heart skip a beat. "How long have you two been standing there?"

They both shrugged. Mark realized their eyes were on him. They were studying him. Had they overheard his true feelings?

An awkward silence in the room. Then Lea stood up and flashed them a broad smile. "Good news, boys. We had a vote here. And we voted two to one. Roz and Axl are going to move to the attic—and you two get to stay in the guesthouse."

She turned to Mark as if challenging him. But he knew when he was defeated.

The twins cheered and did a funny, awkward tap dance of celebration. But their smiles faded quickly. "Only one thing," Daniel said softly. "Samuel and I will take the guesthouse only if you promise us one thing."

Mark narrowed his eyes at them. *Now what? What is their next demand?*

"Only if Ira will come have sleepovers with us," Daniel said.

He saw Lea's chin quiver. The tears were about to flow again.

"Are they angels?" she whispered. "Is that the sweetest thing?"

23

Lea grabbed the car keys and stuffed them in her jacket pocket. She herded the twins toward the back door. "Where's Ira? Ira's coming with us? Did you see him?"

Before they could answer, Elena burst into the kitchen. "Have you seen my necklace? Did you see it anywhere?"

Lea blinked. "Necklace?"

"The one with the amethyst. You know. Grandma's necklace? It was on my dresser. I know I left it on top of my dresser. Now I can't find it anywhere."

"Maybe it fell off, sweetie," Lea suggested. "Did you look underneath?"

"Duh. Like of course. Like I'm not stupid." Elena turned to the twins. "Did you see a necklace anywhere?"

They both shook their heads. "Not me," Daniel said.

"We'll all search for it when we get back," Lea said. "It didn't fly away. We'll find it. Get Ira for me, will you? I'm taking the twins shopping."

Lea drove the twins to the mall at Bridgehampton to buy them clothes. Ira had protested vehemently, but she forced him to accompany them and help select what kids at his school were wearing. The twins had been with them for two days, and he hadn't made a single attempt to be friendly. Now he sat glumly in the front seat beside her, his arms crossed, staring straight ahead through the windshield.

In the Camry's backseat, the twins strained at their seat belts, leaning out the windows to see the passing scenery.

"I don't think they've ever been in a car before," she told Ira.

No response.

"Come on, Ira. Shape up."

"Look at that truck!" Daniel exclaimed. "Couldn't you fit a whole house in that truck!"

Lea found it so touching. These twelve-year-old boys seeing the world for the first time.

She turned into a long parking aisle and stopped while a blue pickup backed out of a spot. "Be nice to them," she whispered to Ira. "Be a help, okay? I'll buy you something special right now. To cheer you up. What would you like? What can I buy you?"

"A candy bar?"

Lea bought all three of them big Milky Way bars. The twins ate them slowly, taking small bites, savoring them, dopey smiles on their faces as if they were drunk from the chocolate.

"You had candy bars on the island, didn't you?" Lea asked.

They both nodded. "I got a Snickers bar for my tenth birthday," Samuel said.

"It was my birthday, too," Daniel said. "We had to share it, don't you know."

Ira stared at them. Lea thought she caught a moment of empathy on his face. Having to share a candy bar was something Ira could feel strongly about.

Still chewing on their giant candy bars, they followed Lea into T.J.Maxx.

"We need to get you boys at least three or four pairs of jeans to wear to school," Lea said. "Ira, what kind of jeans are the kids wearing these days?"

Ira licked caramel off his lips. "I don't know."

"Come on, Ira," Lea snapped. "Help out here. What kind of jeans?"

He shrugged. "I'll know it when I see it."

"Okay. Follow me. Boys' jeans are over there."

She led them to the tables stacked high with jeans. Only a few brands but several styles and colors of denim. Did kids still wear cargo jeans? Most of the jeans in Ira's closet had a dozen pockets up and down the legs.

She picked up a pair of straight-legged, faded denims and held it against Samuel. "This looks about your size. Ira, do kids wear these?"

Ira shrugged. "Maybe."

Lea searched through the pile and pulled out the same size. "You boys will have to go try these on. But wait. Let's find a few more."

Daniel had a smear of chocolate on his chin. "Only one of us has to try them on," he said. "We're the same size."

"But don't you want to pick the ones you like?" Lea asked.

Samuel gazed up at her. "Do we really get more than one? We don't have to share?"

"Yes. You can each pick two or three."

The twins clapped their hands, careful not to drop their candy bars. They let out squeaks of joy.

It takes so little to make them happy, Lea thought. *My kids take everything for granted.*

She had a sudden memory flash: the twins stepping out of the red rain, looking so lost and forlorn. All around them, the devastation, everything down and destroyed. The mournful wails. The heavy, sour smell of death with each breath she took.

She forced the images from her mind. "Here. Go try this smaller size. Take these and try them all on." She watched them race to the dressing room against the back wall. They were so small for their age. Ira towered over them.

Ira hunched beside her, doing his best to look bored and unhappy. "What am I supposed to do?"

"Help me pick out some shorts for Axl."

"Big whoop."

A short while later, success. Jeans were selected. T-shirts added to the pile. A couple of sweaters and long-sleeved shirts. It was April and the weather was still cool and damp.

"Thank you, Mum. Thank you." From Daniel.

Then Samuel: "Thank you, Mum. I'm so happy. I never had new clothes, don't you know."

"Do we love our new mum? Yes!" Daniel exclaimed.

They both hugged her so tight she could barely breathe. Lea was almost overcome by their innocent, joyful gratitude. She carried the pile of clothing to the registers up front.

She dumped everything on the counter. The three boys had wandered off. Where were they? She spotted them near the back wall. They were talking to another boy. A big hulk of a boy with a hard, bulldog face. Lea recognized him from Ira's class.

And there was his mother. Elaine Saltzman. Ahead of Lea in the line. Elaine turned as if she knew Lea was thinking about her. "Lea?"

"Hi, Elaine. How are you?"

Elaine swept her coppery hair behind one shoulder. She motioned toward the boys. "Do you have nephews visiting?"

"No. They're mine. I mean—"

"Yours?"

"I'm adopting them. They grew up on that island off the Carolinas. Cape Le Chat Noir? They lost their families in the hurricane. And I—"

"That's so wonderful of you, Lea. You just brought them here? You're adopting both of them? Do you know anything about them?"

"Not really. But look. They're sharing their candy bars with your son. Look how sweet they are."

Samuel thought the boy was funny-looking. *He looks like a big mean dog. Is he really only twelve?*

The boy's head was enormous, his black hair uncombed, falling wildly over his square forehead. He had such a mean scowl on his face. And those little bulldog eyes.

It didn't take long to see that Ira was afraid of him.

"This is Derek," Ira whispered as the boy lumbered up to them. "Be careful. He's really mean. Be nice to him."

Daniel chuckled. Samuel gave him a look, a warning, to be cool. *Don't be yourself, Daniel,* he thought.

"Hey," the big kid said. He had his eyes on Samuel's candy bar. "What's up?"

"These are my new brothers," Ira told him. His voice was suddenly trembly. *Like a warbling bird,* Samuel thought.

Derek sneered. It made him look more like a pig than a bulldog. "Brothers? Since when?"

"My parents are adopting them," Ira said. "They live with us now."

Derek eyed the twins up and down, sizing them up. "How old are you?"

"Twelve," Daniel answered.

"You don't look twelve. You look six."

Samuel felt a tremor of fear. *Please don't be yourself, Daniel.*

Derek leaned over them, trying to be intimidating. "What are your names? Babyface One and Babyface Two?"

"I'm Daniel and he's Samuel. Or maybe I'm Samuel and he's Daniel. Sometimes I forget."

Derek sneered again. "You're a funny guy." He eyed them slowly. "No. I got a better name for you. You're Shrimp One and you're Shrimp Two."

"I want to be Shrimp Two," Daniel said. "Can I be Shrimp Two?" He had the sweetest smile on his face. Samuel had seen that crazy smile before. It meant he wasn't thinking sweet thoughts.

Derek stretched out a porky hand to Daniel. "I'll finish your candy bar for you."

Samuel saw a hard jolt freeze Daniel's face. And then he caught the warning glance from Ira. Ira took a step back. He had his eyes on Daniel. "Just give it to him," Ira whispered.

"Give it," Derek ordered. He waved his hand in Daniel's face. "I'll finish it." He turned to Samuel. "I'll finish yours, too. You've had enough, right?"

"Right." Samuel had his eyes on poor, frightened Ira. He handed his chocolate bar to Derek. Then he waited to see what Daniel would do.

Daniel kept that sweet smile on his face, but his cheeks were kind of red. Samuel knew that look, too. He knew everything about Daniel. After all, he was almost him. Almost, but a little different.

To Samuel's relief, Daniel stuffed his candy bar into the big porker's hand. "Enjoy it, Derek," he said. "It's all yours."

Derek snickered. "I *will* enjoy it, dude." He took a big bite and chewed with his mouth open so they could see the chocolate chunks smearing over his teeth.

"Aren't you going to say thank you?" Daniel sounded hurt.

Derek chewed noisily. Some chocolate juice ran down his chin. He swallowed. "Funny," he told Daniel. "You're fucking funny. Next time, I'll want a *whole* bar."

Daniel's smile grew tighter. Like a mask.

Samuel felt his heart skip a beat. *Uh-oh.*

He saw the new mum by the front windows waving two big shopping bags at them. He tugged Daniel's arm. "We have to go. The new mum wants to leave."

Daniel nodded. He turned slowly and followed Samuel and Ira. Derek stood in place, a candy bar in each hand, stuffing his face.

Ira pushed between them, his face all sweaty. "You have to be nice to Derek. He's a bad dude. He likes to hurt people. Really. He beat up my friend Ethan behind the playground at school and almost broke his arm."

"Doesn't he ever get caught?" Daniel asked.

"I think the teachers are afraid of him, too," Ira said.

They caught up with Lea. The twins thanked her again. All the way home, they kept thanking her and discussing which shirts and jeans to wear on their first day of school.

"That was so nice of you to share your candy with Derek," Lea said.

"We like to share things, don't you know," Daniel told her.

"On the island, people have to share," Samuel added. "Because there isn't enough to go around."

He saw a sad smile form on Lea's face as she made the turn onto their block.

As soon as they were home, the twins carried the shopping bags to their room in the guesthouse. Daniel closed the door behind them, making sure it clicked. Then he pushed the lock on the handle.

He tossed the shopping bags onto the floor and turned to his twin. "What did you get?"

Samuel pulled the red leather wallet from his back pocket. He handed it to Daniel.

He could see the surprise on Daniel's face. "You got a woman's wallet? What's in it?"

"Didn't have time to look. Someone dropped it on the dressing room floor."

Eyes flashing with excitement, Daniel poked through the wallet and pulled out a bunch of bills. "Yes. Yes. These are fifties, Sammy. Three hundred dollars. You did good." He gave his brother a congratulatory face slap.

Samuel giggled. He liked it when Daniel was pleased with him. "What did you get, Daniel?"

Daniel reached deep into both of his pockets and began to pull out shiny things. Chains. Chains with sparkly things attached.

"Necklaces," Samuel said. "Good boyo. So many sparkly necklaces. How did you get them?"

"Easy as salt clam pie, Sammy. The display case wasn't locked."

He swung the necklaces over his head, round and around, and did his funny Daniel dance. "I like sparkly things," he said. "I'll put these with the necklace we found in Sister's room."

24

Lea stirred the soup in the pot with a long wooden spoon. Behind her, the twins were already seated at the table, eager for their lunch. She smiled. So far they had devoured everything she gave them. They seemed to like any food you put in front of them. Ira was such a picky eater. These boys were a pleasure.

"Is it soup yet?" Mark entered the kitchen, scratching his stubbly face. "What a morning. The guy from the grant committee is coming here."

Lea turned from the stove. "Really? Did he tell you how much they're giving you?"

Mark snickered. He stepped up behind Lea and kissed the back of her neck. "You're such an optimist."

She frowned. "Well, they have to give you at least part of the grant, right? They wouldn't turn you down flat."

Mark shrugged. "Who knows? It's hard times. I know you don't read the newspaper—"

"I read it online. The guy's coming all the way out from the city?"

"He said he has a house out here."

"Why didn't he tell you over the phone? He likes to give good news in person?"

"Your guess is as good as mine. He wouldn't even gi hint."

The soup made a sizzling sound. Lea spun around. She the burner off before it boiled over the side of the pot. "Si We're all having tomato soup. Homemade. I sliced the t and everything this morning."

"What a homemaker." Mark tried to kiss her again ducked her head as she lifted the soup pot from the stove. " you're going away again. Who will make us homemade sou

"Huh? Going away? Mark, I'm going to the city tomorro ing for one night. I'll be back late the following day. You're to make me feel guilty about a day and a half in the city, are

He backed away, raising both hands in surrender. "Just You know I'll miss you even if it's only one night. Every precious to me."

"Shut up. You're not funny."

Ira and Elena were away at friends' houses. She ladled tomato soup into bowls, then joined Mark and the twi table.

Daniel leaned his face to the bowl and took a lor "Smells so good, Mum. Tangy as sea grass drying on the l

"My bruvver is a poet," Samuel said.

"I like the way you boys speak," Lea said, stirring watching the steam rise from the red liquid. "You have cabularies."

"There's no school on the island, Mum," Daniel said. parents, bless their souls, taught us well."

Bless their souls? He sounds like an old man.

An old man, but a charming old man.

She wished Ira could pick up some of their charm a ness. Maybe it would rub off on him. If only he would sp time with his new brothers . . .

"Wonderful soup," Mark said, across the table fron raised the pepper mill and ground a load of pepper into ways added pepper, no matter what the food was.

If I gave him a bowl of pepper, he'd add pepper.

Lea had learned not to be insulted when he reseasoned her food that way.

She raised a spoon of soup and blew on it. "Careful. It's very hot."

The soup bubbled on the spoon. Red. So bright and red. Where had she seen that color before?

She flicked the spoon hard and sent the soup flying over Mark's shoulder. It made a soft splash on the wall.

The rain had come down so hard. Sheets of it. All bloodred. Red as the tomato soup.

Lea raised another spoonful, whipped her hand up, and sent the soup flying across the table onto the wall.

"Hey—Lea?" Mark's startled cry.

The twins laughed. Did they think it was *funny*?

The red rain. The bloodred rain. The rain of all the victims' blood. The dead crying their red tears down on everyone.

The dead. The raining dead. Their red tears steaming in her soup bowl.

Lea flung another spoon of the red rain, the bloodred rain, spoon after spoon splashing on the white kitchen wall. Tears rolling down her face. Sobs wrenching her throat and chest.

The red rain splashed on the wall. Splashed. Splashed again. Till Mark wrapped his arms around her from behind. Wrapped his arms around her so tight the spoon fell from her trembling hand.

"Hold on to me, Mark. Hold on to me." Where did those words come from? "Hold on to me. Don't let me go back there."

25

"When will Mom be back?" Elena lifted the whole toaster waffle to her mouth and bit off an end.

Mark took a long sip of coffee from the white mug in his hand. "She just left an hour ago. She was taking the first jitney. You already want her back?"

Elena gave him the eye-roll. "Just asking, that's all."

"She has meetings today. She's staying with her sister in the Village tonight. She'll be back sometime tomorrow afternoon. Okay?"

"Okay. Why are you such a grouch?"

"Sorry. Just tense, I guess. I didn't want her to go. She seems so shaky. She can't seem to leave that damned island behind her."

"Da-ad. Language." Elena motioned toward the twins having their breakfast at the table.

"Maybe some meetings in the city will do her good. Give her something else to think about," Roz chimed in from the other end of the table, Axl on her lap with an egg-stained face.

Elena swallowed a chunk of waffle. "Does Mom's cell work? I need to talk to her. You're being totally stupid and unfair."

Mark shrugged. "Yes. Everyone tells me I'm stupid. And unfair."

Across from Elena, Samuel and Daniel giggled. Daniel leaned toward Axl. "How's my monkey boy?"

Axl stuck his tongue out, pleased with the attention. But Roz snapped at Daniel, "I wish you wouldn't call him that."

"He likes it."

"I'm fourteen," Elena told Mark, dropping the waffle onto the plate. "All my friends go into the city on their own."

Mark sighed. He spun the coffee mug between his hands. The cuckoo clock above the sink chirped eight times. They were going to be late.

"You know my feeling on this. Why bring it up now?"

Elena's dark eyebrows formed arched Vs over her eyes, the sign that she was angry. "You're a total phony, Dad."

The twins giggled again. That made Axl giggle, too. Roz tried to wipe the caked egg off his cheeks with a paper napkin. Ira kept his head down, concentrating on his Cheerios, keeping out of it.

"Me? A phony?"

"You wrote a book saying parents should let their kids do what they want. But you—"

"That didn't include letting a bunch of fourteen-year-old girls go traipsing around New York City with no plan or idea of what they're going to do."

Elena balled her hands into fists and let out an angry growl. "We . . . don't . . . traipse." Said through gritted teeth.

"Let's table this for later. We're going to be late." He balled up his paper napkin and threw it onto the table. "And stop tossing my book back at me. I know you haven't read it. The book is a piece of research. It doesn't mean I can't make decisions as your father."

"Phony, Dad." The eye-roll again. "You're a phony and a grouch."

Mark watched the twins gobble down the last syrupy pieces of their toaster waffles. "How are you boys doing in the guesthouse? You like it back there?" He had to change the subject.

"We love it," Samuel said. "Our own house. We never had our own house."

"Our house was always crowded with a lot of strangers, don't you know," Daniel added.

"Really? Well, it was nice of Roz to give up her place for you, wasn't it?"

"Mark, they've already thanked me a hundred times," Roz said, obviously pleased. "And they were so sweet. They both helped me carry my stuff up to the attic. They're very hard workers."

Grinning, the twins raised their skinny arms, doing muscle poses, showing off nonexistent biceps.

"Well, I didn't think it was a good idea," Mark said. "But I'm glad if it works out. Your own secret hideout." He glanced at the wall clock. "Come on, guys. Get your backpacks. I'm driving today because Mrs. Maloney wants to meet the twins. Tomorrow you go back to the school bus."

Ira groaned. "I *hate* the bus. I get bus sick every day."

"Get over it," Elena said helpfully. She bumped him from behind. They bumped each other up the stairs to get their backpacks.

Roz stretched and smiled. "It's going to be so quiet here in just a few seconds." That was Axl's cue to start crying. "What are you doing today?" she asked Mark.

"Autumn and I are going over some foreign contracts and some mail. Then I have a meeting. A guy from the Blakeman Institute is coming here at four."

"Weird. He's coming all the way out to Sag Harbor? Is he bringing you a fat check?"

Mark laughed. "You and my wife are a lot alike. She asked the same question."

"Well?"

"I hope so. I'm counting on this grant. I won't get any book royalties for another five months."

"YAAAAAY." The twins came bursting into the kitchen with their brand-new blue canvas backpacks bouncing on their backs.

"Let's go, guys!" Mark said. "The principal wants to meet you two."

"Rule the school!" Daniel cried, pumping a fist above his head. "We're going to rule the school!"

"Rule the school! Rule the school!"

Mrs. Maloney was a solid woman, with short salt-and-pepper hair over a square, no-nonsense face. She wore no makeup. Her green-gray eyes were the most colorful parts of her face. They radiated humor and intelligence and were enough to make people find her attractive.

Her silky tan blouse pulled tightly over her bulge of a stomach, and even from the other side of her cluttered desk, Mark could see that she was straining her stretch-type brown pants. A tube of Pringles and a can of Pepsi on the edge of the desk revealed that she didn't care much about her weight.

She greeted the twins warmly as Mark ushered them into her small office. Daniel took the chair beside the desk. Samuel sat across from the desk. Mark watched from the doorway.

The principal showed them she already knew how to tell one from the other (thanks to a previous visit from Lea). And she gave them school maps and copies of last year's yearbook, which the twins seemed quite pleased with.

Mark knew quite a lot about Mrs. Maloney. She had first been principal at the Sag Harbor elementary school next door before moving to the middle school last year.

Sag Harbor had a large Irish community. They were the carpenters and landscapers and housekeepers, waitresses and pub owners.

Some said they came here because the weather so near the ocean was close to the weather in Ireland. But more likely, they came because they had relatives here. Mrs. Maloney and her husband had emigrated nearly twenty years ago from a town named Wicklow when they couldn't find teaching jobs in the local schools.

She still had her Irish accent, which made her sound as if she were singing instead of talking, and added to her warmth. She joked with the twins, and they seemed delighted with her.

"There's less than two months left of school, lads," she told them, turning serious. "But it should be enough time for you to learn your way around and make some new friends."

"We want to rule the school!" Daniel cried suddenly. That startled her into a laugh.

"Rule the school!" Samuel repeated, as if it was a chant.

"I like that," Mrs. Maloney said, gray eyes flashing. "Miss Montgomery will like that, too." Then she added, "She's your teacher. Normally, I would split you two up. But since it's so late in the school year . . ."

She raised her eyes to Mark, who was still leaning in the doorway. "I know we don't have any school records for these boys. Is there any chance of locating them?"

Mark frowned. "We're trying. But we haven't been able to find *any* records for them. No birth certificate. No family ID or anything. It's such chaos down there."

Mrs. Maloney tsk-tsked, shaking her head.

"The records were all blown away or underwater," Mark continued. "But we have someone looking for us. A woman Lea met down there named Martha Swann is trying to find whatever she can find."

She nodded, then glanced at the wall clock above Mark's head. "I guess that does it. Welcome to Sag Harbor, boys. We're very happy to have you. Mark, will you help them find room 204? It's the second door upstairs."

"No problem," Mark said.

Mrs. Maloney was fumbling her hand over her desktop. She raised her eyes to him. "Did you see my watch? I'm pretty sure I had it right here on the desk."

Mark shook his head. "Sorry. I didn't see it."

She peered under the desk. Pulled open the middle drawer and gazed inside. Then moved a stack of papers. "That's odd. Did you boys see a silver watch here on the desk?"

"No, mum," Daniel answered, eyes lowered to the desktop. "I didn't see it."

"I didn't see it, either, mum. Can we go to class now?" Samuel said.

26

Autumn came to work after her classes. Mark was glad to see her. After his book tour, there was a lot of work to catch up on. But at three o'clock she was suddenly sitting in his lap and his life went out of control.

She showed up a little after one, breezed into his office down the hall from the living room, and dropped a brown paper bag on his desk. "Cheese Danish? I stopped at the Golden Pear."

Mark turned from his keyboard and swung the black leather desk chair around to face her. He made a grab for the bag. "You're the best."

She smiled. Her eyes glowed. "I try to be," she said in a sultry whisper that surprised him. She tugged off her red hoodie and tossed it on his office couch.

Autumn wore a yellow scoop-neck T-shirt over a short, brown pleated skirt. He couldn't help but stare at her bare legs, lowering his eyes to the yellow sandals on her feet.

Her white-blond hair fell loosely over her shoulders. He didn't remember her wearing lip gloss to work before. And that citrus-like scent was new, too.

She grinned at him as if she had a secret she was keeping. He suddenly had the idea she was posing, standing in place so he could admire her.

She glanced back to the door. "No one home?"

He opened the brown bag and tugged off a piece of the Danish. "No. Lea's in the city. I took the boys to school for the first time. And Roz and Axl are doing the grocery shopping."

She leaned toward him. The lemony scent intensified. The low-cut T-shirt revealed more perfect, creamy cleavage. "And what are we doing today?"

"Mostly mail. And I have a number of requests to answer. Appearances. Some radio things."

She sent a strand of hair off her forehead with a toss of her head.

Mark took another bite of the cheese Danish. "I shouldn't eat this. Wish I had more willpower."

Her eyes flashed. "You? No willpower? Really?" She tossed her hair back again. "Are you going to travel more?"

"No. The book tour is over. I've done everything I can. Now it's up to the publisher." He swallowed another chunk. Tried not to stare at her boobs, which were at eye level. She stood so close. "Besides, I should stay around home for a while. You know. Because of the twins."

She turned suddenly and walked to the window. She pushed back the dark drapes and peered out. A gloomy day, storm clouds filling the sky. The mostly bare trees shaking. April rains.

"Mark, how are the boys doing?"

"Okay, I guess. They seemed excited about school. They kept chanting, 'Rule the school! We're gonna rule the school!'"

"Cute. They really are adorable."

"Yes. Lea is totally over the moon over them. Roz thinks they're *too* adorable. She says all twelve-year-olds are monsters. She's waiting for them to pull off their angel masks and reveal their hideous monster selves."

Autumn snickered. "Your sister is weird."

"She's a cynic. True, she's had a tough life. But she was a cynic *before* she had a tough life. When we were kids, I was always shocked because she had something terrible to say about everyone. But, Jesus, she sure could make me laugh. Still can."

He motioned to the narrow, chrome-armed chair beside his desk. "Sit down. I'm going to hand you things." He patted a stack of folders on the desktop.

She lowered herself gracefully into the chair. Smoothed the pleats of her short skirt. Then she reached her hand out and gently flicked a crumb of Danish off the side of his mouth.

His startled look made her laugh.

Should I talk to her about dressing less provocatively?

Well . . . actually, I like it.

He pushed the brown paper bag to the edge of the desk. Then he pulled the stack of folders in front of him, opened the top one, and started going through the varied requests—for autographs, for appearances, for charitable contributions . . . and a few for apologies.

There were several lengthy letters, some of them from other child psychologists, refuting his findings. One particularly venomous letter from a woman in Los Angeles accused him of demeaning the whole profession and "holding all psychologists up to ridicule by espousing this crackpot philosophy designed only to arouse controversy and sell books."

Mark shook his head. "She must have been speaking to my father."

"Your father?"

"He wrote almost exactly the same letter. I told you. He found my book a total embarrassment."

"Your father wrote to you? He didn't call you?"

"We don't speak."

"You're serious? He's a shrink, right?"

"He's not just a shrink. He's a big deal in the New York Psychoanalytic Society. And he's got his Park Avenue office with his celebrity patients and—"

"He *wrote* to you?"

Mark nodded. "He needed to tell me just how much I had embarrassed him. I think my whole career embarrasses him. You know. I didn't match up to his expectations right from the start. I mean, he went to Harvard and I went to Wisconsin."

Autumn chewed her bottom lip. "How do you want me to handle that letter?"

Mark flipped through it. Three pages single-spaced. "My psych advisor at Wisconsin gave me very good advice. She said, 'Never defend yourself.' She said you never can convince anyone, and if you try to defend yourself, you just sound weak. She said to always be positive, never defensive."

Autumn scratched her knee with her long red nails. "So what should I say?"

"Say thank you for your thoughtful letter. I really appreciate your taking the time to write."

That phony reply made them both laugh. Autumn was gazing at him with such total admiration, Mark had to look away.

Such a beautiful girl. He suddenly wondered about her social life. Did she have a boyfriend? He shared a lot with her about his private life. But he didn't dare ask her personal questions. It might seem like prying. It might seem offensive. And she never offered much.

Today she seemed different to him. Not just the sexy clothes. The secret smiles and the long gazes, as if she had some kind of plan, some kind of surprise.

They went through the files. Then she set the stack on the floor beside her chair and stood up. She stepped close to him. "You're a psychologist, right? Can you read my mind?"

He chuckled. "I'm not a mind reader, I'm a psychologist. But yes, I can read your mind. You wish you'd saved that cheese Danish for yourself. Right?"

"Wrong." She took his hand. Tenderly. "You really can't read my mind?" Her blue eyes caught the light. "You really don't know what I've been thinking for the longest time?"

"Autumn. Really, I—"

And then she was in his lap, squeezing his hand, pressing her hot face against his.

"Autumn—no. Come on."

She kissed his ear. Her breath tickled the side of his face.

"No. We can't. I can't. I mean—" He tried to stand up. But he couldn't move.

She turned his head and pressed her mouth against his. He could taste the creamy, sweet flavor of the lip gloss. And then she was opening her mouth, and his tongue moved despite himself.

"No—"

She held the back of his head and kept his mouth pressed to hers. He couldn't speak.

"No. This is wrong. Please—"

Kissing him. She took his hand and moved it between her legs. Kissing him so passionately. Beneath the short skirt her panties were wet. She pressed his hand into her.

"No, Autumn. Stop. We can't."

She uttered low gasps in his ear. "Oh, yes. Yes. Oh, yes."

Like a porno video.

He felt his erection grow. "I don't want this."

But suddenly he did.

She stood up and pulled him to his feet. Then she reached under the skirt and lowered lacy black panties to her ankles. She flipped the short skirt up as she leaned over the desk.

That creamy white ass. So beautiful. She grabbed the far end of the desk with both hands. "Mark—hurry."

Oh, God. Over the desk. From behind.

His khakis were down. And he was inside her.

This isn't happening. How can it be?

Sprawled over the desk, she moaned, rhythmic soft cries. He buried his face in her soft hair. He lost himself in her.

He lost himself.

Lost.

And came inside her. It didn't matter. All the doctors said he could never have more children.

He stayed on top of her for a long moment, breathing hard, gripping the shoulders of her T-shirt, the creamy ass still moving beneath him. Then, heart pounding, he pushed himself to his feet.

She climbed up slowly. Turned to him. Grabbed his shirt, brought her face close, and licked the side of his face. "Am I your best assistant?" A whisper that tingled his skin. "I want to be the best. Am I the best?"

A door slammed.

They both gasped. She squeezed his shoulders, eyes wide in alarm.

Mark heard the twins' voices. Footsteps.

Autumn bent down, grabbed her underpants and tugged them on. She straightened her skirt. Brushed back her damp, tangled hair with both hands. "Oh, wow. Oh, wow."

The footsteps louder in the hall.

He was scrambling to fasten his khakis. Still fumbling with the fly as the twins tumbled into his office, bumping each other, both talking at once.

Zipper stuck, Mark dropped into the desk chair. Crossed his arms over his lap. Forced a smile. "Hey, guys—how was your day?"

27

The twins had their eyes on Autumn, who leaned against the side of the desk, her skirt still crooked, her cheeks bright pink.

"How was school?" she asked them, sounding breathless.

"Good," Samuel said.

"Yeah. Good," his twin added.

"What did you do today?" Mark asked.

"Stuff," Samuel replied.

"Just some stuff," Daniel added.

Mark tried a third question. "Did you like Miss Montgomery?"

"She's nice, don't you know," Samuel said, eyes on Autumn.

"Nice," Daniel echoed.

Mark laughed. "You guys were talking your heads off till you got in here. Now we get only one-word grunts from you. What happened?"

They both shrugged in reply. Daniel giggled.

Mark studied them. They looked too clean, their new jeans and T-shirts stiff, not broken in. Their blond hair lay perfectly in place, like doll heads.

"Did you suddenly get shy?" Autumn asked. She was working on untangling a thick strand of blond hair.

Mark didn't give them a chance to answer. "Where's Ira? Was he on the bus with you?"

"The lad is taking the late bus," Samuel said. "He was doing a project with Ethan."

Mark smiled, pleased to get so many words from him. "So did you boys rule the school today?"

"Not yet," Samuel said with surprising gravity.

"Soon," his twin offered.

Their school day had gone very well, Samuel thought. Miss Montgomery split them up, seating Daniel in the front and Samuel in the back. But they didn't care about that.

Samuel sat next to an open window. The April air smelled fresh and salty. He liked that. He spent a lot of time watching two squirrels collecting and devouring acorns at the base of the old tree across from the school.

Daniel sat next to Ira in the front row. They didn't talk much. They weren't really friends yet. In fact, Ira seemed very uncomfortable around Daniel.

Maybe he was still angry about Daniel trying to take his room from him. Maybe he just didn't want new bruvvers.

He'll get over it, Samuel thought, watching Daniel and Ira ignore each other. *Daniel will win him over—one way or the other. He'll be true blue, that boyo.*

And Derek? Samuel looked for him, but Derek had a doctor appointment and didn't come to school till lunchtime.

Samuel and Daniel ran into him on their way out of the lunchroom. Derek wore baggy cargo jeans and a red-and-white New York Rangers sweatshirt. His eyes went wide, and his mouth opened in surprise when he recognized them.

"How'd you get into this school?" He managed to find his usual bluster. "This used to be a good school."

"It's our first day," Samuel said. "We're in your class."

Derek bumped Samuel's shoulder with a pudgy hand. "You got any money? Mom forgot to give me my lunch money."

"We don't have any," Samuel replied. "We already had our lunch."

"Let's see," Derek said. He grabbed Samuel by the pants, spun him around with surprising strength, and began to dig into his pockets.

Samuel squirmed. "Boyo, stop!"

Daniel moved quickly. He stepped up behind Derek and, with a powerful tug, hoisted Derek's heavy backpack off his shoulders.

Derek let go of Samuel and spun around furiously. "Hey, jerk! You almost ripped my arms off."

"Sorry, boyo." Daniel held the backpack above his head. "You want it? Jump for it."

Derek uttered a low growl. He narrowed his bulldog eyes and glared at Daniel. "*You* jump for it." He lowered his shoulder and bulled into Daniel, sending him crashing against a metal locker.

Daniel giggled. Holding the backpack high, he quickly regained his balance.

Derek rushed at Daniel, both hands outstretched. He grabbed for the backpack—just as Daniel let go of it. Derek couldn't stop his momentum and slammed headfirst into the wall.

The collision didn't faze him. His big belly heaving up and down beneath the Rangers sweatshirt, he grabbed the backpack off the floor and grinned in triumph. Slowly, he slid it onto his back. "You dudes should be careful. I can mess you up totally."

Samuel felt a tremor of fear. *Please, Daniel. Don't be Daniel. Let it ride.*

Daniel raised both hands as if in surrender. "Truce?"

Samuel took a step back.

"Okay, truce." Derek's reply after thinking about it for a while. "You're both new here, so you don't know what's up. I'll give you a break today."

"Truce," Daniel repeated. He stuck his hand out for Derek to shake.

Weird, thought Samuel. *What's up with the handshake routine?*

"Truce," Derek said. He stomped away without shaking hands.

The bell clanged above their heads. Lunchtime was over.

Samuel turned to find Ira, Ethan, and several other kids watching the whole confrontation. "What was *that* about?" Ira asked Daniel.

Daniel's smile made his dimples appear to grow deeper. "You'll see, boyo. You'll see."

Samuel wasn't in on his brother's secret, either. But all was revealed just before the final bell that afternoon. Miss Montgomery dismissed the class. And as the kids all gathered their books, stuffed their backpacks, and scurried from the room, Mrs. Maloney came charging into the classroom.

Her gray eyes gazed around the room and came to a stop on Derek, who was standing in the front. Arguing with a short, red-haired girl. "Derek, could I see you for a moment?" she called.

The girl hurried away. Derek eyed the principal warily as she approached. The classroom was nearly emptied. Samuel and Daniel watched from the doorway.

"Yes, Mrs. Maloney?" Derek suddenly being very polite.

She frowned at him. Rubbed her short salt-and-pepper hair. "Derek, I received a disturbing note this afternoon. About you."

His mouth dropped open. "Huh? Me? Who sent it?"

Miss Montgomery stood up behind her desk and looked on.

Mrs. Maloney's eyes locked on Derek, studying him. "It wasn't signed. But it said I would find something interesting in your backpack."

Samuel glanced at his twin. He recognized the eagerness on Daniel's face. The anticipation. He'd seen it before.

Derek's blue backpack was on his desk. He stared hard at it as if it would reveal some secret.

"Is there something interesting in your backpack, Derek?" Mrs. Maloney asked softly, almost in a whisper.

Derek shook his head. "No way. Just my stuff."

"Nothing in there I should know about?"

"No. No way. Unless you mean a Snickers bar and some Star-burst?"

Mrs. Maloney let out a long whoosh of air. "I'm sure you're telling the truth. But why would someone send me that note?"

Derek shrugged.

"Why don't we just empty out the backpack and settle the whole thing." Mrs. Maloney kept her voice low and friendly.

"No problem." Derek lifted the pack and started to unzip it. "I don't get it. I totally don't."

Holding the pack by the sides, he upended it and shook it hard, spilling the contents onto the desk. Books. Folders. A pencil box. An iPod. A cell phone. A Snickers bar.

Samuel squinted across the room, studying the contents. As soon as he saw the silvery watch slide onto the cover of a textbook, he understood.

Mrs. Maloney raised her hands to her cheeks. "Well, my faith. That *is* interesting," she said softly. She picked up the watch and slid the shiny band through her fingers. "Derek? How did my watch get into your backpack?"

Derek's face had gone pale. His mouth was working up and down, but he didn't make a sound. He shrugged. "I don't know."

"Do you want to think about it?" Mrs. Maloney remained calm. No sign of anger or even surprise.

"I . . . never saw it. Really." Derek's eyes down, shoulders slumped. Looking guilty as hell. "I don't know how it got there. Really."

"But it did tumble out from the bottom of your backpack, right?"

"Yes. But—"

"Derek, why don't you gather up your belongings here and follow me to my office for a talk. Do we need to call your mother? What do you think?"

She raised her eyes to the door and saw Samuel and Daniel standing, watching the scene intently. "What are you two lads lingering there for? This is no business of yours. Go on now. Don't miss the bus on your first day."

"Okay. Bye," Samuel said, turning to leave.

"See you tomorrow," Daniel said, then quickly added, "Good luck, Derek."

28

"We have work to do, Sammy." Daniel pressed his forehead against the window glass as the school bus bounced along Noyac Road, the tall trees along the side making the shadows dance in his eyes.

Samuel shifted the blue canvas backpack in his lap. He knew how impatient Daniel could be. He hoped maybe he would take his time, get to know the terrain, enjoy their new family, their new home at least a few weeks before setting things in motion.

"You gave that lug Derek a good lesson, Daniel."

Daniel tapped Samuel's knee with his fist. "Derek is dead in the pasture. The flies are already circling him."

Samuel laughed. But he could see the growing intensity on his twin's face.

"Work to do, Sammy."

"What's your hurry, Daniel? Haven't we got it made here?"

"We've waited a long time," Daniel murmured, gazing at a deer chewing tall weeds by the roadside. "A long time, boyo."

"But look at us now. We're in Heaven."

Daniel turned away from the window. He shook his head. "Sammy, it may be heaven but there's a devil on our cloud."

Samuel felt a chill, muscles tightening at the back of his neck. "Who is the devil?" He knew the answer.

"The new pa."

"Maybe he didn't mean those things we heard him say."

Daniel narrowed his eyes at Samuel. "He meant them. He said he didn't want us to come. He didn't want Mum to bring us here. And he didn't want us to live in the little house in the backyard. Why? Because he didn't know if he could trust us."

That made Samuel giggle. "He *can't* trust us, boyo."

Daniel didn't smile. His normally pale cheeks had turned rosy pink. "Pa doesn't like us, Sammy. He doesn't want us here. And he shouted at Mum. You saw him shout at Mum because she wants to make us happy and give us everything we want."

"But, Daniel—"

"He doesn't want us to be happy. Pa doesn't want to give us the things we want. You heard him. You heard every word. We have work to do. We have plans, boyo. We cannot let the new pa stand in our way."

Samuel felt the chill again. "What are you thinking, Daniel? Why are you saying all this? We can't *kill* the new pa. We can't. It would make Mum so sad."

"He's a devil, Sammy. A devil in our heaven."

Samuel grabbed his brother's wrist. "Don't think it. We can't do that to Mum."

"You're right. You're the sensible guy, Sammy. As sensible as potatoes in chowder. We don't want to kill Pa. We just have to keep him busy."

Samuel shook his head. The backpack suddenly felt heavy in his lap. He let it slide to the bus floor. "Keep him busy?"

Daniel nodded. He had that thoughtful look in his eyes that Samuel knew well.

"How do we keep him busy? What do you mean?"

A thin smile played over Daniel's lips. "I have some ideas. We can keep him real busy, Sammy. Maybe with the coppers."

29

Mark watched from the front window as the dark blue Audi pulled up the driveway. A young man with a thick head of wavy brown hair and a seriously tanned face climbed out. He leaned into the car to retrieve a slender laptop case, then walked crisply to the front door, straightening his red necktie and buttoning his dark suit jacket as he walked.

Autumn had left ten minutes earlier, weighed down by a tall stack of folders. She offered Mark several meaningful glances as she left. In return, he gave her a comic wave and a goofy grin, keeping it light. *Nothing serious happened here, Autumn. Did it?*

If only he could move back the clock. Would he move it? Maybe not. Moments before, he had kept his eyes on her long, slim legs under the short skirt as she bent to pick up the folders, and felt himself start to get erect again.

Am I crazy? What am I thinking?

Lea, I love you. Why didn't you stay and watch out for me?

Oh, what kind of juvenile thinking is that?

Roz had returned with a trunk load of grocery bags and a screaming, hungry Axl. Mark emptied the car for her. He saw the twins tossing a tennis ball back and forth in the backyard. He thought about joining them. But it was time for his meeting with this man from the institute.

What was his name? Hulenberger? Something like that.

Mark had suggested they meet and have tea at the American Hotel on Main Street in town. That way there wouldn't be kids underfoot, running in and out, demanding his immediate attention. Elena was already angry that he didn't have time for a long discussion about the sleepover she wanted to have with Ruth-Ann.

But Hulenberger insisted on coming to the house. And here he was at the front door, all tanned and prosperous-looking in a designer suit that fit his slender shoulders perfectly and a crisp white shirt that contrasted his tan.

"Mr. Hulenberger? Come in."

"It's Dr. Hulenberger. But call me Richard. Everyone does. Even my kids." A brief, hard handshake.

"Well, call me Mark. Come in. Welcome."

Mark led him down the hall to his office. He could hear Roz in the kitchen, pleading with Axl to sit still. The back door slammed, and he heard Ira calling, "Anyone home? Roz?"

"Nice day," Hulenberger said. "I enjoyed the drive. My wife and I have a house in Sagaponack, but we haven't opened it yet. It's almost May, but it still feels like October, doesn't it? All the rain. Incredible. We probably won't open up till Memorial Day. My wife hates the country. She always says she'd rather be on Madison Avenue. Ha."

Was he talking so much out of nervousness? Or was he just a chatty guy?

Mark stopped at the office doorway and pictured Autumn bending over the desk again. Her short skirt tossed up onto her back, black underpants around her ankles, and that smooth little ass . . .

Oh, God.

Would he see her there every time he walked into the office?

The whole left side of the desktop was empty. The papers and folders had all been swept aside. He wondered if Hulenberger noticed that something was odd.

He led him to the green leather couch against the wall. Hulenberger dropped onto the edge and sat up very straight, lowering his laptop case to the floor. Good posture. He slid a hand down his tie a few times. Nervous habit?

"Nice room, Mark. I like that photo behind your desk. I think I know those trees. From Brisbane, right? Australia? I walked in that very spot and admired those twisty roots all around the tree trunks."

Mark nodded. "My wife is a travel writer. A good photographer, too. She writes about adventure travel. Seems a lot of people are into it."

"Hannah and I were on a food and wine tour. We weren't impressed with the food in Queensland at all. Dreadful. In fact, we didn't have anything good to eat till we got to Sydney. Were you there with your wife?"

"No. She was on assignment. I had my patients. You know. And my book."

Chitchat, chitchat.

Mark suddenly had a heavy feeling in the pit of his stomach. He rolled his desk chair in front of the couch and dropped into it. The room still smelled of Autumn's lemony scent.

"Nice of you to drive out, Richard."

Richard cleared his throat loudly. Adjusted his tie. "Well, I wanted to tell you in person. I didn't think it was right to do it over the phone or by email. Too impersonal."

"You mean—about the grant?" His voice suddenly tight.

"Yes. Should I come right to the point? I think I should. We're not going to give you the grant, Mark."

Can silence be loud?

To Mark the silence in the room seemed deafening. Without realizing it, he slammed his head back against the leather seatback, like someone showing shock in a cartoon.

"You mean . . . you're not giving the whole amount? Only part?"

Richard sat even more erect. Mark saw a single bead of sweat appear above one brown eyebrow. "No. I came to offer our regrets. We can't give you any of the grant money at this time."

"But my studies . . ." *Why can't I finish a sentence?* His hands left wet marks on the leather chair arms.

"We approve of your work. Wholeheartedly. That's why we made the initial offer. We felt that your studies with juveniles would add considerably to the literature."

Mark was distracted by movement at the office doorway. He turned and saw Samuel and Daniel standing there, hands in their jeans pockets, serious expressions on their pale faces.

"How long have you two been standing there?" He didn't mean to sound so irritated. His mind was churning from the news of the grant money turndown. He should shout at Hulenberger, not the boys.

They didn't reply. Both had their eyes on Hulenberger. Staring at him hard, as if giving him the evil eye. Then, without a word, they turned and vanished down the hall, bouncing a tennis ball on the floor.

He turned back to Hulenberger, who was defiantly gazing at him, not backing down, not avoiding his eyes after bringing this devastating news. Macho guy.

"So, Richard . . . Can you explain? If it isn't my study . . ."

"It's your book. Can I speak plainly? It's the book. We understand why you wrote such an inflammatory thing. But that's the problem in a word, see. It's inflammatory."

"But it's a sincere study. It wasn't skeptical in any way. I wasn't just trying to make a buck with a piece of crappy pop psychology. I did my homework, Richard. I did years of research in addition to my own studies."

Whoa. Blowing it. He's sitting there coolly, and your voice is rising to soprano.

Richard kept his green-gray eyes on Mark, his face a blank. No emotion.

This man is a fish. I've seen eyes like that on a cod. He thinks he's terrific. But he didn't just fuck a beautiful twenty-three-year-old girl.

What am I thinking? Am I losing my mind?

"How can I say this, Mark? The book has attached a certain notoriety to you. I'm sure you won't disagree with that."

Mark didn't reply.

"And the grant committee . . . well, we feel we can't risk backing someone in your position, someone with that kind of controversy following him."

Mark remained silent.

Richard sighed and shook his head. "The institute has such limited funds now. You know how much the government has cut our funding. They're almost not subsidizing us at all. It's a crime. This country will pay for the shortsightedness in Washington. In the meantime, we have to be very judicious about where we spend what little we have. And I'm afraid—"

Mark jumped to his feet, visibly startling his guest. "Okay. I get it. Thanks for coming out, Richard."

Richard gazed up at him, swallowing hard. Mark realized he'd frightened the man. Richard thought Mark was about to get violent.

Maybe I should. Beat the crap out of him. What kind of notoriety would that bring me?

But he'd never been in a fight in his life. Not even on the playground. He'd never thrown a punch or wrestled another kid on the grass or come home with a black eye.

Mark was the good kid. The smart kid. The talker. The kid who was interested in how everything works. He always talked himself out of fights. He used *psychology.*

Richard finally climbed to his feet. He grabbed up his laptop case.

Why did he bring it? Did he just feel insecure without it?

He pulled out his phone and checked the screen. Then he tucked it back into his suit jacket. "I'm really sorry, Mark. I can see you are disappointed."

"Yeah. That's the word for it."

"My only suggestion—if you want any advice from me—is to apply again in a few years."

"A few years?"

"Yeah. Wait for the notoriety to die down. In a few years, people will forget your book, right?"

A smile crossed Mark's face. "That isn't exactly a compliment."

Richard blushed. "You know what I mean. Wait for the controversy to fade. People have short attention spans. You know that, right? Apply again. I'm not guaranteeing anything, but—"

Mark led him to the door. "Do you believe in freedom of speech, Richard?"

"Well, yes. Of course."

"But you don't think I should put my findings and theories in a book?"

"I didn't say that. The committee has to be careful. I know you understand that. You have a bestseller, Mark. No one begrudges you that. Some psychologists would *kill* for a bestseller like yours. This grant money—"

"Would have paid my mortgage for the next two years," Mark interrupted. "And would have paid for my *next* book, which I hope will have the same notoriety."

He pulled open the front door. He could see the twins playing catch at the side of Richard's car.

"I'm sorry. I mean that sincerely." Hulenberger stuck out his hand to shake. "I'm just the messenger here, you know. No hard feelings, I hope."

Mark shook his hand. This time it was cold and damp. He watched him walk down the gravel drive to his car. He deposited the laptop in the passenger seat, glanced briefly back at Mark, then climbed behind the wheel.

One of the twins fumbled the tennis ball and went running down the driveway after it. "Be careful!" Mark shouted to them. "Get out of the way, boys. He's going to back out!"

He didn't watch Hulenberger drive away. Mark turned and walked into the house, feeling heavy, a headache forming just behind his forehead. He sighed. *I need a glass of wine.*

He found Roz in the kitchen, stirring a pot of tomato sauce.

She had a gray long-sleeved T-shirt, torn at the neck, pulled down over the baggy denim cutoff shorts she wore nearly every day. She turned when he entered and read his expression. "Bad news?"

"You were listening?"

"No. The twins told me something bad was happening. That guy looked like the kind who'd bring bad news."

Mark opened the refrigerator and pulled out an already opened bottle of Chablis. "Yeah, well. Bad news is right. I'm not getting the grant."

She stopped stirring. "Because?"

"Because I'm too controversial." He found a wineglass in the cabinet and poured it full. "Mainly, I think, because I'm too successful."

"Yes. That's your problem. You're too successful and too rich."

"I wish." He took a long sip. "Guess I'm going to have to fill up my patient list. Put aside the next book for a while."

The tennis ball bounced hard against the kitchen window. The thud made them both jump.

Roz smiled. "The twins are having fun."

Mark took another drink. The wine wasn't helping his headache. "Think they're doing okay?"

"Yes. I think they're happy. I know you don't approve, but they love their little house back there. I'm surprised they've adjusted so well. Aren't you?"

"I guess. I'd like to see a little more interaction between them and Ira and Elena. Of course, twins often keep to themselves." He refilled his glass. The Chablis tasted a little sour. Or was that just his mood?

He thought about Hulenberger. The guy wasn't actually smug, but he was totally unlikable.

"Can I change the subject?" Roz broke into his thoughts. "I've been thinking I need a night off. You know?"

"A night off? You have a date?"

"Is that *your* business? I just need a night off. Think you could hold down the fort? Watch Axl for me? You know. Take care of him for a few hours without killing him?"

Mark grinned. "Axl and I get along fine. I stuff him full of Oreos and tortilla chips and he's a good boy."

"That's what makes you a good psychologist."

"Lea gets home tomorrow night. Maybe she and I will have a special playdate with Axl."

"Sounds like a plan. Go tell our four boarders it's dinnertime, okay?"

Carrying his wineglass, Mark walked to the stairs and shouted up to Ira and Elena. "Dinner. Come down. Now. Okay?"

He opened the front door and shouted to the twins. "Dinner!" But they had disappeared, probably to their house in back. The tennis ball lay in the driveway in front of Hulenberger's car.

Huh?

The wineglass nearly slipped from his hand. Something was wrong. Hulenberger's Audi was still in the drive.

Mark stepped out onto the stoop and squinted into the evening light. Yes. Hulenberger sat behind the wheel. Not moving. And his head . . . it was tilted back, way back.

Wrong. All wrong.

Something was terribly wrong.

"Richard? Hey! Richard?" he shouted.

Hulenberger didn't move.

"Richard! Hey—what's wrong? Are you okay?" He shouted louder with his hands cupped around his mouth.

No. The man didn't move.

Mark started to jog toward the car. But he stopped halfway. Hulenberger's head . . . it wasn't right.

He spun away, his mind whirling. From the wine. From the headache. So hard to think clearly.

Oh my God. Oh my God.

What has happened here?

"Richard? Can you answer me?"

A tightness gripped Mark's chest. A wave of cold washed over his body, a cold he'd never felt before.

He lurched to the car. What was splattered over the windshield? "Richard? Richard?" Breathing hard, he gazed into the open window. Grabbed the bottom of the window with both hands. Leaned toward the wheel.

And screamed. A long, shrill scream of horror from somewhere deep in his throat.

"No! Fucking no! Oh my God! Oh, shit. Oh my God!"

Dark blood splattered the windshield, as if someone had heaved a can of paint over the glass. And Hulenberger . . . Hulenberger . . . The blood had run down his shirt, his suit . . .

Like a sweater. A sweater of blood.

His head tilted back. His throat . . . it had been torn open. Ripped open?

"Oh my God. Oh my God. Fucking no!"

Fighting the tide of nausea, the drumming of his heart that made the blood pulse at his temples, Mark pushed himself back, away from the car. He turned to the house. He saw the twins standing at the top of the driveway.

"Get back! Go back! Don't come down here! Go back!" He waved them away with both hands. They turned and ran.

Had they seen anything?

His hands felt wet. He raised them to his face. They were covered in blood. Hulenberger's blood. He shook them hard as if trying to toss the blood away. Then he staggered into the house. Through the living room, to the kitchen where Roz was tilting the tomato sauce pan over a big bowl of spaghetti.

"Roz! Call the police." So breathless she didn't hear him.

He grabbed her shoulder, startling her. Her eyes locked on his hands. "Mark? Oh my God! Is that blood?"

"Roz—call the police! Hurry! Call the police! Call the police!"

30

"It's a ten-eighty-four, Vince. We're on the scene."

"I gotta learn those numbers, Chaz. I never know what Vince is talking about."

"Forgetaboutit, Andy. No one knows what Vince is talking about."

Pavano peered out the window as his partner, Chaz Pinto, eased the car up the gravel driveway. "Where are we? Why does this look familiar?"

"John Street, dude. You took the call ten minutes ago, remember?"

A dark Audi stood in the drive. Chaz stopped the black-and-white a few feet behind it.

"It's taking me awhile to get oriented, you know. We're by the water, aren't we?"

"Yeah. The bay is over there." Pinto pointed out the side door. They both gazed at the car in front of them.

"The caller was a woman. She didn't say what the problem was. Something about a car in the driveway. The driver . . ."

"I see him. The back of his head. Not moving."

"Heart attack?"

"Hope so. That would make it easy." Pinto leaned toward the radio. "We're going to check out the car, Vince. You there?"

"Of course I'm here. Where else would I be, Pinto? Don't sit there holding hands, you two. Get out and take a look."

"The driver appears to be in the car."

The front door to the house swung open, and a dark-haired man in jeans and a white polo shirt stepped out.

Pavano's eyes went wide. "Hey, I know that dude." His breath caught in his throat. "Oh, wow. Oh no. I don't believe this."

"What's your problem, Andy?"

Pavano pushed the car door open, flipped his half-smoked Camel to the driveway, and lowered his feet to the ground. "I've been here. That night. Remember? The rain? I had the wrong house. I told him his wife was dead!"

Pinto let out a hoarse wheeze of a laugh. "We're still talking about that one. Behind your back, you know. It's classic. We'll be talking about that asshole move for a long time."

"Thanks, partner." Pavano stretched his lanky body, adjusted his black uniform cap lower over his eyes. *Maybe the guy won't remember me.*

Yeah, sure. What are the chances?

Pinto was approaching the driver's side of the Audi. Pavano followed, boots crunching on the gravel driveway, eyes on the man inside the car.

"Hello, sir? Sir? Are you all right?"

The man from inside the house came running down the driveway. "I'm Mark Sutter," he shouted. "This is my house."

Pavano waved him back. "Please stay there."

The driver's side window was down. "Hey, sir!" Pinto shouted loudly into the car even though he was just a few feet away. "Sir? Are you okay?"

"He's not okay. He's fucking dead!" Sutter cried. He didn't heed Pavano's instruction. He ran up beside them, breathing hard. "He's dead. I saw him. It . . . it's horrible."

Pinto and Pavano both stooped and leaned into the window at the same time.

"Oh, my God!"

"Oh, fuck no! Fuck no!"

"I . . . can't believe it," Sutter stammered.

Pavano frantically waved him back. "Please stay back, sir. Let us do our job."

A pair of blond boys were watching from the front door. "Get the kids away, sir. Please!"

The boys stepped out onto the stoop. "Is he sick?"

"Please, Mr. Sutter. Get those boys inside."

"Oh, fuck. This is impossible!" Pinto gasped. "His whole throat . . ."

"It . . . it's open. Opened up. Like ripped open."

"No. It's burned. Totally burned. See the black skin around the hole? The skin is charred. It's flaking off."

Pavano turned away, his stomach tightening into a knot. The man's throat had been cut or ripped open. He shut his eyes and still pictured the dark red flesh inside, blackened. A hole, a gaping hole in the man's neck. Thick, dark blood caked down the front of the man's suit, puddled in his lap.

Someone opened his throat and let him bleed out.

"How did this happen? How *could* it happen? Here in my driveway," Sutter said, shaking his head.

"Mr. Sutter, please go in your house. Wait for us. And keep those boys away from the window. You don't want them to see this."

Sutter started to turn away, then stopped. "Hey, I remember you!"

Pavano ignored him and turned back to his partner. Pinto reached for the door handle, then thought better of it. "Fingerprints. Look. There's blood smeared on the door here. Might be good fingerprints. We need backup here. We need an ME. We need the crime scene guys."

Pavano raced back to the patrol car, flung the door open, and grabbed the radio. "Vince, we have a homicide here. We need backup. We need someone with a strong stomach."

"I take it you don't need an ambulance?"

"No. We don't need an ambulance. This is a murder scene. We need CS guys. We have a man with a giant hole in his neck and—"

"Save the details, Andy. I'm eating my dinner. Ten-four."

"Just hurry, Vince. I've never seen anything like this."

"You haven't seen much—have you, Andy?"

Who told him he always has to have the last word? And who told him he couldn't be serious even for a crime this horrible?

Pavano slammed the patrol car door and made his way back to Pinto. The big, older cop leaned with his hands on his waist, peering into the victim's window. Finally he turned, removed his cap, and scratched his thinning flattop.

"It's like a horror movie, Andy. The skin is all scorched. The hole is as big as a grapefruit. And it looks empty inside. Just burned skin." He swallowed. His teeth clicked.

Never realized he has false teeth, Pavano thought. *And then, why am I thinking about Chaz's teeth when I'm staring at a guy with a giant knothole in his neck?*

Pinto pulled Pavano back from the car. "Stop looking at him. Your face is green. No shit."

Pavano nodded and turned his back on the Audi. It didn't make him feel any better.

I came out to Sag Harbor to take it easy, get away from all the fucking crime in the city, maybe get back with Sari. What the hell happened here?

"We can't do anything," Pinto said. "Not till the crime scene guys get here. Let's go inside and talk to that Sutter guy."

Pavano nodded. "He acted totally innocent. That's the first sign he did it, right?"

Pinto patted him on the back. "Too much TV, Andy."

The sun had almost disappeared behind the house. The sky darkened to gray, and a cool breeze rattled the still-bare trees.

They stepped onto the front stoop. Pinto leaned close. "Andy, tell Sutter *this* time you got it right—the victim really is dead."

"Shut the fuck up, will you?" Pavano could feel his face turn hot. That rainy night on this doorstep had to be the worst moment of his life. And now here he was, ringing the doorbell again.

It took only a few seconds for Sutter to pull open the door. He had a glass of white wine in his right hand. Pavano saw the hand tremble. A few drips of wine spilled to the floor. "How did some-one do that to him? Can you tell me?"

"Hard to say," Pinto replied softly, eyes narrowed on Sutter.

Pavano didn't see the blond boys, but he saw another boy, dark-haired, small, peering down from the top of the stairs.

"Dad, is everything okay? Why are the police here?"

"It's okay, Ira. Go back to your room, all right?"

"But aren't we going to finish dinner? My spaghetti's getting cold."

"We'll finish dinner in a short while. Please—get up to your room. And tell Elena to stay up there, too."

Sutter can't hide how tense he is. Tense because he murdered the guy?

"Sir, I'm Officer Pinto. He's Officer Pavano. As you can see, we're from the Sag Harbor Police Department."

Sutter gazed hard at Pavano. "We've met," he said quietly.

"Sir, can we go somewhere more private?" Pinto had Sutter by the elbow.

"Sure. Come into my office. I can't tell you much about Richard, but—"

"Is that his name? Richard? Do you know his full name?"

They stepped into the book-lined office. Pavano admired the dark wood, the big desk, the floor-to-ceiling bookshelves.

"Well, yes. His name is Richard Hulenberger."

Pavano pulled out his phone. He brought up the memo app and typed in *Richard Hulenberger*. The phone had replaced the little black notebook that cops used to carry in their shirt pockets. Pavano missed his notebook. But he was grateful. He could never find a pencil to write with.

"Is he a friend of yours?" Pinto asked.

Sutter motioned for them to sit on the green leather couch. "A friend? No. First time I ever met him." Hand still trembling, he set the wineglass down near the edge of the desktop.

The two cops remained standing. Pavano typed *Not a friend* into his phone.

Pinto shifted his weight. He gazed around the room. "Mr. Sutter, before we talk about anything else, I need to ask you one question."

Pavano watched as Sutter jammed his hands into his jeans pocket.

"Yes. What?"

Pinto took a breath. For dramatic effect? "Mr. Sutter, do you own a blowtorch?"

Sutter blinked. "Why, yes. Yes, I do."

31

A heavy silence for a moment.

Sutter lowered himself to the edge of the desk, hands still stuffed in his pockets. "I . . . don't understand. Why are you asking me about a blowtorch?"

"What kind of blowtorch do you have?" Pinto crossed his arms over his chest. Pavano noted on his phone: *Blowtorch.*

"Um . . . let me think. It's a fifteen-liter flame gun. I think that's what it's called. It's propane. Do you want to see it? It's in the garage."

Pinto motioned for Sutter to sit still. "The crime scene officers will want to see it. Thank you. But I'd like to ask a few more questions first." He rubbed his chin. "Fifteen-liter? That's a pretty big mother. Why do you have it?"

Sutter twisted his face. Was he confused? Struggling to figure out why he was being questioned about his blowtorch. Or was he pretending?

Pavano admired Pinto for thinking of a blowtorch. It was a good notion. That man's scorched neck wound could definitely be caused by a blowtorch.

"I use it for melting ice," Sutter said. "You know. In the winter. Ice covers the front stoop. It gets treacherous. I melt ice off the driveway with it, too. Why are you asking me—?"

"So tell us, who is Richard . . . whatsisname?" Pinto interrupted.

"Hulenberger. He's from the Blakeman Institute. In the city."

Pavano typed rapidly on the phone keyboard. He let Pinto ask the questions. Pinto was doing a good job. Pavano could see the Audi in the driveway from the office window. So far, the other cops hadn't shown up.

"And you never met him? He drove here from the city be-cause . . . ?"

"He wanted to meet with me. I'd applied for quite a large grant."

"And he came to tell you . . . ?"

Sutter lowered his eyes to the floor. It took him a few seconds to answer. "He came to tell me they were turning me down. No grant."

The bitterness in Sutter's voice brought Pavano to attention. He felt his heart start to pound a little faster.

"He brought you bad news," Pinto said softly. "Very bad news."

Sutter nodded. He didn't raise his eyes.

"And how did that make you feel? Angry? Fucking angry?"

Sutter raised his eyes. His face showed a new intensity. He pulled out his hands and held them tensely at his sides. "Do I need a lawyer?"

"I'm just askin'," Pinto replied with a shrug. "Somebody brings me bad news, it makes me angry. You know? Kill the messenger? Know what I'm saying?"

"I'm a psychologist, Officer," he said heatedly. "I think I know how to control my anger so that I don't murder anyone who brings me disappointing news."

"You're a psychologist with a blowtorch?"

"I explained the blowtorch." He uttered a cry of frustration. "Is that what happened out there? Are you telling me Richard was murdered with a blowtorch? He left my house, sat down in his car, and someone took a blowtorch to him in my driveway?"

Pinto made a calming motion with both hands. Pavano could see this guy was strung tight. But the situation would make anyone a little tense. And, he didn't have much of a motive for killing Hu-lenberger. Not if he was telling the truth.

But was he hiding some things? Did he know Hulenberger better than he was letting on?

We should advise him to call his lawyer.

"It's definitely a homicide, Mr. Sutter," Pinto said, his hands still raised as if warding Sutter off. "The guy didn't take a blowtorch to himself. The crime scene guys will want to see your blowtorch. And they'll have a lot more questions. If you'd feel more comfortable with a lawyer present . . ."

"Yes. I'll call my lawyer. No. Wait. I didn't see anything. I don't know anything. Why do I need a lawyer?"

"Mr. Sutter, please take a deep breath," Pinto said softly.

Pavano could see the turmoil in Sutter's mind. His eyes were darting from side to side. He was thinking hard about something.

"I . . . have to tell you one thing," Sutter said, clasping his hands together in his lap. "There are fingerprints. I mean, I touched the car."

Pinto raised one eyebrow. "Fingerprints?"

"I grabbed the side of the car. You know. The window. I wasn't thinking. I didn't know. I . . . got blood on my hands. Blood from the side of the car. I was still washing it off when you drove up."

Pinto gave Pavano a quick glance. Pinto was suspicious of this guy. "Thanks for telling us," Pavano said, typing on his phone.

The doorbell rang. Pavano and Pinto followed Sutter into the hall. A woman carrying a little boy on her shoulder opened the front door. Pavano remembered her from the first time he was here.

A tall African-American man stepped into the entryway. He had a noticeably big, melon-shaped head, shaved bald, and a silver ring in one ear. He wore a baggy brown suit, wrinkled and frayed at the cuffs. He had a dark brown dress shirt underneath and a blue bow tie tilted under his chin.

"Can I help you?" Sutter motioned the woman away. "I'll take care of this, Roz."

The man ignored Sutter and approached Pavano and Pinto. "Are you the officers who discovered this?"

Both cops nodded.

"I'm Harrison. The ME."

Pinto squinted at him. "You're new?"

"I haven't been new for thirty years. I'm from Riverhead. You've heard of it?"

"You're an ME or a comedian?"

"I'm not as funny as your face. Let's start again. There are CS guys dusting the car right now. Then they'll sweep for fibers. You know. Stuff for the DNA lab guys. You're familiar with that, right? Or are you new?"

"Pavano's new," Pinto said, motioning with his eyes. "He's out here from the city."

Harrison had one brown eye and one blue eye. He focused the blue eye on Pinto. "Am I going to get his thrilling life story now, or are we investigating a goddamn homicide?"

"Sorry, Dr. Harrison," Pinto said. "We've been questioning Mr. Sutter here. He—"

"We'll get to you, Mr. Sutter," Harrison gave him a nod, then turned back to the officers. "Did you touch anything? Open the door? Roll down the window? Shake hands with the victim? Muss up his hair?"

Pinto squinted at Harrison. "Are you for real?"

"We didn't touch a thing," Pavano stepped in. "But Sutter did. He had his hands on the bottom of the window. Smeared the blood."

Harrison squinted at Sutter and tsk-tsked.

"Pinto and I looked into the car, but we stayed back. Then we called in right away," Pavano explained.

"Do you expect a Nobel Prize for that?"

Pinto exploded. "What the fuck, Harrison? What's your problem?"

Pavano just wanted to get out of the house. There were kids upstairs. They were probably listening to all this.

What happened to those two little blond boys?

"Have you examined the body at all, Doctor?" Pavano asked.

Harrison pulled a soiled handkerchief from his jacket and mopped his bald head. "Yeah. I did a cursory exam before the CS guys arrived." He tucked the handkerchief away and fiddled with his bow tie.

"And could you determine the cause of death?"

Sutter uttered a groan. Pavano turned and saw him gripping the bottom of the banister, his face pale. "Are you feeling okay?"

"Not really," Sutter uttered. "I mean, a murder in my driveway? I feel kinda sick."

"Why don't you go sit down. Get a glass of water," Pavano instructed. "We'll come back to you, okay?"

Sutter nodded but didn't reply. He made his way back toward his office.

"Cause of death?" Pavano repeated to Harrison when Sutter was out of hearing.

"Officer, you know I can't say till I do the whole goddamn exam." He motioned them outside. The cool evening air felt soothing on Pavano's hot face.

Harrison led the way to the Audi, where two uniformed officers were combing every inch of it. "You want to know a cause of death from my first cursory exam? Okay, I'd say it was asphyxiation."

Pinto and Pavano both uttered sounds of surprise. Pinto removed his cap and scratched his head. "Asphyxiation? What makes you say that?"

A grim smile formed on Harrison's face. "Here. I'll show you. You didn't eat dinner yet, right?"

"We didn't eat dinner. Why?"

"Because you probably wouldn't be able to keep it down."

"Another one of your jokes?"

The smile faded from the big man's face. "No joke."

He pulled open the back door. He pointed to something stretched across the backseat.

It looked like a wet pink snake to Pavano. No, wait. Some kind of long pasta noodle. Jagged on both ends. Dark streaks along the sides.

"What are you showing us?" Pinto demanded. "What is that?"

"The man's windpipe," Harrison said. "Whoever killed him ripped out his windpipe while he was still alive."

32

Pavano again let Pinto do the questioning while he studied Sutter's sister. Sitting across from them in Sutter's office, Roz kept her hands clasped tightly in her lap, squeezing her fingers. But it was the only sign of nervousness. She seemed like a straightforward woman, and Pavano believed what she told them.

Which was nothing useful.

She had come home from grocery shopping and was in the kitchen the whole time Hulenberger and Sutter were meeting in the office. She had heard voices, but she hadn't seen Hulenberger and definitely hadn't seen him leave the house. She hadn't heard anything unusual. Now she was worried about upsetting the kids.

"You certainly don't think the kids saw what happened?" she asked.

"We have to talk to them. You know. Be as thorough as possible," Pinto said, glancing at the notes on Pavano's phone. "It's possible they saw or heard something helpful."

"Elena and Ira were upstairs in their rooms," Roz told them. "I'm sure they didn't see a thing. And the twins . . . I'm not sure where they were. Probably in the guesthouse out back."

"Ma'am, could you bring them in one by one?" Pinto asked, speaking softly.

"A horrible murder like this could upset them terribly, Sergeant. Ira is very delicate. You might say he's troubled. And the twins just arrived here."

Pavano raised his eyes. "Arrived here?"

"Mark and Lea adopted them. She brought them home less than two weeks ago. It's hard enough for them to adjust. If you—"

"We'll do our best not to upset them, ma'am," Pinto said. "You and Mr. Sutter are welcome to stay in the room when we talk to them."

"Where *is* Mr. Sutter?" Pavano asked. Sutter had slipped away while they were questioning his sister.

Roz sighed. "I think he's trying to phone Lea. His wife. She's in the city."

Pinto shifted his weight on the desk chair. He suddenly looked old and weary. Pavano knew he was ten years older than he, but he looked even older than that. *Frayed.* That's the strange word that popped into Pavano's mind. The frayed life of a cop.

With another warning to be careful, the sister went to round up the four kids. Pavano picked up a pink paperweight from the desk and tossed it from hand to hand. It took him awhile to recognize it as a porcelain model of a human brain.

The color reminded him of the slender windpipe tossed on the backseat of the victim's car. He set the brain back down on the desk.

Elena, the fourteen-year-old, came downstairs first. She was a pretty girl with shiny black hair and lively dark eyes. She seemed confident and mature for her age. She spoke in full sentences, not in teenage grunts and fits and starts. She didn't seem at all hesitant to answer Pinto's questions, but she had nothing to tell them.

She had been in her room since getting home late from school, texting her friends and listening to music. She had glimpsed her father talking to a man in a suit but didn't hear what they were talking about and didn't see or hear the man leave.

Ira Sutter, the twelve-year-old, slunk down on the couch and pressed close to his aunt. He gripped the couch arm tightly with a slender hand. Before Pinto could ask a question, Ira demanded in a tiny voice, "Is Dad in trouble?"

"No, of course not." Roz answered for them.

"Then why is he so upset? Why are all these policemen here?"

"There was an accident. In your driveway." Pinto spoke up before the sister could answer. "We're just trying to find out what happened. No one in your family is in trouble. I swear."

"Ira, did you see that dark car in your driveway?" Pavano asked.

The boy had a slender, pale face. His natural expression appeared to be worry. "I saw it after the police came."

"But not before?"

He shook his head, then glanced at his aunt. Roz gave him a reassuring pat on the knee of his jeans.

"Did you see the man when he was talking to your dad?"

He shook his head again. "No. I was upstairs. Then Roz called us down to dinner but there was no man here."

A few more questions and they let him go.

"Do you want to see the twins together or one by one?" Roz asked.

Pinto sighed and rubbed the stubble on his jaw. "Together is fine. I know this seems like a waste of time. But we just have to do it. You know. So we can say our report is complete."

Somewhere a clock chimed. Was it seven o'clock or eight o'clock? Despite the horror of what they had seen, Pavano was starting to feel hungry.

The twins plopped down on the couch, all blond hair, wide eyes, and innocence. They were very cute, Pavano observed. They looked smaller than their twelve years. Their voices were little boys' voices.

The two cops chitchatted with them for a few minutes. The boys had funny accents, sort of English, sort of Irish. They didn't seem at all fazed by having to talk to policemen.

Their answers turned out to be a lot more interesting than those of the other two kids.

"Did you see the man talking to Mr. Sutter?"

"Yes, sir," the one with dimples seemed to be the one who liked to talk. "We saw him in the den with the new pa."

"The new pa?"

"That's what they call Mark," Roz interjected.

Pinto leaned forward in the big chair. "You saw them in here when you came home from school?"

Both boys nodded. "He was talking to the new pa, telling him bad things."

Pavano's breath caught in his throat. He squinted at the expressionless boy. "Bad things?"

"For sure. He said he had bad news. The new pa looked very sad."

Pinto and Pavano exchanged glances. Pinto cleared his throat. Roz suddenly looked troubled, her lips pursed tightly. She started to say something, but Pinto motioned for her to remain silent.

"So what did you do?" Pinto asked.

"Sammy and I took a ball and went outside to play."

"Did you hear the man have a fight with your dad?"

"No. They weren't fighting. Just talking, right, Sammy?"

Sammy nodded his head solemnly.

"Were they arguing? You know. Shouting."

"No. Just talking," Daniel insisted. "But I think Pa was a wee bit angry."

The quiet one spoke up. "Daniel and I went out to play catch. With a tennis ball."

"Where did you play?" Pavano asked.

"By the driveway. You know. Next to the garage."

"And so you saw the man's dark blue car?" Pinto asked.

They both nodded. "The ball bounced off it a couple of times, don't you know. But it didn't make a dent."

"And did you see the man leave the house?"

They nodded again.

"Did you see him get into his car?"

Daniel nodded. "He got in his big car. And the new pa shouted at us."

"He said get out of the way," his brother chimed in. "He said the man was backing up and we should get out of the way."

"So what did you do?"

"We went back to our house. In the garden."

"Your house?"

"Their room is in the guesthouse," Roz explained. "That's where they're staying."

"You went back to your room? And you didn't hear anything strange? Did you see anyone come to the driveway? Did you hear a shout or a fight or anything weird?"

The twins exchanged puzzled glances again. They shook their heads.

"We didn't hear anything. Not a peep, sir."

Pavano heard a baby crying somewhere.

Roz jumped to her feet. "That's Axl, my little boy. He's waking up from his nap. Officers, I have to go upstairs and get him. I'm afraid this interview session is over."

Pinto climbed up with a groan. Pavano's head suddenly felt like solid granite. *Too much. This is too much to think about.*

They followed Roz to the front. Before they could exit, the screen door swung open. A uniform cop, one of the crime scene guys, poked his head into the house.

"Sergeants, one more bit of info you can add to your report."

"What's that?" Pinto asked. Pavano pulled out his phone to write it down.

"That blowtorch in the garage? We went over it. Looks like it's been used recently."

33

"I wish I was there with you, Mark. I'm so sorry I'm not there to help you. Roz must be a mess, too."

"Lea, is it too late for the jitney? Can you get a train? I'll pick you up in Southampton."

"Mark, you're breaking up. I can't hear too well. Are the kids okay? Are they upset?"

"I don't know if they realize what happened. I think they're mainly confused. I'm going to talk to them later. After the police leave. You know. Try to see how they feel, what they know."

"How can you explain it to them? A murder right at our house?"

"I'll just be straight with them. I mean, I don't know how else to handle it. Just tell them what happened and be there for them."

"Oh, wow. I have the shakes just thinking about it. Right in front of our house. And you didn't hear anything? You didn't see anyone go up to his car?"

"None of us did. Listen, can you—"

"I'm worried about the kids, Mark. Poor Ira. Something like this . . . a horrible murder in our front yard . . . I mean, how much more traumatic can it be?"

"He was up in his room. I don't think he realizes . . . I'm going to sit down and talk to them all. Get their feelings out in the open."

"I can't hear you very well. You keep breaking up. I'll try to get back as fast as I can, darling. I'll cancel my meeting for tomorrow morning. I'll let you know what jitney I'm on. I'm so sorry I'm not there with you, sweetheart."

"Are you feeling okay? I really didn't think you were ready for the city. Those nightmares you were having. And . . . and the tomato soup thing . . ."

"You're breaking up, Mark. What did you say?"

"Do you feel okay?"

"Actually, no. Maybe you were right. Maybe this city visit was too soon. I feel weird. I can't really explain it. Kind of like I can't concentrate. I don't really feel I'm totally in control. It's nothing. I'm sure. Just tired, I guess."

"Please get home as fast as you can. We need you here. I . . . don't know what's going to happen. I mean, when word of this gets out. You know. I'm a public figure now. The publicity. 'Gruesome Murder in Bestselling Psychologist's Driveway.' It could get bad, Lea."

"But you had nothing to do with the murder."

"Don't be naïve, sweetheart. Does that matter? It happened in our fucking driveway. If the details are released . . . Can you see the front of the *Post*?"

"I'm so sorry, honey. I can't hear. I'll text you my jitney."

A soft click. Then silence. The connection was lost.

Mark headed to the bar against the den wall. *I need something stronger than wine.*

And then he felt a stab of anger: *How can she be away when I need her? When we all need her here?*

He knew what he was doing. It was obvious. He was angry at himself for what happened with Autumn. And he was transferring his anger to Lea. Embarrassing to be so obvious.

Autumn, you missed all the excitement.

He thought about kissing her. Fucking her on top of his desk. *Oh, Jesus.*

The two police officers left. He saw two other cops in the driveway, working over the car. They had set up halogen spotlights on poles to light their work. Yellow crime tape had been stretched across the bottom of the front yard. Cars moved slowly on the street. Gawkers wondering what had happened there.

Mark shook his head and took a long sip of his Cruzan Single Barrel rum. *The neighbors must have their binoculars out.*

Luckily, the houses were far apart, separated by tall, old oak and sassafras trees and high evergreen hedges. Mark had no idea who his neighbors were.

Richard Hulenberger's body had been removed. Wrapped and carried away in a silent ambulance. Now, gazing into the white halogen light, Mark saw that the car seats were on their backs on the lawn. One cop was leaning into the trunk, sweeping it with some kind of whirring device. A vacuum?

He gathered the four kids in the den while Roz went to feed and entertain Axl. The den had two brown, soft-leather couches at a ninety-degree angle against two walls, and a matching recliner chair, all facing a fifty-five-inch flat-screen TV mounted on the only wall without bookshelves.

A stack of glass shelves to the right of the TV screen held Lea's stuffed-monkey collection, dozens of specimens. Lea wasn't embarrassed to show off her monkeys. She told anyone who asked that growing up in a house jammed with so many kids, she never had room for any kind of collection. In a way, the mostly hideous monkeys were fulfilling a lifelong dream.

Samuel and Daniel sank into one couch and slumped down, looking uncomfortable, troubled. Elena took the recliner, sitting stiffly on the edge, not tilting back as she usually did. Ira perched next to her on one arm of the recliner.

Mark studied them for a few seconds. Elena wore freshly applied lip gloss. Ira had a tomato sauce stain on his chin.

"As you've probably figured out, something terrible happened in our driveway this afternoon. The man who was visiting me was murdered by someone."

Elena rolled her eyes. "Dad, please—tell us something we *don't* know."

Mark's impulse was to scold her for being so flip. But he quickly remembered that her attitude might be her way of dealing with something frightening.

"Elena, not appropriate."

"Sorry."

"I don't really know much about it," he confessed, standing awkwardly in front of them as if giving a lecture. He had set down his glass but found himself craving another few sips of rum. "But if I can answer any questions. I know you must be upset. And maybe confused."

Ira spoke up first. "Dad, did the killer mean to kill *you?*"

The question made him suck in a burst of air. Not a question he expected. "No. I . . . don't think so, Ira. The police didn't have anything to say about that. I don't think anyone wants to kill me."

Ira screwed up his face, thinking hard. "But will the killer come in the house?"

"No," Mark answered quickly, without wanting to think about that. "No one is coming in the house. We're all safe here. You don't have to be scared. We are all completely safe."

Elena shifted her weight on the edge of the recliner. "Does this mean that Ruth-Ann can't come for a sleepover Friday night?"

Mark blinked. *Is she totally self-involved? Doesn't she react at all to someone being murdered in front of her house? Maybe that's a good thing.*

"I don't see any reason why Ruth-Ann can't come Friday, Elena. But I think the news of what happened here will be out by then. We'll have to talk with her parents."

"Maybe she'll be too scared to come over," Ira suggested in a tiny voice.

Elena wrapped her hands over Ira's shoulders. "Well, you'll protect her—won't you, big guy?"

Ira squirmed out from under her hands. "Shut up."

"Don't tease Ira," Mark scolded.

"Sorry," Elena murmured. She gave Ira a bump with her shoulder. "It's just . . . I'll be so upset if we don't have our sleepover. We've planned it for weeks."

"Shouldn't be a problem," Mark said.

And suddenly both twins were on their feet. Both with the same forlorn expressions.

Daniel's eyes brimmed with tears. He took a tentative step toward Mark. "Can I have a hug?" In a tiny, high voice. He rushed into Mark's open arms.

"Me too," Samuel said. "Can I have a hug, please?"

Mark wrapped them both in a tight hug. He could feel their trembling bodies. They both made sniffling sounds.

Glancing over their heads, he caught Elena's trembling-chinned expression. She was near tears, too. Not as skeptical as he thought. Ira sat with his arms crossed tightly in front of him, staring into the distance.

Mark tried to pull his arms away, but the boys clung to him.

"Hug," Daniel said, burying his face in Mark's shirt.

"Hug," Samuel repeated.

34

Samuel closed the guesthouse door behind him, making sure it clicked shut. The two boys strode into their room. Each climbed onto one of the low twin beds, one against each wall. They stood up and bounced on the beds for a few moments, a gleeful trampoline act.

Bright lights set up by the police officers in the driveway broke the darkness outside their curtained window. The light swooped across the flowered wallpaper and caught the two boys as they leaped and bounced.

"Smoked meat," Daniel said when they finally slumped to their beds.

"Smoked meat," Samuel repeated. "There was Daniel being Daniel again."

Daniel stuck his chin out defiantly. "Smoked meat. Smoked meat. Smoked meat."

Samuel sighed. "Yes, the man was smoked meat. But—"

"This will keep Pa busy for a while."

"I know, Daniel. But, we just got here. Perhaps we need to go slow."

Daniel giggled. "You loved it, too, laddy. I saw your eyes shine. You wanted a taste of that smoked meat."

Samuel bounced lightly on the bed. "Don't be making a joke, Daniel. We don't eat smoked meat anymore—remember?"

Daniel giggled again. "Did you put the blowtorch back where we got it?"

Samuel nodded. "Sure, I did. But I don't really understand why we needed it, boyo."

"To keep Pa busy. To give the coppers something to puzzle about, don't you know."

Samuel's expression changed. He stood up and crossed to his brother. He put his hands on Daniel's shoulders and peered down at him. "I know you like a bit of fun—"

"You too."

"But if we get caught, it's all off. All. Off. And why did we adopt the new mum? Remember?"

Daniel grinned up at him. "To rule the school?"

"Yes. To rule the school. But if we go too fast . . ."

Daniel removed his twin's hands from his shoulders. His eyes flashed. Samuel knew that expression. Thoughtful. Devilishly thoughtful.

"Pa doesn't want us. He doesn't like us. So we have to keep him busy. Out of our hair, don't you know. And then, Sammy . . . And then . . . who will help us rule the school? Do you know? Can you guess? Who will be the first to help us?"

Samuel stuck out his jaw. "I can't read your mind now, can I? Especially not *your* mind."

"The bruvver and sister," Daniel said.

Samuel stared at him. "Who?"

"The bruvver and sister," his twin repeated. "You know. Ira and Elena."

"The two of them? Help us?"

Daniel nodded enthusiastically, eyes aglow. "The bruvver and sister know people, Sammy. They have friends, right? They know things. They will help us rule the school. They'll join us. And then more. And more."

Daniel jumped to his feet and pumped his fists above his head. "More and more and more. And when we own all the kids, we own the town. It will all be ours. All. And what does it take, Sammy? You know the answer. Teamwork, boyo. Teamwork wins the day."

"Daniel, listen to me. What if Ira and Elena don't *want* to join us? What if they tell Mum and Pa?"

Daniel giggled. His grin made his dimples flare. "We'll convince the bruvver and sister."

Samuel stared at him. "Convince them? Okay. But no smoked meat, Daniel. Okay? No smoked meat?"

Daniel nodded. "Total domination, Sammy. You'll see. Total domination."

A hard knock on the door ended the discussion. The door swung open, and Roz edged into the room, carrying a round tray with a bowl and glasses. "You boys didn't get much dinner, what with the police and all. I brought you some Cokes and a big bowl of popcorn."

Sweet smiles on both boys. "Oh, me goodness. Thank you, Aunty Roz," said Samuel.

Daniel's eyes lit up with glee, and his dimples flashed. "Thank you, Aunty. Who loves the popcorn? We do! Pop pop pop."

PART THREE

35

Mark wrapped his arms tightly around Lea's waist and pressed his face against her cheek. "I'm so glad you're here."

She stepped back, nearly stumbling over her overnight bag. Her dark eyes flashed. "It takes a murder to make you miss me so much?"

"Don't make jokes. Please. It's . . . been horrible for all of us."

"I'm so sorry I couldn't get back last night, honey. The jitney was booked. And I missed the last train. Then this morning there was an accident on the expressway, and—look at the clock. It's nearly two."

"It's okay, Lea. You're here now." He pulled her close again and kissed her.

"How are the kids? I worried about them all night. Are they—?"

"Roz and I got them off to school. They seem to be okay. A little quiet, maybe. Ira is glum, but I don't think more glum than usual."

"The morning papers could have been worse," she said, tugging off her red jacket and tossing it on a chair. She straightened her T-shirt and pulled it out from her jeans.

"For sure it could be worse. The police didn't reveal the details. Too sickening, I guess. If they had, it would have been on every front page."

Lea touched his face. "Poor baby. I feel so bad for you. Did you see the . . . uh . . . the body?"

"No. I—" He reached for her again. He had a sudden desire to pull up her T-shirt and kiss her all over.

The doorbell interrupted. Mark glanced over Lea's shoulder and saw two dark-uniformed men peering through the screen door. He recognized the two cops from the night before.

He groaned.

Lea turned to the door. "Hello?"

"It's Sergeant Pinto and Pavano," the big, older cop said. "Sorry to interrupt."

Lea pushed open the door, and they entered, both removing their dark caps. Pinto studied Lea. He had a toothpick riding up and down between his teeth. Mark smelled tobacco on the other one. Pavano held his arms tense at his sides, as if expecting trouble.

He always looks uncomfortable. Like he knows he's chosen the wrong line of work.

"This is my wife, Lea." Mark gestured to the suitcases. "She's just back. From the city."

The cops nodded at her. Pinto's eyes lingered longer than Mark thought they should. Pinto removed the toothpick and shoved it into his uniform shirt pocket. "Sorry for interrupting your afternoon, Mrs. Sutter. We need to speak to your husband for a few minutes."

"I've already answered all your questions," Mark snapped. "Do I need my lawyer?"

"If you prefer," Pinto said. "But then we'd have to have our talk at the station."

"But I've told you everything I know."

"We're making a report for the state guys now," Pinto said. "They're probably going to send their own cops down. They'll ask you the same questions. Then if the feds get into it . . ." His voice trailed off.

"It won't take long," Pavano said. "We have some test results."

"Results? You mean like fingerprints? You got them overnight?"

"The lab guys don't get cases like this very often," Pavano said.

"Perhaps if we could sit down." Pinto motioned toward Mark's office down the hall.

Mark sighed. Lea shrugged. She lifted the overnight bag. "I'll go unpack. Then maybe I'll make a nice dinner before the kids get home." She turned to Mark. "Unless you need me . . ."

He shook his head. "Go ahead, dear. No problem." He turned and led the two cops into his office.

Autumn had left a stack of mail on his chair. She arrived late that morning and didn't have work on her mind. Shining those beautiful eyes on him, she'd slid his hand over her breasts. Then she got all pouty when he told her Lea was coming home.

Autumn was young and beautiful and sexy, but seeing her made him feel sick now. How was he going to deal with her? If he told her yesterday morning was a onetime thing, would she go berserk? Tell Lea?

He couldn't fire her. That would be a definite lawsuit. And it would mean more hideously damaging newspaper stories.

And how did he feel about her? He hadn't had time to sort it out. He knew he didn't want to hurt her. But he also knew that Lea meant everything to him. He had done a stupid, impulsive thing. So unlike him. So totally unlike him.

He knew he needed to think about this all. But with the murder . . .

The two cops were staring at him. Trying to read his thoughts. Did he appear tense to them? Would they misinterpret it and decide he was guilty in some way?

He removed the stack of letters from his chair and sat down. Once again, they took their places on the green leather couch facing the desk.

Pinto dropped his cap onto the floor in front of him. Pavano pulled out his phone to take notes. He tapped a slow rhythm with the fingers of his other hand on the couch arm.

"One more time," Pinto said. "The victim brought you bad news, right? Very bad news."

"Well, yeah," Mark replied. "But I told you, he was just the messenger. It wasn't his fault I didn't get the grant. The board voted. They just sent him to tell me."

"And . . . I know you've already stated this. . . . Your feeling when he told you? Angry?"

"Disappointed," Mark corrected him.

Pavano tapped something into his phone. Then he raised his head and gazed intently at Mark. "The victim's car was in the driveway for how long before you noticed it?"

"Maybe fifteen minutes. Maybe twenty."

"You don't think it's strange that a car could sit in your drive-way twenty minutes, and you didn't notice it?"

Mark shrugged. "What can I tell you? I didn't see it."

"And you never looked out the window and saw anyone approach the car?"

"No. No, I didn't. I told you."

"You never noticed another car drive by or stop?"

"No. I didn't look out the front. So I—"

"You saw no one in your front yard? No one walk up your driveway?"

"This is getting repetitious," Mark said.

Easy. Don't let them rattle you.

Pinto nodded. "I know. We have to do this." He glanced at the notes on his partner's phone. "Mr. Sutter, we have test results that show your blowtorch was recently used."

Mark blinked. His mind went blank for a moment. *What can I say? What can I tell them?* "Yes. Well, yes. I used it. Ira and I were doing a project."

"A project?"

"Yeah. Metalwork. We were building a robot, actually. I do these projects . . . Well . . . They're good for Ira. Help him build confidence."

"So if we ask your son about the blowtorch, he'll back up your story?"

"Well . . . hmmm . . . actually, no. He wasn't home. I used the blowtorch on the robot while he was in school." Mark could feel his face go hot.

Pinto shifted his weight. "Could you show us this robot that you used the blowtorch on? Is it here?"

"Ummm . . . I know this sounds bad, Sergeant. But the robot disappeared. Ira took it to school, and it disappeared from the art room."

They both squinted at him.

"I'm telling the truth. It must have been stolen." His face still felt blazing hot.

"The lab guys seem to think the blowtorch could have been used yesterday. As the murder weapon."

"I . . . don't know anything about that. The garage door was open. Anyone could have taken it out."

A long silence.

"Well, we have fingerprint results on the victim's car," Pavano said finally. He flipped through some screens on his phone.

Mark felt his throat tighten.

"The CS guys found only children's prints," Pinto said. "Children's prints on both front doors. And then there were three other prints. Round. Like a ball had hit the car."

They hadn't asked a question, but they waited for Mark to say something.

He leaned over the desk. He cleared his throat. "I'm not surprised by that," he said.

The two cops waited for him to continue.

"The twins," Mark said. "I believe you talked to them. And they told you they were playing with a tennis ball at the side of the driveway."

"And it's their prints on the car?" Pinto said.

"Pretty good bet," Mark said and then regretted sounding so sarcastic. "They were playing catch. They said the ball hit Hulenberger's car a few times."

The cops nodded. He could see they were studying him.

"And my prints . . . they must have been there," Mark said. "Remember? I gripped the side of the door? Under the window?"

"Actually, the crime scene guys couldn't get any good prints," Pinto said. "The blood was too smeared."

Pavano was flipping through his phone screens. Pinto licked at the side of his mouth. "So the twins saw Hulenberger get into his car. I recall that's what they said. But then they didn't see anyone come up the drive? They didn't see someone come up to the car?"

"I told them to get out of the way," Mark said. "I told them to watch out. He was backing up."

"And do they always obey you really quickly?" Pinto asked, leaning forward.

Mark pushed back from the desk. "I don't understand that question, Officer. What are you saying? That the boys stayed by the front? That they might have seen something?"

Pinto and Pavano exchanged glances. "They might have," Pinto said finally. "And maybe they're afraid to tell us?"

"They were there," Pavano added. "It's hard to believe they didn't see anything at all."

Mark rubbed his chin. The beard was getting long. He needed to trim it. "You may be right. Sometimes when kids are traumatized by something they've seen, they manage to lock it away, push it to a back burner, so to speak. Sometimes the fear is so powerful, they just force it from their memory. Stress-related memory loss is very common."

The cops nodded. Pavano clicked away on his phone.

Pinto climbed to his feet with a groan. His shirt had pulled out over his potbelly. "And sometimes do kids *lie* to stay out of trouble?" he asked.

Mark stood up, too. He didn't answer the question. He knew it wasn't really a question. He didn't know the twins well enough to know how truthful they were.

They seemed sweet and innocent. But, of course, kids can put on quite a show for grown-ups when they want to. If the boys saw something frightening, if they witnessed the murder, he felt terrible for them. What a welcome to their new home.

And then he had a memory flash: *I did see them at the side of the house. When I ran out to Hulenberger's car, the twins . . . were standing at the side of the house. They weren't in back. They were there.*

"We'll want to talk to the boys," Pinto said, studying Mark's face.

Mark returned his stare. "With me in the room?"

"No. But we'll have a psychologist in the room. We'll make sure they are comfortable. You can wait right outside. If you wish to have a lawyer present . . ."

That was a challenge. Mark felt a stab of anger. "Because you think if I'm not there, the boys are going to incriminate me? That isn't going to happen. You know the expression 'barking up the wrong tree,' I'm sure."

They both grunted in reply. Mark led them down the hall and held open the screen door for them.

After they had driven away, he found Lea in the kitchen, stirring an iced coffee. "That was weird." Lea poured in an envelope of Equal.

"You were listening?"

She nodded. She raised her eyes to him. "Mark, why did you lie to the police?"

He blinked. He could feel the blood pulse at his temples. "You mean . . . about the blowtorch thing?"

She nodded. "A robot project? You and Ira never built a robot. Why did you say that?"

"I needed an answer, Lea. I needed to tell them something. They said the blowtorch had been used. I guess I panicked a little. I mean, I couldn't explain it. I . . . thought it would be better to give them *something*."

She studied him. "But, Mark, it wasn't a good lie. They can check it easily. I don't understand—"

"Why are you looking at me like that? You don't think that I—"

"Of course not." She stepped around the counter and took his hand in hers. "But look at you. Your face is all red and—"

He let her hand slide away. "Forget about the blowtorch. That's not important. The twins were out front when Hulenberger left. The cops think they might have seen the murderer."

Lea gasped. "Oh, those poor boys! They must be so scared."

"Actually, they seem fine," Mark said, taking a sip of her iced coffee. "You need more ice."

"You know I don't like it too cold."

"The twins said they didn't see anything. They said they went back to the guesthouse when Hulenberger started to back down the drive."

"And you don't believe them?" Her voice rose a few octaves. She gripped the glass with both hands. "The way you said that, you think they were lying?"

"All honesty? I don't know what to think. I remember seeing them at the top of the driveway. When I discovered the murder . . ."

She shook her head. "Listen, Mark—I know you didn't want those boys to come here. But they are sweet, lovely boys. And accusing them of lying is—"

"We don't know what kind of boys they are, Lea. We don't know anything about them. Yes, I didn't want you to bring them here. But I'm giving them every chance. And I didn't accuse them of lying. If they saw something horrible, it's possible—"

He stopped. Spun around at the sound of a cough. The twins stood side by side in the kitchen doorway.

"How long have you been standing there?" It came out like an accusation.

They didn't answer. Instead, broad smiles crossed their faces. They dove across the room to wrap Lea in enthusiastic hugs.

"The new mum is home! Mum is home! Yaaaaaaay."

36

"Where are we going, Daniel?"

"To find the bruvver."

The twins wore their colorful surfer swimsuits, still crinkly and stiff, and white sleeveless T-shirts that came down nearly to their knees. Their plastic flip-flops clopped on the pavement. Daniel took long strides, eyes straight ahead. Samuel struggled to keep up.

A mail carrier in his tiny white truck waved as he putted past. Samuel returned the wave and watched a chipmunk dart under the truck's wheels. He waited for the bump and then the *squish*. But the little animal scampered out the other side.

"Close call," Samuel murmured.

Daniel didn't reply. He appeared lost in thought. The blue of his eyes had faded, as if all of his energy was retreating into his mind. Samuel had seen him disappear into himself before.

They turned onto Long Point Road, which snaked along the bay. Samuel's flip-flop snagged a clump of tall grass, and he had to stop to free himself. The afternoon sun beamed down on his face, making it feel more like July than May.

"Hey, Daniel—wait up! Do you mind telling me where we're headed, laddy?"

Daniel kicked pebbles into the tall grass along the side of

the street. Tall, leafy hedges hid the houses that lined the water. "Ethan's house," he said finally. He pointed. "Up there."

"Ira is swimming there with his friend," Samuel said. "That's why we're walking there? To swim?"

Daniel wheeled around, startling his twin. "Time to get in the swim, right, Sammy? Get in the swim. You know? Rule the pool?"

Samuel started to laugh but cut it short. He could see that his brother wasn't joking around. "You mean—"

"The new pa doesn't like us," Daniel said, a sneer making his features hard. His eyes suddenly ice instead of sky. "The new pa doesn't want us. The new pa is our enemy."

"Yes, I know that, boyo."

"The new mum will do anything for us. But Pa fights her. He shouts at her. He doesn't want to give us what we want. He is our enemy."

"Yes. So we keep him busy. I understand what you are saying. But what are you thinking? What does it mean, Daniel? Go ahead. Tell me."

Daniel stared so intently at his twin, Samuel had to turn away. "What it means is . . . What it means is . . . we don't have to take our time, Sammy lad. We can make our move now. It doesn't matter. We've no one to impress. We don't have to pretend anymore. That's good news—right? You want to rule the pool and rule the school?"

"But if we waited—" Samuel gazed at two fat yellow bees fighting over a tiny blossom tucked in the hedge beside them.

Even bees fight.

But not like Daniel.

The mailman waved again, moving the other direction in his stupid little cart-truck. This time, Samuel ignored the grinning jerk.

"Daniel, we already murdered someone to keep Pa busy. Maybe if we take our time . . . go a little slow . . ."

"Slow is no," Daniel sneered. He saw the bumblebees, too. He moved quickly, reached into the hedge, cupped them both in his hands, and flattened them between his palms. "Slow is no." He squeezed his hands together, grinding the bees flat.

"Mum deserves a better man," Daniel said, wiping his palms on the front of his T-shirt. "Mum deserves better. She'll want us to rule the school, Sammy. It will make Mum happy. You'll see."

Samuel shrugged. His face felt burning hot, not just from the sun. He knew he'd already lost the argument. "What do you plan to do?"

"Test the bruvver."

"What? Test Ira? You're going to start with Ira?"

"First Ira, then the sister. We have to show him. We have to dominate him—dominate him to win him over. Right, Sammy?"

Daniel didn't wait for Samuel to reply. He turned and started walking again, running his hand along the hedge, making bees fly and butterflies jump. "We have no choice. It's time to start. And we will start by dominating the bruvver."

They turned and Samuel followed his twin up a smoothly paved driveway that led to a wide three-car garage attached to a white frame house. He could hear the splash of water from behind the house and recognized Ira's laugh.

"Are we going to swim, Daniel? Can't we have a nice swim first?"

Daniel kept walking. "We need to test the bruvver."

"What are you going to do?" Samuel jogged to catch up. He grabbed his twin's shoulders and spun him to face him. "What are you going to do to Ira?"

A crooked smile crossed Daniel's face and his eyes regained their deep blue liveliness. "Maybe see how long he can stay underwater."

37

The lovemaking didn't seem the same.

Was it just his guilt?

No. Mark wasn't imagining it. They'd been married fourteen years. Long enough to know each other's every move.

Fourteen years and suddenly he decided to try another woman. No. Not a woman. A girl.

So, yes. Guilt had to play a part here.

Afterward, cradled in her arm, waiting for his heartbeats to slow and his breath to come easier, tapping one finger on his sweat-damp chest, he pictured the young Lea. Only twenty-two when they got married. What could she have been thinking?

He saw the diamond-sparkle of her dark eyes and remembered how sunlight shone in her hair, softer and flowing down past her shoulders then. What year was it? Yes, 1998. In another millennium. She smelled like lemons. Sweet lemons. When did she change her scent?

Once you start seeing the past, pictures fly at you as if falling out of an old album. *Does anyone still keep photo albums?*

He saw Lea's roommate, the lanky, toothy girl with the sexy laugh. Always pushing her coppery hair off her face, twisting it in her fingers, popping her chewing gum with that smile, as if it was some kind of clever joke.

Claire. Lea had moved from Rockford to New York with Claire. Their big adventure. Thank God Claire had a thing for the First Avenue bars, for that's where Mark met Lea. Very romantic. The two of them breathing beer fumes on each other.

Did she feel the instant connection he did? Of course, it was entirely physical. And what a jerk he must have been that night. Trying so hard to impress her with his stories about college life in Madison, and his studies in psychology. He even bragged about his father being such a hot-shit Park Avenue shrink.

Can you imagine? Using his father? Lying beside her, he cringed. Fourteen years later, he shut his eyes and tried to make the hideous memory go away.

Claire. Think about Claire. Claire Shiner. Yes. It took this long for her last name to reboot. Claire got pregnant. What did she expect, picking up men in the bars every weekend? Always so horny and obvious about it. She decided to go home to Rockford to have the baby.

If she hadn't gone home . . .

. . . Lea wouldn't have needed a roommate. Lea, he remembered, worked as an intern at the *New York Press,* a weekly giveaway newspaper. She couldn't afford that East Side apartment she and Claire shared, tiny and sordid and odorous as it was. Would she and Mark have moved in together if Claire hadn't fucked her way back to Rockford?

All so romantic.

The breeze from the open window made him shiver. He wanted to slide under the covers, but he couldn't tell if Lea was awake. *Don't move. This is too nice.*

Too nice. In bed with Lea in the afternoon. A lovemaking matinee like young people. It seldom happened in this crowded house. He listened to the sweep of the curtains making the sunlight dance across their bed.

Silence everywhere else. Ira was swimming at Ethan's house. The twins had pulled on their swimsuits and hurried off to join him. Roz had dropped Elena and Ruth-Ann at the Bridgehampton mall. Roz and Axl were . . . He wasn't quite sure where they were. So hard to keep track of everyone.

So maybe the illicit nature of this rare chance increased his expectations.

No. That wasn't it. Sure, he was eager. He hadn't seen her in a week. And in a way, he wanted to reassure himself that they were okay. That he hadn't screwed up anything.

No. *You're thinking too hard, Mark.*

She had welcomed him with that little sigh from deep in her throat that she always made when he entered her. And he felt the same surge of joy as they began. But it didn't take long to realize that it was different.

Numb.

Such a strangely out-of-place word. But as he moved on top of her, the word invaded his thoughts.

Numb.

And he realized he was doing it all and she was just accepting. She had her arms around his neck and then his waist. But she didn't grasp him with the strength she always had.

And her eyes . . . gazing over his rolling shoulders. Yes, she seemed distant. Numb. She wasn't reacting, and she wasn't trying to hide it.

When he finished, she murmured, "Nice," and her eyes settled on him for a moment before losing their focus and settling back into what seemed to be a hazy world of her own thoughts.

"Lea? Is everything okay? You seem so . . . far away. I could see on your face." He took a breath. "You're still on that island, aren't you?"

It took her a long time to respond. And then she nodded her head, her gaze not on him but at the ceiling. "Yes. Still on the island." Whispered so that the words sent a chill down his neck. "Still on the island. Still back there."

A long sigh. "So many nightmares. Every night. Nightmares pulling me there, pulling me into all that death and horror. I can't get the wailing out of my ears. The wailing and the moaning and the crying. It's like I'm still there. Still there."

She squeezed his hand. "But . . . I want to come back, Mark. I really do."

And then an abrupt move. To break the sadness? Pushing him

aside, she stood up. "The kids will be home soon." It was still a thrill to watch her walk naked across the room. She vanished into the bathroom, and he thought of Autumn.

I can't keep her around. I don't want to ruin my life.

And what could he do to help Lea? The things she saw on that island. He felt as if he could see them, too, in her eyes.

Numb.

She had gone numb.

That will just take time.

He felt a heaviness lower over him, his eyelids suddenly heavy. What a luxury a Saturday-afternoon nap would be. He pulled the quilt up, shut his eyes, and sank into the pillow.

He drifted off. For how long? He didn't know. A gentle tapping sound woke him. He lifted his head to see Lea at her rosewood desk, her head a silhouette in the glow of her laptop monitor, leaning toward the screen and typing rapidly.

She moved her lips when she typed. So cute. It always made him smile. But her back was turned and he could see only the bobbing of her hair, pulled back in a loose ponytail, and the fingers of her right hand tap-dancing over the keys.

"Hi," he called. "How long did I sleep?"

"Not long." She didn't turn around. She was wearing a light green beach cover-up.

Mark pulled himself up. "It's a beautiful day. Feels like summer. Maybe we should round up the kids and drive to the beach. Sagg Main?"

She shook her head. "No. Think I need to get this written."

"The island? Are you getting your experience there in writing?"

She kept typing. Her head nodded toward the screen, then pulled back. "I'm not writing about that."

"What?" He stood up quickly. The breeze from the window tickled his skin. The short sleep had revived him. He did three or four knee bends just to show off to himself.

He walked to the dresser and pulled out a red Nike swimsuit. Tugging it on, he stepped up behind her. "What are you writing about?"

"Something different."

He chuckled and cupped his hands over her shoulders. "You're being secretive?"

"Yes."

He leaned over her shoulder to read what she had written. "You don't have secrets from your husband, do you?"

He thought of Autumn.

She lowered her hands to her lap. "I just . . . have some new ideas."

He squinted at the screen and his eyes scanned her last paragraph:

Tibet's inhuman climate and hard, stony ground makes burial nearly impossible. This is why Buddhists there choose a sky burial. Upon death, the body is chopped into small pieces which are mixed with flour. Then the remains are spread out over a tree to be eaten by scavenging birds.

Mark stood up and released her shoulders. "Lea, what is this? Dead Buddhists in Tibet? Sky burial?"

She turned and raised her face to him. The light from the laptop monitor bathed her in gray. "Death rituals," she said, just above a whisper. "I've been doing some research."

She hadn't said anything funny. Why did she have that strange, guilty smile on her face?

"Your blog," he said. "You're not going to write your travel blog?"

She shook her head. The strange smile remained. "I've kind of lost interest in that."

"But . . . you've put so much time and effort—"

She shrugged and turned her face away. "I can't write it anymore. It's just not interesting to me. You know. I have to write what I'm interested in. I've always been that way."

He blinked at the screen. "But, sweetheart—death rituals? Why death rituals?"

"It's all so fascinating. Did you know there's a province in Madagascar where people pull the dead out from their graves and dance with them? Every seven years, Mark. They dig up their relatives and dance them. Isn't that sweet?"

Sweet?

He took a step back. He watched her type. She leaned toward the screen as if she wanted to dive in. Her eyes were narrowed in concentration.

As if I'm not here.

"Sky burials? Dancing with the dead? Lea? Should I be worried about you?"

38

"Hey, how'd you get here?" Ira raised his head from the fat blue inner tube and squinted at the twins as they pulled back the gate and stepped onto the deck.

"Walked," Daniel answered.

Samuel had never seen anything as beautiful as this pool. It was long and wide, nearly the length of the house. The pool walls were a light blue. Sky blue. The water sparkled with little patches of sunlight. *As if little chunks of the sun had fallen into the pool,* he thought. He wanted to dive in and scoop them up.

He just wanted to sink into the water, immerse himself in the clear, clean cold. Be clear and clean himself. But he knew Daniel had other plans.

"You guys know how to swim?" Ethan sat on the edge of the deep end, blond hair as bright as the sunlight, leaning down to fill a yellow-and-red plastic water blaster.

"We swim," Daniel said. "We lived on an island, remember, lad? Sammy and I swam before we could walk."

"That's cool," Ethan replied. Samuel had never seen a boy so pale, nearly as white as the fence surrounding the pool deck. He could see Ethan's rib cage poking out from his chest.

He's puny for twelve. The boy needs to pump up.

Maybe we can help him. If Daniel doesn't drown the lad today.

Ethan dipped the blaster under the water. Then he raised it and shot a lazy spray of water across the pool to Ira. Floating drowsily on his tube, luxuriating with his eyes closed, Ira didn't even notice.

"Is the water warm?" Samuel dropped to his knees and ran a hand through it. Under the surface, he could feel the spray of cold water shooting into the pool. "Nice."

Ethan aimed carefully and sent a long spray of water into Ira's face. Ira spluttered and dove off the tube. Ethan laughed. He had a dry cackle of a laugh. *Like an old witch,* Samuel thought.

Ira floated beneath the surface. He rose up in front of Ethan and spit a long stream of water onto his legs.

Daniel grabbed the chrome ladder and lowered himself into the water. He pushed himself away from the wall and paddled toward Ira. "How long can you stay underwater?" he asked, bobbing in a spill of gold sunlight.

Ira's head sank into the water again. He rose up and spit another mouthful onto Ethan's legs. Ethan gave him a blast between the eyes with the plastic squirt blaster.

"How long?" Daniel insisted, following Ira across the pool.

Samuel's body felt sticky and drenched with sweat from the walk to Ethan's house. He held his breath and leaped into the deep end. The shock of the cold water made him gasp, and he came up to the surface spluttering.

"Ira can stay underwater for a whole minute," he heard Ethan tell Daniel. "I've seen him."

Daniel eyed Ira. "A whole minute?"

Ira shrugged his skinny shoulders. "Yeah. I guess."

Samuel didn't want to listen. He knew the routine. He ducked underwater and swam the length of the pool. It felt so fresh and cold, and made his body tingle. *Alive. I feel alive.*

When he resurfaced, Daniel was continuing his act. "Do you have a timer?" he called to Ethan.

Ethan set down the water blaster. "There's a stopwatch on my dad's iPhone."

"Go get it," Daniel ordered. "You can time Ira and me." Ethan started to the house. His swimsuit hung on him, down to his knees. "Wait. Ethan, you want to be in the contest?" Daniel's voice made a ringing sound over the water.

Ethan turned back. "I don't want to swim. I have a scrape on my arm. From the cat. And the chlorine makes it hurt."

Ethan is not a superhero, Samuel thought, snickering. He made himself heavy and sank to the pool bottom, then kicked back up. *I could live in the water. Only place I feel alive.*

The kitchen door slammed behind Ethan. Samuel slid onto his back and floated, gazing up at the sun-streaked sky.

"I think I can stay under longer than a minute," Daniel told Ira. The two of them held sides of the tube, bobbing with it. Samuel spotted another inflated float leaning against a green chaise longue. Shaped like a big, gray whale.

That would be fun to ride. But Daniel has his own fun in mind.

"I can maybe do longer than a minute," Ira said without much conviction.

"Want to go first?"

Ira shook his head. "Why don't you go first?"

"Why don't you both go under at the same time?" Ethan said, reappearing on the deck with iPhone in hand.

Daniel slipped off the tube and swung himself around to face Ethan. "No. I want the Ira lad to hold me under."

Ira made a kind of squawking sound. *"What?"*

"Hold my hair," Daniel instructed. "Push me under. Hold me down, okay? You have to hold me or I'll float to the top, and you'll win."

Ira slid off the tube and pushed it toward the side of the pool. "You really want me to hold you under?"

Daniel nodded. "Just grab my hair and push down on my head."

"But how will I know when you want to come up?"

"No worries," Daniel told him. "I'll give a signal."

"You sure?"

Daniel grinned at him, dimples flashing. "Yes, I'm sure. Sure I'll win."

Samuel sighed. He dove under again. Peaceful down below. *Daniel should have been an actor.* Samuel surfaced, shaking water from his thick blond hair.

"Go!" Ethan cried from the deck, eyes on the phone in his hand.

Daniel let Ira push him under the surface. Ira gripped Daniel's hair and held his head down.

"Hold on tight," Samuel said, bobbing closer. "Don't let him come up."

"He . . . said he'd signal," Ira said, obviously not sure about this contest.

Samuel floated in a circle around Ira. Ira kept Daniel down with one hand, paddled the surface with the other.

"Push him," Samuel said. "Keep pushing."

"But—"

"One minute," Ethan called. He dropped onto the edge of a deck chair, concentrating on the phone. Samuel could see that Ethan's slender shoulders were already pink. Sunburned.

"It's kind of hard to keep him from floating up," Ira said.

"Keep pushing," Samuel told him. "He has big lungs. He can stay down a long time."

"He hasn't signaled," Ira said.

Samuel watched his brother float under the rippling water, his arms limp and relaxed at his sides, legs not moving.

"Two minutes," Ethan called.

"I . . . I think your brother wins," Ira said. "Two minutes. Wow. I can't—"

"Hold him under," Samuel said. "Don't ruin his turn. He gets angry if you ruin his turn."

"Did he just signal?" Ira very tense now. The strain showing on his face, pale, his features tight. "I thought I saw him signal." The muscle in the arm holding down Daniel quivered.

"Not yet," Samuel said.

Underwater, Daniel floated perfectly upright, arms limp and relaxed.

"Three minutes," Ethan called, jumping to his feet. "That's

enough, right?" He stepped to the edge of the pool, gazing down at Daniel's unmoving form. "People can't stay under this long—can they?"

"He . . . hasn't signaled," Ira said in a wavering voice.

Samuel and Ira both watched a string of bubbles float up from Daniel's mouth.

"Is that the signal? He said he'd signal."

"Four minutes. Are you sure he's okay?" Ethan lowered the phone. "I mean really. Is he okay? Four minutes?"

They all saw Daniel's head slump forward under the water. His head bent and one last bubble slid up to the surface. Then his legs suddenly splayed, and his arms floated limply to the top.

"Let go of him!" Samuel screamed. "Something's wrong, Ira. Let go of him—now!"

Ira gasped and swallowed a mouthful of water. His hand flew off Daniel's head.

Released, Daniel's body rose to the surface. His face appeared for only a moment, eyes closed, water spilling from his open jaw. Then his body tilted forward and he dropped facedown, arms outstretched and limp.

"Daniel! Daniel! Get up!" Samuel screamed. "Daniel! Daniel!"

Ira uttered another hoarse squawk. He gaped, eyes bulging at the floating, lifeless raft that was Daniel.

"Daniel! Daniel!"

Ira dove toward Daniel. Grabbed his arm. Tried to tug him up.

But he remained facedown, bobbing on the surface, arms and legs floating at such odd angles, as if they were all independent of each other.

"You *killed* him!" Samuel shrieked. He slapped the water angrily with both hands. Slapped it. Slapped it hard until it churned around him. "Ira—no! No! Ira—you *killed* him! You killed my bruvver!"

A hoarse cry escaped Ira's throat.

Ethan stood on the edge of the pool, his body trembling. He had left the phone on the deck. His hands were pressed against the sides of his face.

"Nooooooo." Ira wailed. "He didn't signal. It wasn't my *fault!*" He turned to Ethan. "Get help! Hurry!"

Ethan didn't move. "My parents—they're not home!"

Samuel splashed over to his brother. "Help me pull him out. Maybe we can get him breathing."

Another moan escaped Ira's open mouth. His eyes spun. His mouth twitched.

His face is going out of control. The poor kid is totally dazed.

Ira flailed across the water and grabbed Daniel's arm. And that's when Daniel lifted his head, shot straight up, turned grinning to Ira, and let out a loud laugh.

"Oh." Ira's hand slid off Daniel. The startled kid fell back, dipping underwater for a second before reappearing, his face showing his disbelief.

Daniel gave him a hard two-handed shove and laughed again, shaking water from his hair.

"You're okay? He's okay?" Ethan shouted from the side, his voice high and shrill. "Is he really okay?"

Ira still hadn't spoken. He bobbed in place, eyes on Daniel.

"Why'd you let me up?" Daniel pushed Ira again, more gently this time. "I didn't signal. I wasn't finished."

"But . . ." Ira struggled to find words. "It was five minutes."

Daniel laughed. "Did you forget? I *told* you Sammy and I were swimming before we could walk."

"But . . . that's impossible." Ira shook his head. "Five minutes?"

"I can't believe he's okay," Ethan called. "Hey, get out of the pool. Let's get some snacks or something. Come on. I can't stop shaking. Get out, guys."

Samuel could see that Ira would love to climb out of the water and catch his breath. But Daniel raised a hand. "Whoa. It's Ira's turn."

"Huh? No way." Ira slid back, rippling the water. "No way. I can't stay under for five minutes. You win."

Daniel grabbed Ira's shoulder. "You have to take your turn. Maybe you'll do better than a minute. That would be cool, right, lad?"

Ira didn't reply. "No. You win, Daniel. Let's get out."

Daniel grabbed Ira's hair. "Take your turn. Let's see how you do. Give me a signal. Just wave your arms when your chest starts to hurt. Okay?"

He didn't wait for Ira's reply. He gave him a hard push and sent him sinking. Ira's head disappeared under the water.

Samuel knew the smile on Daniel's face. He'd seen it before.

Behind him, he heard a splash. He turned to see that Ethan had dropped into the pool. He was wading toward them. "Ira can only do a minute. I've seen him."

Daniel gripped Ira's hair tightly. He kept his arm stiff, pushing the boy down. A few bubbles escaped Ira's mouth.

Daniel, still smiling, turned to Ethan. "What about keeping count? What are you doing here? You're supposed to time him."

Ethan peered down at Ira. "I told you. He can only do a minute."

A shadow swept over them as two large birds flapped overhead, squawking loudly. Samuel glanced up quickly. He lowered his eyes in time to see Daniel slide his other hand over Ira's head and push down with both hands.

Ira's legs kicked slowly. Distorted by the water, they reminded Samuel of pale, rubbery snakes. And then the boy's arms shot out. He began waving wildly.

Ethan stared at Daniel. "The signal. He wants to come up."

Daniel pushed down on Ira's head with both hands. The smile never left his face.

Ira kicked and thrashed. He tried to twist his head out from Daniel's grasp. But Daniel held on tight. A stream of bubbles rose up from Ira's mouth.

"Let him up!" Ethan shouted. "He's signaling. He's done."

Daniel held on tight, not moving. His jaw was clenched, nostrils flaring.

"Let him up! Come on, Daniel. Let him up!"

Ira shot his feet out. Twisted his head. Raised both fists above the surface. Beneath the water, his body flopped like a frantic fish caught on a hook.

Daniel scrunched up his face, his eyes shut, and pushed down on the struggling boy's hair, holding his head under the surface.

Samuel wanted to sink under the water and never emerge.

Please, Daniel, don't do it. Please don't do it this time.

Please stop now. Yes, I know why you are doing it. I know the new pa doesn't want us. I know you want to rule the pool. But, please, Daniel. It's too soon.

Please don't do it to Ira. Please.

39

"Why is Axl crying?"

Roz squinted at Mark. "Why does the sun come up every morning? You're the child shrink. You tell *me*."

Mark set down the book he'd been reading, a treatise about how sibling order determines your fate. *So interesting how often the oldest sibling is the achiever in the family.* He pulled off his reading glasses and folded them carefully. He grinned at his sister. "Maybe he's hungry."

"Oh, wow. Genius. I never would have thought of that." Roz rolled her eyes. She tossed the ball of dirty laundry she was carrying onto his lap.

He pulled a red pajama top off his head. "He's bored, that's all. Let's pick up the boys and take everyone to the ocean."

Roz started grabbing up the dirty clothes. "I thought doing the laundry might be more fun."

She turned as Axl came toddling into the room. "Beach! Beach! Beach!" He could always stop crying in a split second.

Mark chuckled. "He was listening to us."

"He listens to everything," Roz said. "He's a little spy."

"Beach! Beach! Beach!" He reached for his mom to pick him up, but her arms were full of laundry. So he wrapped his hands around her knees.

"Where are the boys?"

"At Ethan's house. All three of them. We'll have to pull them from the pool. I'll probably have to bribe them with ice cream to get them to come with us."

"They'll come. Axl, let go of me. I can't walk. Is Lea coming?"

"No. She's working. I'm not sure what's up with her. She's writing a piece about death rituals."

Roz squinted at him. "Odd."

"Yes. Odd."

"It's that island. The hurricane. She saw so much death. I think she's having trouble shaking it from her mind."

"We'll have to be very nice to her." Roz struggled across the room with Axl clinging to one leg. Giggling. He'd turned her into an amusement park ride. "The ocean will tire him out. That's good. Only thing I hate is that he eats the beach."

Mark nodded. "He's definitely a sand eater. I had to pry a huge glob of sand from his mouth last time, remember? Maybe he learned his lesson."

"Learned his lesson? Go ahead. Say something stupider than that. We'll just have to watch him like a hawk."

"Yes. Like a hawk. I'll start loading up the car. We'll take your SUV. More room."

"Do we need food?"

"No. Bring something for Axl. We're only going for an hour. No one will starve. And we can buy them ice cream from the truck in the parking lot."

"Let me just drop this laundry in the machine." She turned back to him. "This is the twins' stuff. It's so clean, you'd think they didn't wear it." She held up a white T-shirt. "But look at this. This ragged, dark spot on the sleeve? I think it's a burn mark."

"A burn mark?"

"Yes. The sleeve was definitely burned. Weird?"

"Weird." Mark stared at it. "Hope they're not playing with matches in their private hideaway back there."

"They love it back there, Mark."

"Really? Think they're happy here?"

"Well . . . I walked by the guesthouse last night after supper and I heard them in there giggling and giggling."

"Think they already feel at home?"

"They have funny jokes. One of them kept saying, 'smoked meat, smoked meat,' and then they'd laugh and laugh."

"I don't get the joke."

"They were being silly. I think they're doing a great job of fitting in. I mean, losing their family and all, moving from their home, it can't be easy."

Mark climbed to his feet. He glanced at his laptop monitor. No email. No one ever emailed him on Saturday. "Well, we'll see how they fit in. I mean, we haven't asked much of them. They live by themselves in the back. They don't share much about school with us. They don't—"

"Mark, there was a horrible murder right in our driveway. Maybe they even witnessed it. But they haven't seemed messed up by it. They haven't acted out or anything."

"I think it's good they went swimming with Ira. That's encouraging. They're the same age, so if they manage to bond with Ira, maybe . . ."

His voice drifted off. He still had major doubts about the whole thing.

He went upstairs to give Lea one more chance to come along with them, but she was captured in the glow of her laptop screen. Were her eyes glassy or just reflecting the light of the monitor?

"We're going to the ocean. I'm going to pick up Ira and the twins. Want to come with us?"

She mumbled something he couldn't hear and kept typing without turning her head. He couldn't help but be annoyed. "Sweetheart, don't you want to spend some time with the boys?"

Another mumbled reply.

He forced a laugh. "I'm going to have to pick you up and carry you away from that keyboard, aren't I."

She waved him away. "I need to get this all down, Mark."

He kissed the back of her neck, changed into a swimsuit and sleeveless T-shirt, found his Tevas, and hurried outside. Roz was struggling to fasten Axl in his car seat. "Just think. Only six more years of this. Lucky, huh?"

Mark laughed. "That's what I love about you, Roz. Always thinking on the bright side."

"Maybe I shouldn't have put the suntan lotion on him first. He keeps sliding out of the seat."

Mission accomplished with Axl, Roz climbed into the backseat beside him and they drove the few blocks to Ethan's house. The sun, still high in the afternoon sky, filtered through the trees, sending flickering light dancing over the windshield. On the side of the street, a dead squirrel had attracted the attention of several hungry blackbirds. The passing car didn't even make them flutter a wing or interrupt their feast.

Mark pulled the car to the bottom of the driveway. The three garage doors were open. No cars in view. Wasn't anyone home to watch the boys in the pool?

He left the air-conditioner running for Roz and Axl and climbed out of the car. It was a hot day, more like summer than May, a great beach day. Sunlight bounced off the front of the white frame house. He took a few steps up the smooth paved driveway. A chipmunk darted out of the garage, into the yard.

A few doors down he heard the low drone of a power mower. Across the street, two little girls rode pink and yellow tricycles up and down a driveway.

Nearly to the front of the house, Mark stopped to listen. The silence disturbed him. No splashing. No boys' voices. Usually they were decimating each other with water blasters, cannonballing into the pool and jumping out, shouting and wrestling and splashing.

Today silence.

They never went indoors when they could be in the pool.

A sudden feeling of dread made the back of his neck tingle. Too quiet. Too quiet. His legs felt heavy as lead as he started to jog toward the back.

Is something wrong back there?

What's going on?

He was breathing hard by the time he reached the white picket fence. Still silent back there. "Hey—where is everybody?"

He pulled the gate. When it didn't budge, he pushed it. He stumbled onto the deck and saw them immediately.

Oh my God.

Was that Ira? Yes. Ira flat on his back. Stretched out straight on the deck beside the pool. Daniel and Samuel on their knees, hovering over him, faces narrowed in concern.

Ira flat, his face pale white, head straight up, arms and legs so stiff at his sides. Not moving.

Not moving.

Ira. Not moving.

40

A few minutes earlier. Daniel pushed down on Ira's head. The boy kept thrashing and squirming under the churning water, but weakly now.

"Be careful," Samuel said, tugging his brother's arm. "Don't get carried away. You just want to scare him, Daniel. You don't want to drown him, do you? *Do* you?"

Daniel's eyes were wild and distant at the same time. Samuel always wondered what he was seeing at times like these. Samuel knew what *he* saw. An endless dark chasm stretching beyond them forever.

"Daniel, please—"

Daniel blinked, as if coming to consciousness. He lowered his hands around the struggling boy's waist and, with a grunt, hoisted him out of the water.

Ira emerged coughing and choking, eyes wide, water rolling off him, legs still churning. Daniel held him high, allowed him to spew up a stream of water, cough and groan and sputter.

Behind them, Ethan shrieked at the top of his voice: "Are you okay? Is he okay? Is he okay? Ira?"

Samuel thought he could see the heartbeats in the boy's bony white chest. Now Ira made hoarse vomiting sounds, dredging up only pool water.

Daniel held him up, his biceps round and hard, too developed for a twelve-year-old. But Samuel knew where his twin's strength came from.

Ira's hair was matted over his face like a clump of dark seaweed. His head was down, arms limp at his sides, legs finally still.

"Is he okay? Is he breathing? Is he going to be okay?"

Samuel gave Ethan a reassuring thumbs-up.

Ira grew quieter. His chest still heaved but the choking and vomiting had ceased. He raised his head slowly, groaning. He brushed the wet clump of hair off his eyes with one hand.

Daniel laughed. "You did it, laddy!" he cried exultantly.

Ira squinted at Daniel, struggling to focus. "Did it?" His voice a choked whisper.

"A minute-twenty!" Daniel declared. "You broke your old record. I knew you could do it!"

Ira just stared at him, his face vacant, obviously trying to decide Daniel's intent. Did Daniel just try to drown him? Was he playing a vicious game? Or was he really trying to help Ira break his underwater record?

Daniel kept the grin on his face. "Way to go, lad. Next time, a minute and a half." He lowered Ira gently into the water. Then he turned to Samuel. "Wasn't that amazing?"

"Amazing," Samuel echoed.

"But you *forced* him," Ethan protested. "Didn't you see he wanted to come up?"

"I knew he could break his record," Daniel insisted.

"C-cold," Ira stammered. "I'm . . . getting out." He started to paddle weakly toward the side, gliding as if in slow motion.

"Get him some more towels," Daniel ordered Ethan. "Maybe a sweatshirt or something."

Ethan splashed out of the pool. His bare feet thudded on the deck, leaving dark footprints as he disappeared into the house. As soon as he was gone, Daniel nodded to Samuel.

Samuel knew the routine.

Each taking an arm, they led Ira out of the pool. "Th-thanks," Ira stuttered. The poor kid was shaking.

"Here. Lie down in the sun," Daniel instructed in his most gentle voice. *Like a harmless little boy,* Samuel thought.

They helped Ira onto his back on the sun-hot deck boards. He stretched out flat, water running off him, still breathing hard, shuddering.

"Ssssh. Relax," Daniel whispered. He turned expectantly to Samuel.

Time for me to go to work.

It was so funny, actually. Daniel was the angry one. The bold one. Face it—the evil twin. Daniel was the one who wanted to act. Daniel wanted to rule the pool or rule the school or rule the fools.

Samuel knew he was different. He was shy. He was peace-loving and calm. No, *not* kind or sweet or feeling. But calm, at least. Not eager.

So funny, since Sammy was Death Man.

Sammy was the killer-man. Sammy had the beam, the ray, the whatever-you-want-to-call-it. Sammy had the heat. The burn. The furnace. Go ahead—say it: the fire of *Hell.*

Yes, together on the island where the dead met the living, they stepped out of a blood rain. Yes, the blood was on their shoulders and in their hearts. The blood splashed at their feet and puddled all around them, ran down their faces and stained their skin as well as their clothes.

Like a nightmare. I know we are nightmares.

And the strange part: Daniel brought the anger. But Sammy brought the death.

Now Daniel eyed him eagerly. Samuel leaned over Ira, brought his face close to the shivering boy's, and began to fire up his eyes.

Samuel's eyes clicked as if someone had bumped a switch. And they began to light instantly. The white around the pupils darkened to pink, and then the pupils disappeared into the growing red glow.

Like the coiled burners on an electric stove, Samuel's eyes reddened and the heat began to radiate. His eyes were bright fire now, hot neon, red and hypnotic.

So hypnotic, Ira made no attempt to move or look away.

"Easy," Daniel warned, bumping Samuel's arm. "Don't burn

him. Back off a bit. You'll blind him. We don't want to hurt him. We only want to open his mind. Easy. Easy. We don't want Mum to see that he is changed."

"Okay, boyo. I'm being careful," Samuel whispered. "Hurry. Ethan will be back." He could see the red-glare reflection of his eyes in Ira's eyes. "I'm just holding him. Not burning him. Go ahead. Tell his brain who is boss."

Samuel was always surprised that he couldn't feel the heat. Burning embers. No. Burning lasers. His eyes radiated blistering heat. But he couldn't feel a thing.

Daniel leaned over the prone figure. Ira was hypnotized in the red glow.

"Okay, bruvver, I helped you today," Daniel said, eyes on the glass doors of the house, watching warily for Ethan's return. "Now we will stick together, boyo. Stick together like bruvvers. Yes?"

Silence for a second. Samuel kept the light on Ira's face. "Yes," Ira answered. Robotlike. But he gave the correct answer.

"Bruvvers forever," Daniel murmured. "Even closer than bruvvers. And we'll all be together day and night, all together we'll rule the school."

"Yes," Ira said, this time without hesitating. He almost sounded enthusiastic.

Good boy.

Daniel gave Samuel the nod. The job had been done. Ira's mind had been fixed. Samuel shut his eyes. He could feel a little prickling heat on the backs of his eyelids. He kept his eyes shut until they cooled.

When he opened them, he saw the new pa burst through the gate and stride onto the deck, his chest heaving up and down. "What's wrong? Hey—what's wrong?" In a panic.

Daniel helped Ira to a sitting position. "Wave at your pa," he whispered.

Ira waved.

"Is Ira okay?" The new pa hurried up to them. Samuel saw the sweat stain on the front of his sleeveless tee.

"I'm fine, Dad. We were just taking a break," Ira said.

"We had an awesome swim, don't you know," Daniel said. "Then we did some tricks in the water. And had some contests."

"Ira can hold his breath a long time," Samuel told him.

Ira nodded. "I beat my old record, Dad."

The new pa studied Ira's face, as if he still thought something had gone wrong. "When I saw you lying on the deck like that . . ."

"Just relaxing," Ira said. "What's the big deal, Dad?"

"Where's Ethan?"

Ethan reappeared as if on cue, carrying a stack of towels. "What's up? Is Ira okay?"

"Of course I'm okay," Ira insisted.

Ethan squinted at Ira, confused.

"Ethan, want to come to the ocean with us?" the new pa asked, wiping sweat off his forehead with the front of his shirt. "We have room."

"No. Thanks. My mom said I had to stay home. She went to Cromer's to get dinner. She'll be back any minute."

"Okay. Next time. Let's hurry, guys. I left Roz and Axl in the car."

Daniel helped Ira to his feet. He kept his arm around Ira's shoulders as they made their way to the car. "I see you two are bonding," the new pa said.

No one replied to that.

At the gate, Samuel turned back to Ethan. "Can I borrow this towel?" He held up the ragged white towel.

"No problem," Ethan called. "Bring it back next time, okay?"

Samuel followed the others to the black SUV at the bottom of the drive. The boys greeted Roz and Axl. "Put beach towels down on the seats," she told them. "Don't get the car all wet."

"Roz, it's a beach car," Pa told her. "It's supposed to get wet."

"Wet," Axl repeated, and laughed.

Ira climbed into the passenger seat next to Pa. Samuel followed Daniel to the back. They climbed up next to the beach basket and supplies.

The car bumped off the driveway, onto the street. At the side of the road, Samuel saw big blackbirds feasting on the carcass of a stiff, dead squirrel.

After they had driven for a few minutes, Samuel poked his twin. Daniel turned from the window. Samuel grinned at him. "You win a prize," he whispered.

Daniel's eyebrows slid up. "What did you get?"

Samuel slowly unrolled the towel. Then, grinning, he revealed the prize inside. The iPhone Ethan had used to time the underwater contest.

Daniel started to giggle and soon Samuel was giggling too.

"What's so funny?" Roz asked.

"We're just happy lads," Daniel answered.

41

At police headquarters on Division Street in Sag Harbor, Andy Pavano didn't have his own office. There was a cubicle by the men's room that had been promised him. But it was filled nearly to the ceiling with junk, mainly old computer equipment and fax machines, and no one in the department seemed eager or even willing to clear it out for him.

Maybe they were waiting for him to do it himself, Andy thought. In the meantime, he was squatting in the office of Angie Donato, the one woman in the department, who was out on maternity leave. The only redecorating he had done to make it his own was to turn all her family photos to the wall because her four kids were really ugly. Beasts. No exaggeration.

Waiting for a meeting in which he knew he and Pinto were going to be bounced off the Hulenberger murder case, he sat on the edge of his (her) desk with the phone pressed to his ear, enjoying Sari's voice even though she wasn't saying anything promising to him.

The air-conditioning was on the fritz, so a large floor fan hummed and squeaked in the corner, making it hard to hear her. "What did you say? You what?"

"Rod and I are serious about each other, Andy. I mean, I don't know how serious. But—"

"Sari, please tell me his name isn't Rod. You're not going with a guy in a tennis hat named Rod."

"You're making jokes. He's a nice guy. He's nice to me. He—"

"You know you still feel something for me. At the theater the other night . . ."

"I told you that was nothing. Sure, there are leftover feelings. From before. Sure, we both have them. But come on. That's what they are. Leftovers."

Marie, the office secretary, began having a heated conversation with a lanky young cop in the hall outside his door. Andy turned his back and tried to drown out their voices.

He missed some of what Sari was saying. He just caught the name *Susannah*.

"Sari, what? What about Susannah?"

"How long were you married, Andy? Did you cheat on her, too?"

Ouch. That brought a physical pain, a sharp stab to the pit of his stomach.

"That's cold, Sari. That's not fair. You don't know anything about me and Susannah. And I didn't cheat on you. I—"

"You were a shit, Andy. You were a total shit."

"How about lunch?"

He heard her breath catch.

"Just a quick lunch at the Paradise. We won't be serious. No serious stuff. Just talk. Like old friends."

"You sound too desperate."

"Does that mean yes?"

She laughed. "Can Rod come, too?"

"Aaaaagggh." He let out a frustrated growl.

Pinto poked his big balding head into the doorway. "Are you having phone sex again?"

Andy tried to wave him away.

"Big Pavano is calling. Time to have our heads chopped," Pinto said, motioning for him to come to the chief's office.

Since Andy arrived on the force, the chief was always referred to as Big Pavano, which was a joke, since Andy was a head taller and had him by at least thirty pounds. But rank was everything, even on a police force of seven.

Andy waved Pinto away again and pressed his face against the phone. "Have to go. We'll set a date for lunch, okay?"

But Sari had already hung up.

Michael Pavano—as stated to anyone who commented, no relation to Andy Pavano—did not have the cliché looks of a local Long Island police chief. Yes, he had been a marine. Had a pretty good career, working his way up the ranks to master sergeant because he was smart and obedient and liked to follow the rules, felt more comfortable following the rules, liked a structured life and the sense of order the corps offered.

But when it was suggested he be moved to internal affairs, he balked and then resigned his commission. He had no interest in plotting investigations of men who had worked hard enough to become U.S. Marines.

The switch to a uniform in the Boston Police Department seemed natural, but he struggled to find the kind of structure he had as a marine. Of course, it didn't exist. So when a friend suggested the job opening in the Sag Harbor Department, it seemed like an escape and an opportunity at the same time.

To Andy's mind, Big Pavano didn't look like a marine or a cop. For one thing, he was short and slender. (He said he'd made the marine height requirement by standing on tiptoe, a rare joke for someone normally humorless.) He didn't have the beer pouch of an ex-soldier who had relaxed his standards. He had a full crop of straight black hair, streaked with gray at the sides, and a friendly face, warm blue-gray eyes that somehow always managed to look sympathetic.

There was a sadness about Big Pavano, Andy thought. Maybe because he'd always been married to his post, never had a wife or family.

He had three folding chairs waiting facing the desk in his small, nearly bare office, and motioned for Andy and Pinto to sit down.

As they did, a toweringly tall, light-skinned black man in a blue cop uniform ducked his head under the doorframe and stepped into the room.

"This is Captain Franks," Pavano said, "from the State Criminal Investigation Bureau. I called him in because . . . well . . . you know why."

"Morning, Sergeants." Franks nodded solemnly to them. He had short black hair receding on his broad forehead. His dark eyes studied them with interest, moving from Pinto and Andy. His broad nose had obviously been broken a few times. He had a long scar, old, across his chin.

Tough dude.

He was broad-chested, built like a heavyweight fighter, his uniform jacket stretched tight over his uniform shirt. His state cop badge caught the light from the ceiling fluorescents. Andy saw that he had a standard Glock .22—the policeman's favorite—in the black holster at his waist.

Chief Pavano dropped into the folding chair next to Andy, perching as erect as a marine. Franks stepped behind the desk and leaned his massive fists on top of the scattered papers on the desktop.

"So what do we have here?" he asked. He had a James Earl Jones voice, booming despite his attempt to speak softly. He wasn't asking a question, Andy knew. No one tried to answer.

"We have a man murdered in bizarre fashion inside a car in another man's driveway." Franks answered his own question. "The method of murder indicates that the killer had some strength and also used some sort of heat-producing weapon. Am I correct so far?"

Big Pavano coughed. "That's what we have, all right, Captain."

Andy scraped at some loose skin on the back of his thumb. He knew that he and Pinto were being removed from the case and Franks was taking charge. Why did Franks have to put on a show first?

"Now, we have blood all over the man's car," Franks continued, almost as if talking to himself. "The victim's windpipe is fucking tossed on the backseat, ripped from his throat. And his throat has been burned open. We have a gaping hole there, right, and the skin is scorched black. Like someone tried to fucking barbecue him."

Chief Pavano nodded grimly. Andy and Pinto stared straight ahead. Andy's stomach rumbled. He pictured the wet, blood-tipped pink noodle stretched on the backseat of the car. It made him sick every time he thought of it.

"With all that blood and ripped skin, we should have some evidence," Franks boomed. "The weapon. Fingerprints on the blowtorch? The killer had to reach in through the open window, yes? So how about a fingerprint or two on the side of the fucking car?"

"We took that car apart in the lab in Riverhead," Chief Pavano told him. "I mean, bolt by bolt, Captain. We dusted it and X-rayed it and lasered it and micro—whatever those guys can fucking do these days. We did everything but *taste* it. And we came up with nothing. Prints from a tennis ball. Kiddie prints."

Franks rubbed the scar on his chin, gazing at Chief Pavano thoughtfully. "Well, what *don't* we have here? We don't have a psycho serial killer, right? We don't have a Hannibal Lecter. At least the killer didn't *eat* the fucking windpipe. And God knows, we haven't had similar murders we can tie to this one."

"We don't have a lot of murders in Sag Harbor, Franks," Pinto murmured. "It's a quiet little village, you know."

Franks nodded. He pulled out a small key chain and twirled it in one hand. "So . . . we rule out serial killer. We have to look closer to home, don't we? I think I've gone over this story enough. Try this on for size. The psychologist, Sutter, writes a book that people don't like. He has a book tour. He gets booed and yelled at in one city, then another. Everywhere he fucking goes. City after city, people are angry at him. He comes home. Maybe he's upset. Maybe he's overwrought from all the abuse. Maybe the sonofabitch is about to lose it.

"So how does it go down? He needs money to pay the mortgage on his beautiful house by the bay. And he and his wife have just adopted two more kids. She doesn't work. The load is all on him. It's making him crazy. Nothing but stress and anger and abuse.

"He thinks he's going to get a big grant. He's *counting* on the fucking grant to keep him afloat. Then this guy Hulenberger arrives and tells him no way, José. Like a punch in the face, right? And Sutter fucking loses it. He runs outside, grabs his blowtorch from the garage, runs to the car in the driveway in a fucking insane rage and makes a mess of Hulenberger."

Silence for a long moment. Andy heard phones ringing down the hall. He heard Marie at the front desk laughing about something. A siren started up with a growl in a black-and-white out in the parking lot.

"Sutter seemed distressed by the murder in his driveway. But he didn't seem whacked-out or overly stressed," Pinto offered. "He seemed to have it together whenever Andy and I talked to him."

Franks frowned at Pinto. "So?"

"He had an excuse for the blowtorch. So we combed the house," Big Pavano said, shaking his head. "I mean, every inch. Tore up floors and everything, Captain. No other weapon."

Franks turned his glare on Pavano. "So?"

Silence again.

Franks turned to Andy. "Any thoughts?"

Andy realized he was tapping one shoe on the floor. He forced his leg to stop. "Maybe you're on the right track," he said, thinking hard. "It's just . . . no one saw anything. His two boys, the twins . . . they were playing ball in the front yard. They didn't see anything or anyone."

"Are they lying?" Franks demanded, leaning over the desk. "They're twelve, right? Twelve-year-olds can lie, yes? If they're frightened? If somebody scared them or threatened them?" He twirled the key chain. "Or if they want to protect their new father?"

Andy shuffled his feet. Did Franks want them to *disprove* his theory? Or was he the kind of cop who only wanted to be backed up in everything he said?

"We've talked to the twins twice with a psychologist in the room, Captain," Big Pavano said. "She found no evidence—"

"I think we have our suspect," Franks interrupted, slapping his hands together like cymbals. "There's a lot we don't know—yet. But we know it's Sutter. So let's get back to work and fucking nail him."

Chief Pavano jumped up and, adjusting his black uniform tie, stepped behind the desk to get to Franks. Leaning their heads together, they started to talk in low tones. Andy and Pinto remained seated, exchanging glances.

Finally, Andy spoke up. "You mean . . . Chaz and I . . . we're still working this murder?"

"We're sticking with you," Franks said. "You haven't screwed it up too badly so far. I'll be here. I'll be watching over everything. With your captain, of course. You go ahead and nail this sonofabitch. You'll be stars. You want to be fucking stars—don't you?"

Andy wasn't so sure. He nodded to the two captains and followed Pinto out of the room. When they were back in Andy's makeshift office, they both let out long whooshes of air, although there was no reason to feel relieved.

"You think Sutter did it?" Andy asked.

"I do now" was Pinto's reply.

PART FOUR

42

Breakfast Monday morning. Mark pulled on gray sweats. He thought maybe he'd run on the sand along Long Beach this morning. Downstairs, he was surprised to find Lea already in the kitchen, coffee made, a stack of frozen waffles ready for the toaster.

She wore a short, sheer green beach cover-up over a black one-piece swimsuit. Her hair was tied loosely back with a green hair scrunchie. She turned and smiled as he entered the kitchen. When he walked over and picked up a white coffee mug from beside the coffeemaker, she raised her face to him and kissed him tenderly behind the ear.

The kiss sent a tingle down his neck. He turned with a smile. He rubbed her cheek with two fingers. "What was that for?"

"An apology," she said. Her dark eyes stayed on his.

"Apology?"

"I've been . . . sort of distant since I got home. I'm sorry."

"I noticed," he said. "The island?"

She turned to the counter, lifted her mug, and took a long sip of black coffee. "I . . . I dream about it every night. Really. Every night."

He took her by the shoulders. "I'm really sorry."

"I hear those people screaming and crying. I see all those bodies.

Bodies piled up everywhere. *Parts* of bodies. Houses all broken and destroyed. Will I ever get over it?"

"Sure, you will," he said. Stupid, inadequate answer. He drew her close. He kissed her. Coffee breath, but he didn't mind. "Maybe you should see someone. I know some doctors in the city you might feel comfortable with."

She hesitated. "Maybe."

He kissed her again. Then he pulled his head back and studied her. "The twins. Daniel and Samuel. Do they keep reminding you of all the horror you saw? Are they keeping you from pushing it from your mind?"

She raised a hand to his mouth. "Stop. Don't even think it. You have to stop being so negative about them, Mark. I really care about them."

"Sorry. As long as—"

"I'm going to be better. I promise. I'm back. You'll see. It's just the shock of everything. Now that the travel blog is over, I—"

"Are you sure you want to end it? I know you're not a quitter. You came to New York with a goal and—"

She lowered her eyes. Her hair fell over her face. "I'm not quitting. I'm just changing."

"Well, at least you won't be traveling. Nice if you'll be home all the time." He raised his hands to her cheeks and started to kiss her again. But a cough interrupted.

Elena appeared in the doorway. "Yuck. Are you two kissing this early in the morning?"

"No." Mark lowered his hands from Lea's shoulders and took a step back. "Well, maybe yes. So what if we were?"

Elena didn't answer. She pulled open the fridge door. "Isn't there any cranberry juice? You know I hate orange juice. No one here drinks orange juice. It's too fattening. Why do you keep buying it?"

"So you'll have something to complain about," Mark said. "And hey, maybe I drink it? And maybe Axl drinks it too?"

She pulled out a yogurt container and closed the door. "Could you buy better juice? You know Ruth-Ann is coming for our sleepover Friday night. Do we have to have this grocery-store apple juice? Can't you at least buy Martinelli's?"

Mark laughed. "I had no idea juice was so important in your life."

"Dad, do you think you could stop laughing at me just for a few minutes?"

That caught him by surprise. Was he teasing her too much? Fourteen-year-olds were so sensitive.

"Where's your brother?" Lea said, pouring more coffee into her mug. "Is he getting dressed?"

"I don't know." Elena checked the date on the container bottom. Then she tugged off the top and started to stir the yogurt. "He wasn't in his room. I thought he was down here."

Lea blinked. "Not in his room? What do you mean?"

Elena stopped stirring. She scrunched up her face, as if concentrating. "You know, I think his bed was made. Like he hadn't slept in it."

"Huh?" Lea uttered a sharp cry. "Are you serious?"

"That's impossible," Mark said. "Go get him."

"Can't I finish my yogurt first?"

The kitchen door opened. Daniel and Samuel walked in. Mark squinted at them. They looked more disheveled than usual. Their hair hadn't been brushed and stood up in white-blond clumps over their heads. Daniel's jeans had a stain in front. Samuel's black T-shirt was wrinkled, tucked in in front but hanging over his jeans in back.

"Morning, Mum and Pa," Daniel murmured.

As they made their way toward the breakfast table, Mark and Lea gasped at the same time. "Whoa. What's on your faces?"

Mark nearly did a coffee spit. Each boy had a two-inch blue arrow, pointing up, on one cheek. "Hey, stop right there." He set down the coffee mug before he spilled it.

"Those aren't tattoos—are they?" Lea demanded.

The twins giggled. "No. Just the face paint, don't you know," Daniel answered.

Elena stood gawking with her yogurt spoon halfway to her mouth. "You painted arrows on your cheeks?"

The boys nodded. Daniel's wide grin made his dimples flare.

Mark reminded himself he needed to stay calm and not overreact. "But—why?" He kept his voice low and steady. "What do they mean?"

"We're going *up,*" Daniel said, his grin not fading.

"We want to be cool," Samuel added. He popped two waffles into the toaster and pushed them down.

"That is *definitely* not cool," Mark said.

He stared at the arrows, so shiny and dark on the boys' pale skin.

"Definitely not cool," he repeated. "You have to go take them off. I can't let you go to school like that."

"But, Pa—" Daniel started.

"He's right. For once," Elena said. "Not cool, guys. Actually, we're talking freaky here."

The grin finally faded from Daniel's face and his blue eyes appeared to darken, as if a storm cloud had rolled over them. "We want to rule the school, Pa," spoken in a low voice just above a whisper.

"We want to rule the school," Samuel repeated.

Mark watched them both carefully. Daniel was always the leader. Samuel seemed to go along with everything Daniel said. He wondered about their birth order. Did Daniel come out first?

"I'm sorry, boys, but I can't let you go to school with arrows on your faces. Mrs. Maloney will just send you home. You don't want to get in trouble with her, do you?"

"She won't be sending us home," Daniel replied.

Such certainty, Mark thought. *They seem meek a lot of the time, but then they show tremendous confidence.*

His mind spun away from the issue at hand. *Maybe they* will *make an interesting book. I could do it as a diary of their development as they adapt to a whole new world.*

Lea had her arms wrapped tightly around the front of her beach wrap. She looked tense, but so far, she hadn't said a word of protest.

They stood defiantly, eyes locked on Mark. Stone statues.

Elena couldn't hide her surprise at their stubbornness. "You two are *weird*."

Lea pulled Mark to the back door. "You can't win this fight," she whispered. "Remember trying to get Ira to zip his coat in the freezing cold last winter? They get these ideas about what's cool and what isn't, and you can't ever win those fights. Kids are stronger and crazier than we are."

"Then what am I supposed to do?" he snapped, eyes on the twins. "Just do whatever they want? Is that really your policy? So far, you haven't said no to them once."

"Let them go to school. The other kids will let them know how dorky the arrows are. They'll learn soon enough. From their peers."

Mark shook his head unhappily. He shrugged. "Okay, I give up. I surrender." He turned to Elena. "Where's your brother? Go get him. He's going to be late."

Elena turned toward the hallway door and shouted. "Ira—get *down* here. You're going to be late!"

"Don't shout. Go get him," Mark snapped.

Elena groaned and pushed between the twins to get to the kitchen doorway. But the back door opened, and Ira came walking breezily in from outside. "Hey, what's up?"

Mark couldn't hide his surprise. "What were you doing in the backyard? Why weren't you in your—"

He stopped midsentence when he saw the blue arrow on Ira's right cheek. "What the hell—"

That made the twins giggle.

Mark rubbed his finger down Ira's cheek. "No, Ira. No. No way."

"I'm going to rule the school," Ira said brightly.

Mark shook his head. "No. No arrow. Please. Tell me I'm dreaming this."

"We're going to rule the school," Daniel repeated. He raised his palm, and Ira slapped him a high five.

"Go remove it. All three of you," Mark insisted.

"Why weren't you in your room?" Elena asked Ira.

He pointed to the twins. "I'm living with *them* now."

Mark's breath caught in his throat. "You're *what*? You're giving up your room?"

Lea: "When did you decide this?"

Ira shrugged. He seemed to have no idea of how poorly this was going over with the rest of his family. *Or maybe he doesn't care?* Mark thought.

But that didn't make sense. Timid, fearful Ira always needed the acceptance and support of Mark and Lea. He was desperate for their attention, their approval.

"It's cool," Ira said. "I moved some of my stuff out last night. The twins and I—we're going to stick together."

Mark took a long breath. "Isn't this something you should probably discuss with your mom and me? You can't just move out of the house without telling us. I mean, whose idea was this?"

He turned to the twins, who were spreading grape jelly onto their toaster waffles. "Was this *your* idea?"

Before they could answer, the phone rang.

Mark squinted at the ID screen. "I don't recognize the number." He picked up the phone from the kitchen counter and clicked it on. "Hello?"

"Hello, Mark? This is Ginny Margulies. Ethan's mother?"

"Oh, yes. Hi, Ginny. How—"

"Is Ethan there? Did he stay over there last night? I'm really worried. He wasn't in his room this morning and . . . and . . . is he there with you?"

43

Mark felt his throat tighten. He turned to Ira. "Did Ethan spend the night here last night?"

Ira nodded.

"Are you *kidding* me?" Mark exploded.

Ira grabbed a toaster waffle. The twins giggled.

"Ethan is here?" Mark demanded. He heard Ginny Margulies shout something in his ear. "Where is he?"

"Out back," Ira replied. He loaded the waffle into the toaster.

"Your mom and I were out. Didn't Roz check on you last night? She said she checks on the guesthouse every night."

Ira shrugged. "Axl was crying a lot. Roz didn't come."

Mark looked to Lea to say something. But she stood frozen, leaning against the refrigerator with her arms crossed. *Just watching. Why isn't she giving me a little support here?*

"You're not going to school till you explain this," Mark said to Ira. "And you are all going to remove those stupid arrows from your faces."

"I don't think so," Ira said softly.

"Is my family getting weird?" Elena chimed in.

"Ethan is here," Mark said into the phone.

"Oh, thank goodness." He heard a long sigh at the other end.

"But we didn't know—"

"You don't know who's staying in your own house?" Her worst fear over, the woman quickly turned angry. "I don't understand. Why didn't he call me and tell me where he was? Why didn't *you* call me? Somebody?"

"Please. Calm down. Ethan is fine. There was a mix-up, that's all. My sister was supposed to check on them."

Mark wanted to end the conversation. But he knew there was just more confrontation facing him after he hung up.

What is Ira's story? Why is he acting so un-Ira-like?

"Can I at least talk to him?" Mrs. Margulies's voice was tight and challenging.

"Well, no. I don't see him yet. He—" Mark realizing how feeble he sounded.

"Well, where *is* he?"

Mark lowered the phone. "Ira? Can you go get Ethan? His mother wants to speak with him."

Ira took a bite of toaster waffle. He stared back at Mark as if he didn't understand the question.

The twins giggled again.

Elena rolled her eyes. "What is your *problem* this morning?"

Lea finally uncrossed her arms. "We should have a family discussion later, don't you think?" She turned to the twins. "If you have guests back there—"

"We're not exactly guests," Ira interrupted. "We live there now."

"The school bus!" Daniel cried, pointing at the window that looked out on the driveway. "Let's go!"

"Not so fast!" Mark made a grab for Ira. But Ira dodged out of his hands and burst out the kitchen door.

The twins followed, shouting their morning chant, which was beginning to sound more and more unpleasant to Mark. "Rule the school! Rule the school!"

Maybe there's a meaning here I'm not getting.

Out the back window, he saw Ethan run out of the guesthouse and catch up with Ira and the twins. "Oh no," Mark groaned. "Is that a blue arrow on Ethan's face?"

Lea raked her hands through her hair, making it stick out in frazzled clumps. "I don't really understand. . . ."

Mark heard a chattering sound. He lowered his eyes to the phone. He forgot he was still holding it.

"Ginny? Ginny?" It took awhile to make her stop shouting. "Ethan just got on the school bus," he told her. "He's on his way to school."

"But what about his backpack? What was he wearing? What about his lunch? Did he have any breakfast?"

"I'm sorry. I really can't answer those questions. This is all a surprise to Lea and me, too. The boys slept in the guesthouse last night and . . . we didn't know."

"Excuse me? The guesthouse? You allow twelve-year-old boys to sleep by themselves in your guesthouse? And you don't even know who's there?"

"Normally, we check on them all the time. But I guess the boys had a sleepover together and forgot to tell us." *Lame.*

Silence at the other end.

Mark raised his eyes to Lea, who was pacing back and forth, hands in the pockets of her beach cover-up, hair still spiked like lawn divots.

"Ira is a nice boy," Mrs. Margulies said finally. "But I'm not so sure I want Ethan to come to your house."

"I'm sorry, Ginny. I feel as badly as you do."

"I read the papers, Mark. I know what happened at your house. The murder, I mean. You must be under a lot of pressure. I think Ethan should stay away."

"Well, if it makes you feel any better—" He realized she had clicked off.

He slammed the phone onto the counter. He turned to Lea. "Nice morning, huh? That was a warm family moment."

She narrowed her eyes at him. "Are you blaming the twins? You're going to berate me again for bringing them here?"

Elena backed away, hands raised. "I don't want to hear this."

"How are you getting to school?" Mark spun on her. He didn't intend to sound so angry.

She backed up against the kitchen table. "Ruth-Ann's dad. He's picking me up. You don't have to chew my head off. I didn't do anything."

Before Mark could apologize, he heard footsteps coming down the stairs. Roz stormed into the kitchen, still in her long blue flannel nightshirt and carrying Axl in her arms. Her hair was unbrushed. Her eyes darted around the kitchen.

"Roz—? Are you okay?" he started.

"Who did this?" she demanded. "Who was it?"

Elena squinted at Axl. She was the first to see it. "Oh my God."

"Who snuck up to the attic last night?" Roz shouted. "Who would do this to my baby?"

Mark took a staggering step toward her, then stopped short when he saw what Roz was talking about. The fat blue arrow, pointing up, on Axl's left cheek.

44

The halls at Sag Harbor Middle School smelled of some kind of strong disinfectant. The sharp odor made Samuel's eyes water and his nose burn. He had always been very sensitive to smells.

When he was younger, the pungent aroma of burning meat from the island's smoker pits always made him nauseous. But he had outgrown that a while ago.

The four of them walked past the principal's office and turned the corner into the long hall that led to Miss Montgomery's classroom. Daniel walked with an arm casually draped over Ira's shoulder.

Samuel kept close to Ethan, who still seemed reluctant to devote himself wholeheartedly to ruling the school. His assignment from Daniel was to keep close to Ethan and make sure his transition was smooth.

Samuel glimpsed a few kids turning from their lockers and staring at them as they passed. He wasn't surprised that the face arrows would draw some attention.

Two dark-haired sixth-grade girls, fresh from a morning basketball team practice in their blue-and-white team uniforms, noted the arrows and giggled. But they didn't stop to comment or ask what the arrows meant.

"You know those girls, boyo?" Daniel asked Ira. "They're pretty awesome."

Ira shrugged. "I know them, but they don't talk to me. I—I'm not really popular, you know."

Daniel chuckled. "You will be."

Samuel saw the big bulldog-faced kid, Derek Saltzman, bending over the water fountain on the wall. Derek raised his head as the four boys approached.

He narrowed his beady gaze on Ira. "Hey, Sutter. Did you have a shower this morning?"

"No. Why?" Ira said.

Derek filled his mouth with water, then turned and sprayed Ira's face and the front of his jacket. "There's a shower for you, dude." His laugh sounded more like hiccupping, a series of high whoops.

Ira wiped water off his cheeks with his hand.

Derek noticed the blue arrows for the first time. "What's up with that?" He took his thumb and smeared it over Ira's cheek. "Hey, it doesn't come off."

"Want one?" Daniel said.

"Yeah, boyo. Join the club," Samuel said.

Ethan hung back, almost using Samuel as a shield. Samuel knew Ethan was afraid of Derek.

"You look like fucking freaks," Derek snarled. "Here. Want to wash it off?" He spit another stream of water into Ira's face.

Daniel stepped in front of Ira to confront Derek. "You're a tough lad. Want to spit water in *my* face?" Daniel's features hardened, and he gave Derek an icy stare.

Oh, please, Daniel. It's early in the morning. Don't spoil the whole school day.

But Derek wasn't intimidated. "Fuck yes!" He sucked in a long drink and spit a stream of water in Daniel's face. Then he laughed his whooping laugh.

Daniel didn't move a muscle. Just let the cold water run down his cheeks and chin.

Daniel. Please.

"You forgot to add something to those arrows on your faces," Derek said, returning Daniel's unblinking stare. "You've got to put the words *I'm with Stupid.*"

Some boys across the hall burst out laughing at that. Samuel spun around, surprised to find a small crowd watching the confrontation. He recognized the two girls from the basketball team and five or six other kids from his class.

Daniel and Derek continued their staring contest. Derek leaned his back against the porcelain fountain and crossed his beefy arms in front of him.

Samuel watched his twin clench and unclench his fists. Samuel's stomach tightened in dread. He knew this meant trouble. A lot of trouble.

But couldn't it wait till later? Couldn't they have a quiet school day first?

A hush fell over the hall as the two boys continued to glare at each other. No locker doors slammed. No footsteps on the tile floor. No voices.

And then heavy footsteps. And a ringing shout. And before anyone could move, Mrs. Maloney bulled her way through the crowd.

"What's going on here? What is the fuss and commotion, may I ask?"

Samuel took a step back. The principal wore a long gray crewneck sweater and a plaid skirt over black tights. Her beaded earrings jangled as she walked.

She pushed past Samuel, Ethan, and Ira, and strode up to Daniel and Derek, her eyes moving from one to the other. "Well, boys, I like shows. I like to be entertained. Can anyone explain to me what this show is about?"

They didn't answer.

"Well, there must be a show because I see you've got an audience." She motioned to the crowd of onlookers blocking the hall.

Neither boy spoke.

The principal narrowed her eyes at Derek. "Is there a problem here? I hope you haven't been giving our new students a bad idea of our school."

"He spit water on the new kid," a boy shouted from the back of the crowd.

"He spit on Ira, too," another boy chimed in.

Mrs. Maloney sighed and shook her head, making her earrings jangle. "Oh, Derek, Derek, Derek. After that nice long talk we had in my office the other day? You do remember that talk, don't you?"

Derek nodded his head and grunted.

"Well, we don't spit on people in this school. Lordy no. Do we need to have another long talk? Maybe call your mother in again?"

Derek's cheeks turned red.

Daniel tapped Mrs. Maloney on the arm, startling her. Samuel watched him turn on his sweetest, most angelic smile. "He didn't mean us any harm, mum," Daniel said in a tiny voice. "It was a joke, see."

Mrs. Maloney reacted with surprise. "A joke? Spitting on other kids is a joke?"

Daniel's dimples flashed. His blue eyes widened in innocence. "He meant it to be funny. He wasn't being mean."

"Yeah. It was a joke," Derek claimed. "I saw someone do it on TV."

Suddenly, Mrs. Maloney didn't seem to be interested in Derek. She was squinting at Daniel. Then her eyes moved to the other boys.

"Oh, good Lord in heaven!" she exclaimed, slapping her cheek with one hand. "I didn't even notice. My eyes must be going."

Samuel knew she had just seen the blue arrows on their faces.

This is not going to be a quiet morning.

"Well, goodness. Big blue arrows on your handsome faces. Ira, did you boys start a *gang*?"

Ira swallowed. "N-no."

"Do we allow gangs at Sag Harbor Middle School?" she asked, running a stubby finger down Ira's cheek. "I don't think so."

"It's not a gang." Daniel stepped in. "It's a club."

The bell clanged right above their heads. The sound made Samuel jump. The disinfectant smell had given him a headache. The tension in the hall wasn't helping. He thought about soft waves, frothy, clean, and cold, splashing on yellow sand.

"Everyone get to class." Mrs. Maloney waved them all away with both hands. "You too, Derek. Everyone but the Blue Arrow Gang."

Derek flashed Daniel a nod, as if to say thank you. He thought he'd escaped punishment this time. But Samuel knew he was mistaken.

Mrs. Maloney herded the four boys to her office. She brought in folding chairs and motioned for them to sit. Then she sat down heavily behind her desk and thumbed through a few pink phone-message slips.

She wasn't really reading them, Samuel thought. She was getting herself together, preparing what to say.

When she glanced up, her expression was stern. "Please explain these face tattoos to me."

"We want to rule the school," Daniel replied without hesitating.

She blinked. "I don't understand."

Daniel wore his most innocent face and spoke in his high, little-boy voice. "The arrows point *up*, see? It means we want to go *up*."

"Up with Sag Harbor Middle School," Samuel added, always ready to help his twin. "Up with our school."

Mrs. Maloney rested her head in her hands. "So you lads are telling me you want to be cheerleaders?"

"Not really," Samuel answered. "We want to show that we are together, see."

"No, I don't see." She turned to Ira. "I know your father believes that kids should do whatever they want. But did he really approve of you painting arrows on your faces?"

"Not exactly," Ira replied in a whisper.

Mrs. Maloney sat up straight. She tapped one hand on the desktop. "Well, I'm glad you lads want to do well and show some pride in your school. But I think you've gone about it the wrong way. I'm afraid I can't allow it."

"Yes, you can," Daniel said in his little voice.

She blinked at him. "I want all four of you to go wash those arrows off right now."

"No, we won't be doing that, mum." Daniel's matter-of-fact reply.

She used the desktop to push herself to her feet. "Go to the boys' room now. Stay in there till the arrows are gone. Go!"

No one moved.

"We won't be doing that," Daniel said. He stood up and nodded to Samuel.

Okay. Heaven give me strength. Here we go.

Samuel concentrated. It took so much energy to heat up his eyes.

Mrs. Maloney crossed her arms over the front of her sweater. "Daniel, I don't understand. At your old school, did you talk back to your principal and disobey him or her?"

"We want to rule the school," Daniel said.

"Answer my question. Why are you acting like this? I know you are new here and things may be different for you. . . ."

Daniel turned to his twin.

Samuel saw only red now. A billowing sheet of red in front of him. His eyes made a sizzling sound, like bacon frying.

Burn time, Mrs. Maloney.

"Daniel, if you don't obey me, I have no choice—"

"You have no choice," Daniel said.

45

Mrs. Maloney uttered an alarmed cry. "Samuel? Your eyes! What's wrong with your eyes?"

"Are you going to burn her?" Samuel heard Ethan's voice behind him.

"Are you going to *kill* her?" From Ira, alarmed.

Samuel saw only shimmering sheets of red. But he could feel the excitement in the room.

"Ouch! Stop it! Are you *crazy*? What are you *doing*?"

I hate it when they scream like that.

Did we remember to close the office door?

Samuel felt his brother's hand on his arm. "Careful. Careful. Not too much," Daniel whispered. "Just enough to let me get inside her brain."

Mrs. Maloney was silent now. Samuel kept the fiery beam trained on her head.

Burn. Feel the burn.

Silence, except for the pop and sizzle of the red heat.

"Almost done," Daniel said calmly. "Ease up, boyo. I'm almost there. Ease up. Ease up. We don't want to leave burns. We don't want her to remember, do we?"

Samuel pulled the heat back. It was easier to harness it than to fire it up. He could feel his eyes cooling. His headache was gone. He gazed around the room and saw the principal slumped in her leather chair, a dazed smile on her face, arms dangling down the sides of the chair.

Ira and Ethan sat expressionless watching with silent awe.

Daniel still leaned over Mrs. Maloney, staring into her eyes. He patted her broad shoulder gently. He brushed a hand over her head, straightening her short hair. He lifted her hands and placed them in her lap.

"Did it work?" Samuel asked.

He grinned. "No doubt. No worries. Be happy."

He dropped back into the chair between Ira and Ethan.

Mrs. Maloney shook her head, as if waking up from a short nap. She squinted at the four boys for a long moment. Then she smiled.

"I'd better make that announcement now," she said.

She stepped around them to a table with a microphone and a stack of electronic equipment. She threw a switch. Cleared her throat. Leaned over till her mouth was a few inches from the microphone.

"Attention, everyone," she said.

Samuel could hear her voice echoing from classroom to classroom all down the hall.

"Attention, everyone. This is Mrs. Maloney. I have a special announcement this morning."

The speaker squealed. She jerked her head back. Then resumed:

"Our school has a new slogan I think you will all be proud of. It's *Up with Sag Harbor Middle School*. And we have a new school symbol. It's a wide blue arrow pointing up. Because we *all* want to move up, don't we?"

A pause. She turned and flashed Daniel a grin.

"So I'd like every student to stop by the art room at some point before you leave today, and we will have the school arrow painted on your face. I want you to wear it proudly. Don't forget. Everyone must stop in the art room and receive your school arrow *today*. Have a *special* day, everyone. Up with Sag Harbor Middle School."

46

"Lea, please come away from there. You're not even writing. You're just staring at the screen. Please—"

"I . . . can't, Mark. There's so much more to write. I'm sorry."

"I'm going to pull you away. You don't leave this room. We have to talk."

"Maybe when it's finished . . ." She turned on the desk chair to face him, her face pale, eyes tired.

"I'll take you to lunch in town. Where shall we go? We need to talk about the kids. The boys. How we're going to deal with this arrow thing."

She uttered a sigh. "The arrow thing. It's so silly, isn't it?"

"Well, yes and no. We need to figure out how we're going to handle the twins. I mean when there's conflict. You and I have been at each other's throats."

"No. We haven't. We—"

"Yes, we have. You're always the good guy, Lea, and I'm forced to be the bad guy."

"But you *are* the bad guy."

He stared at her. "Was that a joke? Are you *serious*? You're joking, right?"

She shrugged. "I can't do lunch today. I'm so sorry. I have to work."

"But you don't have a deadline, do you? You're not even writing it as an assignment for anyone."

She spun her chair back to face the laptop monitor.

"The kids are worried about you, Lea. Elena asked why you never talk to her anymore. The twins—well, you see they need some guidance, some care. You have to admit you've been neglecting them. And poor Ira—"

"Do you think he'll always be called Poor Ira?"

"That's not funny, Lea."

"I'm not neglecting the twins. The twins and I have a special bond. Even if we don't spend time together . . ."

"You're not making sense, sweetheart. Please get changed and come to lunch with me? It's a beautiful day and . . . and . . . I love you. I want to spend time with you."

She turned. Her eyes went wide. Her whole face constricted. He realized she was staring at the bed.

"Mark—why do we have black sheets? Black sheets mean *death*!"

"Huh? We've had those sheets for years. We—"

"No!" She jumped to her feet, face wide with alarm. "No! Black sheets are death! *Death!*"

"Lea—what are you doing?" He made a grab for her. Missed.

She dove to the bed. Grasped the end of the top sheet. Tugged it up. She gritted her teeth. Uttered an animal growl. And *ripped* the black sheet between her hands.

"Lea—stop!"

She ripped the sheet. Pulled hard. Ripped it some more.

"Lea—please." He ran over to her. Grabbed her arm. "Please stop."

She tore frantically at the sheets, growling and grunting. "Black sheets are *death. Death. Death. Death.*"

47

After school, Samuel could see how surprised Derek was when he and Daniel showed up at his front door. The twins knew Derek's house because it was one of the first school bus stops.

Derek had a stack of Oreos in one hand and a smear of chocolate on his front teeth. "Hey, you two weren't on the bus," he said, blocking the doorway.

"We walked," Daniel said. He eyed the Oreos. "After-school snack?"

Derek nodded. "Sorry. These are the last ones."

We didn't come for cookies, stupid.

"Nice house," Daniel said, peering into the front room.

It *is* a nice house, Samuel thought. Big, with lots of tall glass windows reflecting the afternoon sunlight, at the top of a gently sloping front lawn, surrounded by leafy old trees.

"You want to come in?" Derek couldn't hide his surprise at seeing them. The uncertainty seemed to change his personality. As if he'd momentarily forgotten to act tough.

He led them into the front room, all chrome and white-leather furniture, big glass tables, and a zebra rug on the light wood floor. Tall paintings of beach scenes, crowds in bright bathing suits, people swimming. High cathedral ceiling with a wide skylight.

Derek swallowed the last of the Oreos. He wiped his face with the back of a pudgy hand. "Hey, thanks." To Daniel.

The twins were gazing around the bright white sun-sparkling room. They'd never stood in such luxury.

Too bad. Too bad.

Along with the anticipation, Samuel actually felt a little trepidation.

We walk into this clean perfect sunlit house, and what do we do?

Daniel finally turned back to Derek, who stood awkwardly, leaning on the back of a low, white couch. "Thanks," Derek said again. "You know. For what you did this morning?"

Daniel gave the big kid a blank stare. Like he didn't remember what Derek was talking about.

"You saved my ass," Derek said. "With Mrs. Maloney. That was totally cool."

"Well, it was all a joke, right?" Daniel said, but he didn't say it in a friendly way. There was no smile in his voice. "When you spit the cold, cold water on me. All a joke, right?"

"Yeah, sure." Derek instantly saw the change in Daniel's face.

"You just lost your head, right, boyo?" Daniel definitely menacing now.

"Huh? I lost my head? Well, yeah. I guess."

Daniel gripped Derek's face by the chin and turned his head from side to side. "Hey, lad, you didn't get your school arrow."

Derek's cheeks turned pink. He pulled free from Daniel's grasp. "I . . . forgot. You know. I didn't get to the art room. Maybe I'll go tomorrow."

"Probably not," Daniel said. He nodded to Samuel.

Samuel took a deep breath. Then he gritted his teeth and started to warm up his eyes.

Daniel wrapped a hand over Derek's beefy shoulder. "Can we see your room?"

48

Pavano wasn't fucking Sari. He was making love to her.

He wondered if she felt the same strong feelings he did. As she moved on top of him, he smoothed his hands over her ass and thought about how different this was. Sex with real feeling and not just sex.

How long had it been?

The last year with Susannah had been all the wrong feelings. After sex, he felt guilty. Sex with Susannah had been an assault. So much anger mixed in, anger that caught him by surprise. It was all too many feelings at once.

I'm a simple guy.

Why was he thinking of Susannah? *Damn it, go away, bitch.*

He wanted to be in the moment. But it seemed impossible to keep memories out of his mind. He remembered the birthmark on the back of Sari's knee. And her salty scent. And the way she cooed—like a dove—with each move.

He had been surprised when she agreed to lunch at the New Paradise Café in town. And then amazed when she led him back to her little cottage of a house off Noyac Road.

And then it seemed natural to find themselves in her bedroom. And comfortable. Yes. Natural and thrilling and comfortable at the same time.

Pavano shut his eyes and thought how smart he was to come back. How smart . . . how smart . . . how smart . . . Ohhhh, yes . . . how smart. Oh God.

When it was over, he reached to throw an arm over her waist. But she sat up quickly, reached down to the floor, and pulled on her red underpants. Her long black hair fell over her face. In the slanting afternoon light from the tiny bedroom window, her skin had a sheen of silvery sweat.

"Sari, come back. What's your hurry?"

She picked up her bra from the floor and slid it over her breasts, fastening it in back. Then she brushed back her hair with both hands. Her dark eyes locked on him for a moment, then turned away.

"Have to talk to you, Andy."

He patted the bed. The sheets felt damp and still warm. "Come back here. We can talk."

"No. I mean, we have to talk." She pulled on her jeans. Then she dropped into the small red armchair across from the bed. "Remember the other night at that theater?"

Why is she looking at the floor? Is she avoiding my eyes?

"Sure. Of course I remember."

"Remember I said it didn't mean anything? When I kissed you? Remember?"

"Yeah. So?"

"Well, today . . . this meant something." She finally raised her eyes. She spread her long fingers over the arms of the chair, then tightened her hands into fists.

"To me too," he said. He could feel himself getting hard, getting ready again. What the hell? He had time. He wasn't on duty till six.

"What it meant was good-bye." Sari was staring hard at him now.

"Huh?"

"I wanted to say good-bye, Andy."

"But . . . we just said hello."

She shook her head. A smile crossed her face. It seemed so out of place. "Andy, you're sweet."

"Sweet?"

"But you're such a jerk."

He blinked. He waited for her to continue.

"We had lunch, right? We sat across from each other? We talked. We ate. We even held hands for a few minutes?"

"Yeah. So?"

"So you didn't see the ring on my finger? You're supposed to be a cop, Andy. You're supposed to see everything?"

She waved her left hand in his face. The ring sparkled in the sunlight from the window.

He felt the muscles tighten on the back of his neck.

"I married Rod, see."

"What the fuck? You married the tennis hat guy? When?"

"Sunday. We got married last Sunday. So I wanted to tell you. You've been calling me and following me and trying to bring back the past and—"

"Only because I still have feelings for you."

Stop sounding like a girl.

"That's why I wanted to say good-bye." She stood up and searched for her T-shirt on the floor. "I have nice memories, too, Andy. So now we had another nice memory and a nice good-bye."

"Jesus, Sari."

His phone beeped. It took him a moment to remember it was in his uniform pants draped over the bench at the foot of the bed. He heard Chaz's voice: "Pavano? You there? Got an early call. Pavano?"

Andy lurched to the bottom of the bed and fumbled the phone from the pants pocket. "Chaz? What's up?"

"Where are you? Got to roll."

"Uh . . . Nowhere. I can meet you."

Sari, straightening her T-shirt, squinted at him. "Nowhere?"

Pinto gave him an address on Madison Street.

He clicked the phone off and stuffed it back in the pocket. He scrambled out of bed and grabbed up his clothes. "Hey, Sari—it's been real. Happy marriage. I enjoyed the honeymoon."

49

"I can't do this, Chaz. I admit it. I don't have the stomach for it." Pavano hung in the doorway, unable to step into the small bedroom.

Pinto scowled at him. "Are you actually trembling? Pavano, how long were you a cop in the city?"

Pavano swallowed. His Adam's apple rode up and down his throat. "You know I was Housing Authority. I never . . . I never saw anything like this. I . . . don't think we should fucking be here."

"We're fucking here, aren't we?"

"First the guy in the car. Now this. I'm having such a bad day. This isn't working out for me."

"It didn't work out too good for this kid, either," Pinto muttered. "Actually, you're doing better than he is. That cheer you up?"

"You're a riot," Andy said, eyes on the window. Avoiding the corner by the bed. Avoiding it.

A few minutes ago, I was in bed with Sari. And now . . . a fucking horror show.

Pinto softened his tone. "Look, we got the call. We'll do what we can do. You saw me radio Vince. The crime scene guys are on their way."

"Chaz, there's no one here. Who made the call?"

"A neighbor. Said she smelled something bad."

"Yeah. Smells bad, okay. Maybe we should wait for the CS to get here."

"Take a breath, Andy. You're not a fucking rookie. Be a pro."

"I . . . I never—" Pavano stopped himself. He forced himself not to look in the corner.

But what *was* that sick, sharp smell? It smelled like when Susannah burned a roast.

The bedroom was spotless. Not a thing out of place. A kid's room without even a dirty sock on the floor. No sign of a weapon. A row of track lights across the ceiling sent bright circles of white halogen light over the room. Brighter than daylight. Cheerful.

Posters of New York Rangers hockey players on one wall. A movie poster hanging a little crooked over the desk. Pavano recognized Buzz and Woody.

His eyes moved too far and he glimpsed the dark lake of blood on the carpet. And were those chunks of . . . burnt skin?

"He's burned up, Chaz. I mean, like someone took a torch to him. Like the guy in the car. It's fucking sick."

"You're babbling. Just shut up."

"But where are the parents? Where are the fucking parents? Why was he alone in the house?"

Pinto removed his cap, scratched his thinning flattop. Beads of sweat glistened on his broad forehead. His little bird eyes trained on Pavano. "Now you're starting to think like a cop."

Still eyeing Andy, Pinto slid the cap back on. Then he turned and took a few steps toward the corner.

"Saltzman. The mailbox said Saltzman, right? I think I met the kid's mother. On the pier one night. She's divorced. I remember she's divorced. She said the kid was troubled."

"He ain't troubled now. Come over here. Take notes."

"Wh-what are we looking for?"

"Are you stuttering now? Are you totally going to lose it?"

"I feel sick, Chaz. I mean really."

"Suck it up, man. We've got to look for clues. For anything. Till the ME gets here."

"Then what?"

"I don't fucking know."

Pinto leaned over the perfectly smooth white bedspread. Nothing to see. "You going to toss your dinner? Do it downstairs. Don't contaminate this room."

"The room—it's totally clean. It's almost like it's *sterile* or something. A kid's room without a piece of paper out of place. No dirty clothes. No backpack hanging over a chair. Nothing. But there *had* to be a fire or something. Right? It smells like there was a fire."

"Yeah. Smells like a barbecue."

Chaz bumped open the closet door with his hip, careful not to leave fingerprints.

He sighed. "No sign of a murder weapon."

"This is worse than the guy in the car. I've never seen anything like this."

Chaz whirled around. "Do you think I have?" His cigarette-hoarse voice went up two octaves. "It's a fucking nightmare."

Andy froze at the sound from the hall. Footsteps on the stairs.

"Vince radioed for CS backup," Chaz said. "Has to be the ME. And he had to tell Franks. Franks will probably bring some state guys. Now we got some kind of fucking serial killer creep, right?"

The red-haired woman burst into the room, eyes wide with fright, a raincoat flying behind her. "What are you doing here? This is my house. What are you doing here?"

Andy recognized her from that night on the pier. This was the same Saltzman, the victim's mother.

"Get her out!" Pinto waved to Andy with both hands. "Get out of here. Get her out!"

"I don't understand," the woman planted her feet and glared at Andy. "Why are you here? Where is my son? Where is Derek?"

"Get her out!" Pinto lurched toward Andy. "Out. Now. Out of here."

Andy felt in slow motion. Like coming out of a nightmare. Pulling himself awake slowly.

He took the woman by the shoulders. Too late.

"I don't understand!" Fear replacing anger. "I don't understand. Tell me—"

"Get her out! Get her out!"

Andy couldn't budge her. She saw. She saw the kid's body.

"My Derek! Is that my Derek? I don't understand. I don't understand. Do you hear me? Talk to me. Please. I don't understand."

"Come with me." Andy tried to turn her away. He held her shoulders and spoke softly. "Come with me. Please."

"I don't understand. I don't understand."

I've seen people go into shock before. But I'm not trained for this.

"Is that my son? Is that Derek?"

"Pavano—get her out of here. Don't stand there. Get her *out*!"

"Is that my Derek? But where is his head? Where is his *head*?"

Pavano managed to wrap his arm around her shoulders. She was screaming now, shrieking and sobbing. It took all his strength to force her into the hall.

Two uniformed cops were on the stairwell. Pavano motioned them up. "Take care of her. Call a doctor. This is her house. It's . . . her son."

He passed the screaming woman on to them. The two cops struggled with her on the stairs. She stumbled and they had to block her to keep her from tumbling down the stairs.

His stomach churning, Pavano returned to Pinto. He found him bending over, hands on his knees. "Pinto? You okay?"

"Not really."

"Huh? What?"

"Look under the bed, Andy. What's that thing under the bed?"

Andy sucked in his breath. He squatted down and peered at the round, dark object half hidden in shadow near the wall under the bed. "What the fuck?"

Pinto straightened up. He sighed. "Andy, I think we just found the kid's head."

50

Mark gripped Autumn around the waist of her white tennis shorts. He intended to lift her off his lap. But she took one of his hands and slid it between her legs. Then she lowered her face to his and began to kiss his neck. Slowly, she moved her lips to his cheek, then his mouth.

"No. Autumn."

She giggled and nibbled his ear.

"Lea is right upstairs. She could come down—"

"But she won't," Autumn whispered. "She never stops working up there."

She sat up straight, her white-blond hair falling over her eyes, holding his hand against the front of her shorts. "What is she writing?"

Mark glanced nervously to the office door. He could feel his erection pushing against his jeans. "I'm not even sure. A long piece. Something about death rituals. She used to share her work with me."

"And now?" Brushing her hair against his cheek.

"She stays up there day and night. I'm really worried about her. I can't even drag her away for meals. She's . . . not right."

"That's why I'm here for you, Mark." Whispered against his ear so that the skin tingled all down his body.

"No. Autumn—please." He worked his hand free and gripped her waist again. "Get up. Come on. Really. I'm serious."

She made a pouty face, her round blue eyes wide, mouth all satirical. "Don't you like me anymore?"

"We can't do this." Another glance to the door. Did he hear footsteps or just the house creaking? "Roz is home, too. And the boys are out back."

She nuzzled his neck. Her lips were hot and dry. "Doesn't that make it more exciting for you?"

"No. It just makes it more wrong."

"Wrong?" Her smile faded. "You don't really think it's wrong, do you?"

Is she delusional?

"Yes. Wrong. I mean, look. I have too much to deal with now. I'm so worried about Lea and stressed about the kids and . . . We can't do this. We—"

The front doorbell chimed.

Autumn scrambled to her feet. She frowned at him as she smoothed her short hair with both hands. Then she tugged down the legs of her shorts. "Wrong?"

"Of *course* it's wrong."

What's that song? "How Can It Be Wrong If It Feels So Right?"

"Mark. It's those two policemen again." Roz's shout from the front entryway. "Shall I send them back to your office?"

Mark stood up and straightened his blue polo shirt over his jeans. He squinted at Autumn. "What the fuck?"

She began straightening the stack of files on the desk. "Guess I'll go home. Say you'll miss me."

Mark didn't answer. He was trying to figure out why the police had returned. He heard their clomping footsteps, heard their voices as they made small talk with Roz.

Autumn slid out with her pouty face on. She glanced back as the two cops entered, then vanished down the hall.

Mark had a sudden fright. *Do I have lipstick on my face?*

Then he remembered Autumn wore only a clear lip gloss.

The two officers entered and apologized for disturbing him.

They sat down in their usual places on the couch. The one named Pavano looked tired, weary, as if he hadn't been getting much sleep. His partner didn't waste time getting to the point.

"Mr. Sutter, I'm sure you're aware that one of the students in your sons' class was murdered last Wednesday."

Mark nodded. "Yes. It's so horrible. So shocking. I spoke with our three boys—Ira and the twins—and tried to see if they needed counseling."

"Well, Officer Pavano and I think—"

"My wife and I—we know the Saltzmans. I mean, we knew them before the divorce. My wife was in a reading group with Elaine Saltzman. She . . . she must be beyond devastated."

The two cops nodded. Pavano tapped something into his phone.

"My son Ira wasn't friends with Derek. But they knew each other since fourth grade, I think. Ira is very sensitive. I think he had a nightmare last night. You know. About Derek."

"Sorry to hear that," Pavano said, glancing up from his phone. "They brought in grief counselors to the school."

Mark cleared his throat. "Yes. That's smart. I'm trying to work with Ira on my own."

"We went to the school yesterday," the big cop, Pinto, continued, keeping his small eyes steady on Mark, as if studying every reaction.

They couldn't think I had anything to do with the kid's murder. Why are they here?

"We spoke to Mrs. Maloney and to the teacher. What's her name?"

"Montgomery," his partner offered.

"You know. We're trying to cover every angle. Grasping at straws, really."

He and Mark stared at each other. Mark waited for him to continue. He could smell Autumn's lemony perfume. Was it on his cheek?

"We asked the principal to go over everything that happened on Wednesday," Pinto said. "We just asked if anything concerning the deceased stuck out in her mind that day. Anything at all."

"What were you looking for exactly?" Mark asked. He leaned forward and crossed his arms over the desk.

"We didn't know," Pinto said. "Just trying to get an idea of the boy's day."

"I don't understand," Mark said. "You talked to the principal. So . . . why did you come here?"

"Well . . ." Pinto removed his cap and tossed it onto the arm of the couch. "The principal remembered that Derek Saltzman had a fight with your boys that morning."

"Huh? A fight?"

"A spitting fight."

Mark felt his cheeks grow hot. "I don't think so. My son Ira would never spit on anyone."

"Mrs. Maloney recalled that Derek Saltzman spit water on your son Ira and on your twin boys as well."

Mark shook his head. "First I've heard of it. I do know that Derek has been in trouble before."

"Well, we thought your boys might have some kind of information or recollection from that day," Pavano chimed in. "Something that might give us a clue."

"That's pretty fucking desperate," Mark said, tapping the desktop with both hands.

"We agree," Pinto said quickly. "But there's one more detail." He turned to Pavano, as if asking for permission to continue.

Pavano gave an almost invisible shrug.

"This isn't being given out to anyone," Pinto said, playing with his cap, twirling it on one hand. "If you could keep it confidential. I mean, not spread it around to people in the community."

"Yes. Of course," Mark said.

"Well, you see," Pinto continued in a voice just above a whisper, "the boy's murder is very similar to the murder that occurred in your driveway."

Mark couldn't hide his surprise. "How do you mean?"

"The victim was burned," Pinto said. "Like with a blowtorch. Very similar. Only in the boy's case, his head was burned completely off. We found his skull—no skin on it or anything. We found his skull all scorched . . . under his bed."

Mark stood up. He took a deep breath and held it, fighting down his nausea.

"Horrible," he muttered. "Like a fucking horror movie."

The two cops nodded. Pinto spoke first. "So, since the murders were similar, and since your sons had the spitting fight with the victim on the morning of his death, we just thought it wouldn't hurt to talk to them for a few minutes. With your permission, of course."

"But tell me again. You certainly don't suspect—" Mark started.

Pinto waved a hand. "Of course not. No kid could do what we've seen in these murders. Pavano and I, we're just trying everything."

"You know, I've thought a lot about the murder in my driveway," Mark said, sitting up straight, leaning his head against the back of the desk chair. "I mean, it's hard to *stop* thinking about it."

"That's for sure," Pinto replied.

"I mean, it's not like you guys leave and I just turn it off. I think about it day and night."

"And?" Pinto said, showing a little impatience.

"Well, I just think you're looking in all the wrong places. I mean, coming here? That's a waste of your time. These murders . . . They're so violent. And nothing like this has happened in Sag Harbor before, right? So you need to check out new arrivals. Find someone who's moved here very recently, someone with a violent past. The summer people haven't arrived yet. That should make your job easier. I'm not a cop, but I'd be checking mental hospitals and—"

"Thanks for your advice. But you have to understand *you're* our number one suspect," Pavano blurted out.

Mark felt his face grow hot. He saw Pinto flash an annoyed scowl at his partner.

"A guy comes to your house with bad news," Pavano said, ignoring Pinto's displeasure, "he ends up dead in your driveway. A kid gets into a fight with your boys. The kid ends up dead in his room."

Mark wished they wouldn't concentrate their stares on him like that. Yes, he could feel he was blushing. But blushing could mean all kinds of things. He'd written a paper on it. Why was he think-ing about that paper now?

"I can testify that Mark isn't a murderer."

The voice made Mark jump. Lea came floating barefoot into the office, in a sleeveless blue top and blue short shorts. Her hair fell loosely around her face.

Mark thought she looked beautiful, except for her eyes, which were red and tired from staring into the laptop screen all day.

The two officers climbed slowly to their feet. They all nodded at each other solemnly.

"Mark can't even kill a lobster," Lea said. "He's so squeamish, I have to drop them in the pot. He looks the other way. Really."

Pinto studied Mark. "I'm allergic to shellfish," he said.

"Too bad," Lea offered.

"Mrs. Sutton, you were away when the murder occurred in your driveway," Pavano said.

"I was in the city. I had some meetings. But I hurried home. I knew the kids would be upset."

"They've been very edgy and out of sorts," Mark added. "I've tried to get them to talk about it, but . . ."

Pinto turned back to Lea. "The twin boys were out in the front yard when the victim was murdered. Have they said anything to indicate—"

"That they saw anything?" Lea interrupted. "No. Not a word. Mark asked them directly more than once. They say they were in back. In the guesthouse, in their room. They didn't see a thing. And I believe them."

"The twins have had their lives turned upside-down," Mark said. "Losing their parents and their home on the island, moving to a very different place. I've been watching them very closely. I think I'd know if they were keeping something from me."

"Well, we appreciate all your help," Pavano said.

"We came to ask the three boys just a few questions. Do you think that would be okay now?"

Mark turned to Lea. "Roz was going to take them into town to buy dinner," Lea said. "But go ahead."

"I guess it would be okay," Mark said. "But if the talk begins to upset them—"

"We'll know when to stop," Pinto said, glancing at his partner.

"I'm happy to cooperate, even if you think I'm your number one suspect. But as I said, this is pretty ridiculous, a total waste of time," Mark muttered, walking to the office door.

"We have to do everything," Pinto said. "This isn't our usual kind of case."

"I'll go get the boys," Lea said. She turned to Mark. "I'm going back to my work. Roz will take the boys and get dinner when they're finished here."

Mark turned to the cops. "The boys are out back. In the guesthouse. They've been hanging out there. All three of them. My son is shy and difficult. But I think he's bonding with his new brothers."

"Nice," Pavano muttered.

Mark realized that was too much information.

I'm their top suspect. God. How stupid is that?

He heard the boys clomping down the hall.

I'll cooperate the best I can. But of course my main goal has to be to protect my kids.

51

A few minutes later, the three boys stepped in. They glimpsed the two police officers and lingered near the office door.

All three boys wore loose-fitting denim jeans and oversize dark T-shirts. Ira carried his game player in one hand. The twins had sweet smiles on their faces, which seemed strange to Mark. Why were they always so happy?

Pinto motioned for them to sit on the floor. He squinted from one to the other. "Those arrows on your faces."

"We saw them on kids at your school," Pavano offered. "The principal said—"

"It's our new school symbol," Daniel interrupted. He turned his face to show off his blue arrow.

"What does it mean?" Pinto asked.

"Up," Daniel replied. "Up with Sag Harbor Middle School."

"Nice," Pinto said. But he gave his partner a look that said it wasn't so nice. "Is everyone at your school wearing them?"

"They will be," Daniel answered. "It was the principal's idea."

"Different," Pavano commented.

"We just want to talk to you for a few minutes about your friend Derek Saltzman," Pinto said, leaning toward the boys with his hands on his knees. "Of course you heard about what happened to Derek."

The boys nodded somberly. "It's very sad," Daniel said softly.

"Is that how you feel? Sad?" Pinto asked.

The three of them nodded again.

"He wasn't very nice," Ira said, eyes down. "But he shouldn't be killed."

"Not very nice?" Pinto's eyes widened.

"He was mean to a lot of kids," Ira said, glancing at Mark.

Mark nodded, signaling him to be honest about Derek.

"Was he mean to you?" Pinto asked Ira.

Ira nodded. He stuffed his hands into his jeans. "Yeah. He took things from me. Candy and stuff. He did that to everyone. My friend Ethan, too. He took their stuff. He bossed kids around. A lot."

"It's . . . very scary," Samuel chimed in. "What happened to Derek." Mark saw a tear glisten on his cheek.

Daniel's shoulders trembled. "I'm scared," he said, eyes on Mark. "Why did a killer do that to Derek?"

Samuel and Daniel both sobbed. Tears tracked down their faces. Ira kept his head down. He kept picking at a scab on his thumb.

"I think that's enough for now," Mark told the two cops.

Pinto leaned closer to the boys. "Are you feeling too sad to answer a few more questions?"

Silence. Ira spoke first. "It's okay."

"You said Derek was mean. Is that why you got in a fight with him Wednesday morning?"

The question made Mark clench his jaw. But the boys didn't react at all.

"It wasn't a fight," Daniel said, raising his blue eyes to the cops. He wiped tears off his cheeks with both hands.

"It was just a joke, don't you know," Samuel told them. "That's all. A water-spit joke. We didn't have a fight."

Pavano tapped notes into his phone. Pinto studied their faces.

"You didn't get angry when Derek spit water on you?"

"Just a joke," Daniel muttered. "The boyo was joking us."

"Mark? Can you come here a minute? I need some help." Mark heard Roz call from the kitchen.

He jumped to his feet and motioned to the two cops. "Be right back." He hurried from the room.

Pinto scratched the side of his face. "Just one more thing. I need to ask you twins one more question."

They raised their eyes to him.

"You see, we talked to the school bus driver. He told us you two weren't on his bus Wednesday afternoon. Is that true?"

Daniel and Samuel exchanged glances. "Yes," Daniel answered. "We missed the bus, don't you see."

Pinto: "Where did you go?"

"To Derek's house."

Both officers leaned forward. Pinto studied the twins' faces. "You went to Derek's house after school? Why?"

"To tell him no hard feelings," Daniel said in a tiny voice. "We told him we weren't mad at him. You know. About the water spitting."

Pavano typed furiously on his phone. Then he stopped. "Does your father know you were at Derek's house?"

They both nodded. "He came to pick us up," Daniel said. His shoulders started to tremble again. His twin wiped tears from his eyes.

Pavano and Pinto exchanged glances again. "Funny. He didn't tell us about that."

"It was *so* scary," Daniel uttered. "Samuel and I—we were scared." Both twins looked to the doorway, checking to see if Mark was there.

"Why were you scared?"

"Pa yelled at Derek," Daniel replied, voice trembling. "Pa yelled at him. He was real mad. For spitting on us, I think. And Pa slapped Derek. He slapped Derek twice."

Both boys were sobbing now. "We were so scared," Samuel said.

"Pa made us promise not to tell," Daniel added, glancing to the door. "But it wasn't right. Pa shouldn't have done that. It made us scared."

52

"I need to talk to you boys." Mark burst into the guesthouse. "This is serious." His head was spinning. His muscles felt tight from . . . anger.

He wasn't expecting the scene confronting him. Ira and Ethan on the floor, backs against the wall of the small bedroom, books in their laps. Two lanky, dark-haired boys Mark didn't recognize, hunched on the twin's beds with video games in their hands. A boy and two blond girls in front of the TV on the dresser.

"Hey, what's going on?"

The twins appeared from the closet in back. They carried bed-sheets and pillows in their arms. Their eyes went wide when they saw Mark.

"Put those down," Mark snapped. "We need to talk." He gestured around the room. "If you two want to invite friends over, you have to tell us." He knew he should get his anger under control before he talked to them—but how could he?

"Sorry, Pa," Samuel said softly.

"Some friends from school, don't you know," his twin added. "It's Friday night, so—"

"I don't care what night it is. Come over here. I've been questioned by those two policemen for the past hour. Did you tell them that I was at Derek Saltzman's house?"

Mark felt himself lose it. He grabbed them both by the shoulders. Hard. "*Did* you? Don't lie to me. Tell the truth."

"Ouch." Daniel squirmed under his grip. The cry made Mark realize what he was doing. He let go and took a step back. The other kids were all watching him.

"Sorry. Tell me what you told the police. Did you lie about me to the police?"

"No," Daniel said. "Sammy and I wouldn't lie, Pa."

Mark stared at them both. He was breathing hard. His head throbbed. Daniel was lying to him. His face was as innocent as ever, but he was lying.

"Samuel, did *you* tell the police I was at Derek's house?"

"No, Pa. I didn't tell them anything. Why are you mad at us?"

"You're lying. You're both lying, aren't you?"

He saw the frightened faces on the other kids. Ira was watching him warily, chin trembling.

And then Mark saw something else.

Something sparkly in the open drawer of the bed table. He strode across the room, in front of the two boys he didn't know, reached into the drawer and pulled it out.

Holding it by its silver chain, he raised it to his face. Then he turned to the twins. "Isn't this Elena's necklace? The amethyst necklace? The one she is missing?"

The twins gazed at it as if they'd never seen it. They didn't speak.

"This is ridiculous," Mark said. "Are you two *thieves* as well as liars?"

For some reason, that made them giggle.

"It's not funny!" he exploded. "You all have to go home! Go on. Get out of here. All of you! I have to talk to these two."

"But we *are* home," one of the blond girls said. When she turned, he saw the fat blue arrow on her cheek. They *all* had the arrow, he realized.

Mark motioned to the twins. "Come with me. Now. We're going to get to the bottom—"

"Mark!" Through the open window, he heard Lea's shout from the house. "Mark? Are you out there? We're going to be late."

I should cancel tonight. I've got a serious problem with these boys.

I won't be good company, that's for sure.

But it's the first night I've been able to persuade Lea to go out—

"Mark? Where are you? We have to go."

He waved a finger at the twins. "Later. We're going to have a long talk later. When I get home. We have to get at the truth here, do you understand?"

They both nodded. Mark turned to Ira, on the floor against the wall, but Ira avoided his eyes. Mark spun away, clenched his fist over the amethyst necklace, and stomped to the door.

"Bye, Pa," Samuel called.

"Yes. Bye, Pa," Daniel echoed.

"Bye, Pa," they called in unison.

"Look. Look at this." Mark ran into the kitchen, waving the amethyst necklace in front of him. "Lea—"

Her head was tilted to one side as she adjusted a dangling red earring. "What's that?"

"It . . . It's Elena's necklace. The one that's missing. The twins had it. They stole it. They *stole* it, Lea."

She straightened up. Brushed back her hair with both hands. "Calm down, sweetheart. You sound like a crazy person."

He let out a long breath. "Are you listening to me? The twins stole this from Elena's room. They are thieves, Lea, and—"

She took the necklace from him and smoothed the chain through her fingers. "I'm sure there's a good explanation, Mark."

"No. No, there isn't." He didn't intend to sound so frantic, but he felt he might explode with anger. "And—and they lied, Lea. They lied to the police. Didn't you wonder why I was in there being grilled for an hour?"

"I was getting ready, dear. I thought you wanted to go out and have a good time. This is what you wanted, isn't it?"

"You're not even listening to me. Those boys you brought here—"

"I know how you feel about them." Her voice suddenly sharp. "You've made it perfectly clear."

"We've got a real problem, Lea. Can't you understand that?"

"I understand that your *attitude* is a real problem."

"No. No, that's not the problem. They are liars and thieves and . . . and God knows what else."

She startled him by grabbing the front of his shirt with both hands and tugging it hard. "They're *my boys,* Mark. Do you understand? *My boys. My boys. My boys.* And you're not going to ruin it for me. Understand?"

He pried her hands off him as gently as he could. Her eyes were wide with anger. Her shouts had been like animal growls. *I have to back down. She's losing control.*

"We'll talk about it later, okay, sweetheart? Okay? Let's go out and have fun and get drunk and enjoy ourselves. Okay?"

She nodded, but her glare didn't soften. "Okay. Let's go. Let's go have fun."

53

"I want that one." Elena stabbed a finger at the laptop screen. "Just a tiny black-and-red flower. Subtle, see?"

Ruth-Ann brought her face close to the screen. "Too subtle. It'll look like a birthmark or a mole or something."

Elena gave her friend a shove. "No, it won't. It will look like a perfect little flower."

"Where will you put it?" Ruth-Ann demanded. "On your butt?"

They both laughed.

"On my ankle," Elena said. "Right here." She touched her bare ankle with one magenta fingernail. Then she scrolled down the screen of tattoo designs. "Which one do *you* want?"

"I don't want color," Ruth-Ann said. "I don't like the colors. I just want black. There. Look. Those Chinese letters. What does that say?"

"I don't read Chinese," Elena said.

"There's a caption. Read the caption," Ruth-Ann leaned closer. "There. Yes. That's the one I want. In English it means *Sexy Beast.*"

Both girls collapsed laughing. The laptop started to slide off Elena's lap. She caught it before it fell to the floor.

Ruth-Ann shifted her weight on the edge of the bed. "Can you imagine? All these people walking around with Chinese tattoos, and they think they say *Life* or *Hope* or *Peace* or something. But they really say *Kick Me*."

"No. *Eat me.*"

They laughed some more.

Yes, they were a little giddy tonight. Elena felt more excited to see her friend than usual. Sure, they'd had sleepovers before. But not since the murder in the driveway.

Ruth-Ann's parents kept calling from L.A., telling Ruth-Ann she shouldn't spend the night at Elena's, "just to be on the safe side."

But Ruth-Ann persuaded Mrs. Ellison, the woman hired to take care of her, that Mark and Lea weren't ax murderers, and her parents were being extra strict only because they felt guilty about being away in L.A. for so long.

And so here they were, picking out tattoos online and texting boys in their class, and laughing a lot. They pretty much had the house to themselves on this Friday night. Roz had retired up to the attic with Axl. The boys were in their private house out back. Mark and Lea had gone to see friends in Sagaponack.

"How about a cute ladybug?" Elena asked, returning to the tattoo thumbnails.

"Lame," Ruth-Ann said. "Why do you want a bug crawling on you? Hey, Elena, think your parents would let you get that tiny flower tattoo? Your dad says kids should do whatever they want, right?"

Elena snickered. "That's total bullshit. No way they'd let me get a tattoo even if you needed a microscope to see it. We're fourteen, Ruth-Ann. You know what that means."

"No. What?"

"It means anything we want to do, we're not old enough yet."

Ruth-Ann thought about that, chewing her bottom lip. "Hey, you're right. You got it. That's exactly what fourteen means."

They tapped on their phones for a few minutes.

"Look at this." Elena shoved her phone into Ruth-Ann's face. "This photo Roshanna sent me. Roshanna kissing her dog. Look. With tongues."

"Eeuw." Ruth-Ann made a face. "Which one's Roshanna?"

That made them both laugh. "You're cruel," Elena said.

Ruth-Ann nodded. "It's my best quality."

Elena heard a sound. She glanced up to see Daniel and Samuel in her bedroom doorway. "Hey, guys."

"Hey, guys." Daniel mimicked her words like a parrot.

"You've met Ruth-Ann, right?"

"Hi. What's up?" Ruth-Ann poked Elena and whispered, "They're totally cute."

"What's up?" Daniel echoed. They stepped into the room, their blue eyes catching the ceiling light.

Like big cartoon eyes, Elena suddenly thought.

They wore matching denim cutoff shorts. Daniel had an orange T-shirt with a bright yellow sun on the front pulled down nearly to his knees. Samuel had a black sleeveless T-shirt that revealed his slender, pale shoulders.

Daniel held up something in his hand. A brown wallet. "Pa left his wallet on the floor in his office."

"Well, just put it back on his desk," Elena said.

Daniel nodded. "I'll do that." He tucked the wallet into the pocket of his shorts.

Elena clicked her laptop shut and set it beside her on the bed. "What's going on in your private little kingdom out back? You're not doing anything bad back there, are you?"

"You'll be wanting to come see," Daniel said. He kept his eyes on Elena, as if he was trying to tell her something.

"I don't think so," Elena replied. "Ruth-Ann and I are kind of busy here."

The boys stepped up to the bed, walking side by side, their faces blank.

Elena felt a tremor of misgiving. "What do you guys want?"

"Want to see our friend Roshanna tongue-kissing a dog?" Ruth-Ann offered. She reached behind Elena for the laptop.

"No. Don't show them that." Elena wrestled Ruth-Ann away. "They'll enjoy it too much."

She expected the boys to laugh or at least smile at that, but their stony expressions didn't change.

"You'll be wanting to come with us now," Daniel said, so earnest and innocent at the same time, she had an impulse to hug him.

"And why would we want to do that?" Elena demanded.

"Does your brother ever talk?" Ruth-Ann offered, her eyes on Samuel.

"I'm the quiet one, don't you know," Samuel said.

"I'm quiet, too," Ruth-Ann told him.

Elena poked her in the ribs. "Shut up. When are you ever quiet?"

Ruth-Ann laughed.

Daniel took Elena's hand and tried to tug her up off the bed.

She pulled back. "Hey, what's your problem?" She slapped his hand away.

He didn't seem to register the rebuke. "You'll be needing a bag or something. For the two of you."

"For what?" Elena jumped to her feet.

Ruth-Ann had a grin frozen on her face. "You dudes are weird tonight."

"You need to gather your things," Samuel said. "So you can join us and rule the school."

Elena frowned at him. "Does that make any sense at all?"

"Is this some kind of dare?" Ruth-Ann said, still enjoying it.

Elena felt on the verge of being creeped out. Her parents were away. And these boys were acting like . . . robots? Their eyes were icy, she thought. She couldn't see any joke in them.

I don't really know them at all. They've been part of my family for only a few weeks. And I don't really know what they are like.

"Do you have a bag to carry your things?" Daniel asked.

"You will come as well," Samuel said—very formally—to Ruth-Ann.

She leaned forward and placed her hands on Samuel's shoulders. She expected them to feel soft, but she could feel only hard bone. "What do you want to show us back in your little house? You're not explaining anything. What do you want?"

"To rule the school," Samuel replied. He didn't move. Didn't try to free himself from her hold on him.

"Yes. Rule the school," his twin echoed.

"I don't get it," Ruth-Ann said.

"I think that's why they've got those stupid arrows painted on their faces," Elena told her. She realized it was the first mean thing she'd said to them since they arrived. But they were starting to annoy her.

She had spent a lot of time telling Ruth-Ann how cute they were, how adorable they acted together. But they weren't being any fun tonight.

"If Ruth-Ann and I go down and see what you want to show us, will you leave us alone?"

"No." Daniel returned her stare.

Ruth-Ann laughed. "You *won't* leave us alone?"

"No." The two boys in unison.

"You will stay with us. You will help us rule the school."

"Stop saying that!" Elena snapped. "We're not going to stay with you, and we're not—"

Ruth-Ann grabbed her hand to silence her. She leaned over the boys, who were at least a foot shorter than her. "Why do you want Elena and me to stay with you? Are you frightened of something?"

That made them smile for the first time.

"We're not afraid," Daniel said. "We don't know fear of things, don't you know." His smile faded quickly. "You will both live with all of us. You will help us."

Elena squinted at him. "*All* of you? Don't you mean just you and Ira?"

"There are others," Samuel said. "We have others now who want to go *up*."

Elena and Ruth-Ann exchanged confused glances. "You have other kids living with you out there? Do Mom and Dad know about this?"

"They're joking," Ruth-Ann muttered.

"They don't look like they're joking."

Elena's phone chimed. A text message. She ignored it.

"Let's go," Daniel said, motioning with his eyes to the bedroom door.

"Bring your things. Hurry," Samuel said.

Both girls crossed their arms defiantly. "No way."

"Beat it, you two," Elena snapped. "You're annoying us. Get lost."

"You're my sister," Daniel said to Elena. "You will join us now. We are bruvvers and sisters."

"Sisters? Leave me out of this," Ruth-Ann insisted.

"Go away. I mean it," Elena insisted. "You're not allowed in my room, remember? Ruth-Ann and I want to be alone."

"This isn't your room, lassie," Daniel replied, his brogue suddenly growing thicker. "You will be living among your bruvvers now."

"Are you nuts?" Elena was a patient person, but they were pushing the limits here. She took a breath. *Don't lose it. Maybe this is some weird game they played on the island. Maybe it's a big tease.*

"Where's Ira? Why are you leaving him alone down there?"

"He isn't alone," Daniel replied. "I told you, there are others now. And they are waiting for you." He scraped a finger down her cheek. "I will be putting the arrow on right here. It will look so lovely."

"Get your hand off me. Hey—"

Her breath caught in her throat when she saw the change on Samuel's face. His eyes—those wet blue eyes—they were suddenly fiery red.

Ruth-Ann uttered a gasp. She bumped up against Elena.

Elena stared into the glowing red eyes. "Samuel? What's wrong with you? Are you okay? Your eyes—"

"We don't want to hurt you," Daniel said in a low voice just above a whisper. "But you cannot be insulting your bruvvers."

Elena heard a sizzling sound. Like something frying on the stove. It took her a long moment to realize the crackling and sizzling came from Samuel's glowing red eyes.

And then she felt the searing heat on her forehead, lowering over her face.

"Oww! That *burns*! Stop it! Stop it!"

And Ruth-Ann was screaming, too. The two of them screaming in pain as Samuel glared from one to the other, and the scorching heat pierced their skin.

"Stop! It hurts! Stop it! You're *burning* me!"

54

Lea yawned and dropped her bag on the blue granite kitchen counter. She shook out her hair. "God, I'm tired."

Mark tossed the car keys beside her bag. "It was an interesting group of people."

"Interesting makes me tired." She kicked off her shoes.

He brushed his lips against her cheek. She could smell the wine on his breath. "At least I got you away from that laptop for a few hours."

She made an ugly face. Then she pulled a bottle of Poland Spring water from the fridge and took a long drink.

Mark decided to change the subject. He didn't want to bring up the twins again. He'd been thinking about them all night. He knew he had to handle the problem on his own. It was so impossible to talk to her about them.

I'm still feeling the wine. Maybe I should wait till morning.

"Huntley had some good jokes." He started to unbutton his Hawaiian shirt. "The *Wall Street* guys always hear the best jokes. I always wonder where they come from."

"Where jokes come from?"

He nodded. "Yeah. They don't just spring up from nowhere."

"Boring," she murmured. She capped the water bottle and set it down on the counter.

He put on a fake pout. "Boring? You think I'm boring?"

"You're not boring, sweetheart. Jokes are boring. I mean, all you can do is laugh at them. That's not interesting." She pulled off her silver bracelet and shook her hand as if it had been too tight. "What I can't understand is why Nestor keeps all that African art in a summerhouse. I mean, really."

"I don't think that's strange, Lea. He just likes to have it around him. If you were into collecting African art, you'd want to be able to see it. Besides, he said his apartment in the city is filled up. He doesn't have any room left."

"But he's taking a hell of a risk, Mark. Anyone could break into his house when he's away in the city. It's all glass. And some of that art is valuable. The death masks—"

"Those are so interesting. Scary, really. The white carved ones. I wouldn't want them on the wall staring at me all day."

"They're not carved, actually. They're molded. Molded on the dead person's face after he dies."

"Oh, I forgot." Mark took the water bottle and twirled it between his hands. "You're the expert on death rituals now."

She slapped his wrist gently. "Don't make fun of me, sweetheart. You know, some tribes believed you could communicate with the dead person through the mask. The dead spirit was on the other side, but the mask was on *this* side, so you could talk through it. Sometimes, the mask was to protect the dead person from evil spirits. You know, disguise him so the evil spirits wouldn't recognize him. It's kind of how Halloween masks started."

"Lea, why are you doing all this research into death rituals? Tell me."

"It's what I'm interested in now. Can't you accept that?"

He rubbed his hand over his face. "Know any good jokes?" He dodged away so she couldn't slap him.

Lea yawned again and stretched her arms at her sides. "It's late. We should get to bed. I have a lot of writing to do tomorrow. I—"

Elena entered, carrying a balled-up bedsheet and pillow. Ruth-

Ann followed, arms loaded down with jeans and tops and other clothes.

Lea blinked as if she was seeing a mirage. The girls didn't offer a greeting. They moved past Lea and Mark on their way to the kitchen door.

"Where are you going?" Lea finally managed to say.

"Out back," Elena replied without turning around.

"Why?"

"Don't you say hello? Are we invisible or something?" Mark said.

"Hello," Elena offered. She shifted the bedclothes in her arms.

"Come back," Lea said. She shut her eyes. "Explain this to me." She opened them and squinted at her daughter. "You're taking all that stuff out back because—?"

"Moving in with our brothers."

"No, you're not," Mark said sharply. "You're definitely not."

"Both of you?" Lea squinted at them, confused.

"Are you crazy?" Mark's voice slid up a few octaves. Then he saw the blue arrows. "Huh? Oh my God! No! You too? I don't believe it. What is this about?"

Elena moved a hand up to the arrow on her cheek. "It's just a symbol. You know, *Dad*." *Dad* said as a word of disgust.

Mark shook his head. "No. I don't know." Through gritted teeth. "Tell me. Why did you let them put those arrows on your faces?"

Lea took another long drink from the water bottle.

"We want to move *up*," Ruth-Ann said. She tucked her chin over the ball of clothing she carried. "That's all. No big deal."

"No big deal?" Mark cried. "It *is* a big deal. Believe me. It's a big deal." He shook his finger at Elena. "You will *not* be moving back there with the boys. You will be staying in your room. Of all the stupid, crazy ideas. I thought you were the sensible one."

"I *am*!" Elena insisted with all the nastiness she could get into her voice.

"No arguing. No more talk. Take that stuff back upstairs to your room."

"Let's pretend this never happened," Lea said quietly.

Those words seemed to send a shock wave through the air. The girls froze, wide-eyed. Mark felt it, too.

Pretend it never happened?

But what was actually happening?

Don't we have to hear an explanation? We can't just pretend it didn't happen.

"Come back here. I mean it!" Mark cried.

But the girls were out the door. Mark could hear loud music and laughter from the guesthouse. The door slammed behind them, the window glass rattling.

The sound made Lea gasp. "Mark—what is going on?"

"It's . . . the twins."

"There you go again. The twins. The twins. How can you blame the twins if these two girls—"

"I could storm out there and yell and scream and send everyone home," he said. "But I'm kind of drunk, Lea. And I think maybe if we get calm first—"

"Get calm?"

"If we go screaming after Elena and Ruth-Ann and threaten to physically pull them back to the house, it's war. And we're the ones starting it. We need to be the adults here. I need to talk to the twins. But I need to go into the house and be the calm, reasonable one."

"Do you hear all the voices out there? It sounds like a mob. How can there be *room* for them all in that tiny guesthouse!" she said.

The kitchen phone rang. The sound made them both jump. Lea glanced at the clock above the sink. Nearly midnight. Who would be calling this late?

Mark made a move toward the phone but let her reach it first.

She recognized the voice of one of the class parents. Alecia Morgan. She sounded agitated. "Lea, is Justin over there? Is he with you?"

She hesitated. "I . . . don't think so. Was he—"

"He said he was going over to Ira's. He was supposed to call so we could pick him up. I've been calling him since nine-thirty, but I only get his voice mail."

"The boys are out back," Lea said, staring hard at Mark. He was mouthing something but she couldn't understand him. "In our guesthouse. They like having their own little hideaway."

The woman's voice turned cold. "I just want to know if he's there and why I haven't heard from him."

"I'll check. I—" A long beep. "Uh-oh. I'm getting another call. I'll get Justin and tell him to call you."

"Lea, wasn't anyone supervising them?"

Lea cut off the call without answering her.

"Mark, go see if Justin Morgan is out back with the boys."

He nodded and started to the door. But stopped to listen to the next conversation.

"Your daughter?" Lea made a shrugging motion to Mark. "Debra? No. I don't think so, Mrs. Robbins. Elena is having a sleepover with Ruth-Ann. But I don't think—"

"Would you check, please?" The woman's voice quavered. "I'm going out of my mind. She was supposed to be home three hours ago."

"Well, of course I'll check. Do you want to hold on? I'll—"

The doorbell chimed.

"I can't believe Roz can sleep through this," Mark muttered.

Lea waved him to the front door. She told Mrs. Morgan she'd call her back. When she stepped into the front hallway, Mark was talking with a smiling, middle-aged man in a gray running suit, a high forehead, square-shaped eyeglasses catching the entryway light.

"Oh, hi, Mrs. Sutter. I'm Steve Pearlmutter. Rex's father. Sorry I'm late picking him up. There was an accident on Noyac Road and the cars were backed up for over an hour. No way to turn around. Unbelievable."

Mark and Lea exchanged glances. *Rex Pearlmutter?*

Lea spoke up first. "Sorry you were stuck for so long. Let's go out back and find Rex." She turned and led the way to the kitchen. "It's been a crazy night. Our kids invited a lot of their friends over. I hope they haven't been too wild. Mark and I had to go out and—"

Pearlmutter's eyes grew large behind the square glasses. "You mean the kids aren't in the house?"

"They're right out back," Mark offered. "They love hanging out in the guesthouse."

Pearlmutter smiled. "We didn't have a guesthouse when I was a kid. My friends and I had to play in the basement."

"Is your son in Ira's class?" Lea asked, pulling open the back door.

Pearlmutter nodded. "Yes. And I think they know each other from tennis camp."

Mark shook his head. "Ira only lasted a few days at tennis camp. It was too rigorous for him. He got blisters."

"They worked them pretty hard," Pearlmutter agreed. "But Rex learned a lot. Really improved his technique." He laughed. "He's only twelve and he can pretty much keep up with me now."

They stepped outside. Low hedges clung to the back of the house. Rows of just-opened tiger lilies, bobbing in a light breeze, led the way along the path to the guesthouse.

Music blared from the guesthouse. Lea's bare feet sank in the dew-wet grass. The ground felt marshy even though it hadn't rained. She felt something brush over her feet. It scampered into the flowers, making them shake. A chipmunk? A mouse?

She raised her eyes to the guesthouse. The lights were all on. Two tall pine trees stood as sentinels on either side of the red wooden door. The light from the windows made their long shadows loom over the yard.

"Pretty loud in there," Mark murmured.

"They like their music loud," Pearlmutter offered. "We used to—right?"

"I guess you're right," Mark said.

"Rex is usually an early bird," his father said. "He uses up so much energy during the day, he's exhausted by eight-thirty or nine. Staying up past midnight is a special treat for him."

Lea stopped at the door. She had a heavy feeling in the pit of her stomach. She thought of Elena and Ruth-Ann. And who was the other girl? Debra Robbins?

Why would these snobby, sarcastic fourteen-year-old girls want to hang out with a bunch of immature twelve-year-old boys? Did that make any sense?

No.

And the blue arrows on their faces. Would fourteen-year-old girls really want to join a club for elementary school kids?

These thoughts made her hesitate with her hand on the brass doorknob. "Should we knock first?"

"Let's go in, see what they're up to," Mark said, motioning with his head.

Pearlmutter snickered. "Catch 'em in the act."

Lea pushed open the door. Music roared out. Bright yellow light spilled over them. The bedroom was in the front of the house. Behind it, a narrow hall had a bathroom and a long, thin dressing room on one side, a closet on the other.

"Oh, wow," Lea murmured, her eyes moving around the room. The bunk bed and the twin bed beside it had been stripped. Bare mattresses. No pillows. Nothing on the blue-green carpet. No clothes strewn about or tortilla chip bags or soda cans.

"Hello?" Mark called, squinting into the bright light. He moved quickly to the back of the room and swung open the hall door. "Hello?"

Lea's eyes went wide. She turned to Pearlmutter, whose knotted face revealed only confusion, and murmured in a voice that seemed to be coming from someone else, "There's no one here."

55

Saturday morning, Samuel followed Daniel onto a pale blue local Hamptons bus that took them on the old Montauk Highway to Hampton Bays. It was a warm, sunny morning, one of those beautiful May mornings with no humidity and the sweet fragrance of spring flowers in the air.

Samuel gazed out the window as they passed a green college campus. The sign said: Stonybrook Southampton. Trees were just sprouting leaves and the lilac bushes were spreading their violet flowers.

How good to be among the living, Samuel thought.

Living is so special.

Deep thoughts for a Saturday morning as the bus bumped along the narrow two-lane road, twisting past an inlet of the ocean now, sparkling waters under the clearest of blue skies.

What a shame. What a shame.

Samuel wished his brother could enjoy being among the living as much as he did. If only Daniel had the same appreciation for the spring air and the delightful aromas, the brightness of the morning, and that special vibrant green on the trees you see only in springtime.

But Daniel had a different agenda. And, of course, it had to be

Samuel's agenda as well. For he was the Burner, the Fire Man, the Punisher. And as sure as the lilacs opened every spring, Daniel had people to punish.

If Daniel could use his hypnotic powers without help, Samuel would be content to watch. And yes, enjoy. But wherever the power came from—Hell, most likely—it joined the two of them together the way no twins had ever been joined.

The bus bounced along the highway, past a model of an Indian teepee and a cigarette trading post. Some kind of Indian reservation, probably.

Samuel read somewhere that all this land had belonged to an Indian tribe. Now their territory seemed to be squashed down to a cigarette store on the old highway.

The road turned. They were rumbling through a suburban neighborhood of nice houses. The sun and the sky appeared brighter here.

Samuel and Daniel sat two seats from the back. No one else on the bus except for an elderly woman in the front seat, sound asleep with her head bobbing against the window.

Samuel thought about the big move. It had gone smoothly. And was very timely, since Mum and Pa had arrived home earlier than expected. Now they had room to spread out. And room to welcome the dozens of new kids flocking to them in order to move Up with Sag Harbor Middle School.

Monday will be the first hard day, Samuel knew.

We should rest up and enjoy our new home for the weekend. We should make sure that all the new minds are set. That the new followers are clear about the goal.

But no. Daniel had his other plans.

Pa had seen too much. Pa knew too much. Pa could ruin everything.

And so, it was important to keep Pa busy. Very busy.

And that's why it was so urgent and important to kill Autumn Holliday.

56

The twins found Autumn's house easily, on a street just off Dune Road near Hot Dog Beach. Set back on a small square of grass, it was a squat, two-story redbrick with white trim and white columns on either side of the front door.

The house was old and not very well kept up. One side had darkened, the bricks rutted and cracked. The paint was peeling from the two columns.

"Let's be quick, boyo," Daniel said. "We don't want to neglect the newbies, do we?"

They climbed onto the narrow stoop, up to the screen door. Samuel pushed the doorbell and they heard it buzz inside.

Footsteps. Then Autumn pulled open the door and stared through the screen at them.

"Huh? You two? Really?" Blue eyes wide with surprise.

"Hi," Daniel said shyly, smiling so his dimples would flash.

"Did you boys come all this way to see me? How did you find me? How did you get here?"

She pushed open the screen door before they could answer. Samuel followed Daniel into the small front room. He sniffed. The stale air smelled of coffee and cigarette smoke.

The brown leather couch on the back wall had a duct tape repair on one arm. He saw two folding chairs, a small flat-screen TV playing a cooking show. Fashion and gossip magazines were strewn over the low coffee table. A huge landscape painting of grassy sand dunes covered the wall over the couch.

"Not very fancy," Autumn said, as if reading his thoughts. "Not like *your* house. Oh, this stuff isn't ours." She gestured around the room. "My sister and I are renting the house just till we figure out what our lives are going to be about. Oh, wow. I wish Summer was here. I'd love for her to meet you guys. I've told her all about you. But she's in the city this weekend."

"Your sister's name is Summer?" Daniel asked.

She nodded. "Yeah. Autumn and Summer. Do you believe my parents? Good thing I don't have a brother. Spring is such a bad-news name for a guy." She giggled.

She's a beautiful girl. Too bad. Oh lordy, too bad.

Autumn's white-blond hair was like a smooth helmet, parted in the middle and cascading down to her shoulders. She wore a blue midriff top that matched her eyes and revealed several inches of creamy white skin, down to the red short shorts that showed off her long, slender legs.

Samuel's eyes stopped at the red shoes. They were velvety with red straps at the top, had tall spiked heels, at least four or five inches high, and thick platform soles.

"You're a giant!" Samuel blurted out.

She giggled again. "Are these *awesome*? I was just trying them on when you arrived." She pointed to the shoe box on the floor beside the coffee table. "They're sooo expensive."

She did some awkward strutting. The heels made tiny round imprints in the faded brown carpet. "This takes practice. It's like being in the circus. You know. A balancing act."

"They're pretty," Samuel murmured.

Daniel glared at him. They had a job to do.

"How did you boys get here?" She ruffled her hand through Daniel's hair as she made her way to the couch, tilting one way, then the other. Finally, she dropped onto the edge of the brown cushion.

"Bus," Daniel said, smoothing his hair back into place.

"Do your parents know you came all this way by yourselves?"

"I don't think so." Daniel's reply.

Autumn fiddled with the straps on one of the shoes. "So why did you come? Just to visit? For an adventure? That's so nice of you."

"No. We came to kill you."

Subtle, Daniel. Always the subtle lad.

Autumn let go of the red straps and raised her eyes to Daniel. "What did you say?"

Samuel clenched his jaw tight and started the fire in his eyes. He felt the warmth immediately. The light changed as if he were viewing the room through a filmy red filter. The warmth washed down his neck, his back, a rippling heat that swept over his whole body.

"We came to kill you," Daniel repeated, his face blank, eyes trained on hers.

Autumn giggled. "Why would you kill *me*? Is this a game? Something for school? No. A war game?"

"You did bad things with Pa," Daniel said, taking a step toward her. "We saw you."

Autumn didn't giggle this time. Her face creased as she narrowed her eyes at Daniel. She was beginning to realize he was serious.

"You—you two were watching us?" She stood up, awkwardly on the tall, spiked shoes. Grabbed the taped arm of the couch for support. "Really? You're serious? You were spying on us?"

Samuel blinked as the red before his eyes pulsed and began to sizzle.

"We saw you," Daniel said quietly. "You did a bad thing with Pa."

Autumn's mouth curled in anger. "That's none of your business. How is that your business? You're a kid. You don't know anything about grown-ups. Did you really come all the way here to tell me you were spying on me?"

"Now we have to do a bad thing to Pa," Daniel said.

"Listen, you don't know what you're saying," Autumn told him, hands on the waist of her shorts. "You're just a kid. You don't have to worry about any of this. You got yourself all stressed out over nothing."

She started to walk past him toward the front door. "I think you two have to leave now. And don't tell your parents—"

She stopped midsentence when she saw Samuel's eyes, and her mouth dropped open. Startled, she stumbled and backed into the wall.

"Samuel? What's wrong? Your eyes—"

"We have to do a bad thing to Pa," Daniel repeated. "It's important. You have to burn."

"No—wait! What's going on? What are you *doing*?" She pressed her back against the wall and raised her hands as if preparing to fight as Samuel moved close.

He raised his eyes to her and steadied his fiery gaze on her throat.

She uttered a cry. Grabbed her throat with both hands.

"Stop it! That *hurts*! Are you fucking *weird*?"

She pressed her hands around her throat. Samuel raised his eyes to her forehead. The heat crackled like electric current.

Still gripping her throat, she ducked her head. Slid down against the wall, struggling to avoid the painful attack.

"Stop! You fucking weirdo! Damn it! Damn!" She sank to the floor, covering her face.

Samuel aimed the red beam at the top of her head.

Beside him, Daniel watched, unblinking, his smile gleeful, hands balled into fists, thumping the air as if cheering his brother on at some kind of sports event.

"Damn! Damn! You're *hurting* me! Damn it! Stop! Fuck you!"

Samuel the Punisher, the Fire Man, Samuel the *Avenger* aimed the beam at the part in her hair. He saw a line on her scalp darken, saw the hair along the part blacken in the scorching heat. Saw the darkening skin start to peel open.

So sorry to make a big hole in such a pretty head.

Autumn, you are the prettiest one yet. So sorry it didn't help you survive.

You were so pretty and so bad.

Rolled into a tight ball, Autumn had stopped screaming. When she made her move, it was a blur of motion to Samuel. He stared down at her through the thick, pulsating curtain of red. He could see vague shapes and the direction of his heat beam. But he didn't see clearly enough when Autumn suddenly untucked herself.

Grunting like an animal, she made a wild grab at her foot, slapping at it, fumbling frantically. With a hoarse cry, she tugged off one of the red shoes.

Then she rose to her feet, her hair smoking, thrusting the shoe above her head.

"Look out, boyo!"

Daniel's warning came too late.

Samuel's vision was a blur of red.

Eyes wild, hair burning, Autumn lunged toward Samuel. She gripped the shoe by the toe with the spiked heel pointing out.

Like a sword blade. That was his thought as she swung it down on him. Plunged it down with all her strength, aiming for his eye.

He saw the long spike driving toward his face. And then felt Daniel push him, shove him back. He stumbled.

The heel missed his face—and she drove it deep into his chest.

Samuel saw it in slow motion. Saw it puncture his shirt. Felt it dig into the skin. Felt it. Felt it. Felt it slice into the tender spot just below his rib cage.

He dropped to his knees. The red curtain faded from his eyes. Everything went black for a moment, then his vision quickly returned.

The shoe hung tight to his chest. The spiked heel had been driven all the way in. He gripped it in one hand and watched Autumn stumble to the front door, staggering on one shoe.

Daniel made a grab for her. Missed. She hurtled through the screen door and dove screaming into the street.

The screen door slammed behind her.

Daniel started to the door, then thought better of it, and turned back to his brother, Samuel on his knees on the carpet. Daniel's eyes were wild. His whole body trembled.

"Sammy, what are we going to do? She got away."

57

"No, she didn't," Samuel told his brother. "No one escapes me. She's as good as dead, boyo."

He saw the panic on his brother's face. He knew he had to be brave, put on a good front. Daniel had never encountered failure. It frightened Samuel to think how his twin might handle such disappointment.

Samuel could still hear her screams out in the street. He motioned with his head to the shoe. "Help me."

Daniel hesitated for a moment, his face locked in horror. Then he wrapped his hands around the heel of the shoe—and pulled it out of his twin's chest.

It slid out easily, making a *sssllliick* sound like pulling a spoon out of a jelly jar.

Daniel tossed the shoe across the floor. Then he smoothed down the front of Samuel's T-shirt. "Afraid you've got a hole in your shirt, bruvver."

Samuel jumped to his feet. "Let's go."

"Whistle while we work," Daniel said. He whistled a short tune. *Daniel being Daniel.*

They burst out through the screen door together. Jumped off the stoop. Samuel saw Daniel remove something from his jeans pocket and drop it beside the steps.

The morning sun was high over the shingled roofs of the little houses that lined the street. Houses not much bigger than cottages. Each with a trimmed square lawn. An SUV parked in the driveway.

Not a fancy Hamptons neighborhood, Samuel thought as they took off running in the direction of the shrill screams. *This is where the workers live.*

Saturday morning and everyone must be sleeping in, for there was not a person in sight. Oh, yes. A man in khaki shorts watering his flower garden with a hose in the next block. A small brown dog sniffing around him.

Samuel saw Autumn pounding frantically on the front door of a small brick house down the block. No one answered. She leaped off the front stoop and, screaming all the way, fled into a sandy, pebbly alley lined by wooden fences that snaked behind the houses.

"Nice of Autumn to scream like that and let us know where she is going," said Daniel, trotting beside his brother, eyes straight ahead.

"She's a nice girl." Samuel's earnest reply.

They caught up with her behind a stack of blue and yellow boogie boards tilting against a wood picket fence. The boards formed a low tent. Autumn probably thought she would be hidden by them.

They found her huddled behind the boards, her body hunched and shaking, her breath coming in loud wheezes.

Panting like a dog. Like a cornered dog.

Samuel set his eyes to glowing. He felt anger now and new dedication to the task. No hesitation.

Did she really think she could wound the Avenger? The Heater? Punish the Punisher?

"Please . . . Oh, please . . . please . . ." She was begging now. Actually wringing her hands in front of her. She climbed to her feet. "Please?"

Samuel trained his gaze on the white skin of her tummy between the top and her low-riding shorts.

She shrieked in shock and agonizing pain as he cut a long line across the bottom of her stomach. Reflexively, Autumn grabbed at the deep opening in her skin and spread both hands over it.

But she couldn't keep her insides from spilling out.

The twins watched in intent silence, as if watching a medical demonstration, as her intestines came sliding out over her hands and poured like long pink sausage links to the ground.

She made a hoarse choking sound, grabbing frantically at the waterfall of shiny wet organs spilling out. Spilling out of the deep slit across her belly. A gusher of pink and yellow sausage oozing through her fingers.

She choked and gagged until her eyes rolled up and her knees folded and she slumped face forward with a loud *splaaat* into the still-throbbing puddle of her insides.

The twins gazed down at her in solemn silence.

Samuel waited for his eyes to cool. Then he stepped back, let out a sigh, and called down to her, "Oh, poor Autumn. Lassie, where are those beautiful new shoes now?"

Daniel laughed and gave him a shove. "You're a poet." He stared down at the young dead woman. His smile faded. "You know, bruvver, we don't have to worry about Pa now."

That made Samuel laugh. "I think Pa is deep in trouble," he said softly. "Come on, bruvver. Let's find our way back to the Harbor of Sag."

"A poet," Daniel murmured. "My bruvver is a poet."

It was a beautiful morning, just starting to warm up, the air so fragrant and fresh. White butterflies danced over a flowering hedge. A soft breeze tickled his skin and cooled Samuel's hot face.

It made him think of the island. The ocean breezes over Cape Le Chat Noir. The simple life. Waves splashing as he and Daniel and Ikey ran along the cool, wet sand.

"I think the bus stop is over here," he told Daniel. "It's such a pretty day. I know we're going to have a nice ride."

58

When Lea's Skype bell rang on Saturday morning, she was tempted not to answer it. But when she saw it was Martha calling from Cape Le Chat Noir, her curiosity won out over her weariness.

She clicked to take the call, and a second later, Martha's pale blue eyes gazed out at her from the laptop screen. Martha's short blond hair was wrapped in a colorful kerchief, but her face appeared pale and lined, and she wasn't smiling.

"Martha? What a surprise." Lea adjusted the laptop to get her face in the frame.

"How are you, Lea? Is this too early?"

"Well, no. Actually, I'm still up from last night. Look at me. I'm still dressed in yesterday's clothes. I . . . didn't get any sleep."

"Well, I'm sorry to call so early."

"That's okay. Really. It's nice to see you. We haven't been in touch for a few weeks."

"You look awful, Lea. What's going on there? Why were you up all night? Is everything okay?"

Martha's image froze on the screen. Her face didn't move but her voice continued. Then the screen popped, and her mouth caught up with her words.

Lea sighed. She rubbed her eyes with her finger and thumb. "It's a long story, Martha. What a horrible night."

"Why? What on earth happened?"

"The kids are gone. I mean, disappeared."

Martha's mouth dropped open. The screen stopped again with her face frozen in her startled expression.

"You mean the twins? You can't find them?"

"No. All the kids." The words tumbled out of Lea in a trembling voice. "The twins. Ira. Elena. Her friend. And a lot of other kids." She sucked in a deep breath. "Oh, Martha. I don't know what's happening!"

"I don't understand, Lea. You called the police?"

A bitter laugh escaped Lea's throat. "Oh, yes. The police have been here. Local police. State police. The FBI. They've been here all night, Martha. All night asking Mark and Roz and me questions. Questions. Like it's our fault. Like we're hiding something from them. Like we know something we're not telling."

"Oh, wow. It sounds like hell. Do you want me to get off? I could Skype you some other time. Or I could email—"

"No, it's fine. Actually, it's good to have a friend to talk to. I can't see straight I'm so frazzled and worn out. But it's good to have a friend."

"Well, where do they think your kids are? Do they think—"

"It's not just my kids. There are maybe seventy or eighty kids missing in Sag Harbor, Martha."

"Huh? That's *insane*."

Lea rolled her eyes. "Insane but true. At first the police thought it started here. You see, a bunch of kids were hanging out in our guesthouse in back."

"Seventy?"

"No, not seventy. A few. Several. I . . . don't know. Mark and I went out last night and—"

"Are you sure you want to tell me all this now? You look so tired and—"

"I don't understand it, Martha. They're just *gone*. Where would they go? How could they all sneak off together? It can't be a mass kidnapping. Whoever heard of that?"

"What do the police think? The FBI?"

"At first they didn't believe us. There's been some other trouble here. With Mark. And we had all these totally upset parents calling us and coming over. All night. Expecting Mark and me to know where their kids were. Angry at us. I mean, they blamed us for . . . for . . ."

"And no trace of any of them? No clues at all?"

"Not yet. The Sag Harbor police station—they started getting call after call. All from frantic parents reporting their kids were missing. So they finally caught on it wasn't just Mark and me. It was happening all over town."

"And so—"

"But that didn't stop them from searching our house. And tearing up the guesthouse. I don't know what kind of clues they expected to find. A map leading them to the kids? A ransom note for seventy kids? I—I—"

"Take a breath, dear. This must be so *horrible* for you. I can't believe what you are going through."

"No, you can't." Lea wrung her hands. "Elena is so sensible. I can't imagine . . ."

"Well, I'm sure they'll all be found soon. Such a big group of kids can't stay hidden for long, can they?" Martha leaned toward the camera. "Have the police considered this might be a big prank?"

"Huh? A prank?"

"You know. One of those mass jokes people dream up and spread over the internet?"

Lea shut her eyes. "No. No one is treating it as a joke," she said in a whisper.

"Well, I don't think I'm going to tell you why I Skyped," Martha said, rubbing her cheek. "Oh, wait. Maybe I'd better. Actually, as I think about it, what I called to show you might help."

Lea swallowed. Her throat felt dry as dust. "Help?"

Martha nodded. "I've been doing some photo research. You

know. That's what I do for a living. I promised you I'd do some checking."

Lea nodded. "I remember. Did you find something interesting?"

"Interesting, yes," Martha replied. "But not good news, Lea. In fact, it's totally disturbing."

Lea rolled her eyes. "Oh my God, Martha, what did you find out?"

"Let me email you the photos. I think you'll understand why I wanted you to see them right away."

"Okay. Send them to my gmail account, Martha. We can talk about them as I look at them. But what did you find? What is so disturbing?"

"Just wait. I'm sending them now. There are three JPEGs in all."

Lea watched Martha's fingers move over her keyboard. Her expression was tense, almost bitter.

"I'm really sorry to burden you with this, Lea. Especially with the hell you're going through. I hate being the messenger, really. James and I care about you. We think you did such a brave thing. I mean, adopting those boys. But you need to see these photos."

Martha blinked and typed some more. "Also, James and I . . . we kept something from you. We kept a big secret. We thought you'd be better off not knowing. We did it for your happiness, Lea. But the secret . . . I guess I just have to come out and say it. It's making us feel too guilty."

"What the hell, Martha? What are you talking about? Such a big fucking mystery? Maybe this isn't the best time. I—"

"Did you get the photos, Lea? You should have gotten them by now. Check your email. I'll just wait."

Lea slid the mouse and opened her in-box. Yes. There was the email from Martha.

Lea clicked twice to open the attachments. She waited for them to download, watching the little line slide across the screen. Her heart started to pound.

She clicked again, the Picasa program came to life, and a thumbnail photo appeared on the screen. She clicked it. And watched as it sprang up full-size.

A black-and-white photo. A beach scene? No. "Is it Cape Le Chat Noir?"

"Yes." Martha's reply in a soft voice.

"Oh, wow. I see. It's after the hurricane. All the houses are down. And the trees. I see."

She saw several forlorn people huddled in the background, fuzzy and out of focus. And near the camera . . . Standing together, one with his hand around the other's shoulder . . . Yes. The twins.

No mistaking them. Daniel and Samuel standing close together, surrounded by the hurricane's destruction.

"Martha, I see the twins."

"Take a good look, Lea."

"I *am* taking a good look. The twins are standing there together after the hurricane. They're holding on to each other and looking very alone and forlorn."

Her eyes scanned the photo. "I don't see anything else, Martha. Am I missing something? Why is this photo interesting?"

"Well, do you notice the photo is in black-and-white?"

"Yes. So?"

"It wasn't taken after the hurricane here last month, Lea."

"I don't understand."

"The photo was taken in 1935. The day after the hurricane of 1935."

59

The morning went by in a blur, and even two cups of strong black coffee at eleven didn't wake Mark's mind. Half an hour earlier, he had lifted his head, not recognizing where he was.

It took him a few seconds to remember he had fallen asleep after five in the morning on the couch in the den, the soft couch, his favorite napping couch, in the clothes he had worn to Nestor Bridger's house.

The police. The angry, frightened parents. They hadn't left till five. And then, his head throbbing, he had collapsed on the couch.

But who could sleep with Ira and Elena and the twins gone—missing—and at least seventy other children, and after an endless night of the phone ringing nonstop with frantic parents at the other end, and police and FBI and who-knows-what invading every corner of his house. And the questions . . . the accusing stares.

Could they possibly think he had kidnapped seventy kids? Where would he keep them? In the basement? In an upstairs closet?

Somewhere around three in the morning, they asked if he wanted a lawyer. He'd gone into a long rant—he should have held it in—but the wine and the exhaustion, not to mention the anxiety, made him open up and tell them how stupid they were to think he had any answers or anything helpful to say or anything to do with the disappearance of the kids.

Maybe his rant encouraged them to leave. No. Now he remembered. More angry, frightened parents showed up at the door, and the round of questions grew even more intense.

He pictured the two Sag Harbor officers he'd become very acquainted with, Pavano and Pinto. They'd been pushed to the back. Too low on the ladder to speak, they watched the whole thing, leaning against the living room wall, occasionally muttering among themselves as their superiors—who was that big guy, Franks, who paraded back and forth with his Glock hanging out of its holster?—asked all the questions.

The officers and agents didn't leave until after five. Mark sprawled fitfully on the worn-soft couch, the questions tumbling through his mind, struggling to think clearly about a theory of his own. It wasn't forthcoming. He didn't have a clue.

He was just as puzzled upon waking up. And where was Lea? A glance at the clock. Ten-thirty. *This is Saturday, right?*

She must be up in our room. Can she sleep? This is late for her not to be downstairs.

Rubbing the dark stubble on his cheeks, he shuffled into the kitchen for coffee, feeling stiff and not at all rested and in need of a shower. He squinted at a note in Roz's handwriting: *Axl upset by all the noise last night. Took him to the beach. Home after lunch. Have my phone. Call with any news.*

"No news, Roz."

He peered through the kitchen window at the guesthouse. Dark and silent.

His eyes burned. He suddenly craved a cigarette. Crazy. He hadn't smoked since college.

Don't be crazy. Don't give in. You have to be the sane one.

Lea printed out the three photos and sat at her desk gazing at them over and over. The first two—the twelve-year-old twins in 1935—came as a frightening shock.

The twins were twelve in 1935 and twelve today. Cape Le Chat

Noir . . . It's the island where the living coexist with the living dead.

"It can't be! Oh, shit. Oh, shit. Please. It can't be true!"

She sat in the glare of the monitor, gazing from one photo to the other, screaming at them without even hearing herself. Screaming at the beautiful twelve-year-old twins. Beautiful more than seventy-five years ago. Beautiful today.

"Oh, shit. Oh, shit. I brought them here. Martha warned me. Mark warned me. Oh, shit. It's all my fault." And then: "But I care about them. They *made* me care about them."

She slammed the two printouts onto the desk and gazed at the third one. This photo was *not* a surprise. She had suspected it. She prayed and prayed it wasn't true. But somehow, all along, Lea knew.

Martha had signed off, and her apologies reverberated in Lea's mind.

"So sorry. Really so sorry. I think I warned you not to rush into adopting those boys. I just had the feeling there was something *off* about them."

Not much of an apology, really. Of course, Martha was sorry for the way things turned out—*not* sorry for providing Lea with the truth.

And what did she mean by something *off* about them? Martha said she would send an email—immediately—with all the information she had been able to dig up about the boys. "It's not good news, Lea. I'm so sorry. I wish it weren't true. I'll send it right now."

And as for the third photo, Lea could see even on the grainy Skype image how uncomfortable it made Martha and how reluctant she was to discuss it at all.

"James and I hoped we were doing the right thing."

After that, Martha made an excuse to end the conversation. And repeated her apology, sounding a little more heartfelt this time. "I only wish . . ." No finish to that sentence. And then she was gone, and Lea sat in front of the screen, her eyes shut tight, but not tight enough to keep the pictures from her mind.

And things began to come clear, began to connect, starting with the twins, and moving to the murder in the driveway and the murder of Derek Saltzman and the disappearance of Ira and Elena and some seventy other kids.

Starting with the twins, who weren't really twelve. The twins, who had to be ungodly evil creatures she had brought home with her.

Was it coming clear? Did she have the connections right? It wasn't like she was blaming two innocent, adorable boys with such glowing blond hair and twinkling blue eyes. She wasn't condemning angels. She was starting to see demons.

But I care about them. I have such strong feelings for them.

And then Martha's email arrived, confirming her worst, most terrifying fears.

She couldn't read it all. Her eyes blurred the words. She didn't want to know the truth. Not *this* truth. She scanned through it, catching phrases that made her heart skip.

. . . Both died in the hurricane. The priest was summoned to perform the Revenir rite.

. . . The priest came too late. They'd been dead too long. He should never have revived them.

. . . They brought the evil of the grave back with them.

. . . They can kill. They can hypnotize. Like their bodies, their minds never advanced. They are still twelve.

. . . They lived in isolation on the island. People were afraid of them. They lived by stealing. No one was brave enough to stop them. They waited all these years for someone to take them away.

. . . They hate adults. They only care about controlling other children. They never got to be real children. So now they want to be leaders of children . . . To hold power over children . . . The only thing they care about . . .

Lea shut her eyes. "Oh, shit. Oh, shit. It's too much. It's all too horrifying. What will happen to Ira and Elena? How can I face Mark? How?"

Martha's words brought another revelation. The thought had been lurking in her mind. The email suddenly forced it to her consciousness. *The twins hypnotized me. They used their powers on me. They made me care about them. My connection to them . . .*

that feeling of love I thought I felt . . . it wasn't real. They used me. Used me to get here. No wonder I've agreed to their every wish. No wonder I never opposed them. . . .

She opened her eyes and shuffled through the three printouts again, as if hoping to see something she missed. Something redeeming. But there was no reassurance here. The past—and her future—held only horror.

Oh, poor Ira and Elena. Maybe there was time to rescue them. She *had* to try.

Carefully, she folded the three photos in half. She tucked them into the big pocket of her silky blue robe.

She heard a cough. Was that Mark stirring downstairs? The aroma of coffee made her stand up. She stretched her arms over her head.

Yes, she could feel her heart like a hummingbird in her chest. And the coffee aroma suddenly nauseated her.

Mark has to know.

She glanced at the clock on the bed table. Just past eleven. The morning had slipped past. But so what? What did a few hours matter when there was nothing to look forward to but more tears and grief and disbelief and anger and regret.

She moved to the dresser, adjusting the robe and tying it more securely, and picked up her hairbrush. She swept it back slowly through her straight black hair. It felt real. The touch of the bristles through her hair, the scrape against her scalp.

She brushed for a long time, leaning her head back, appreciating each stroke with a soft sigh. This was real. Nothing else in her life felt as real. Nothing else could be as real.

Oh, poor Elena. Poor Ira. What has Mommy done to you?

She forced herself to set the hairbrush down. Then she took a long, shuddering breath. She fingered the folded-up photos in her robe pocket and murmured out loud, "I'm going to tell Mark now."

Face the music, Lea.

Isn't that what her dad always said every time she had to be punished for some crime large or small?

You did the dance. Now face the music.

Did that make any sense at all?

The punishment was always the same: *Go to your room and stay there till I tell you to come out.*

She pictured her brothers smirking as she trudged off to her room, red-faced, fists swinging at her sides, ready to face the music.

Well, after all the years, now she was *really* facing the music.

She started to the stairs but stopped at the bedroom door when she heard the sirens. Approaching sirens, and there seemed to be a lot of them, a blaring concert of sirens, warring with each other.

Lea spun around and trotted to the bedroom window.

Several dark vehicles squealed up the gravel driveway. She saw the yellow letters *FBI* stenciled on one SUV. Two Sag Harbor black-and-whites, two unmarked SUVs, windows blackened, heavy like armored cars.

She gripped the windowsill and stared down at them all, her mouth hanging open, uttering small cries of shock.

Four or five dark-uniformed policemen lined up in front of the house, standing stiffly a few feet abreast of each other, weapons tensed in front of them. Were those automatic rifles?

She recognized the big black state police captain from the night before as he came roaring out of the backseat of an SUV. Was his name Franks? Yes. He had a pistol in one hand and motioned to the others leaping from their vehicles to follow him to the house.

They all had guns raised. All of them.

Do they plan to kill us?

"Mark?" Lea screamed, squeezing the wooden windowsill. "Mark! Do you hear them?"

Finally, she forced herself away from the window. She spun to the doorway, her robe tangling around her. And went running to the stairs.

"Mark! Can you hear me? Mark? What do they *want*?"

60

At first Mark thought people were screaming. The sound made him drop his coffee mug on the kitchen table. And as he hurried to the front of the house, he realized they were sirens.

And, strangely, the wailing cacophony made him angry. Because they had just been there, just invaded his house and his life, and he didn't want them back with their foolish accusations and misguided questions and insulting stares.

I'm sick of the bullshit. I just want my kids to be safe.

Why are they back here? What are they doing to find my kids?

Mark clenched his jaw tight and squeezed his fists until his fingernails dug into his palm. And then the pounding on the front door and the shouts shook him out of his anger.

He heard Lea calling his name. Turning, he saw her halfway down the stairs, her hand gripping the banister, her eyes wide with fright. "Mark?"

The pounding on the door drowned out the rest of her words.

"Mr. Sutter, police. Open the door." Barked. *Just like on TV.*

Mark pulled open the door. An army of men—it seemed like an army—led by Captain Franks, who came in with his shoulder low like an NFL blocking tackle, pushed into the house.

Mark stepped back, blinking at the force of it all. The sheer invasion. The anger. He saw the weapons raised. They forced him against the fireplace.

He heard Lea scream.

"Mark Sutter, you are under arrest for the murder of Autumn Holliday." Franks spitting the words in his face. Standing so close, Mark could smell the coffee on his breath.

"Huh? Autumn? What?"

Did the words make any sense?

Beside him, a wavy-haired cop was reading him his rights from the screen of an iPhone.

"Wait! Wait!" Mark raised his hands in the air.

The cops all tensed their weapons.

"What did you say?" His voice shrill, almost unrecognizable, shouting over the droning voice of the cop still reading off the phone screen.

"Did you say Autumn? Killed?"

He couldn't help it. He pictured her bent over his desk. Her hands gripping the edge of the desktop. That creamy white ass moving under him.

"Noooooooooo!" A howl of protest burst from deep inside.

Two cops stepped toward him menacingly, guns raised. He saw Pavano and Pinto holding back, still in the doorway, as if guarding against any escape attempt.

Were there cops outside in case he made a run for it?

What a joke. The child psychologist makes a run for it.

How could Autumn be dead? Why? Why Autumn? And why did they think he was the murderer?

"I—I can't . . . believe it." He felt sick. He grabbed his stomach. He felt the coffee rising up his throat. "Not Autumn."

He let out a long sigh, shut his eyes, and leaned back against the mantel.

"No. There's some mistake. Why are you arresting Mark?"

He heard Lea's trembling voice. Opened his eyes to see her step warily past Pavano and Pinto into the living room.

The officers ignored her and kept their eyes on Mark, weapons tensed.

"You don't have to answer any questions until you have a lawyer present," Franks said, the only calm voice in the room. "But you can help yourself by—"

"When was Autumn killed?" Mark interrupted, narrowing his eyes at Franks. "Last night? You know I was here all night. You were here with me."

"How was she killed?" Lea asked, moving up beside Mark, gripping his hand.

Her hand is ice cold. She's as terrified as I am.

"Our initial report says she was murdered this morning. Perhaps an hour or two ago." His dark eyes locked on Mark's, probing. "Mr. Sutter, if you'd care to cooperate. Could you tell us your whereabouts this morning?"

"Huh? My whereabouts?" The word didn't make sense to him. He knew he wasn't thinking clearly. The word didn't seem like English.

"Did you go out this morning?" Franks rephrased the question. This version sounded more like a threat.

"N-no. I was asleep. On the couch in the den. I woke up and made some coffee." Again he felt his stomach lurch. He held his breath, forcing it down.

"You didn't go out this morning?"

His answer came out in a sharp scream. "No. I fucking told you. I didn't go out. I've been in here all morning. Do I have to spell the fucking words for you?"

Franks didn't react. He turned his gaze on Lea, holding on tight to Mark's hand. "Mr. Sutter, can anyone vouch for your whereabouts? Can anyone confirm that you were here all morning?"

"Lea can."

Franks waited for Lea to speak up. Mark saw she was breathing hard. She'd gone very pale. "Actually, I was upstairs. In our bedroom. Mark was down here. But I know he didn't go anywhere this morning. You kept us up all night, remember?"

"So you were upstairs and didn't see him this morning?" Every question Franks asked sounded like an innuendo and a threat.

Mark gasped, startled by the anger that built up so instantly inside him.

You should be out finding my kids.

"I didn't see him," Lea started. "But—"

Behind Franks, a state cop dangled a pair of silvery handcuffs in front of him.

"You're wasting your time," Mark told him, unable to keep a trembling sneer from his face. "If someone murdered Autumn, the real killer is out there. And you're standing here arresting me, a child psychologist who's never even been in a fucking playground fight."

"Very eloquent," Franks commented drily. "Listen, Mr. Sutter, cooperate with us now and we can clear this up very quickly."

Mark blinked. "What are you talking about? What do I have to do?"

Lea let go of Mark's hand. "I'm going to go call Nestor." She turned to Franks. "He's our lawyer. He's in Sagaponack. I don't think Mark should say another word until he gets here."

"What do you want me to do?" Mark concentrated on Franks. "How do we clear this up? *Tell* me."

"Show us your wallet," Franks said. "That's all. Have you got your wallet, Mr. Sutter?"

"Of course I have my wallet."

Franks nodded. "Then will you be so kind as to show it to us?"

Mark thought hard. Where did he leave it? His brain was so churned up. His stomach rumbled with anger. He could feel every muscle in his body tensed and tight.

Where? Where?

"I left it on my desk last night." He started into the hall.

Two cops rushed forward and grabbed him roughly by the arms.

"We have to come with you," Franks said. "You're in our custody, remember?"

"I know I left it in my office." Mark let the two cops walk on either side of him. Franks followed right behind. "I can picture it next to the phone."

Into the office. A strong breeze rattling the blinds in front of the open window. Mark gazed at the desk.

Autumn, how can you be dead? Who would want you dead?

Autumn, you were so beautiful.

No wallet.

He fumbled his hand over the desktop. He shoved a stack of folders out of the way. He pulled open the desk drawer and shuffled through it.

Don't look frantic. Don't make them think you're frantic.

But he couldn't control his hands from shaking. Emotion had taken over. Rational thought always lost out to fear, to panic.

"I know I left it here yesterday. I was at my desk and I needed one of my credit cards to buy something over the phone and—"

"Do you want to search for it in any other room, Mr. Sutter?" Franks's deep voice, mellow and calm.

Sure, he's calm. What does he have to worry about? He's so pleased with himself, so pleased with his false arrest.

"Yes. Yes. Let me look for it upstairs. In the bedroom. Maybe I left it on the dresser. Sometimes I leave it there. I—"

"Can I save us some time?"

Franks's question made Mark spin away from the desk. He squinted at Franks. "Save time? What do you mean?"

One of the officers handed Franks a plastic bag. It looked like a food storage bag. Franks shoved it into Mark's face. Mark squinted at a wallet in the bag. "Is this yours?"

Mark reached for it, but Franks swiped it away from his hands. "No. No. Don't touch. It's evidence. Trust me. We saw your driver's license inside. Your AmEx card."

A dizziness fell over Mark. No. Not dizziness. Falling, a free fall. Like he was dropping down an endless black hole.

"Okay. That's my wallet."

Franks nodded to the cop at the office door. "Put the handcuffs on him." He turned back to Mark, shaking the wallet in front of Mark's face.

"Mr. Sutter, your wallet was found this morning in the grass next to Autumn Holliday's front stoop. My advice, sir: Don't say another word to me until your lawyer gets here."

61

As the solemn-faced cop moved forward raising the silvery hand-cuffs, Mark had one of those flashing-lifetime moments he had always believed to be only a staple of fiction.

The room grew dark and Franks and the other officers appeared to fade into the wallpaper. A white light formed like a glaring spot-light in his mind, and the images began to whir past—not of his childhood, not of the history of events that led him to this madden-ing moment.

In the two-second flash of bright light, the events of his *future* swept past him, a frenzied slide show of despair and ruin. He saw a clear picture of his office, now a closet piled high with cartons. His career over. The house empty. His family scattered. Bold newspaper headlines bannering his disgrace. He saw the sad faces of Ira and Elena, two hardened, disillusioned kids.

And Lea . . . Where was Lea? Gone? No picture of Lea?

And the last image of himself, handcuffed in a tiny gray prison cell, clanging the bars with the handcuffs, pounding out his anger, shouting, "But I'm innocent. I'm innocent!"

The light faded. The room came back into focus. And Mark, startled, found himself shouting, "But I'm innocent!"

"Wow. No one ever told us that before," Franks said.

Maybe it was Franks's sarcasm that set him off. Or maybe it was the frightening images of the future that flashed before him, almost like something in a science-fiction movie. Or maybe it was the burning outrage that was making it impossible for him to breathe.

This isn't right. I didn't murder anyone.

I couldn't murder anyone. I couldn't murder Hulenberger. I couldn't murder Autumn.

My kids are missing. My kids are in terrible danger.

Why are they arresting me? Why aren't they finding my kids?

Something clicked in his mind. He thought he heard the *snap.* It was too much. Too much. Without thinking, he started to move.

He saw Lea push her way past the cops in the doorway. And he heard her sharp cry: "It wasn't Mark! It was the *twins!*"

He heard her blame the twins. Yes, he heard her shout to the officers: "It was the twins." And he saw Lea pull some papers from her robe pocket.

But he couldn't stop himself to hear more. He was already moving. He already had the back of the desk chair gripped in both hands.

With an animal grunt, he gave the chair a hard shove. Thrust it forward on its metal wheels. Sent it skidding into the cop with the handcuffs.

He saw the seat cushion bounce into the cop's midsection. Heard the unsuspecting guy utter a startled groan and saw him toss his hands up, off-balance.

And then Mark dove to the open window. Both hands on the sill, he flung himself out, swung himself like some kind of circus acrobat.

Surprise, everyone!

He dropped onto his back on the hedge beneath the window. Scrambled like a turtle to right himself, arms and legs spiraling at once.

And yes, the element of surprise had helped him. No one was staring out of the window yet. As he forced himself to his feet, ignoring the bramble scratches on his back, his eyes gazed around the backyard. No cops back here. The idiots thought he would submit without any trouble to them.

He heard shouts and angry cries. Heard Franks's deep voice booming from the window. "Sutter—stop. Are you *crazy*? Stop or we'll shoot!"

But he was already around the side of the guesthouse, his sneakers pounding the hard ground, into the cluster of trees that bordered the yard. The ground sloped down, leading him into woods thick with ancient oak and sassafras trees, their fat trunks tilted and tangled and hugged by fat evergreen pines.

Every sense alert, his eyes darting to find a path through the thickening underbrush, Mark heard no shots. The shouts had faded far behind.

He couldn't think clearly. The rush of adrenaline and the blood pulsing so furiously at his temples kept his mind from focusing. He was an animal. An animal running to safety.

He leaped over a fallen trunk covered in green and yellow lichen. Pushed through two pine bushes, stumbled on the thick carpet of dead leaves under his shoes, caught his balance and kept running.

Small creatures scuttled out of his way. Chipmunks? Moles? Over the rushing in his ears, he heard the loud *caw* of birds high in the trees, and he imagined them calling to the police, reporting his location.

He realized he had never ventured into these woods behind his house. This was nature, the uncivilized world, and he was civilized. An author. A father. A husband.

But what was he now?

Running for his life, his freedom, what was he now?

And where was he going?

62

"I think we have a gang or something," Pavano said, chewing the end of his breakfast burrito. "I mean, something organized, don't you think?"

Pinto nodded. He drove past the middle school and turned the patrol car onto Ackerly Street, his eyes surveying the suburban-style houses, the neat lawns and paved driveways.

"Two burglaries on a Monday morning, and it isn't even eight yet," Pinto agreed. "I'd say it was the same guy."

"Couldn't be just one guy." Pavano wiped cheese off his chin with the back of his hand. His eyes were on the sidewalks. Perhaps they could catch them red-handed.

That would feel like an achievement. So far, my life here has been total frustration.

"Look at what they took, Pinto. Flat-screen TVs, desktop computers, phones, handheld video games. One guy by himself couldn't boost—"

"It's the food I don't get." Pinto burped loudly. He'd already finished his burrito. "I mean, emptying the fucking refrigerators? What kind of thief takes all the food, too?"

"A hungry one?"

"Ha-ha. Don't try to be funny, Pavano. You know what you are? You are antifunny."

"I'm not a fucking riot like you, Pinto. True. Let's try to think about this." He pushed a chunk of scrambled egg into his mouth. "This town has gone crazy, Pinto. Three fucking ugly murders. All those kids kidnapped. Now we got houses robbed and—"

The radio beeped. "Where are you girls?" Vince, able to sound harassed in only four words.

"We're on Ackerly near the school," Pinto answered.

"Good. I got another break-in for you. This one's on Clinton. Woman just got home. Thinks she saw the thieves running off. Maybe you can catch them. How fast can they run with computers and TVs?"

"Maybe they have a truck," Pavano offered.

"Maybe they have a flying saucer. Get over there."

The patrol car squealed like in the movies as Pinto made a high-speed U-turn, the car rolling over the curb, spinning up grass, then bumping back to the street.

"Vince, you sending backup?" Pinto, leaning over the wheel, eyes on both sides of the street at once.

"You're joking, right? Every other guy I got is with the feds and the state clowns, searching for Sutter. They're all over Sag Harbor yesterday and no one comes up with a footprint or a trace of the guy."

"You see the *Post* this morning?" Pinto slowed the car down as they approached the house on Clinton. "'Psycho Psychologist'?"

"Pretty good," Vince replied. "Hey, don't expect backup for anything. I got twenty more missing kids. The parents are out in front of the station banging on the door. Like a lynch mob or something. Where are you? You see any kids?"

"Of course I see kids," Pinto said. "We just passed the middle school. I see kids going in."

"School's gonna be a little weird," Vince said. "We got at least a hundred kids gone missing."

"Maybe there *is* a flying saucer," Pavano said.

Silence on Vince's end. The radio squealed, then cut off.

"There's the woman, waving to us on the porch," Pinto said. "Like we couldn't read her fucking address."

"People get upset when their house is robbed," Pavano murmured.

"Hey, you know what? You're a fucking genius."

"And how come you're in a total shit mood this morning?"

Pinto grunted. "I guess cuz everything is going so well in this town."

Pavano shoved the last chunk of burrito into his mouth. The car turned into the driveway. "You know, I don't think Sutter is guilty."

Pinto scowled at him. "Maybe I agree. But no one is asking us, Andy. Franks and the feds got their mind made up. They got the dude's wallet. They got the other two murders. And the fucking guy ran."

"It's not much when you think about it." Pavano reached for the door handle. The woman was running down the driveway toward them. "He just doesn't seem the type, you know."

"I don't know," Pinto said. "He seems pretty squirrely to me. That wallet thing. Does he ever look like he's telling the truth? No. And why did he run?"

"Just saying," Pavano murmured. "It's like a hunch, you know. Only stronger. I think he was totally shocked when he heard about his assistant being murdered."

Pinto grunted in reply. It was obvious he didn't agree. He cut off the engine. The two cops pulled themselves out of the car.

The woman was tiny, middle-aged, pretty. She was dressed in a white top and white leggings. She was screaming as she ran. "They cleaned me out! The little bastards cleaned me out."

Pinto stepped up to her. He was about a foot taller than she. Her streaked blond and brown hair was wild around her face. He squinted down at her. "Little bastards? You saw them?"

She nodded, breathing hard. "Yeah. Kids. A bunch of kids. I mean like little kids. Eight, nine. I screamed and they took off. Little bastards took my new iPad."

Pavano started up the driveway toward the house. "Can we come in? Look around?"

Behind him, he heard the radio in the patrol car squeal. He and Pinto both trotted to the car. Pavano got there first. "Vince?"

"Forget the burglary, Pavano. Get out of there."

"Why? What's up?"

"We're onto something. A neighbor spotted some of the missing kids. I need you over there now."

"Over there? Where?"

"They're in the school."

63

A buzzer rang and echoed in the line of classrooms down the hall. The signal to start class. But today no classes would be started.

Samuel knew the doors were locked, and the teachers had given up trying to enter the building. A group of seventh-graders had been given sentry duty, and they kept watch at all the entrances for any attempt to force open the doors.

Of course, the kitchen workers had been greeted warmly and ushered inside. They arrived first, just before seven, to begin preparing breakfast for the kids in the meal program. They soon got over their surprise at finding the new order, the new regime, as Samuel thought of it. The blue arrows were applied to their faces, and they immediately became pliable under Daniel's will.

Now they were in their white uniforms and aprons, preparing breakfast as usual, only this time for the new arrivals and for the robbery team who returned from their missions with great appetites.

The morning sunlight slanted into the classrooms as kids settled into their new rooms. Some of the light spilled in patches into the crowded, bustling hallway. The mood was cheerful and filled with anticipation for the adventures to come.

Of course, Daniel set the mood, sending his signals to anyone wearing the painted blue arrow, and he could alter the mood,

change the emotions and feelings of the two hundred or so followers simply by changing the direction of his thoughts.

Now Samuel followed him down the line of kids who were
showing off what they had stolen. He stopped in front of a frail,
young-looking blond boy with a galaxy of freckles across his nose.

"What's your name?"

"David."

"How old are you, lad?"

"I'll be eleven next week."

"Well, I'm impressed, David. *Two* laptops. Good work! You're
going to be on my special electronics team."

Samuel watched as a proud smile broke over the kid's face. Samuel patted the arrow on the boy's cheek, then pointed him toward
the computer room, which had been a sixth-grade classroom but
now was a storehouse for stolen computers.

Samuel gazed down the long hall, crowded with followers, some
presenting their stolen items for inspection, a group of new arrivals seeking instructions, a girl who carried her brown short-haired
dachshund with a blue arrow painted on the right side of its face, a
sixth-grade boy with long stringy brown hair, leaning against one
wall, softly playing a guitar, several kids hanging back, watching
warily as the twins made their way through the patches of dull sunlight in the hall.

"Why did you take these sweaters?" Daniel asked a lanky red-
haired girl with red-rimmed glasses.

"I liked the colors," she said. "And I think they're my size."

Daniel motioned with his head toward the girls' hall. "Go try
them on. If they don't fit, put them in the clothing storeroom."

She nodded and hurried off with her armload of stolen sweaters.

"So much to organize, boyo," Daniel said, giving Samuel's face a
gentle slap. "You know. Bright beginnings, right?"

"This school is *ours*!" Samuel declared. He pumped his twin a
hard high five. His excitement actually made it hard to stand still.
He wanted to hop and dance and bounce off the tile walls. What
an amazing day! He hadn't felt this alive in many years.

Daniel may be the match, but I am the fire.

Samuel glanced through the window of the art room. He could see Ira standing at a table with several cans of blue and white paint. He was applying a blue arrow to the cheek of a chubby sixth-grade girl with braces.

"It's so simple. Once the arrow goes on, they're one of us," Daniel said, watching Ira work. "Better than hypnotizing them, my lad. They don't even know I'm putting thoughts in their brain."

"Ira is getting good with the paintbrush."

"Ira is a good bruvver." He flashed Ira a thumbs-up. "Feel like some breakfast, Sammy? We've worked hard this morning. But it feels like play, doesn't it, lad?"

Samuel nodded. "We rule, Daniel. It's what we always wanted. We waited so many years."

Daniel had a faraway gaze in his eyes. "It's a full school. And we rule. But we've only just started."

Samuel snickered. "I know your mind, Daniel. I know you want all the kids, all the kids . . . *all*."

"All." Daniel still had the dreamy look. "All. It's a start, right? Does it make you feel alive, Sammy? Does it now?"

Before Samuel could answer, someone stepped in front of them, someone large, blocking their path. Her appearance was so sudden and unexpected, it took Samuel a few seconds to realize he was staring at Mrs. Maloney, the principal.

She wasn't in her usual school outfit. She had an oversize man's white dress shirt pulled over sloppy, faded jeans. Her bird's-nest hair was matted in spots as if it hadn't been brushed. She kept blinking and gazing down the hall, as if trying to force away a bad dream.

"Well, what a surprise. To find so many of my lovely chickadees in school so early. What are you all doing here?" she shouted over the chatter of conversations. "Can any of you darlings explain this to me?"

Daniel stepped up to her. "How did you get into the building, mum?"

She lowered her gaze to him. "Daniel? Are you here, too? And your brother? What are you doing here? Why are the doors locked? Can you be telling me what's going on?"

"But how did you get in?" Daniel repeated.

The principal dangled a ring of keys in one hand. "I know some hidden entrances. This is my school, don't you know."

"No. You don't rule the school, mum." Daniel spoke softly, blue eyes probing hers. "We rule the school."

My bruvver looks calm but I can feel his agitation. We made a mistake last week. We forgot to paint an arrow on her cheek. We let her get away.

"Daniel, lad, you don't make any sense," she said. Her eyes were over his shoulder. Samuel could see her counting, taking a tally of the kids in the hall.

They had all grown silent. All eyes were on the confrontation between Daniel and the principal. And the tension was evident in the heavy, ringing hush over the hall.

"Who brought you all here?" She raised her head and shouted. "Did someone force you to come here?"

Silence. No one moved now.

"Somebody tell me what this is about. I don't want to punish you all. But you will give me no choice."

Daniel nodded as if he agreed with her. He signaled to Samuel with another nod of his head.

Samuel took a deep breath and started to heat up his eyes.

Mrs. Maloney seemed like a nice woman. She should have stayed home. Now she will be sizzling like Irish bacon.

"The police have been notified," the woman shouted. "They are on their way. I saw a crowd of people outside the building. Many of them are your parents, waiting to see you. How many of you would like to go out and see your parents right now?"

No hands went up. A boy giggled. That made several other kids laugh.

"What's funny, kiddos?" Mrs. Maloney demanded. "Someone tell me, what's funny?"

The red curtain had started to form over Samuel's vision. But he could see the uncertainty in her eyes, and he saw the uncertainty turn to fear.

She tried again. "Your parents will be so happy to see you. Come on, everyone. Follow me. Let's all go outside." She motioned toward the front doors and took a few steps. But no one made a move.

"You don't understand, mum," Daniel said almost in a whisper. "We rule the school."

Her eyes widened in surprise. "Daniel? You? You are behind this bizarre behavior? You and your brother? I . . . don't believe it. You are good lads, I know. What—?"

And then Samuel turned his eyes on her, aimed the full heat of his power at her forehead. He misjudged. Aimed a little too high, and her hair caught fire. That bristly steel-wool hair burst into red flames.

She screamed and grabbed at her head with both hands. And he lowered the beam to her forehead. The skin peeled open, blistered, and split apart.

Her head is opening up. Like a flower blooming.

She raised her hands and pressed them against her burning face. Dropped heavily to her knees. And Samuel sent the fire to the top of her head, a powerful blast that made him dizzy for a second, made him quake, his knees threatening to buckle.

Her head burned like a torch. Her eye sockets lay black and empty now. And her nose was gone, just a dangling flap of charred skin.

The eyes burn so quickly. How quickly a face melts.

The fire moved down her neck, crackling, popping, setting the shirt ablaze. She toppled forward. Her charred head hit the hard floor with a *smack*. Her big body a beached whale, a pile of kindling.

She ended her life as a bloody bonfire.

Samuel shut his eyes. Kept them closed, waiting for them to cool, listening to the sizzle of Irish bacon.

A hard pounding, a deafening *boom*, jarred him from the pleasure of the moment. He turned to Daniel as a deep voice on the other side of the front door bellowed: "Open up! Police! Open this door—*now*!"

64

Pinto and Pavano arrived at the middle school less than five minutes after they got the call. Pinto bumped the black-and-white onto the curb and muttered, "Oh, shit."

Pavano saw the crowd move toward them. Maybe twenty or thirty people. Parents? "How the fuck did they get here before we did?"

The two cops had no choice. They climbed out of the car. The shouted questions were like an attack.

"Are our kids in there?"

"What did you hear? Who brought them here?"

"Are they hostages? Is this a kidnapping?"

"What's going on? What are you going to do?"

A jumble of frightened voices.

Pavano spotted three people, two men and a woman, at the side of the building. It took him a few seconds to realize they were about to climb into an open classroom window.

"Hey! Stop!" Pavano took off, shouting as he ran. "Back away! Now! Back away from that window!"

A young man in gray sweats turned to face him. "We want to get our kids out."

"We'll get your kids," Pavano said, struggling to catch his

breath. "But we don't know who's in there. If this is a hostage situation, you could put your kids in even greater danger."

The three parents stared hard at him, a tense face-off.

"Step back. Let the police handle this. We have to figure out what is happening here."

The parents finally relented. Pavano led them back to the sidewalk.

The parents formed a circle around the two officers. The women were dressed in shorts and T-shirts, some in morning-run or workout sweats or tights. A few of the men appeared dressed for work. A very tanned man wore a black swimsuit and flip-flops and had a blue beach towel over his shoulder. A gray-haired couple held each other around the waists of their maroon sweats, tears rolling down their faces. *Must be grandparents.*

Pinto crossed his arms on his uniform shirt. He had a distant look in his eyes, as if he was willing himself away from this. Pavano raised his hands for quiet, but the shouts and frantic cries only grew louder.

"We know how worried you are. But don't do anything crazy. We're going to take care of this. Your kids will be safe." He told them what he thought they wanted to hear.

He glanced up the lawn at the school building. The red morning sunlight glowed in the long row of classroom windows. No sign of anyone near the school or at the double doors of the entrance.

Pavano let out a sigh of relief as, sirens blaring, a convoy of cars pulled onto the grass. He saw Franks in the first car, an old Ford Crown Victoria, black, with *New York State Police* emblazoned in yellow on the door. Followed by two more state cars and then the feds in three unmarked Escalades.

The state guys went to work, pushing back the crowd, herding them off the lawn and toward the street.

Jogging along the sidewalk, his brown suit jacket flapping around him, Franks waved both hands, motioning Pinto and Pavano toward the building. "Let 'em know we're here."

As if the sirens weren't a tip-off.

Pavano trotted after Pinto, up the long stone walk to the front entrance, past the bare flagpole, past an abandoned red backpack in the grass, the flap open, obviously empty.

"What's the plan here?" Pavano said, a heavy feeling rising in his stomach as they stepped into the shade of the three-story school. "We just knock on the door and they come out?"

"Beats the shit out of me." Pinto picked up the abandoned backpack, inspected it, and tossed it back onto the grass. "Do I know what the hell is going on? Kids go missing on Friday and Saturday. All found in school on Monday? Does that fucking make sense? Why would kidnappers take a hundred kids to school? It's fucking insane."

Pavano stared hard at his partner. Pinto was already red-faced and breathing hard, beads of sweat glistening on his broad forehead despite the coolness of the morning.

"You read the reports from yesterday. Just about every parent said the same fucking thing. Their kids vanished without a word. No sign of violence. No break-ins. The kids were just gone."

"I read 'em all," Pinto said, eyes on the entrance. "And what was that shit about blue arrows on their faces?"

"Just like Sutter's kids, remember? They said it was a school thing. The principal told them to do it."

Pinto grunted. "It's an alien thing, Andy. The kids were all abducted by aliens. They're slaves on another planet by now."

Pavano snickered. "Neighbors saw kids coming into the school this morning carrying laptops and TVs. No way they can be on another planet if they're robbing every house in the neighborhood."

"Just sayin'." Pinto didn't smile.

A shadow passed over them. Cawing birds swooping overhead made Pavano glance up. The clouds overhead were jagged and torn, as if a big cloud had been shredded into long pieces, the sky as frenzied and chaotic as everything down below.

Pinto took the front steps two at a time. He tried one door, then the next. "Locked." He raised both fists to the double doors and pounded against the wood. "Open up! Police! Open this door— *now*!"

Before they could detect any response, Franks stepped up behind them, badge dangling on his suit lapel, followed by four federal agents with *FBI* stenciled in red on their gray flak jackets.

Franks raised both hands in a halt signal. "Hold up. We've got to deal with these parents first. Make sure they're out of the way— in case there's trouble."

Trouble? Pavano wondered what the captain was expecting.

Franks rubbed the scar on his chin. "If this is a mass kidnapping or a hostage situation, we might face weapon fire. There could be explosives—"

The rest of his words were drowned out by the shouts of the parents. Ignoring the outnumbered state cops, they surged forward, stampeding to the bottom of the wide concrete steps.

"We want our kids."

"How are you going to get them out of there?"

"Who locked them in? Who brought them here?"

"What are you doing? You're just going to pound on the door?"

The parents glared up at the officers, their faces frantic, voices shrill. In their utter confusion and helplessness, they all shouted at once, anger rising over their fear.

Pavano saw one of the state cops hand Franks an electric megaphone and Franks began to plead for quiet. "I need you to step back. Quiet, everyone! Quiet! Everyone, please be quiet and step back."

His requests were unheeded. The shouts grew angrier and more desperate. Pavano saw more SUVs pull up and more frantic parents running to the steps. A young couple tossed their bikes to the grass and came jogging to join the others.

As Franks continued to plead, his voice washed back at him as if by a powerful wave. Two officers flanked him. They assumed a defensive position, their faces hard, and unholstered their revolvers.

That's what it took to quiet the crowd. Pavano let out a long whoosh of air. He hadn't realized he'd been holding his breath.

"What now? Their guns are drawn? They're going to fucking *shoot* the parents?" Pinto murmured, close to his ear.

Pavano shook his head. "Can't blame the parents for being in a panic. If it was your kid in there . . ."

Pinto spit in the grass. They stood just behind Franks. Pinto crossed his arms in front of him. Pavano stood stiffly, hands clenched into tight fists.

"We have no information at this time," Franks declared, his voice magnified like the voice of God, booming over the nearly silent crowd.

The exact wrong thing to say, Pavano thought. *What a fucking jerk.*

And yes, it ignited the parents again. Cries of alarm and a barrage of frantic questions.

When the cops finally restored quiet, Franks took a different tack. "We are going to get your children out of there. And we will get them out safe and sound."

Some muttering, but the reassurance seemed to calm them a little. Gazing down at the crowd from the steps, squinting into the spreading glow of sunlight, Pavano recognized Lea Sutter. She stood near the back of the crowd, dark hair down around her face, arms crossed, wearing a pale blue sweater.

Next to her, he spotted Sutter's sister. Roz. She stood with her hands on the shoulders of her squirming little boy, leaning over him, trying to get him to stand still. Lea Sutter stared straight up at the school building, frozen like a statue.

She has four kids in there. What must she be feeling? What horror is she going through? Four kids . . .

Pavano had read the report taken by a state cop late Saturday night. The Sutter kids were reportedly in the guesthouse out back with some friends. And all vanished, kids and guests, leaving no trace. He pictured the twin boys she and her husband had adopted from that hurricane-devastated island. What a tough introduction to American life those poor boys were getting.

He swallowed. *Especially if their new father is a murderer.*

And then he couldn't stop the gruesome images from playing through his mind. The young girl with her stomach burned open, lying facedown in a pile of her own intestines. If only he hadn't seen that. And the boy with his head completely burned off. And . . . and . . . the man in the car . . .

If only he hadn't seen the three victims. Then he wouldn't see them in his dreams. Or when he closed his eyes for a moment. Or when he woke up. Every day. He saw them every day.

I'll probably see them forever.

And if Mark Sutter was the murderer . . . Pavano wondered if Mark Sutter was haunted by the murders, too. He claimed he thought about the first murder night and day. Really? Did he think about the victims and think about how he had burned them . . . burned them open like some kind of monster from hell?

But Pavano knew Franks was wrong. He knew Mark Sutter wasn't the murderer. Sutter didn't have it in him. Pavano could read him. He didn't have the anger. He didn't have the insanity. He didn't have the *balls.*

And there stood Lea Sutter, on the edge of the crowd of frantic, shouting parents. Silent and still. Standing so stiffly beside her sister-in-law. No kids and no husband.

Your husband isn't a murderer. I know it.

So why did he decide to run?

Pavano knew the cops were no closer to finding the murderer of those three people than they were to knowing how a hundred or more kids disappeared from their homes and, presumably, were locked in this school building.

And thinking this, with Franks fading into the background of his mind, yammering on through his megaphone, Pavano suddenly felt the full weight of all his regret. It came so suddenly and as such a surprise, he felt his knees start to give as the heaviness swept down over him.

All the wrong choices he had made in his life suddenly confronted him, just as the crowd of parents confronted Franks. Such bad timing, but he couldn't shake it off. If only you could command your mind to think what it *should* be thinking.

But instead he thought of Sari and then back to Susannah, how he messed up his marriage. It could have worked if he had tried harder, if he hadn't been such a fucking jerk. And Sari . . . Again Sari. What the fuck? What made him think he could step into the past and just claim her as if he hadn't walked out on her before? Didn't he move to the Hamptons to step into his *future*? Well, she fucking showed him you can't go home again.

All the wrong choices. All wrong. Every decision of his life.

And now what?

What was happening? A young blond woman with a red polka-dot bandanna around her neck had stepped forward and was talking to Franks. Their conversation quieted the crowd as the parents strained to hear.

"You're a teacher here?" Franks said, lowering the megaphone.

"Yes. I'm Rhea Seltzer. I teach eighth-grade science. I arrived the usual time. A little before eight. With everyone else." She gestured to some other teachers, who stood apart from the parents. "The door was locked. We tried shouting for the custodians. We thought it was a mistake."

"Then what did you do?" Franks asked, brushing a fly from the broad shoulder of his jacket.

"We . . . didn't know what to do. We looked for Mrs. Maloney. The principal. She usually arrives about the same time we do."

"But you couldn't find her? Is she here?" Franks shouted into the megaphone. "Mrs. Maloney, are you here?"

"We saw her car. It's a white Camry. It's in the teachers' parking lot. But we couldn't find her." Seltzer pointed to a short man with a mane of curly black hair. "Mr. Munroe had her cell number. We tried it several times, but we only got her voice mail."

One of the cops leaned forward and said something in Franks's ear. "Are the teachers always the first to arrive?" Franks asked.

"No," the woman answered. "The cafeteria workers get here first. They have to make breakfast for the meal-plan kids. They arrive before seven-thirty."

"Where are the cafeteria workers?" Franks demanded, shouting as if at a rally. He raised the megaphone. "Are you here? Please step forward."

"Their cars are here. But they're not out here," the teacher Munroe called out.

"They must be inside," Seltzer suggested.

Pavano thought about it. The food workers arrive and are ushered in. Then the doors are locked. Are they hostages? Were they let in to cook for the kidnappers? For the kids?

Franks had to silence the chatter of the crowd again. Pavano turned to the building and gazed along the row of windows. The morning sun, yellow now and slowly rising over the trees, reflected in the glass. He couldn't see anyone inside the classrooms. The third window from the right was open, but no sound came out.

"My son has a cell phone but he's not picking up," a man in a dark blue running suit said.

"I found my daughter's phone in her room. She would never leave the house without it."

"I've been trying to call my daughter all morning. No answer. I don't understand it."

"My son is new in this school. Why did they take him?"

"Are you going to get them out or are you going to stand there asking questions?"

That shout made Franks's face twitch. He was a big, imposing man. He radiated strength, athletic prowess, and power. But his stance wasn't impressing this crowd of frightened parents.

They wanted action. Why weren't the police storming the building? Or at least trying to make contact with whoever was inside? It was obvious they thought Franks was stalling, that he had no clue what to do here.

And they were right.

Pavano's eyes surveyed the crowd. He stopped at Lea Sutter, still standing near the back, her arms crossed tightly over her chest. She hadn't moved.

Did she know where her husband was hiding? Sutter had eluded all three police departments for two days now.

A man in a white T-shirt and khaki shorts came along the side-walk, walking his French bulldog on a leash. He stopped in surprise and stumbled over the fat dog when he saw the crowd. "Is this a school event?"

Some parents turned to set him straight on what was happening.

"Has anyone received a ransom demand?" Franks boomed, sweeping the megaphone from one side of the crowd to the other. "Has anyone received a communication from *anyone* inside the school building?"

The answer was a definite no.

One of the state cops said something to Franks, pointing to the school. Franks let the megaphone slide to the ground. He motioned Pavano, Pinto, and the other cops forward.

"Can't wait to hear his brilliant plan," Pinto muttered. "He probably wants to blow the fucking school up."

"That would get us home in time for lunch," Pavano replied, eyes straight ahead on Franks.

Pinto stopped him. "Whoa, partner. You're not developing a sense of humor, are you? Did you forget? I'm the sarcastic one?"

"Sorry," Pavano murmured. "The strategy just seems kind of obvious to me. I mean, there's an open window, right? So . . . we fucking go in and see what we find in there."

"And if the kidnappers start shooting?"

"Pinto, do you really think there are kidnappers? Kidnappers who grab a hundred kids, take them all to school, and make no demands?"

Pinto shrugged. "What else could it be, shitbrain?"

"We're going in," Franks announced. "Weapons in hand."

The weapons order drew loud howls of protest from the crowd. Franks motioned toward the open classroom window. "Ignore the crowd. If you see someone holding the children, shoot first. Just don't hit any kids. Shoot anything else that moves."

What movie did he get that line from?

Guns drawn, the feds in the FBI flak jackets strode to the open window. Pavano had to squint. The windows all gleamed as if the sunlight was coming from inside.

Pavano, Pinto, and three other local cops followed, almost as an afterthought. Pavano glanced back at the street and saw Big Pavano in his blue-black captain's uniform standing by himself. His cap was tilted over his head. His gun was holstered. He was shaking his head as if he disapproved of the whole thing.

"Where the hell has he been?" Pavano asked.

Pinto spit on the grass. "The captain likes a big breakfast."

"Franks probably hasn't kept him in the loop," Pavano suggested. "It's a miracle the feds are letting Franks run with this."

"Waiting for him to hang himself," Pinto muttered.

They were approaching the open window. Pavano still couldn't see any sign of life inside. He felt his chest tighten. Each step made him feel a little more tense and a little more alert.

What kind of madman kidnaps one hundred kids? What is he doing to them in there?

He pictured the boy with his head burned off.

Oh, God. What are we going to find?

"Here we go," he muttered without realizing it.

Pinto leaned close. "I've been in some tough situations," he said softly. "I always think of a line from a country song I heard." He poked Pavano. "You're a country music guy. You probably know it."

Pavano didn't reply. He waited for Pinto to tell him what song.

"'God is great, beer is good, and people are crazy.'"

Pavano grinned. "Yeah. I know that song, Pinto."

"It ain't a song, Andy. It's my Bible."

Pavano heard the French bulldog start to bark, as if warning them away from the window. Franks stepped up beside the feds. Cautiously, he raised his head to the window and shouted inside. "Can anyone hear me? We're coming in!"

Pavano and Pinto tensed their weapons.

"We're coming in!" Franks shouted again. "Police! We're coming in! Police!"

Pavano could see only the back of Franks's head. From his vantage point, the classroom was a sunlit blur. Was anyone in the room? Or even nearby?

Weapon in hand, Franks motioned for the feds to let him go in first. He started to raise himself over the window ledge.

Something caught Pavano's eye. He turned in time to see the front doors of the school building swing open. He heard parents gasp and shout in surprise.

"They're coming out! The kids are coming out!"

65

Lea leaned close to Roz, her hair brushing her sister-in-law's cheek. "It's all my fault," she whispered.

Axl let out a cry and tried to break free from Roz's grasp. But she had him securely by the shoulders, and he only succeeded in pitching himself off the grass, his tiny sneakers kicking air.

"Lea, what? I can't hear you." She lowered her arms around the little boy's waist and held him tight. "Take it easy, Axl. Be a good boy and I'll buy you some candy."

Lea wiped a tear from her eye. "I said it's my fault. All of this."

Roz narrowed her eyes at her. "What are you saying? I don't get it."

"Ira and Elena. I've put them in so much danger. I love them so much. I . . . couldn't bear for anything to happen to them. They're my children, Roz. My children."

"Lea, please—"

"Mark warned me but I didn't listen to him. I wanted those twins so badly. I mean, I *thought* I wanted them. And now, look what I've done, Roz. Look what I've done."

"Lea, you're not making sense. Of course you're upset. I'm upset. Look at everyone here. We're all going out of our minds with worry. But how can you blame yourself? You didn't—"

"I brought them home. I should have known. Why didn't I listen to Mark? To Martha? I can't believe it, Roz. I tried to tell the police it's the twins. I tried to show them the photos. But then Mark ran and they . . . they ran after him. They wouldn't have believed me, anyway." She couldn't hold back the tears any longer. Wrenching sobs escaped her throat.

Roz let go of Axl and wrapped Lea in a hug. "Stop. Stop it. You're saying crazy things. How can it be the twins? You know that can't be true. Lea, no one blames you. Mark doesn't blame you."

"He *should*. Don't you see? He *should* blame me. When he knows . . . Oh, Roz, when he knows . . ." Another uncontrollable round of racking sobs.

"Aunt Lea is sad?" Axl gazed up at Lea. He looked about to cry, too.

She forced herself in control for his sake.

"Yes, Aunt Lea is sad, but she'll be happy again soon. You wait and see, honey."

"Evil. So much evil. I have proof, Roz. I have the photos. I wanted to show the police. But they wouldn't look at them. I know you think I'm crazy. I know—"

"I don't think you're crazy, dear. I just know you haven't had time to recover from that horrifying hurricane."

"Recover?" Lea cried. "*Recover?*"

"Take it easy, please, Lea. You're frightening Axl." She wrapped him in another hug.

"Now here I am, I'm standing here helplessly while poor Ira and Elena are in there. My babies. They're in such danger, and there's nothing I can do. It's—it's too late!"

"Lea, the police are here. The FBI. Look at them all. They'll get the kids out. I know they will."

"No. You don't understand. They're helpless. They're completely helpless. They can't get them out. They can't save anyone against so much evil. Martha warned me. Martha emailed me again yesterday. All the details. All the horrible details."

Holding Axl between them, Roz pressed her cheek against Lea's. "Stop. Stop. It'll be okay. You'll see, dear."

They stood that way for a long moment. And then Lea pulled back when she heard cries and shouts of surprise from the crowd of parents.

"The front door is opening. Someone is coming out!"

66

A kid appeared in the doorway. Then two. Two blond boys.

It took Pavano a few seconds to recognize the Sutters' twins. He struggled to recall their first names. Old-fashioned names.

Everyone seemed to move at once. The feds and the cops stepped back from the window. The parents pushed toward the kids at the door. At first they cheered, but then a strange silence descended as the doors slammed shut behind the twins.

When the parents realized that no more kids were coming out, the shouts and confused cries rose up again.

The two boys stood rigidly side by side, hands balled into tight fists at their sides. They wore jeans and matching black T-shirts. The sunlight made the blue arrows on their right cheeks shimmer.

At the side of the building, Franks tossed down the megaphone and went running toward the twins. "I've got you! Come with me! You're safe!"

One of the twins raised both hands in a halt signal. "Stay back! Don't touch us!"

"Don't touch us!" his brother echoed.

Franks stopped short. "Why? Is there a bomb? What did they do to you? Did the kidnappers put explosives on you?"

"Stay back. Stay away." Both twins motioned Franks to retreat.

Pavano saw Lea Sutter push her way through the crowd. She stretched her arms out to the boys as she made her way toward them. "Daniel! Samuel! What are you doing?"

How totally fucking weird.

Pavano stared hard at Lea. She stopped at the edge of the crowd. She didn't run up to her two boys.

How totally fucking weird. She didn't ask if they were okay.

Instead, she asked what they were doing.

Wouldn't a mother want to know how her kids are being treated? If they are in danger?

"What are you doing?"

Pavano watched her as she repeated the question. Was that concern on her face? A mother's concern? No. The question seemed to be a challenge.

"Boys, can you get over here?" Franks called. "You're safe. We'll make sure you're safe."

The twins made no attempt to heed him.

"Who's in there?" Franks demanded, his voice amplified over the crowd, now hushed, tense faces watching the boys, watching the doors. "Were you kidnapped? How many are there? Is everyone okay in there?"

Pavano saw Lea Sutter take several steps toward her twins.

"Stay back, Mum," the one with dimples called. They both motioned Lea back. They were twelve, but their voices hadn't started to change yet. They had tiny angelic voices to match their faces.

Franks turned to the cops and agents behind him. "Careful. Those two aren't moving away from the school. I think someone planted bombs on these kids." That comment drew gasps and horrified cries from the crowd of parents.

"Get back, everyone!" Franks shouted. "Get back—*now!*"

"This is fucking weird," Pinto muttered. Pavano nodded in agreement. The twins didn't appear frightened at all. In fact, they had grins on their faces.

"We RULE!" the one named Daniel shouted. He thrust his fists above his head. "We rule the school!"

The other boy—Samuel—shook his fists in the air.

What the fuck are they saying?

"WE RULE THE SCHOOL!" they declared in unison.

Pavano saw Lea Sutter sink back into the crowd, her face pale with horror. Did she have tears streaming down her face? She turned away. Pavano couldn't see.

"We need you to step away from the building," Franks shouted. He moved toward the twins. The four feds followed him, hands on their holsters. "Put your hands down, boys, and come over to me. Slowly."

"We rule! We rule!" The twins screamed. "Bright beginnings! Bright beginnings, everyone!"

Franks tossed the megaphone to the grass. He motioned his officers forward. "Okay, boys. We're not going to hurt you. We're just going to take you to safety."

"I don't think so," Daniel replied. "We rule now. Bright beginnings!"

Pavano glimpsed something strange about the other twin. Samuel. What was he doing with his eyes? His face was turned away from the officers.

"Let's get them!" Franks cried. Flanked by the other lawmen, he took off, trotting toward the twins, arms outstretched.

Screams burst out as a blast of red light—like a solid flame— shot over the crowd of parents. Silent but blindingly bright, it bulleted over the cars, over the street, leaving a fiery trail against the pale blue sky.

Startled, Pavano ducked. By the time he overcame his shock and turned to follow the fiery beam, he heard what sounded like the crack of a lightning strike—the hiss and crackle of a powerful electrical charge.

He gasped along with others in the crowd as the dark-shingled roof of the house across the street burst into flames. The flames licked across the top of the roof, then spread quickly down the sides. A tall tree leaning over the right side of the house crackled as the top limbs caught fire.

Andy froze in confusion. He saw Big Pavano running to his car, most likely to call the fire departments. Franks squinted at the fire, revolver raised helplessly. He had taken a defensive stance, as if ready to do combat.

Screams rang out again as another beam of fiery light—like a laser rocket—soared high over the crowd. Seconds later, the next house on the block, a tall Tudor-style house rising high over a wall of green hedges, burst into flame. Windows shattered. Flames danced along the hedge tops.

Pavano heard horrified shrieks as the front door burst open and people came running out of the burning house. The front of the house was lost behind a wall of fire now. Trees burned. A flaming limb came crashing down on an open convertible in the driveway.

He saw Big Pavano, still on his radio, frantically waving people away from the burning car. The gas tank could explode at any moment.

Quickly, the hiss and roar of the fires threatened to drown out the horrified screams and cries. And a strong breeze brought choking black smoke sweeping over the crowd.

"They've got a *weapon*!"

The two blasts forced Franks to stop his pursuit. But it didn't take him long to recover. "The kid's got a weapon!" he bellowed. "Get 'em! Grab 'em! Get that weapon away from them!"

Ducking his head like a running back, Franks took off toward the twins.

"Oh my God. Oh shit. Oh my God!" Pinto cried. He grabbed Pavano by the arm as the red laser smacked Franks in the chest, sending him sprawling backward.

A *sploosh* sound escaped Franks, like someone diving into a swimming pool, and a gusher of bright scarlet blood gurgled straight up from his body. Pavano saw bright flames scorch a deep hole in Franks's chest, a hole at least as big as a cannonball. And before Pavano could move, the big cop was down on the grass, roaring and rolling and writhing in an agony of blood and fire.

67

Lea turned her eyes from the big black police captain. He had finally stopped writhing and moaning. At the end, he had flung his arms in the air, flung them up again and again, as if he wanted to take off and fly away from the burning pain.

Now he lay on his stomach in a lake of dark blood. The FBI agents were down on their knees beside him, shaking their heads.

Lea saw the twins—her twins—edge back into the school building. The doors slammed hard behind them.

Sirens squealed on the street as three hose-and-ladder fire engines, flashing bloodred lights, roared onto the block. Lea turned to see the wall of fire. She couldn't see the houses behind them. Trees burned, swaying under the weight of the roaring flames.

The whole block is on fire. Like hellfire. They're turning Sag Harbor into Hell.

"They killed a cop!" an old man in a gray sweatsuit was screaming, his eyes bulging, waving his arms like a madman. "They killed a cop! They killed a cop!"

Lea coughed and covered her face as waves of thick smoke rolled over the schoolyard. Two more fire trucks screamed onto the block. One bumped over the curb, nearly smashing the back of an SUV.

They must have called other towns, Lea knew. The Sag Harbor firefighters were mostly volunteer, not up to battling a fire this big.

"They killed a cop! They killed a cop!"

The police seemed in disarray now. Several dark-uniformed cops ran to the front doors of the school building and began to pound with their fists.

Lea spotted the two officers who had come to her house. They had moved to face the crowd of terrified parents. They were shouting something, but Lea couldn't hear them over the shrill squeal of the sirens and the shouts of firefighters as they leaped off their trucks into action.

Were the cops trying to get parents to leave the school grounds? They were shouting and motioning frantically as wave after wave of charcoal smoke, thick as cotton candy, rolled over everyone, turning the world dark and making people choke and gasp for air.

Like one of those black-and-white horror movies Mark likes so much.

"They killed a cop! They killed a cop!"

Couldn't anyone shut the poor guy up?

Lea turned and realized she'd lost Roz and Axl. *They were right beside me. Maybe Roz wanted to get Axl out of the smoke.*

Someone had covered the dead officer with a canvas tarp. The FBI agents were conferring in a circle with the uniformed cops.

As Lea watched, her panic swelled. She thought about Elena and Ira. A sob escaped her throat. She clenched her jaw. Bit her tongue, hoping the pain would force back her panic.

Without realizing it, she had moved up the lawn, toward the circle of law officers. She stopped when she heard the FBI agent's voice, raw and raspy: "They killed a cop. Prepare your weapons. We're going in."

Lea stifled another sob. She stumbled back.

Ira and Elena must be terrified.

She spun away, choking from the smoke, her throat burning as if *she* was on fire. She strode toward the street, toward the flames, the crackling trees trembling their limbs as if pleading for help, the frantic men hooking up long hoses, the flames, the flames, such a horrifying twitch and dance of the flames.

She walked quickly toward her car at the end of the block, fumbling in her pocket for the key.

All my fault. All my fault.

I have no choice. I have to find Mark.

I'll wait in the car, away from the choking smoke. As soon as the kids are safe, I'll find Mark.

And tell him everything.

68

Pavano joined the tight formation of agents and cops as they moved toward the open classroom window. Birds squawked, circling crazily overhead. He glanced back. The fire had spread to the next block. People ran screaming from burning houses.

Smoke and fire as far as he could see. The trees were being consumed by the roaring flames. On the street, five or six cars burned. People ducked and tried to cover their heads from the choking waves of black smoke, swirled by sharp gusts of hot wind from the fire.

The crowd of parents appeared to have been blown apart, people running frantically in twos and threes, in all directions. He saw some ducking low as they ran, covering their heads, making their way to the back of the school. Andy knew they might be in the way if the law enforcement people needed to use the back entrances, but there was no time to warn them or move them away. The FBI guys seemed determined to go in there and confront whatever awaited them without any further delay.

"Maybe we all get mowed down," Pinto said, sweat drenching his forehead. "That kid had a fucking laser blaster like in a movie. Did you see his eyes light up? Fucking weird."

Pavano struggled to hear him over the wail of sirens as more firefighters poured onto the block, adding to the snarl of the fire, the screams of the frenzied onlookers and the cries of terrified people fleeing their burning homes.

How could a quiet neighborhood erupt so quickly in such screaming terror?

"Did that blast really come from his eyes?" Pavano asked Pinto. "That's impossible, right?"

Pinto shrugged. "Beats the shit out of me. But I think we know how those three murder vics got burned. And it wasn't Mark Sutter."

They followed the backs of four FBI agents. The front row stopped under the window and ducked beneath the stone window ledge. Pavano could see their features tighten, their faces unable to hide their fear. He knew they were picturing Franks screaming and writhing on the ground as his body flamed and burned.

Suddenly, Pavano knew what he was going to do. He had known it for a while. It was there in the back of his mind, waiting . . . waiting for the moment he knew would come.

He pushed through the agents and cops to the window. He could see inside the classroom. It was empty and dark.

His heart suddenly beat so hard, he had spots flashing in his eyes. His mouth instantly became as dry as straw. He took a deep breath, willing himself to go ahead with this.

Because it was time to do something brave. Time to do something in his life that he wouldn't regret later no matter the outcome. Time to do *something*.

He couldn't remember which of the agents was in charge. Was it the good-looking guy with the steel-gray eyes and the short blond hair and the high movie-star cheekbones? Or the short, stern-looking older dude?

Pavano decided to try them both. "Let me go in."

They squinted at him as if he was speaking Martian. "Say again?"

"Let me go in first. Alone."

"Why?"

341 • RED RAIN

Because I've screwed up everything else in my life. Maybe I can be an actual hero today.

"I know those boys," Pavano said. "I've spoken to them before. They'll remember me. I can talk to them. I can reason with them. They'll listen to me."

They reacted with hard stares. Like he was totally mental.

"Maybe I can find out what's happening in there," he heard himself say. "Without any more casualties. If I go in by myself, maybe . . ."

The two agents exchanged glances. Behind them, Pavano glimpsed Pinto, casting him questioning looks, like, *What the hell are you doing?*

"Go ahead," the short bald one said. "One shout and we'll be there behind you."

Pavano blinked. "Really?"

The agent motioned to the window. "Better you than me, Sergeant. I hate the smell of burning meat."

69

It took Samuel a moment to realize that the gray-haired woman in the hairnet and crisp white uniform was a cafeteria worker. She carried in two plates heaped high with scrambled eggs, bacon, and hash brown potatoes, just as the twins had ordered. Like all the workers, she had a blue arrow stenciled on one cheek.

Daniel motioned for her to set them down on the teacher's desk, where the twins had settled after returning from their triumphant moment in front of the school.

Samuel lowered his face near the plate and inhaled. He loved the aroma of scrambled eggs. He could eat eggs all day long.

The cafeteria worker stopped to gaze at the poster hanging on the wall behind the twins. It was a portrait of the president of the United States, and someone had painted a blue arrow on his cheek.

"Go back and make eggs for everyone," Daniel told her.

She nodded obediently and turned to leave.

A window to a seventh-grade classroom Daniel had claimed as headquarters was open, and snakes of gray smoke billowed in, dissipating under the bright fluorescent ceiling lights.

Samuel leaned over the desk, dug his fork into the pile of eggs, and started to eat. The twins weren't alone in the classroom. Several boys sat at desks, playing handheld video games, reading books, joking with one another. Samuel knew they were restless, awaiting their next assignment. Were there more houses to break into? Some other mischief to perform to demonstrate who ruled the school?

Samuel knew what was coming next. Daniel would order them to round up more kids. More kids. More. Until all the kids of the town were together, and the helpless parents would go away, and Samuel and Daniel would rule forever.

He and his twin had waited all these years for someone to take them off the island. Sag Harbor was the perfect place for them. Small enough to be quickly conquered. Big enough to show how easy it was to take control.

The perfect place.

Samuel picked up a slice of bacon and bit off a big chunk. Crispy, the way he liked it. Chewing slowly, savoring it, he turned and saw that Daniel hadn't started his breakfast. He had a faraway look in his eyes that Samuel knew well.

The lad is going to spoil our breakfast.

"Ira"—Daniel waved to their brother, who sat at the back of the room talking with some friends—"Ira, come here. I need you to do something for me."

The other boys laughed at something Ira said. Then he climbed to his feet and shambled down the long aisle, hands in his jeans pockets. He stopped in front of the desk, eyeing the big breakfast plates. "When do I get breakfast, Daniel? I'm hungry."

"Don't be worrying about it, bruvver. I'm going to take care of you. First, I need you to do a tiny favor."

Ira tossed back his dark hair. "Favor?"

"Find our sister and bring her here. Do you know where Elena is?"

Ira nodded. "With Ruth-Ann and some other girls. In the eighth-grade room, I think."

"Tell Elena her bruvvers want to see her, all right, boyo?"

Ira nodded again, turned, and walked out the door.

Samuel took a big forkful of eggs. He watched his twin warily.

"When the bruvver and sister come back," Daniel murmured in his ear, "I'll need your help."

"Daniel, why? What do you want?"

"We don't want them anymore." Daniel's face hardened. His eyes appeared to freeze over.

"Don't want them?"

"We need to burn them, Sammy. It's important."

Samuel took a deep breath. He gazed down at the plate of food. He felt sick and knew he wouldn't be able to eat another bite. "Are you sure, Daniel? Both of them?"

Daniel nodded, then raised a finger to his lips. Ira was leading Elena into the room and down the aisle to the desk.

Samuel shooed the other boys out of the room. "Perhaps you lads would leave now." They hurried out, shoes clumping on the hardwood floor.

"Hi, guys," Elena said brightly. She wore a pink sleeveless shirt over white tennis shorts and pink flip-flops. Her hair fell loosely around her face. "What's up? Are we having breakfast?"

"No. Actually, we have to say good-bye," Daniel said, speaking matter-of-factly.

Ira squinted at the twins. "Good-bye?"

"Yes. We don't want you anymore," Daniel said. He stood up, hands pressed on the desktop.

Samuel saw the shock and confusion on their faces. Elena pressed her hands to her hips and strode up to the desk. "Daniel, what are you *talking* about?"

"We need to say good-bye to you now. We want Mum to ourselves, don't you see."

Samuel had his eyes shut. He concentrated and felt them begin to warm up.

"Whoa." Elena shook her head. "You're joking, right?"

"No joke. We want Mum to love us—not you. It leaves us no choice. We have to say good-bye."

Daniel turned to Samuel and gave a casual wave of his hand. "Go ahead, Sammy. Burn them both now."

Samuel opened his eyes, felt the heat, the incredible heat, and turned it on Elena first.

70

Pavano holstered his Glock and grabbed the window ledge with both hands. The granite ledge was shoulder high, and it didn't take much effort to hoist himself up onto his belly, turn, and lower himself into the classroom.

He waited for his eyes to adjust to the dim light. Smoke from the fires had drifted in through the open window, and he had to squint, as if peering through a heavy fog. The classroom, obviously a room for little kids, judging by the drawings hung on the walls, was empty and appeared untouched, in perfect order.

Pavano heard voices out in the hall. Kids' voices, he quickly determined. His legs suddenly felt heavy, his shoes rooted to the floor. He forced himself to move, stride silently to the door, where he stopped and listened for adult voices. For any clue as to who was giving the orders.

He realized he had grown used to his rapid heartbeats and the cold fear that prickled the back of his neck and made his hands so clammy and stiff.

Leaning against the doorframe, he peeked into the hall. No one in view, but the voices were nearby. Rectangles of light washed out from several classrooms. He stared down the row of gray metal lockers. Several of them had blue arrows painted on them, blue arrows facing up.

Pavano started to draw his weapon, then thought better of it.

I came in here to talk, not to shoot.

But it was impossible to force the ugly pictures of Franks's last moments from his mind. And impossible not to keep asking how that kid possessed the powerful and deadly weapon that had burned Franks to a crisp and made all the houses in sight erupt in flames.

His eyes darted from side to side, trying to take everything in as he stepped into the hall. Trying to act like a real cop who knew what he was doing in an insane, dangerous situation like this.

Pinto's country song flashed into his mind. *God is great, beer is good, and people are crazy.* No help. It might be Pinto's Bible but it was no help to Pavano now.

His eyes scanned the large blue-and-white banner that had been hung over a row of lockers. WE RULE THE SCHOOL.

That stupid phrase the twins had spouted when they emerged to face everyone at the school entrance. Was this really all about taking over the school? The twins weren't really the leaders, were they? Had they been hypnotized by their kidnappers? Had all the kids been victims of some kind of mass hypnotizing or mind control?

Pavano tried to force the questions from his mind as he moved slowly, step by step, toward the next room. After nearly tripping over a pair of white sneakers on the floor, he noticed a tall water bottle standing in front of an open locker. The locker was piled high with books and notebooks. Nothing unusual.

He kept his back against the tile wall, his hand poised over the holster. He edged up to the next room. A small sign on the wall read *Library*. He listened to the voices. Kids' voices. They spoke in normal tones. A girl laughed. A boy angrily told her to get away from him.

Pavano peered behind him, then to the end of the hall. So far, no one had noticed he had entered the school. He was about to reveal himself to the kids in the library. Would it send off some kind of alarm?

Does anyone else in here have that weapon, that incredible fire-breather?

He could no longer ignore his pounding heart. His chest ached, and he could feel the blood pulsing down his left arm. He sucked in a deep breath and held it, but it didn't help relieve the wave of panic swooping down on him.

He stepped into the rectangle of light at the library doorway.

"Hello. What are you kids doing?" His voice came out more shrill and menacing than he had planned.

He saw several kids sitting at low tables with books in their hands. Three girls were side by side in front of desktop computers. Bright games on the screens. A boy near the back of the room had his head down on the table, most likely napping.

All of the kids had blue arrows on their cheeks. Except for the napping guy, they all turned at the sound of Pavano's voice. "What are you doing?" he repeated, a little more softly. He took a few tentative steps into the brightly lit room.

Posters for children's books covered one wall. Four square columns that divided the room had book covers posted up and down them. One column had a long blue arrow pointing up on one side.

"Just doing library stuff," a red-haired girl said with her hands still on her computer keyboard.

"But . . . why are you here? Who brought you here? Are you being held against your will? Were you kidnapped? What's happening here?"

They stared at him. Made no attempt to answer his volley of questions.

"We rule the school," one of the boys said finally.

"Yes, we rule the school," the red-haired girl repeated.

"But who brought you here? Have you been kidnapped?"

They stared at him blankly. "Why did you leave your homes?"

Again, no one answered.

Pavano decided he'd better move on. He knew the FBI agents outside wouldn't give him much time. He wanted to solve this. He wanted to at least *learn* something before they came barging in. So little time, but he'd waited a lifetime to prove himself.

He edged back into the hall. Music echoed off the tile walls from a room somewhere in the distance. He could hear only the drums and the bass rhythm. Voices in the next room made him stop. Another locker stood open, this one with a photo of a white dog on the inside of the door. The locker was empty.

The small stenciled sign on the wall beside the next room read *7th Grade*. Pavano heard voices inside. He edged to the open doorway and listened.

"We don't need you anymore."

"We want Mum to ourselves."

"We need to say good-bye to you now."

Pavano recognized the high, little-boy voice of one of the twins.

He took a breath and stepped into the room. The twins stood stiffly behind the teacher's blond-wood desk. There were plates of food on the desk. On the wall behind them, a poster of the president with a blue arrow on one cheek.

He recognized Ira and Elena Sutter hunched in front of them, cowering together, hugging each other in terror.

"Remember me? Sergeant Pavano? I'm . . . a policeman." The words sounded wrong, as if he were speaking a foreign language. But he knew he had interrupted something.

Ira and Elena spun around, eyes pleading with him. "Help us. Don't let them burn us." They started to run up the aisle toward Pavano. But something . . . some kind of unseen force . . . stopped them halfway between him and the twins. Unable to move forward, they sank back against the chalkboard on the wall.

Daniel shook his head and stared at Pavano. "What a shame. What a shame. Don't you agree, Sammy?"

"What a shame," Samuel echoed.

Pavano felt a chill. "What do you mean? What's going on here?" He avoided Samuel's red eyes. Maybe if he ignored them . . . "Listen. Your mom is waiting for you outside. I need you to come with me now. I need you to trust me. Will you come with me?"

No one budged. Daniel narrowed his eyes at Pavano. "I don't think we can be trusting you, sir."

"Why not?"

"We trust ourselves now. We rule the school."

"I heard that. But it doesn't explain what's going on here."

"We don't have to explain." Daniel nodded to his twin.

Samuel stood taller, then aimed his eyes at Pavano.

"Hey, what the hell. What the hell are you doing?"

Samuel aimed a glowing scarlet beam of light. And Pavano felt a burst of pain, just above his eyes, like a searing hot knife blade in the middle of his forehead. Then he heard a tearing sound—like fabric ripping—and felt hot blood spurt down his face.

With a cry of pain, he ducked his head, tried to elude the scorching beam from the kid's eyes. He cried out again as another beam seared his hair.

Too dizzy to stand, he dropped to the floor and rolled between the desks. Ira and Elena, still pinned against the wall, cried out.

A red beam shot over Pavano, made a sizzling sound as it slanted over the floor behind him.

I'm not going to fail this time. I'm not going to die. I'm not going to fail.

Head reeling, blood trickling into his eyes, Pavano tightened his muscles, readied himself. With an animal roar, he leaped to his feet, tried to dodge the blast of light, but the roar turned into a scream of pain as his shoulder exploded.

The blast knocked him back to the floor. He writhed on his back, unable to shake away the scorching waves of pain, tasting the hot blood flowing from the gash that split his head.

With an agonized moan, he managed to pull himself onto his side. Through the wash of blood, he glimpsed the classroom doorway. Saw the figure move quickly into the room. And gasped: "What are *you* doing here?"

71

Mark didn't answer as he burst into the room at full speed. He saw Ira and Elena huddled in terror in the middle of the room and he knew he had to move fast. He knew he had surprise on his side.

A jumbled text message from Lea had made him think the kids were being held in the school. It read: *Kids school help.* Her second text was just as frantic: *Twins evil dangruss.*

When Mark sneaked in through the basement entrance, he nearly fell over the charred body of Mrs. Maloney. The sight of her corpse, burned black and tossed on the basement floor near the furnace room, sent him into a breathless panic. *Ira? Elena? Are the kids being burned, too?*

Now he tore into the classroom, intent on saving his children. He had seen the cop go down. Saw the tear in the cop's scalp and the blood flowing down both sides of his face. Saw the cop thrashing on his back in pain.

Mark roared down the aisle and heaved himself over the teacher's desk. Eggs and potatoes went flying, and the plates crashed to the floor.

Startled, the twins froze.

Sliding over the desk on his stomach, Mark shot out both arms in a desperate grab for the two boys. He tightened his fingers in their hair and *smacked* their heads together as hard as he could.

The collision made a *clonnnk* sound like wood smashing against wood.

Samuel grunted in pain, as the fire in his eyes dimmed like a car cigarette lighter dying.

Cursing, Daniel squirmed and tried to spin away.

Hold on. Hold on. You can do it.

Mark squeezed his fingers into their hair, and with a grunt of effort, smashed their heads together again with all his strength.

Without even a groan, their jaws went slack and their eyes rolled up. Mark loosened his grip on their heads, and they slumped to the floor behind the desk.

Gasping for breath, he lowered himself to the floor, then turned and motioned frantically to Elena and Ira, frozen in the aisle, gaping at him in shock. "Dad! How did you get in here?" Ira cried.

"Hurry! Out of here!" He hurried over to them and wrapped them in a tight hug. "You're okay? You're not hurt?" They nodded. Mark glanced at the twins, still unconscious, piled on top of each other on the floor. He knew they wouldn't be out for long.

"No time! No time! I have to get everyone out." He guided them urgently toward the open window and watched as they eased their legs over the ledge and disappeared over the side.

"I'll be back!" he called to the cop thrashing in pain on the floor. "I'll come back for you."

He sucked in a deep breath, coughing from the smoke-filled air, and took off running down the long hall to the front doors, shoes skidding on the tiles. He grabbed the door handles, fumbled with the bolt that held them locked, shoved it aside, and flung the doors open wide.

Then he turned and tore back down the hall—all a blur of shadows, the walls, the rows of dark lockers, the classroom doors.

You can do this. Keep going. You can do this.

"Out! Everybody out!" His hoarse screams rang off the walls. "Everybody outside!"

Flinging open doors, he shouted at the kids sitting at the tables, on the floor, on window ledges. "Out the front door! Your parents are waiting! Out! Get moving!"

The halls were suddenly alive with jubilant shouts and excited kids stampeding to the doors. Whatever hold the twins had over these kids had ended, and they rushed to celebrate their freedom.

Heart pounding, Mark remembered the wounded cop. He dove into a classroom, careened off a wooden table, bounced to the window, and threw it open. Through billowing curtains of black smoke, he saw cops and feds in several windows down the row.

"Cop down!" he screamed. "There's a cop down inside! He needs help."

FBI agents and uniform cops swarmed to the window, and then black jackets were everywhere, in his window and at the door. They didn't seem to recognize him or remember that he was a fugitive.

"It's the twins! I knocked them out. But the cop was hurt. The twins did it. You have to take them." Mark realized he must sound crazy.

A stern-faced cop grabbed Mark's arm. "Just take us to the cop, okay?"

He led them into the hall, nearly silent and empty now. Trotted toward the classroom. Was this the right room? Yes. He saw the poster of the president with the blue arrow on his cheek. Black smoke billowed into the room from outside.

Pavano had pulled himself to a sitting position and was gripping his head with both hands to stanch the flow of blood. Two cops rushed to his side, one of them shouting into a radio-phone for help.

Mark waved the FBI agents to the front of the room. "The twins. It's the twins. They're the killers! I'll explain later. Just grab the twins!"

He saw their skeptical looks. They hesitated, then moved toward him, suspicious. "Who are you, mister? How'd you get in here?"

Mark shook his head. "I'll explain everything. But you've got to get these twins. I knocked them out. Get them. Behind the desk. Watch out . . . Watch out for the eyes."

The agents drew their weapons and he stood back. He watched them go into a stalking stance as they approached the desk.

"The twins. They're on the floor. I . . . I knocked them out. We got them. We *got* them!"

Two agents lurched behind the desk. They appeared to freeze, as if someone had pushed a pause button. Slowly, one of them raised his gaze to Mark. "No one here. No one." He glanced at the open window. "We're too late, I think. They got away."

72

Mark saw Lea walking determinedly down the middle of the Sag Harbor pier, eyes searching for him among the two rows of parked cars. He could see her distress from her body language, arms tensed at her sides, hands balled into fists, shoulders slumped, strides clipped and rapid.

He waited at the far end of the pier, the meeting place he had suggested that morning. Behind him, the water of the bay lapped darkly against the pilings below. The white yachts lining both sides of the pier stood as still as if on land, too big to be rocked by the gentle waves. One enormous yacht had a red Porsche parked on its wide stern and white-uniformed staff carrying breakfast trays to the main cabin.

Mark stepped out from behind a black Mercedes SUV, watching the pier behind Lea, making sure she hadn't been followed.

The morning had started out cloudless and bright, but now the sky was leaden with acrid smoke. Mark glanced at his watch. Not quite eleven o'clock, and the pier was pretty empty. In an hour or so, as lunchtime approached, the parking spaces would all be filled. He watched men unload shrimp and lobsters from the back of a white panel truck and carry them across the pier into the small, shingled Dock House clam bar.

He took a deep breath, expecting to smell salt water. But sour smoke burned his nose. *That fire must still be out of control.*

A man and a teenage boy walked past carrying fishing rods. The boy pointed to a spot on the side of the pier, but the man waved him off, and they kept walking. No one else in sight. Mark slid out from the SUV and called to Lea.

She stopped short, as if surprised to see him there. Then she came running, dark hair bobbing at the sides of her face, no smile for him.

"Lea—"

"Oh, Mark, here you are."

He wrapped his arms around her and pulled her against him. He wanted to squeeze her tight, hold her there for a long time. She was his old life, his good life, and he desperately wanted to hold on to her. He kissed her, then pressed his stubbly cheek against her face.

"Mark." She pulled away, out of his arms. "I got your text. You're okay? How did you get away from the school?"

"The FBI agents didn't recognize me. I slipped out while they were searching the classrooms." He held onto her. "Thank God the kids are okay."

He felt her shudder. "I saw Ira and Elena. I talked with them. They're fine. Roz took them home. It's so wonderful, Mark. You got them all out."

She raised her face to him. "The twins? Did you see them? Are they—?"

"They got away. I knocked them out, Lea. I . . . I slammed their heads together. I think it broke their spell over the kids. But they escaped. I don't know where—"

"Oh, Mark . . . you were so brave, sweetheart. But . . ."

But?

He waited for her to continue, but she didn't. When she raised her eyes to him, he could tell she was holding something back. She changed the subject. "Where did you stay all weekend?"

"At Nestor's. In his poolhouse. The police came to the house, but they didn't search the poolhouse. I hid in a tiny closet. But they never searched back there."

Her dark eyes locked on his. "Thank God you're safe. You look horrible."

"I . . . haven't slept much. I've been worried—"

She pressed a finger to his lips. "So much to tell you." More tears welled in her eyes. "The twins. I'm so sorry. I should have listened to you. I didn't know—"

A green BMW pulled in beside the Mercedes. Mark guided Lea away toward the Dock House.

"It's our last morning, Mark."

Her words sent a chill to the back of his neck. He squinted at her, unable to respond.

"Maybe we could try to have a normal morning, okay? Wouldn't that be nice? A last normal morning?"

"Lea, what are you saying? You're talking in puzzles. Tell me about the twins. What do you know about them? What did you find out?"

She ran a finger down his cheek. It made his skin tingle. He had rescued the children. They were safe. Why were her eyes so sad? What was she hiding from him?

"A normal hour or two," Lea said. "Look how pretty it is. The white yachts, the pier stretching into the bay, the seagulls against the sky. This is one of my favorite spots in the Hamptons. It always reminds me of Sausalito. Remember that weekend in Sausalito? That restaurant down by the water? We were so young."

He grabbed her shoulder. "Lea, you need to tell me what's going on. Why are you talking about Sausalito? Why are you acting like this? You are really frightening me."

She forced a tense smile and turned away. "I think the waffle cone place is open. Let's get waffle cones, Mark, and maybe walk through town. You know. Like a normal couple. Just stroll aimlessly up and down Main Street and people-watch, the way we used to. We can do it, Mark. The police won't be looking for you anymore."

"No. Not till you explain to me." He grabbed her by the arms and locked his eyes on hers, trying to see her thoughts.

She turned away, as if his stare was too much to bear. "I . . . I'm so sorry, Mark. It's all my fault, don't you see. That's why I feel so bad. I feel so bad for you, Mark. Especially for you. Because you've been so wonderful and loving and trusting. Yes, trusting. And I . . . I've ruined everything."

"But—how? What are you *saying*?"

A sob burst from deep inside her. "Don't you understand, darling? This is the last hour? It's our last hour. Don't you *see,* sweetheart?"

"No. It can't be. Come here." He tried to hug her but she stood rigid, her dark eyes finally coming to rest on his face.

"Don't you see, Mark? I guess you can't. I guess I have to say it. Okay. Okay. I'll tell you. I died on Cape Le Chat Noir. I died there, honey. I'm so sorry. I died in the hurricane."

73

Mark felt a tingle of fear run down his back. Overhead, a seagull screamed as if reacting to Lea's words. A burst of wind off the bay ruffled Lea's hair.

He held onto the sleeve of her sweater. "Lea, you're not making any sense. We need to get you home. The stress—"

"No. It's true, Mark. I . . . didn't want to tell you, darling. I suspected it all along. Didn't you notice how different I was when I returned from the island? I suspected it. I fought it. I fought it every day. I hoped against hope. But I knew. I knew. And then Martha emailed me . . ."

"Lea, you're not dead. You're standing here with me. You're just very distraught, and we need to find you help. I know several good doctors—"

Another seagull cry rang in Mark's ears. He glanced up and saw two fat gulls circling them low overhead.

"I didn't want to leave you. I didn't want to leave Ira and Elena." Tears glistened in her dark eyes and rolled down her cheeks.

"You don't have to leave. I'll take care of you."

"No." Her voice turned sharp. "No. You can't. I have proof, Mark. I have proof right here. I know you don't want to see it, honey. Telling you this . . . doing this to you . . . it's like I'm dying again."

"Stop saying that!" He didn't mean to sound frantic. How had she become so delusional? Did she see something unspeakable on the island? *Is that why her mind has snapped?*

Lea fumbled with her small black leather bag. Some makeup tubes and a mirror fell out. The mirror shattered on the asphalt.

Seven years bad luck, Mark thought. But he immediately scolded himself for having such a superficial thought when his wife was in such distress.

She pulled out some folded-up papers and uncreased them with trembling hands. She made no attempt to wipe away the tears that glistened on her face.

"Here. Oh, here. I'm so sorry. Martha sent these. I'm so sorry, Mark." She pushed the papers at him. Photographs, he saw.

"This is proof?"

She nodded.

He raised the first photo to his face. Black-and-white, very grainy. His eyes focused on a scene of destruction. Fallen houses. Debris everywhere. And then his eyes settled on the two blond boys standing forlornly in the foreground.

"The twins?" He gazed over the photo at her. "Samuel and Daniel? Taken after the hurricane?"

"Oh, Mark." A long sigh escaped her throat. "Yes. The twins. Taken after the hurricane . . . but a different storm, Mark. A different storm. The hurricane of 1935."

The papers nearly flew from his hand. "Lea, please. You're not making sense."

"The second photo, too. I *am* making sense." She struggled to pull out the second sheet for him. "Martha is a photo researcher. I told you that. She found these photos from 1935. Then she emailed me, Mark. Yesterday. She emailed me all the details. She found the truth, Mark. You won't like it, sweetheart. It's all so sad and horrible. You won't like it but you have to hear it now."

Mark took the photo and gazed at the twins standing bare-chested in the midst of the rubble. "I don't believe it," he said softly, "but let's say it's true. What does it mean, Lea? Tell me."

She nodded, tangles of hair, wet from tears, falling down the sides of her face. "There's a ritual on Le Chat Noir. It's called *Revenir*. It means *return*. It's performed by a priest." She stopped and pushed his hand away. "Don't look at me like that. I'm not crazy, Mark. I *wish* I was crazy but I'm not. Just let me finish."

He took a step back, the photos fluttering in his hand. "Okay. Sorry."

"The priest who performs the *Revenir* rite can bring back the dead. It sounds insane but I saw it. I saw it done. I didn't believe it when I was there. But it's true. He brings back the dead, Mark. And in that hurricane of 1935, the priest brought back the twins. The twins died in the hurricane, and the priest brought them back. But—"

He grasped her shoulders gently. "Take a breath. I'm listening. I won't interrupt you. But you're forgetting to breathe."

She swallowed. Her chin trembled. More tears glistened in her eyes. "The priest brought the boys back, but he did it all wrong. There were so many deaths to deal with. He messed it up, Mark. He . . . he waited too long. The boys were dead too long. And when they came back, they had all of death's evil in them. They looked the same. They seemed the same. They were alive again, but they were alive with evil."

What am I going to do? I've got to get her to a hospital. I know some doctors who can treat this. I can make some calls.

"The twins came back to life with evil powers, Mark. Hypnotic powers and powers to kill. The priest brought them back from the world of the dead. But he made mistakes. He told Martha he made mistakes. The boys have been the same age since 1935. Martha says they lived by themselves all these years, waiting . . . waiting for someone to take them off the island so they could work their evil. And I . . . I was the one. I brought them both here. I brought them into our family, our lives, and, and . . . I'm the only one who can take them back."

"Lea, stop. Please. Please stop. Let's not talk about it anymore. How about that waffle cone? Would that make you feel better?"

Anything to make her stop talking this insane nonsense. Why didn't I see that she was having a breakdown? How could I not have seen?

"No. It's too late for ice cream now, honey. Look at the third photo. Martha sent a third photo. I knew what it would show. I mean, I had a strong feeling. But there it is. There's my proof, Mark. I . . . I didn't want to show it to you. I don't want to leave. But I don't have a choice."

"You're not leaving. You're not going anywhere. Stop saying that. I love you. The kids love you. They need you. We won't let you go anywhere."

She pushed the papers. "Just look."

The third photo was in color. It showed a strange-looking man in a red robe. He had a large blue tattoo on the top of his bald head. He had one long-fingered hand raised . . . raised over Lea. Yes. He was leaning over Lea, who sat in a chair with her eyes closed, head tilted back.

Mark raised his eyes to her. "What does this prove?"

"I died in Martha Swann's house. Part of the roof came down in the hurricane. It landed on me, and I died. Martha and James— they knew where to find the priest. They risked their lives out in the storm. They brought him and he performed the *Revenir* rite on me. I came back, Mark. He brought me back. But I wasn't the same. Much as I tried, I wasn't the same. I've been obsessed . . . obsessed with death. I . . . don't really feel as if I belong here."

Her shoulders trembled. A sob racked her entire body. "If only I hadn't brought the twins home, maybe we could have gotten along for a while. Maybe I could have pretended. But . . . I ruined our lives. If only . . ." Her voice trailed off and she grabbed him and pulled his arms around her and pressed her tear-drenched face against his chest.

He held her tight. The photos fluttered across the pier. He wanted to wrap her up and keep her safe. He knew she could be okay again. Of course she could. The island hurricane had been a terrible trauma. So much horror—it could affect *anyone,* especially someone as sensitive as Lea.

Her head pressed against him, he saw the twins over her shoulder. He saw them walk past the old colonial windmill near the street and come toward them, down the center of the pier.

Lea turned, as if sensing they were approaching.

The boys strode rapidly side by side, past the Dock House, past the rows of parked cars on both sides, their eyes straight ahead on Mark and Lea. Mark felt Lea shudder.

As the twins drew close, he called to them. "How did you get here? What are you doing here?"

Daniel's answer came back in his high little-boy's voice. "We came to hurt you."

74

Mark studied their faces. Hard, jaws set tight, eyes like frozen blue ponds.

If they were twelve in 1935, they'd be nearly ninety years old. Ridiculous.

"Come here, boys." Lea stepped in front of Mark and stretched out her arms. "Come here. How did you find us?"

They hung back. "We saw you at the school, Mum. We followed you here. Pa tried to hurt us. Now we need to hurt Pa."

Both boys had dark bruises on the sides of their faces.

"Pa did a bad thing," Samuel said.

"Now, wait—" Mark's breath caught in his throat. "Let's put a stop to this right now. Answer me. What did you think you were doing in that school?"

They ignored him, eyes on Lea. "Pa did a bad thing," Daniel said.

"A bad thing," Samuel repeated. "Pa hurt us. We were ruling the school. But Pa ruined everything."

Mark felt his face grow hot. "Stop saying that. I . . . had to stop you."

"Mark had no choice," Lea told them. She stretched out her arms again. "Come here. I know how hard it's been for you boys.

I know the whole story. Please—come to me. Let me give you a big hug."

"We can't have a hug, Mum," Daniel replied, almost sadly. "We have to hurt Pa now." He turned to Samuel. "Are you ready, Sammy lad?"

Mark uttered a sharp cry when he saw Samuel's eyes blaze.

"Move away, Mum," Daniel warned.

"No. Stop," Lea protested. "Listen to me, boys. We need to talk. The three of us have to stick together now."

"Move away, Mum. We don't want to put the burn on you, too."

The fiery glow of the boy's eyes was so bright, it brought tears to Mark's eyes. Samuel swung his head around, and a blast of heat grazed Mark's chest.

In that second, Mark's questions were answered, and he knew that Lea was telling the truth. He understood how the murders had been done. He understood that the twins had murdered, scorched and murdered. And now he felt the searing heat from Samuel's eyes burn his chest.

They're going to kill me now.

He lowered his head and took off.

"Samuel—stop it!"

He heard Lea's frightened plea over the pounding thuds of his shoes on the asphalt pier. He didn't turn around.

A blazing burst of pain exploded on his back. He heard his shirt sizzle and felt his skin erupt in a circle of fire. Mark dropped to his knees and rolled toward the row of parked cars across the pier. Slid between two cars as another scorching beam cut the air. The blue Honda beside him burst into flames.

With a cry, Mark jumped to his feet. Gasping from the pain that radiated over his back, he stumbled toward the tiny shingled Dock House. When he ducked under another red ray of fire, it sailed over his head and died in the water beyond the pier.

Lea's shrill screams . . . Daniel's shouted instructions to Samuel . . . the boys' pattering footsteps as they pursued him—all became a blur of sound beneath the bass-drum pounding in his chest.

Where am I running? How can I escape them?

He couldn't think straight. No time to make a plan. The terrifying beam from Samuel's eyes could barbecue him in seconds. And as that thought raced through his mind, he also realized that Lea was probably telling the truth about herself. And that he could lose her.

Lose her. Oh no. Oh no. Lose her.

A hoarse cry escaped his throat as he started to heave himself through the open door of the food shack. He thought better of it. Wheeled around and ran crazily, off-balance, in a wild stagger, and stumbled to the far side of the little building—just as it burst into flames.

He heard shrieks of horror, turned, and saw three or four workers run out, pushing each other as they fell through the doorway, crying and shouting their shock and horror. The long apron on a young red-headed woman was on fire. She struggled with the straps, then dropped to the ground on her belly, trying to smother the flames.

A second explosion sent flames shooting off the low, flat roof. Mark glanced back. The twins were ambling toward him, not even bothering to hurry. So relaxed and confident. And why not? Mark was helpless against the boy's unnatural weapon. Helpless against the evil magic Lea had warned him about. Sure, he could run. But where? He couldn't escape. And he couldn't turn and face them down.

Over the crackle of the flames, he heard shouts. People came running out of the waffle cone shop and from the restaurant at the end of the pier. He didn't have long to watch them. Another scorching stab of pain caught him in the back of the leg, hobbling him. Forcing him to his knees.

This is it. It's over.

A sharp stab in his right shoulder and the skin split open. He felt the burn run down his arm. With a scream of horror and pain, his leg throbbing and aching, he lurched to the edge of the pier. Swung his body around—and glanced to the water.

Will I be safe in the water?

He gripped the low, white metal railing at the edge of the pier.

His right arm throbbed. He could barely hold on, but he started to lower his body toward the rolling water. Glancing back, he saw Daniel's intense stare and the pulsing red eyes of his twin as they made their steady way toward him.

A powerful heat blast bounced off the metal railing, shook the rail, and made a *craack* like a lightning bolt. Another shot sent an explosion of heat over the top of Mark's head.

He glimpsed the dark water below. He took a deep breath and prepared to loosen his hold on the rail.

And then stopped.

He gripped the rail tight and stared across the pier as Lea caught up to the boys. They had all their attention on Mark. Daniel was pushing his brother forward, moving them in for the final burn. They didn't see Lea come up behind them.

Ignoring his pain, Mark hung on the rail and watched Lea move up behind the boys. She stretched out her arms as if to tackle them both. Instead, she wrapped her arms around them, pulled them into a tight hug from behind.

They struggled to free themselves. The three of them moved in an awkward dance, held together in Lea's tight embrace.

As she wrestled with them, she called to him. "Good-bye, Mark. Good-bye, darling. It's the only way. I have to take them back."

"Lea, no!"

Gripping the rail, he watched helplessly as Lea spread her hand over Samuel's blond hair—and turned his face to her. Turned his burning eyes on her.

Took the beam of fire. Turned it on herself.

Mark couldn't stop the howl of horror that burst from his throat. Working his legs against the pier wall, he struggled to pull himself up. To get to her. To reach her in time.

But no.

Lea burst into flames that consumed her instantly, rising like candlefire, straight, without a flicker. She didn't move or struggle or make a sound. The boys squirmed and thrashed. But even as she burned, Lea held them close, pressed them to her. And the fire swallowed them, too.

Unable to breathe or cry out, Mark watched all three of them in the fire, statues in a dark embrace, then ash, crumbling ash, a sinking pile of ash inside the single tall flame.

Then gone.

Gone, and the fire vanished with them, leaving the asphalt unmarked.

Mark felt hands grip his arms. Saw faces above him. People tugging him up from the pier side. He heard screams and cries. Sirens approaching. Smoke swept over him from the still-flaming Dock House. People came running onto the pier, faces tight with alarm. Seagulls screamed in the sky.

He let it all fade to the back of his mind. He pictured Lea. Her smile. Her bright, dark eyes.

Gone. Lea was gone.

As he stared, the fire that had consumed her went out with an almost-silent *husssssh*.

75

Mark found Roz in the flower bed at the side of the guesthouse. She was on the grass, digging with a trowel in a square of black dirt. Axl, in red shorts and a sleeveless red T-shirt, sat nearby in a clump of freshly planted petunias, stabbing at the ground with a plastic shovel in imitation of his mother.

Roz looked up and brushed a bee away from her shoulder. "Who was that on the phone?"

Mark hunkered down beside her. He liked the smell of the fresh dirt. Like rich coffee. "Sergeant Pavano. You remember. The cop."

Roz nodded. "Of course I remember him. What did he want? To arrest you for some other murder you didn't do?"

Mark snickered. "Don't be bitter. He had no choice really."

"Of course he did. And I'll be as bitter as I want. He was a total idiot."

"Not total," Mark said. "Don't forget. He was brave. He tried to rescue Ira and Elena and the other kids. He went in before any-one."

She shoved the trowel into the dirt. "So what did the big hero want?"

"Actually, I think he called to apologize for the way the police treated me. But he never got around to it. He just asked how everyone is doing. You know. With Lea gone."

"What did you tell him?"

"I said Ira and Elena hadn't really accepted it yet. But they were doing the best they could. What else could I say?"

Roz sighed in reply.

Mark twisted his face in a frown. "Pavano says he's going back to New York City. He said the city is a lot safer than out here."

Roz concentrated on the trowel. "Maybe he's right."

"Look this. Look this." Axl called to them, holding up his yellow shovel.

They turned to see what the little guy was staring down at. Mark saw two fat brown insects in the scoop of the shovel. "Those are called beetles," he said.

Axl held the shovel close to his face. His dark eyes studied the two bugs. "Look what Sammy teached me. Sammy teached me this."

Roz's mouth dropped open. "What? What about Sammy?"

"Sammy teached Monkey Boy."

Mark felt his heart skip a beat as Axl's eyes flared. In a few seconds, they were fiery red. Axl lowered his glowing gaze to the shovel, and all three of them watched as the beetles sizzled and burned.

Acknowledgments

First, I need to thank Stacy Creamer, whose excitement and enthusiasm for this novel gave me the courage to venture through the red rain and complete what was a very ambitious project for me. I'm so appreciative of her support.

Andrew Gulli of the *Strand Magazine* must be thanked for coercing me from my day job of scaring children into the world of scaring adults.

My friend and longtime (and long-suffering) *Goosebumps* editor, Susan Lurie, was an enormous help, as was my wife, Jane Stine, who is painfully insightful and always right about my books.

Finally, I need to mention three old horror movies: *Village of the Damned, Children of the Damned,* and *Island of the Damned.* While this book is not a reimagining of those films, the horrifying children in all three of them gave me the inspiration that disgustingly evil children might be a fitting subject for me.

Thanks, all.